Anne of Green Gables

a graphic novel

Mariah Marsden &
Brenna Thummler

Andrews McMeel
PUBLISHING®

To Lucy Maud Montgomery,
who reminds us that nothing is more powerful
than a girl with an imagination.

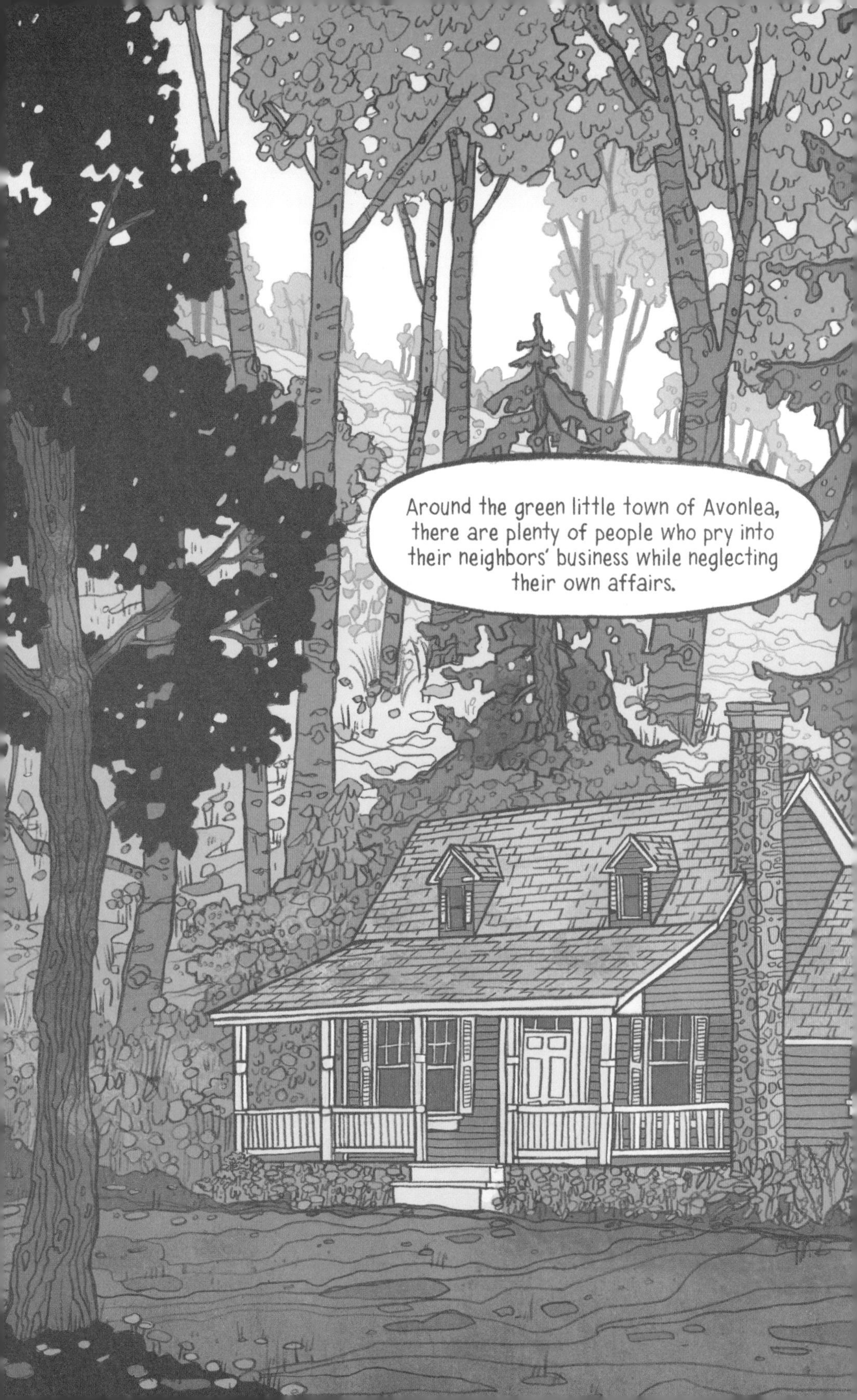
Around the green little town of Avonlea, there are plenty of people who pry into their neighbors' business while neglecting their own affairs.

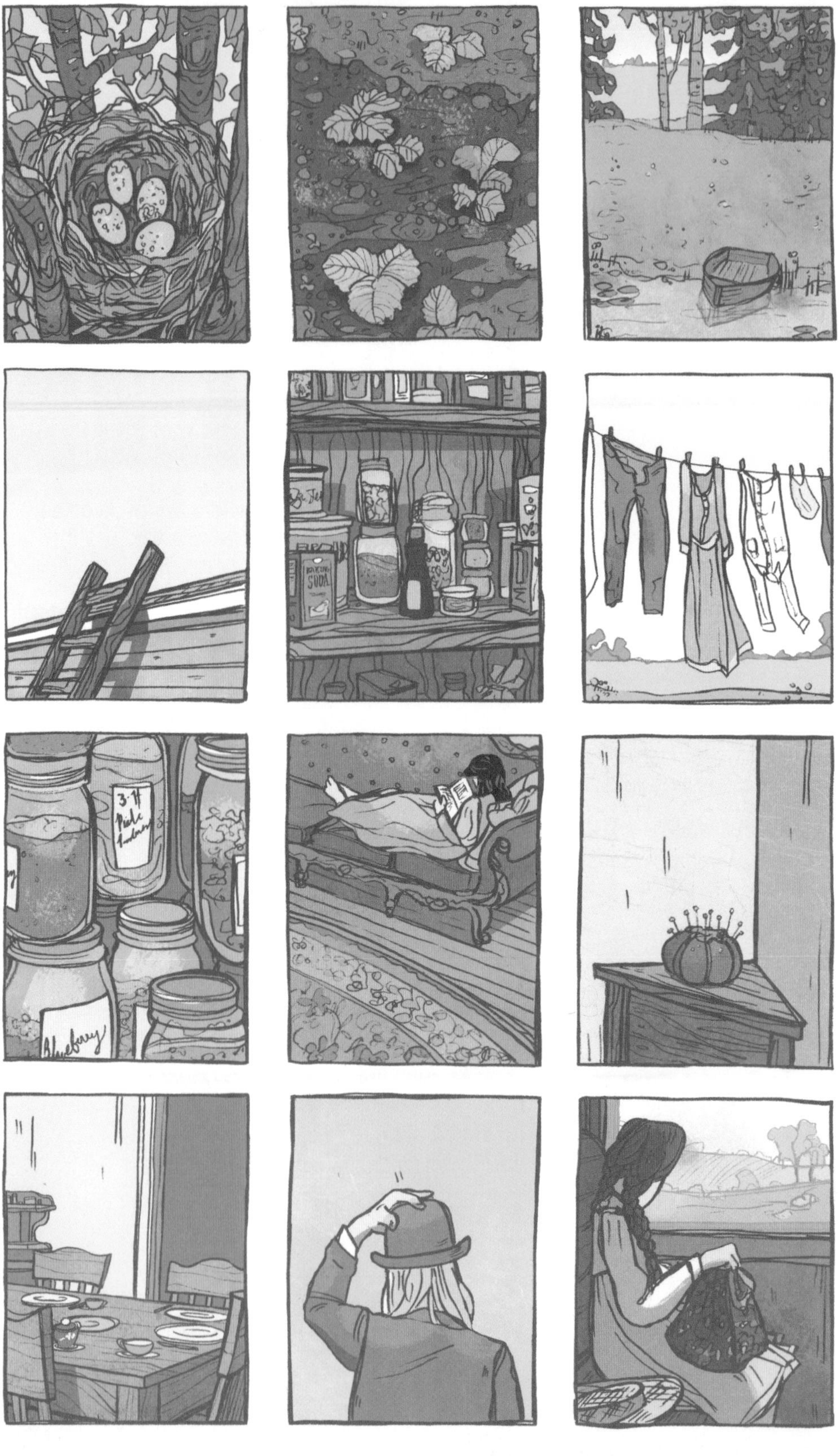
Blueberry

A talented few can juggle both at the same time. Rachel Lynde was skilled in this art and always kept a watchful eye on her own neighbors: Marilla and Matthew Cuthbert, a brother and sister who lived just down the road at a place called Green Gables.

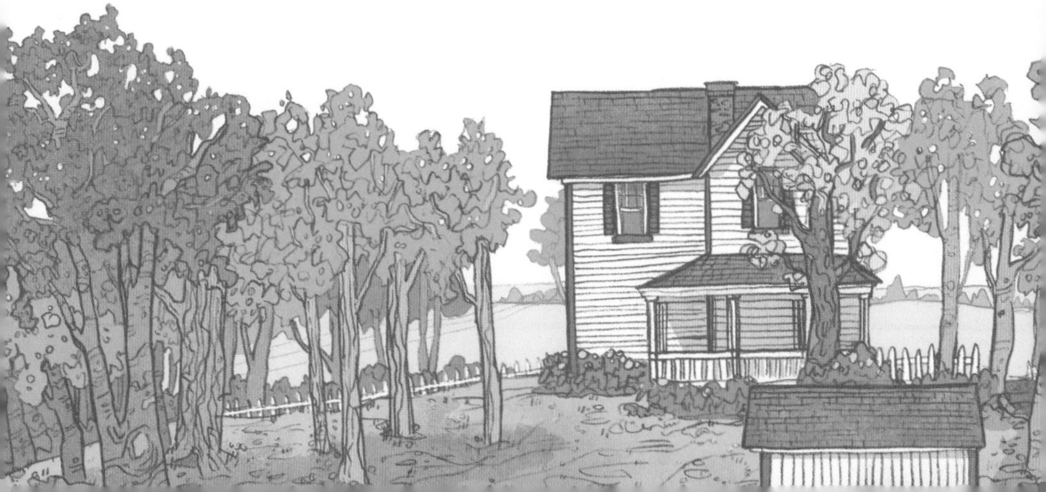

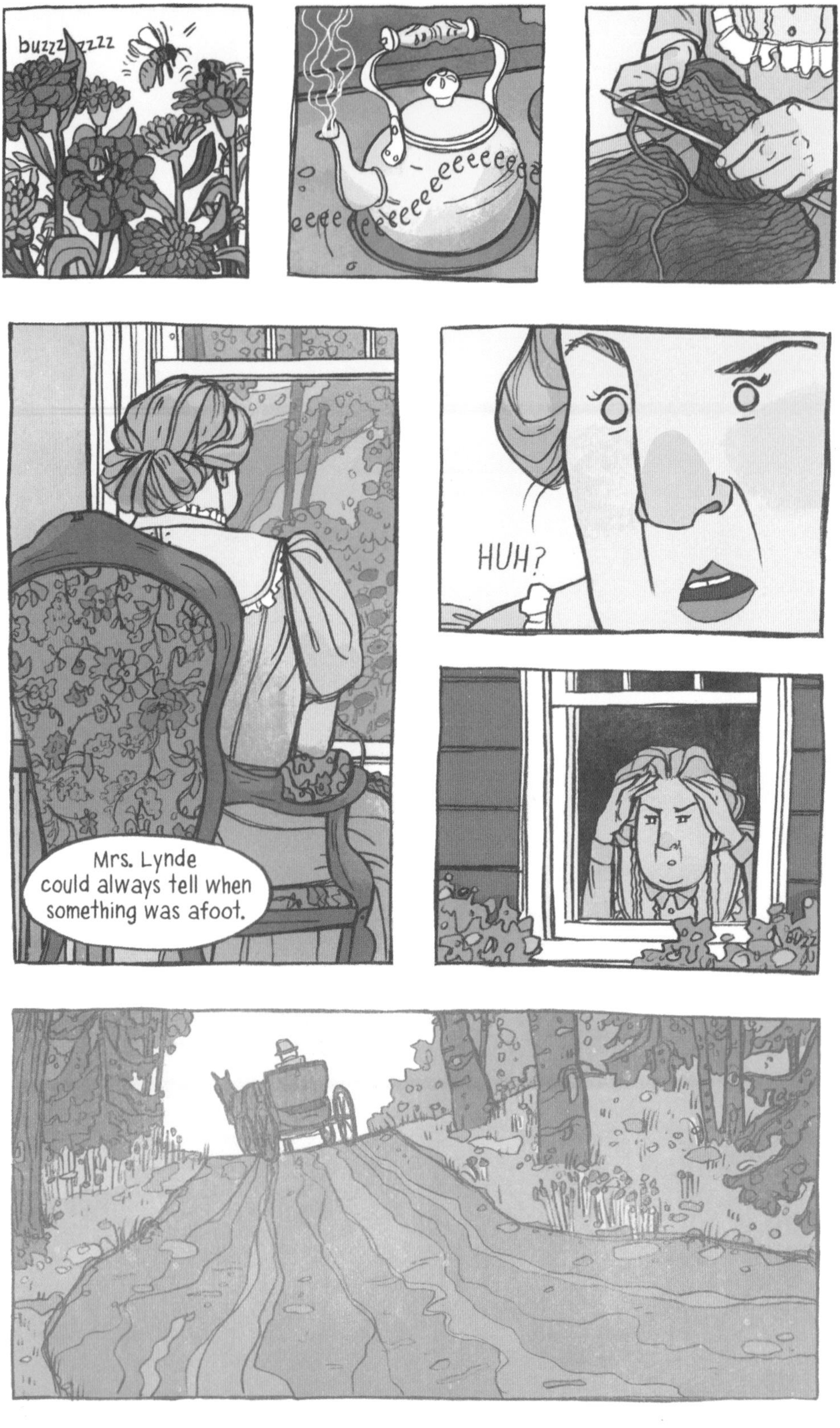
buzzzzzzz
eeeeeeeeeeeeeeeeeee
Mrs. Lynde could always tell when something was afoot.
HUH?
BUZZ

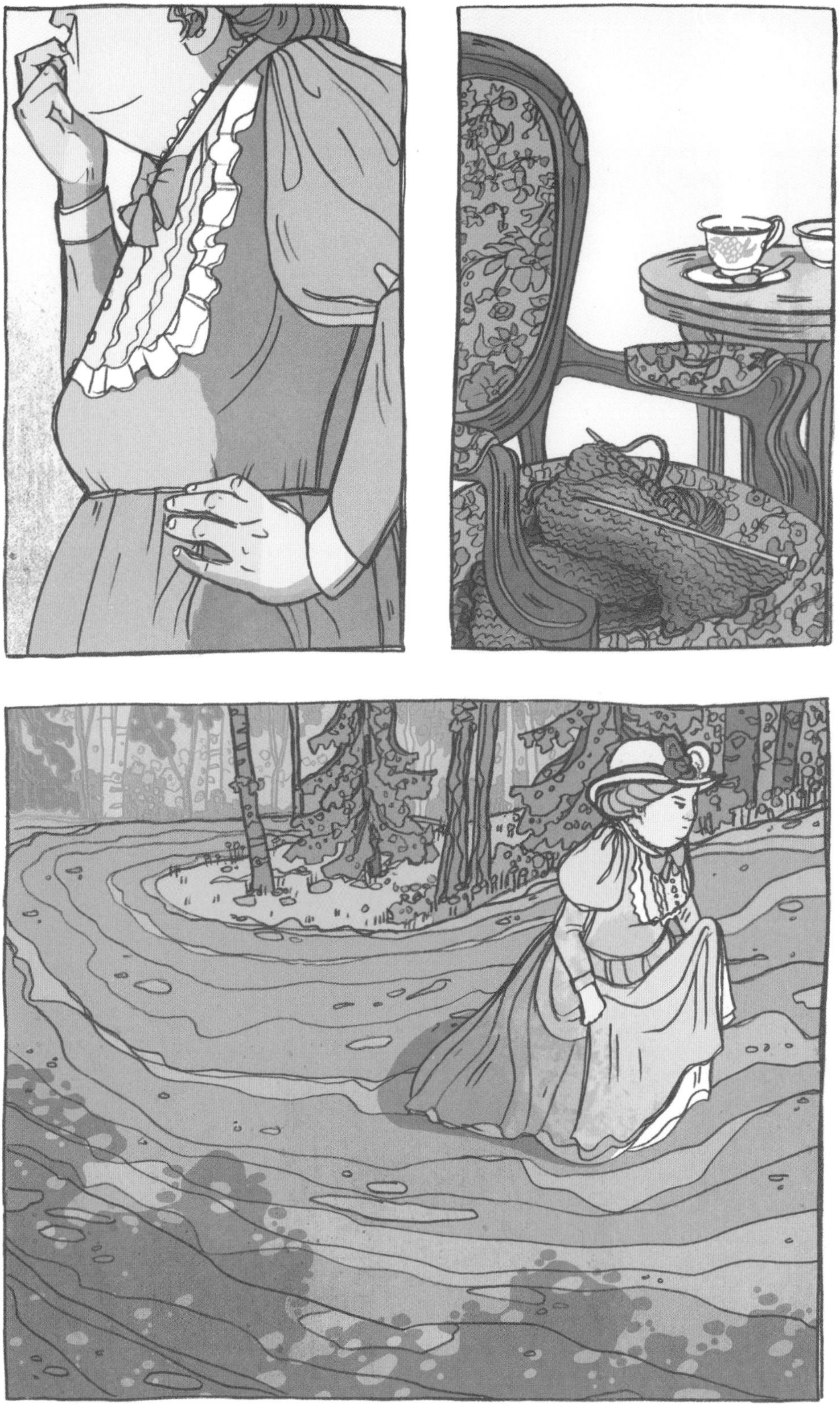

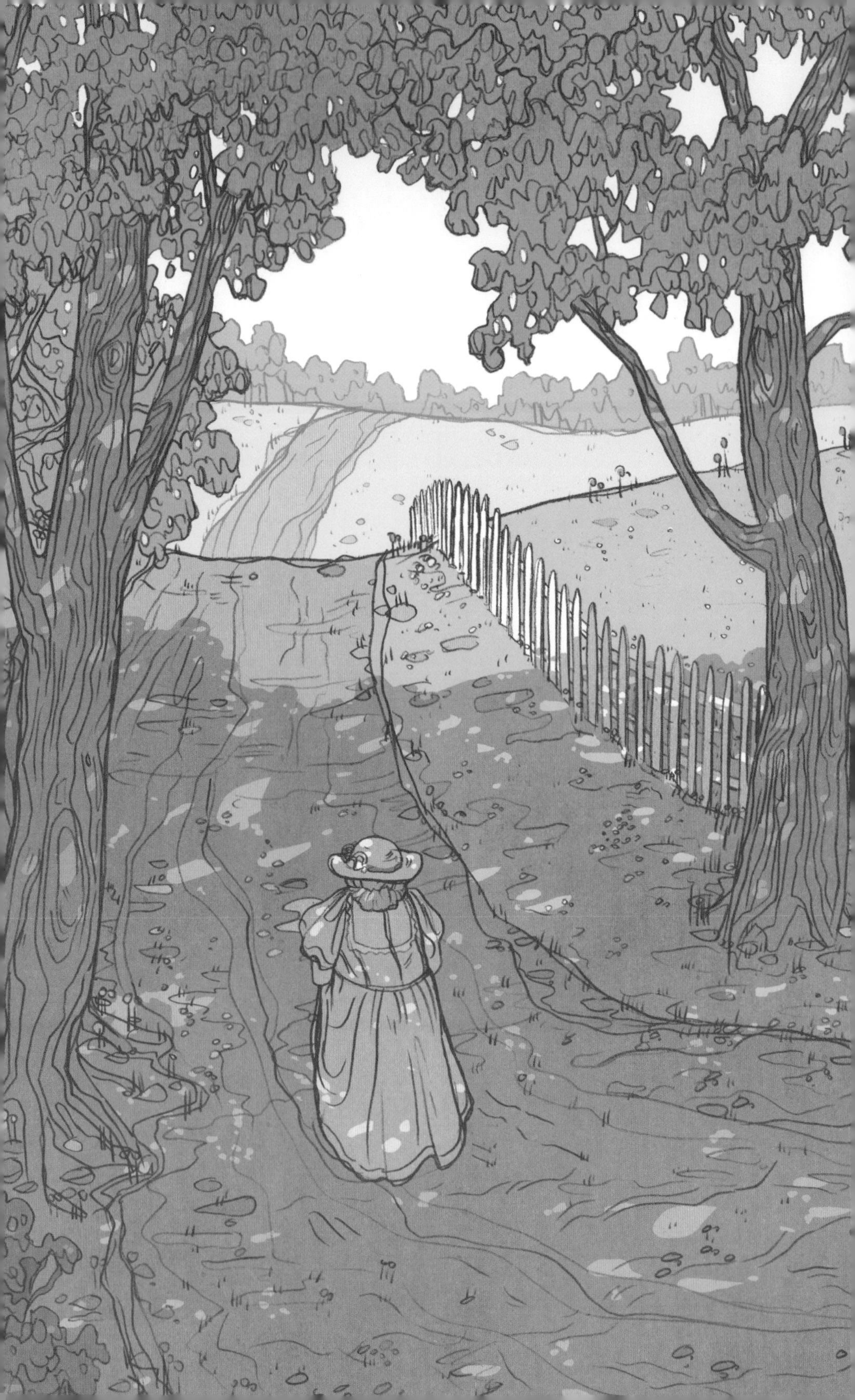

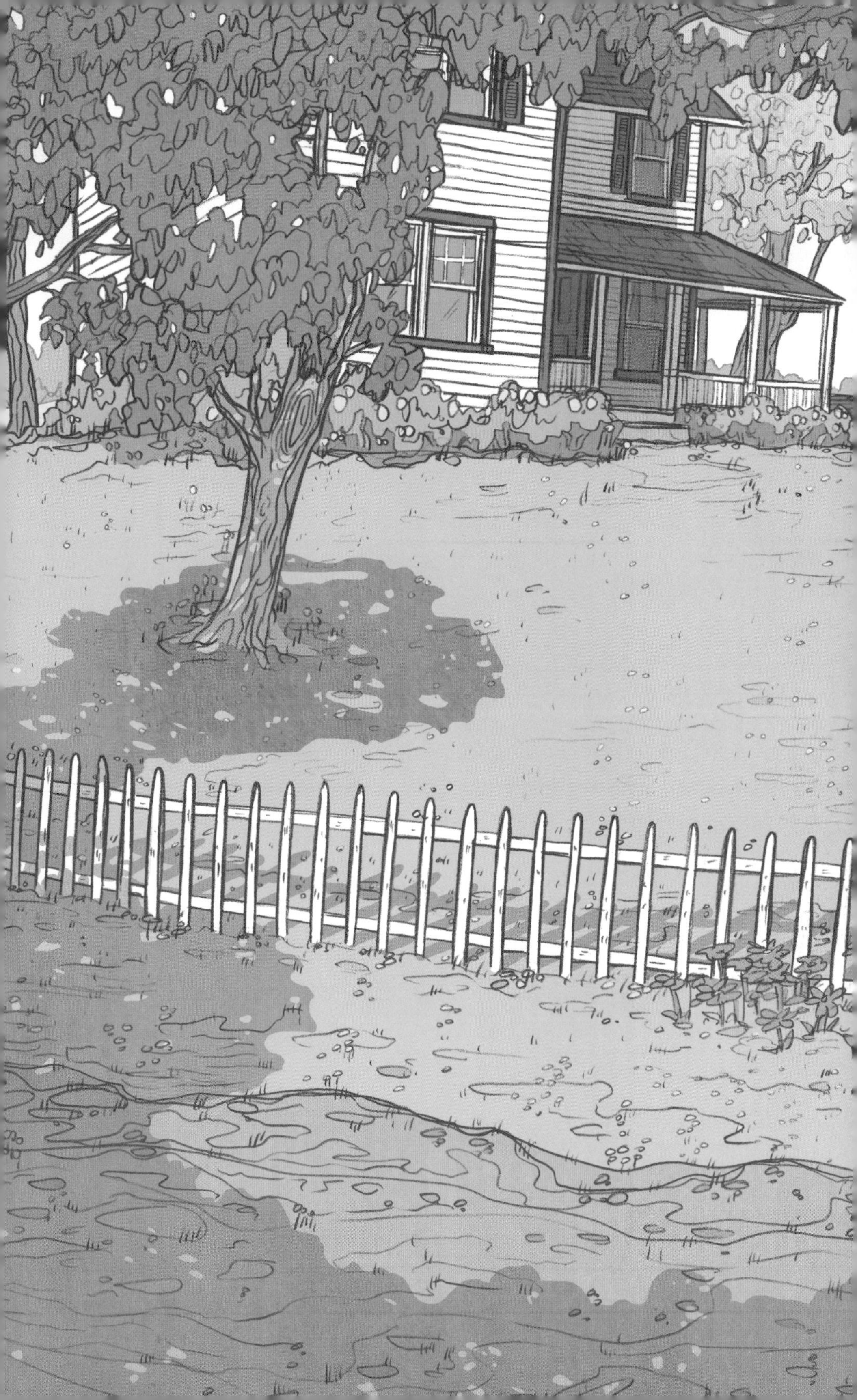

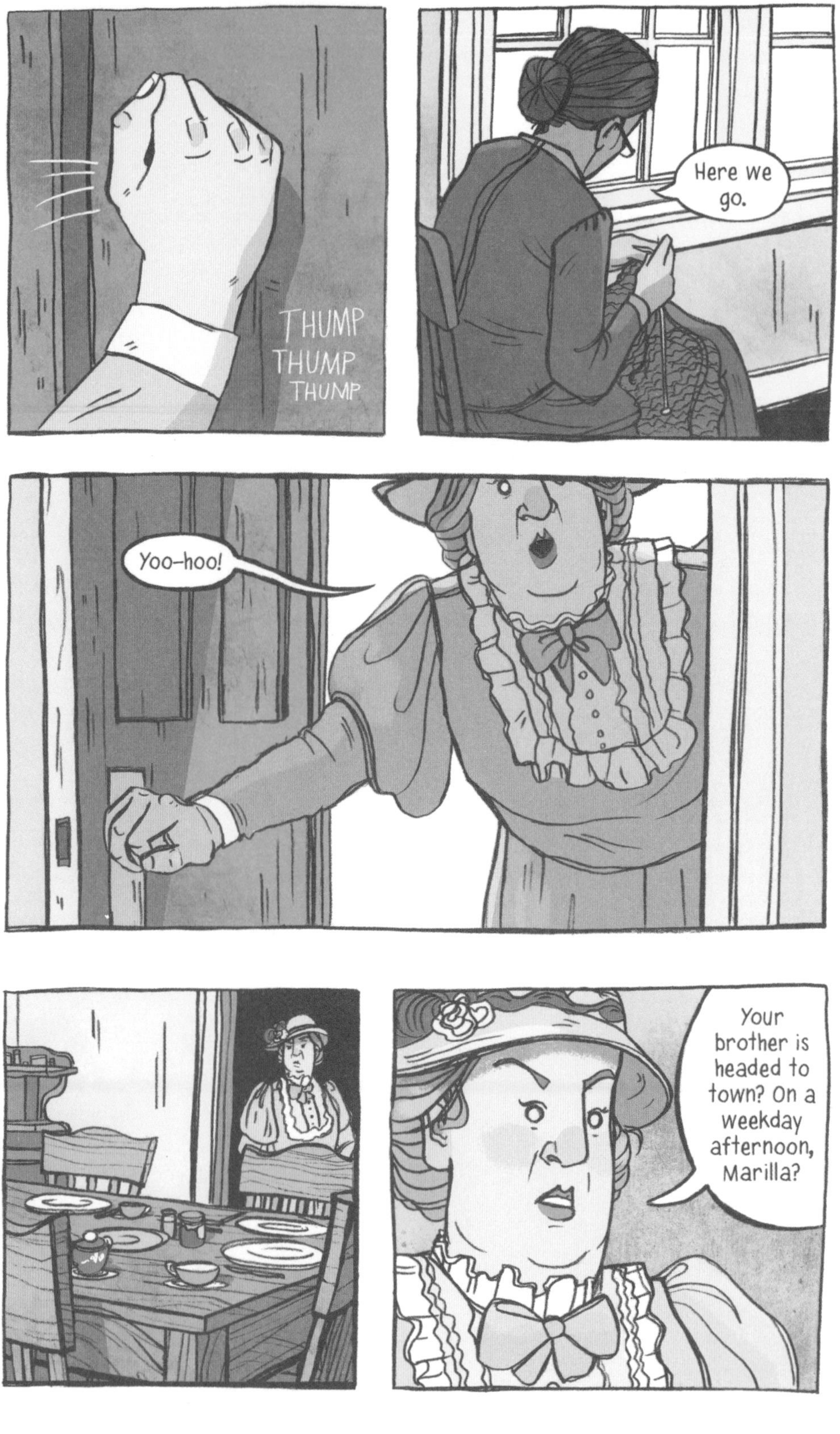
THUMP
THUMP
THUMP
Here we go.
Yoo-hoo!
Your brother is headed to town? On a weekday afternoon, Marilla?

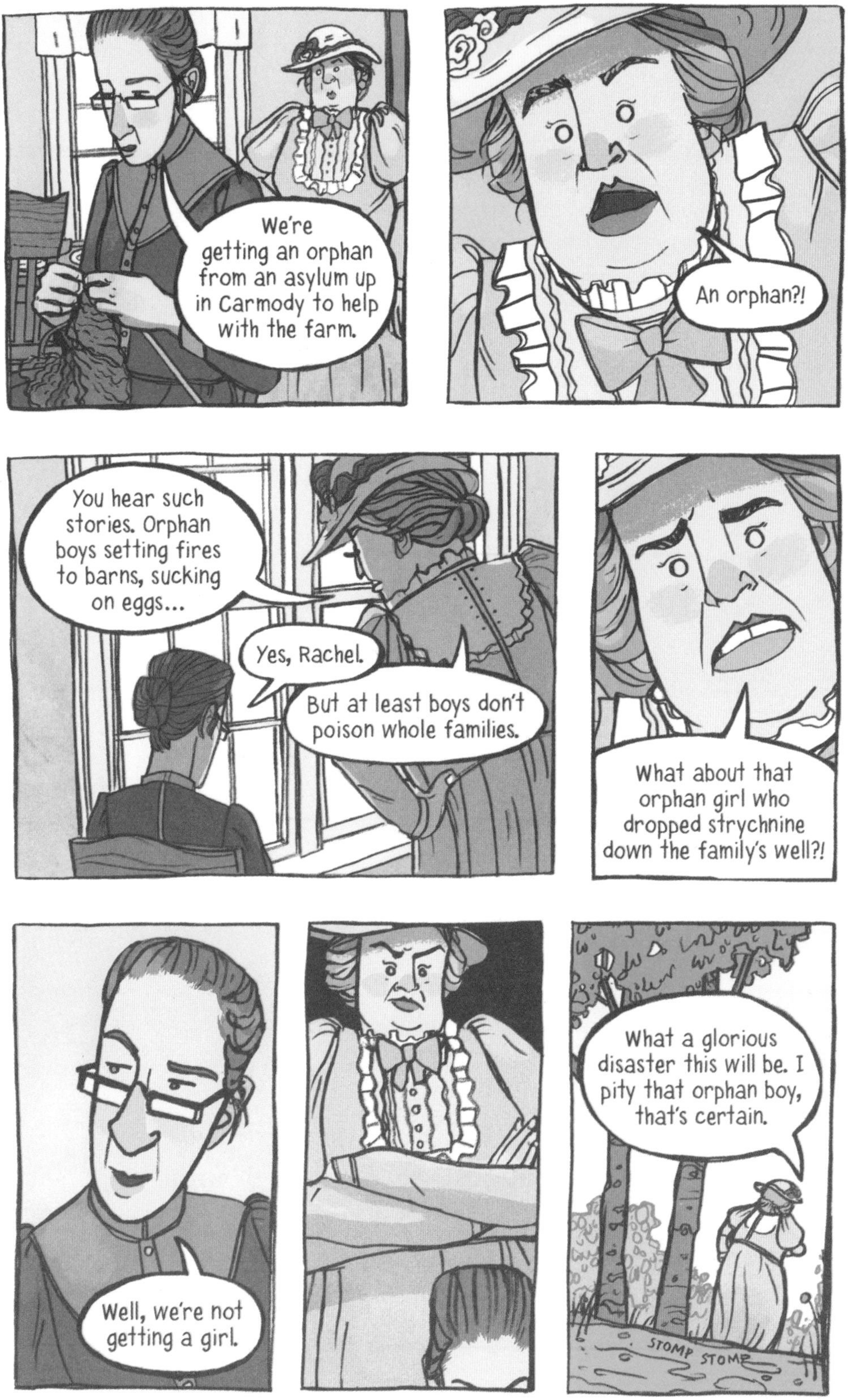
We're getting an orphan from an asylum up in Carmody to help with the farm.
An orphan?!
You hear such stories. Orphan boys setting fires to barns, sucking on eggs...
Yes, Rachel.
But at least boys don't poison whole families.
What about that orphan girl who dropped strychnine down the family's well?!
Well, we're not getting a girl.
What a glorious disaster this will be. I pity that orphan boy, that's certain.
STOMP STOMP

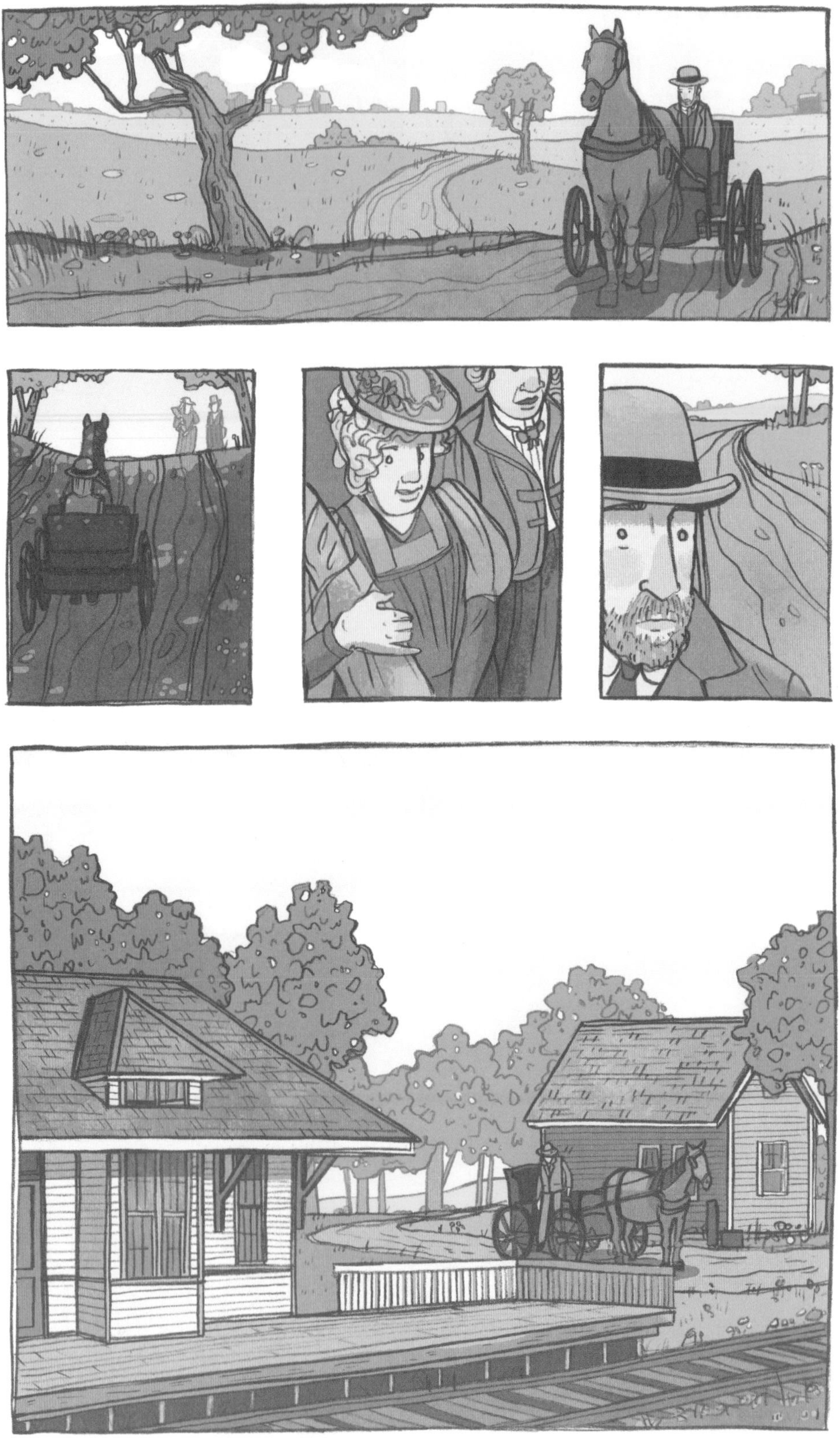

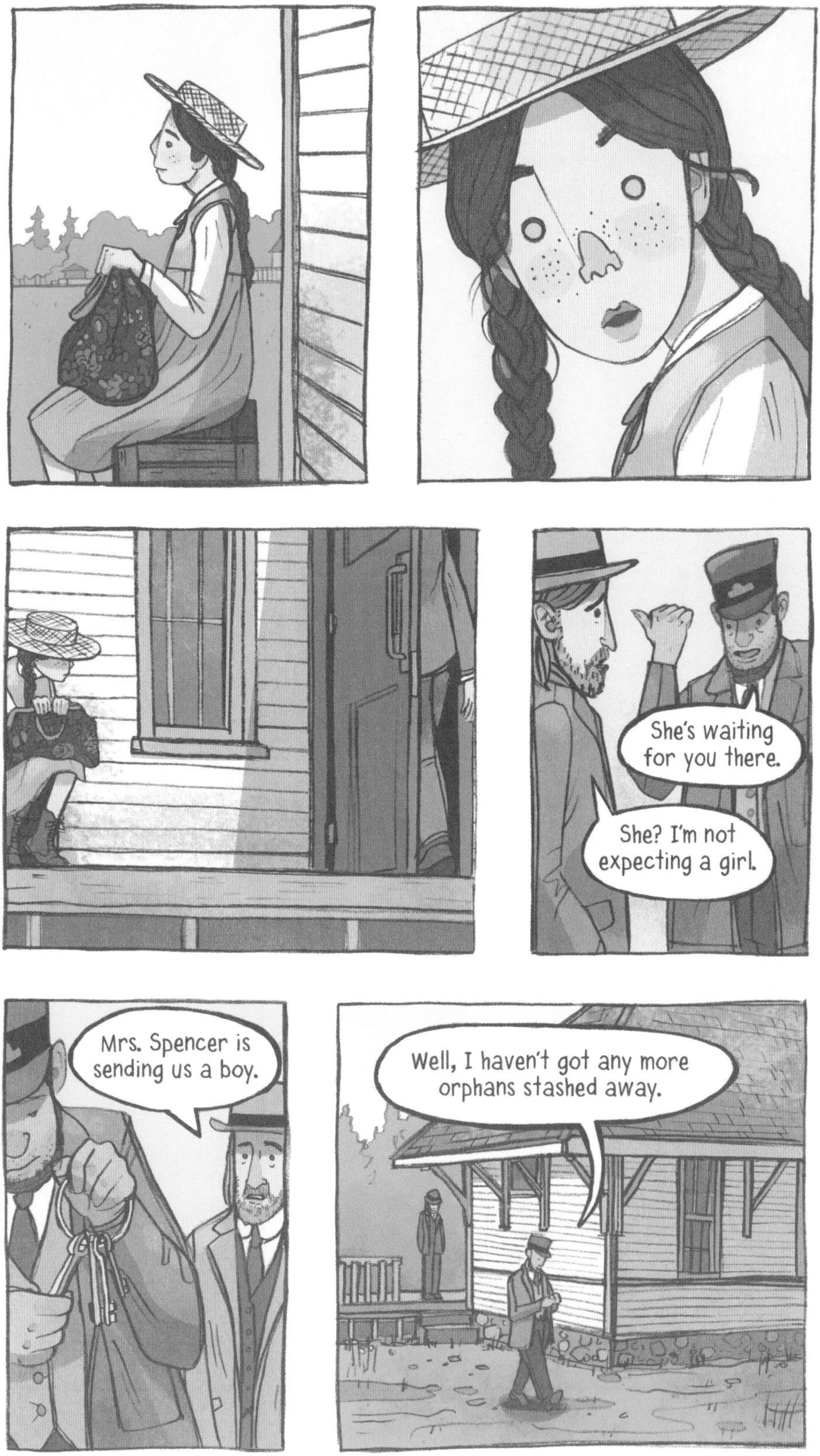
She's waiting for you there.
She? I'm not expecting a girl.
Mrs. Spencer is sending us a boy.
Well, I haven't got any more orphans stashed away.

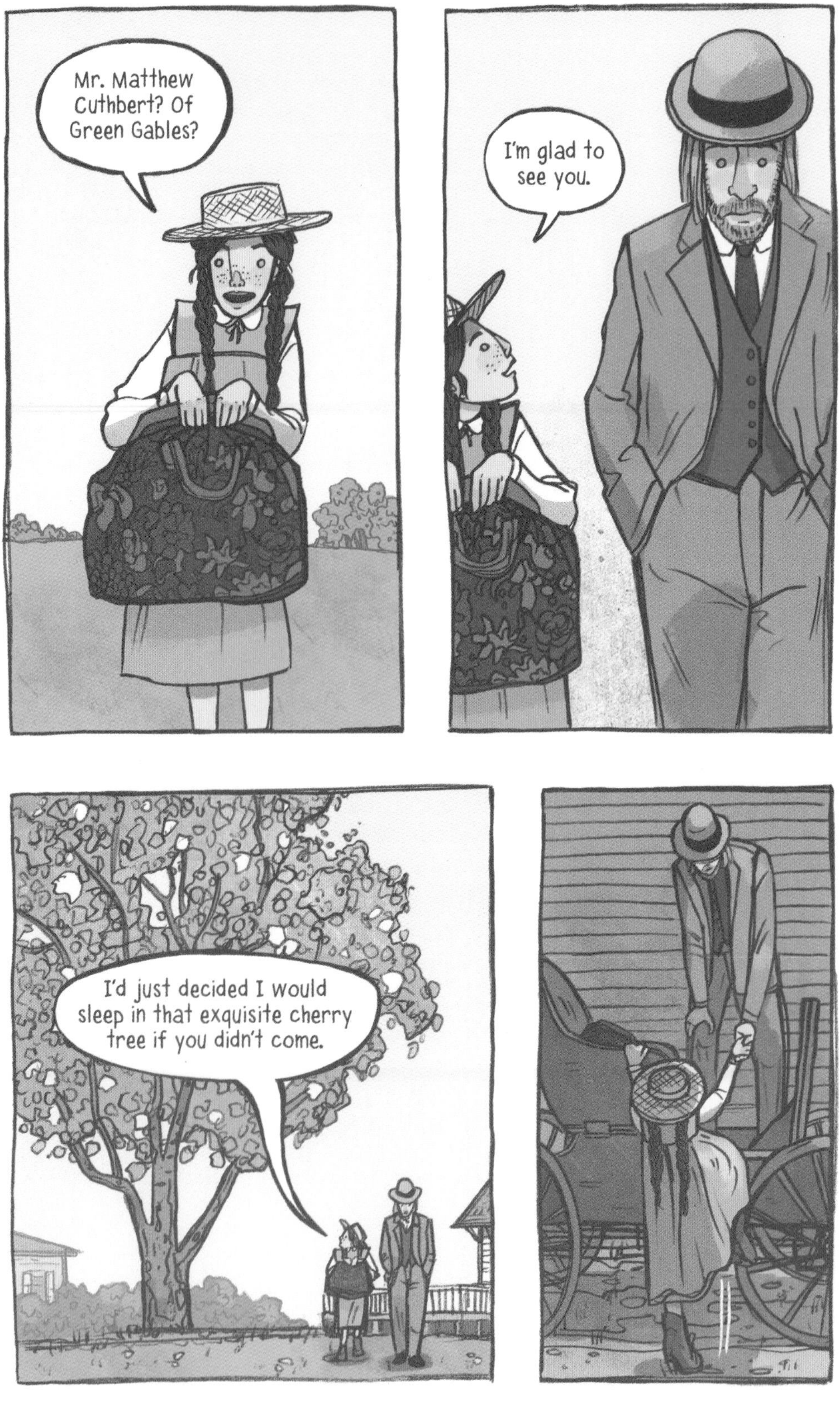
Mr. Matthew Cuthbert? Of Green Gables?
I'm glad to see you.
I'd just decided I would sleep in that exquisite cherry tree if you didn't come.

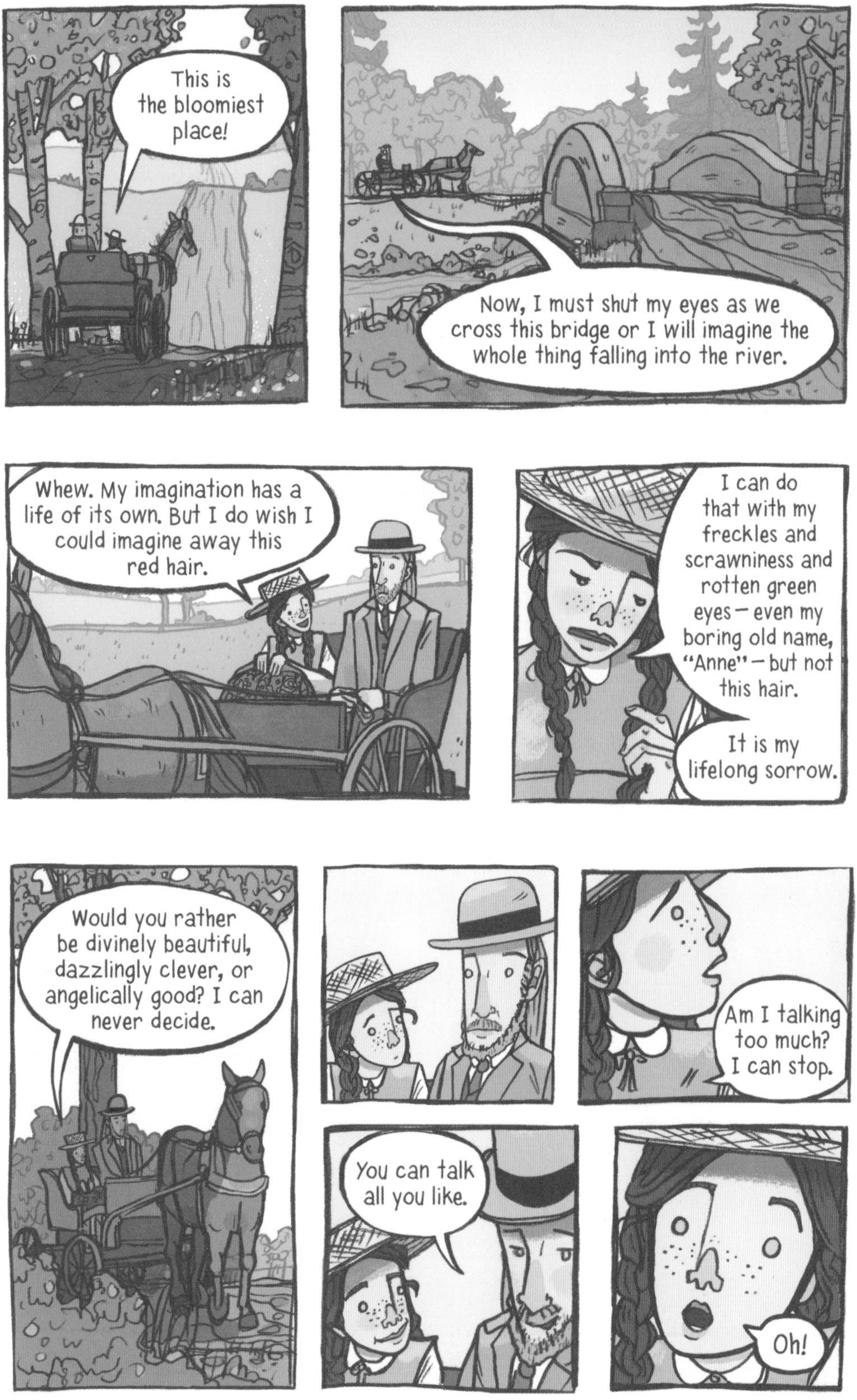
This is the bloomiest place!
Now, I must shut my eyes as we cross this bridge or I will imagine the whole thing falling into the river.
Whew. My imagination has a life of its own. But I do wish I could imagine away this red hair.
I can do that with my freckles and scrawniness and rotten green eyes—even my boring old name, "Anne"—but not this hair.
It is my lifelong sorrow.
Would you rather be divinely beautiful, dazzlingly clever, or angelically good? I can never decide.
Am I talking too much? I can stop.
You can talk all you like.
Oh!

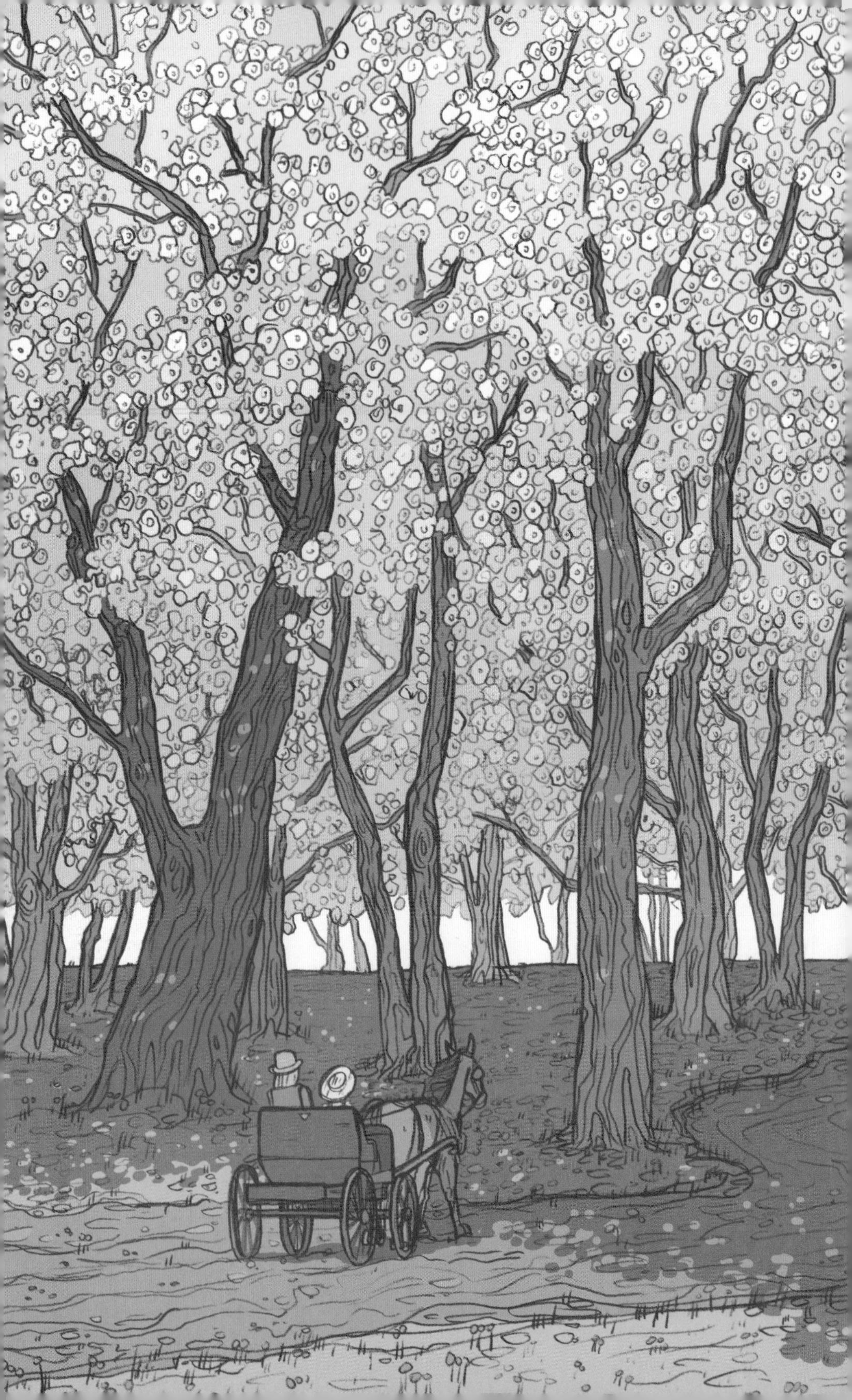

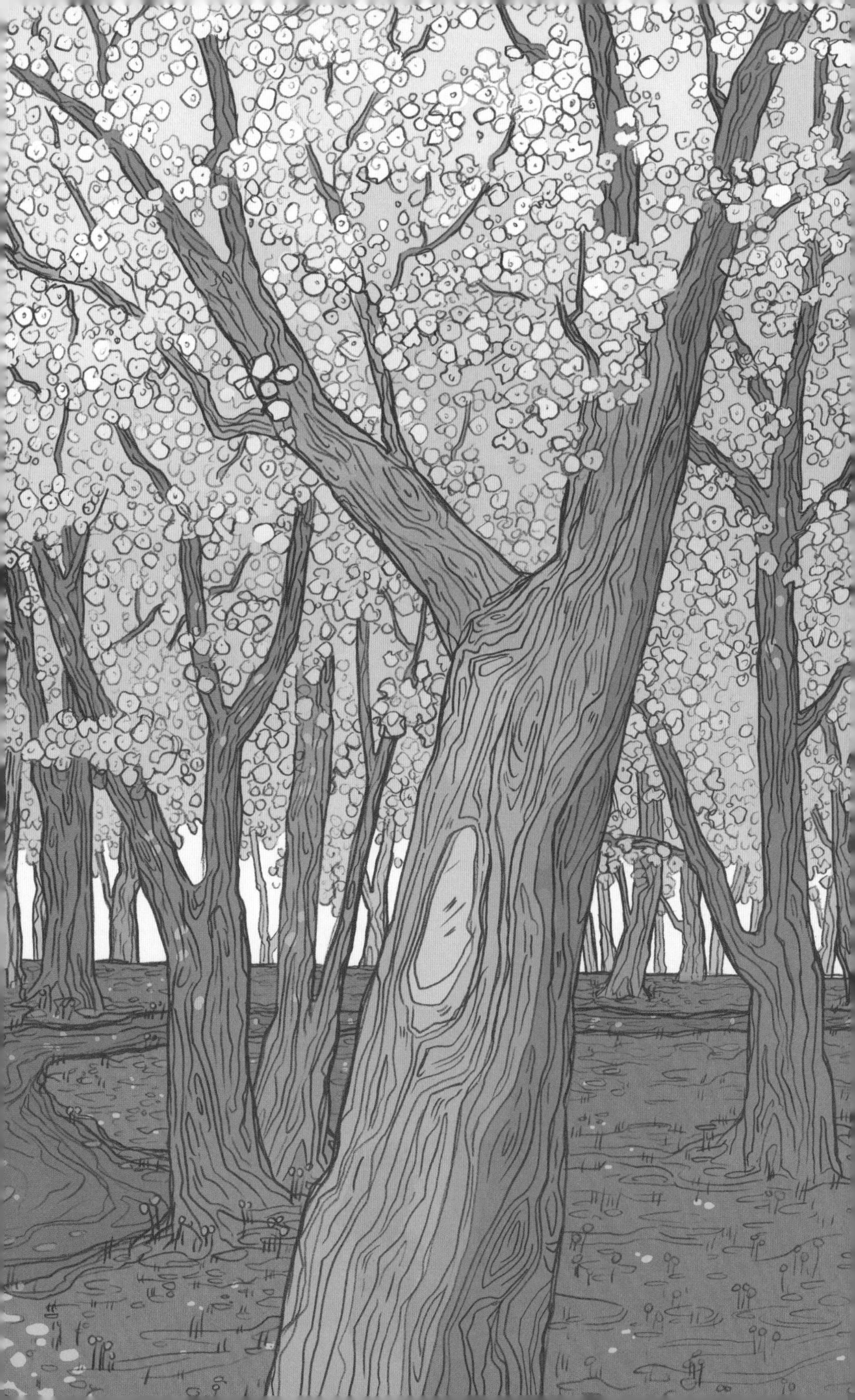

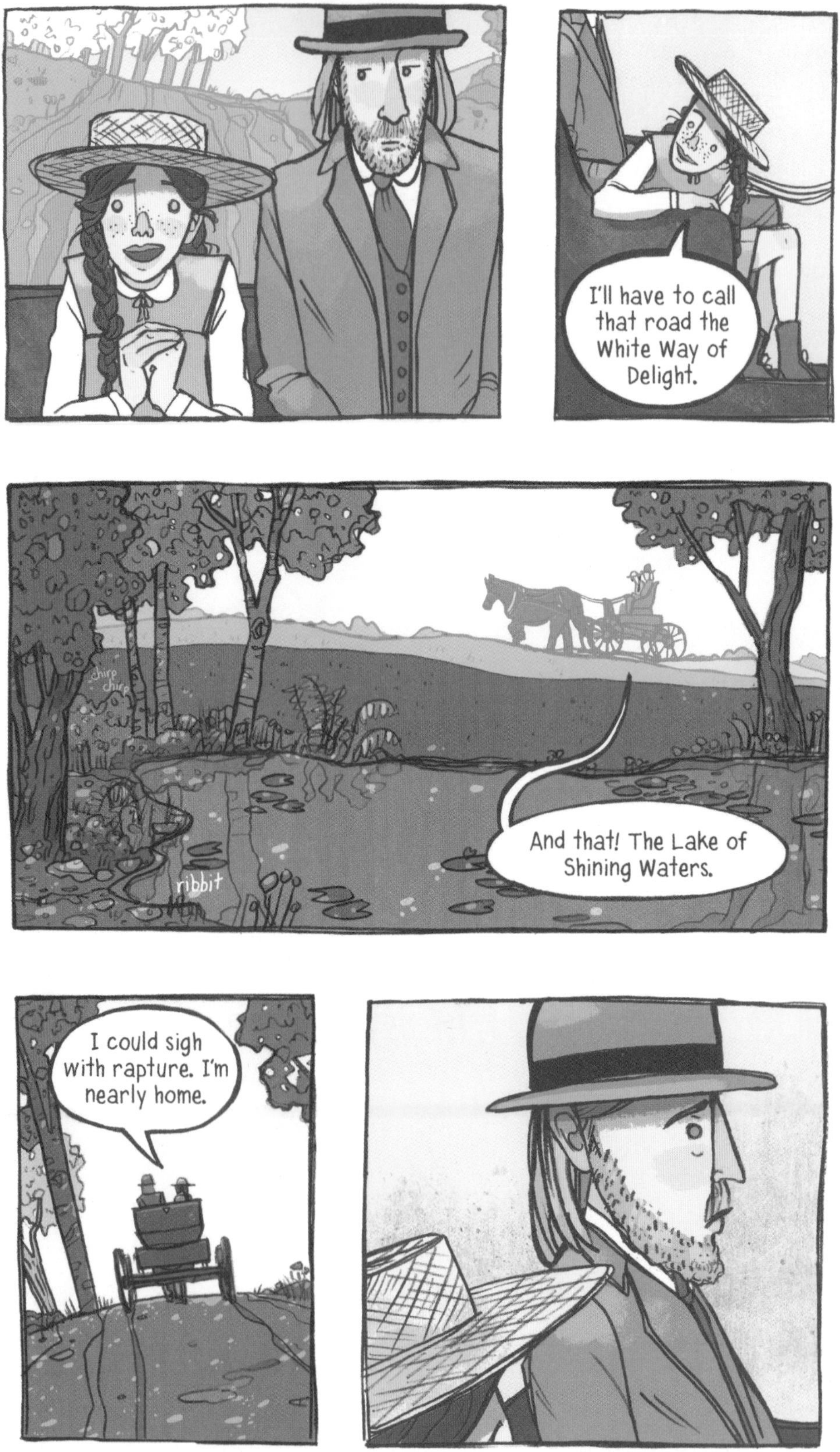
I'll have to call that road the White Way of Delight.
chirp chirp
ribbit
And that! The Lake of Shining Waters.
I could sigh with rapture. I'm nearly home.

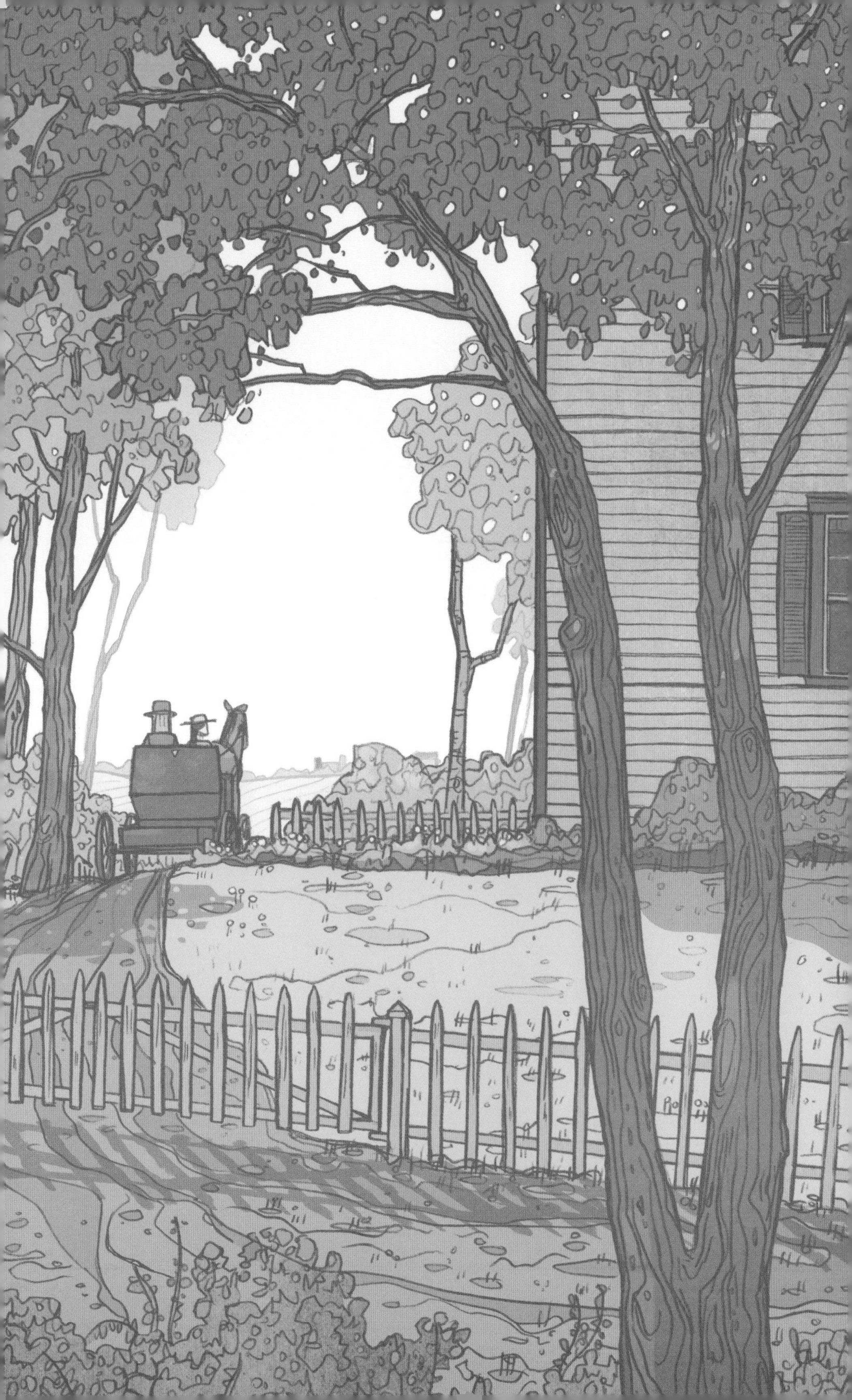

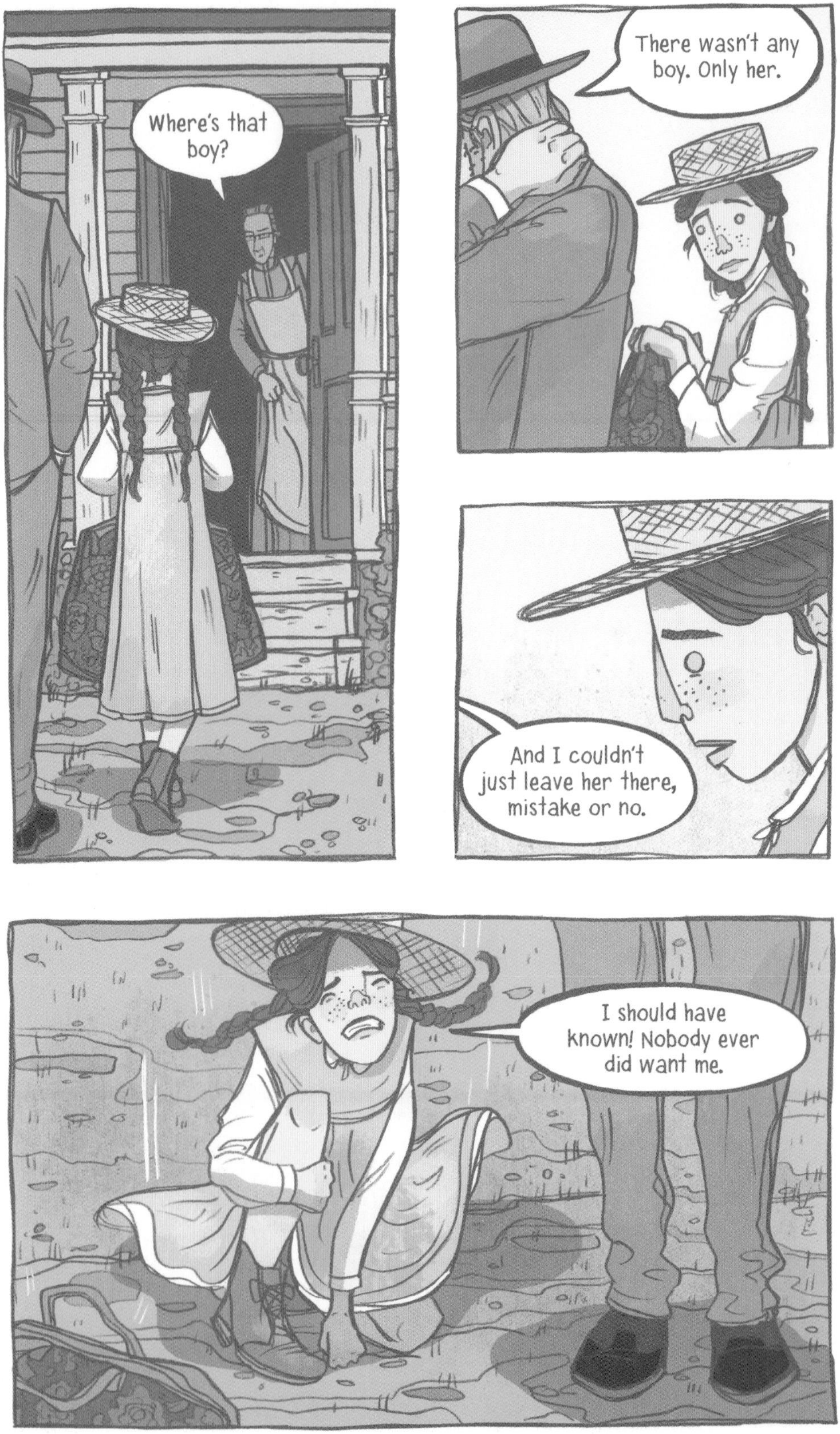
Where's that boy?
There wasn't any boy. Only her.
And I couldn't just leave her there, mistake or no.
I should have known! Nobody ever did want me.

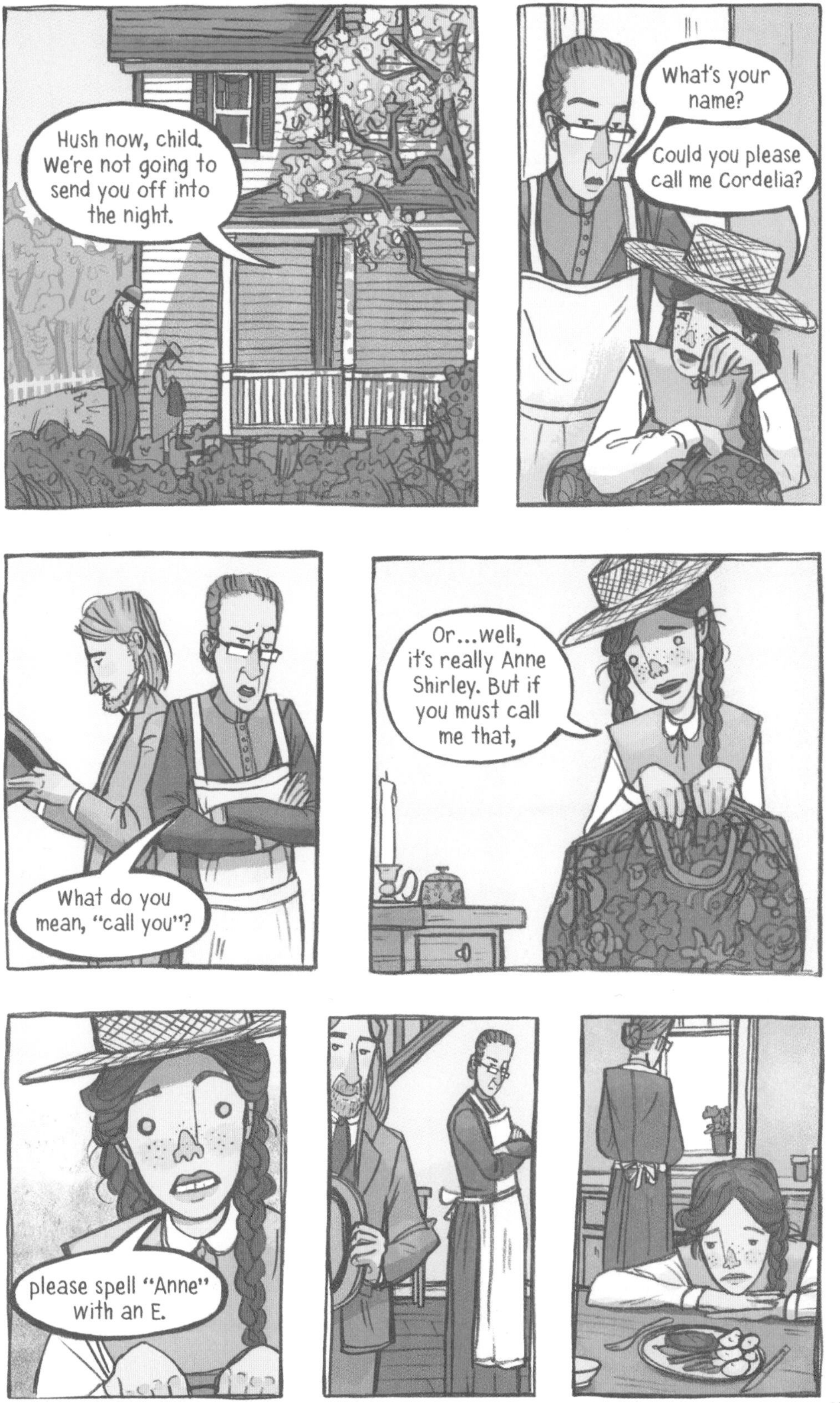
Hush now, child. We're not going to send you off into the night.
What's your name?
Could you please call me Cordelia?
What do you mean, "call you"?
Or...well, it's really Anne Shirley. But if you must call me that,
please spell "Anne" with an E.

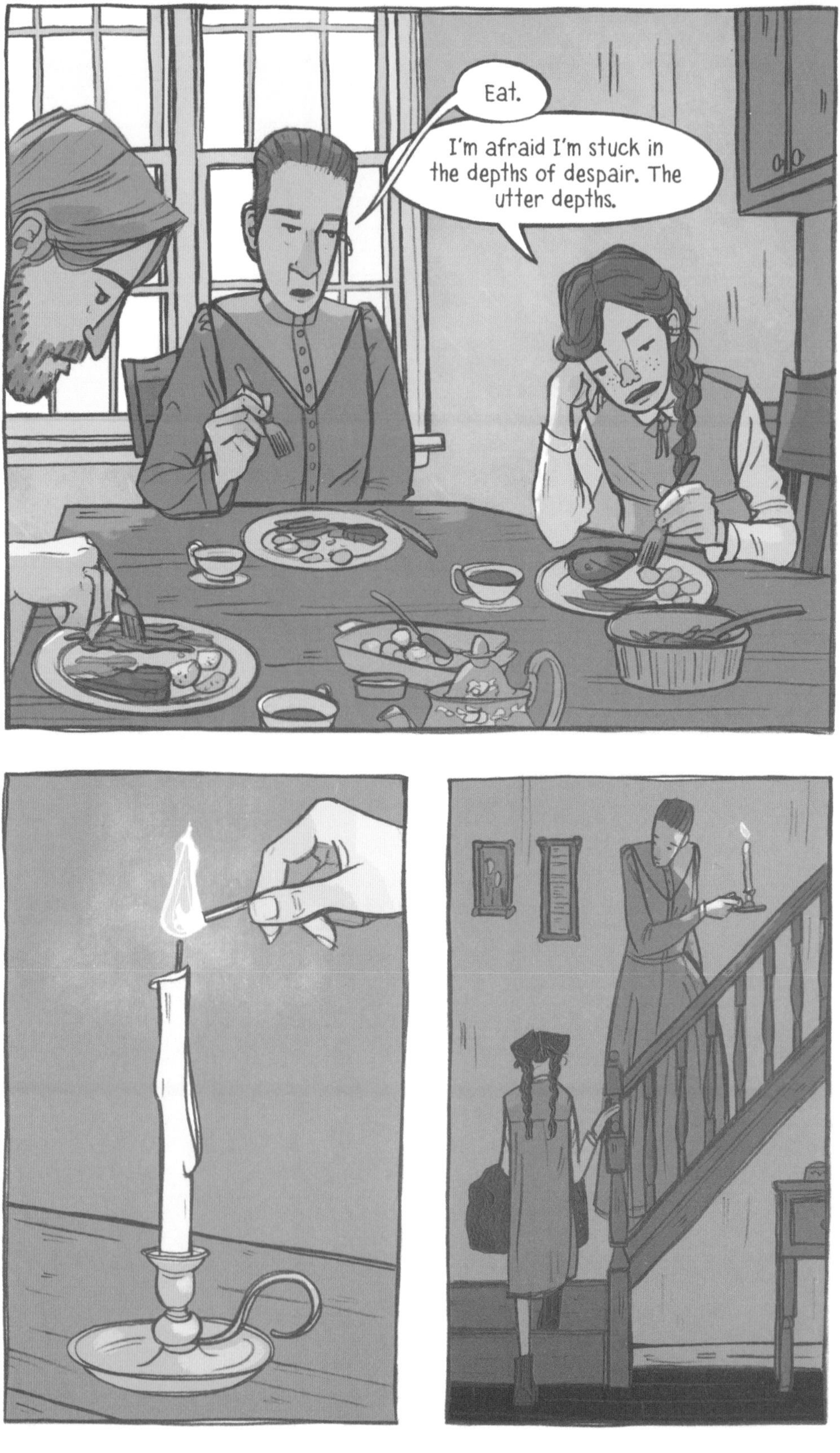
Eat.
I'm afraid I'm stuck in the depths of despair. The utter depths.

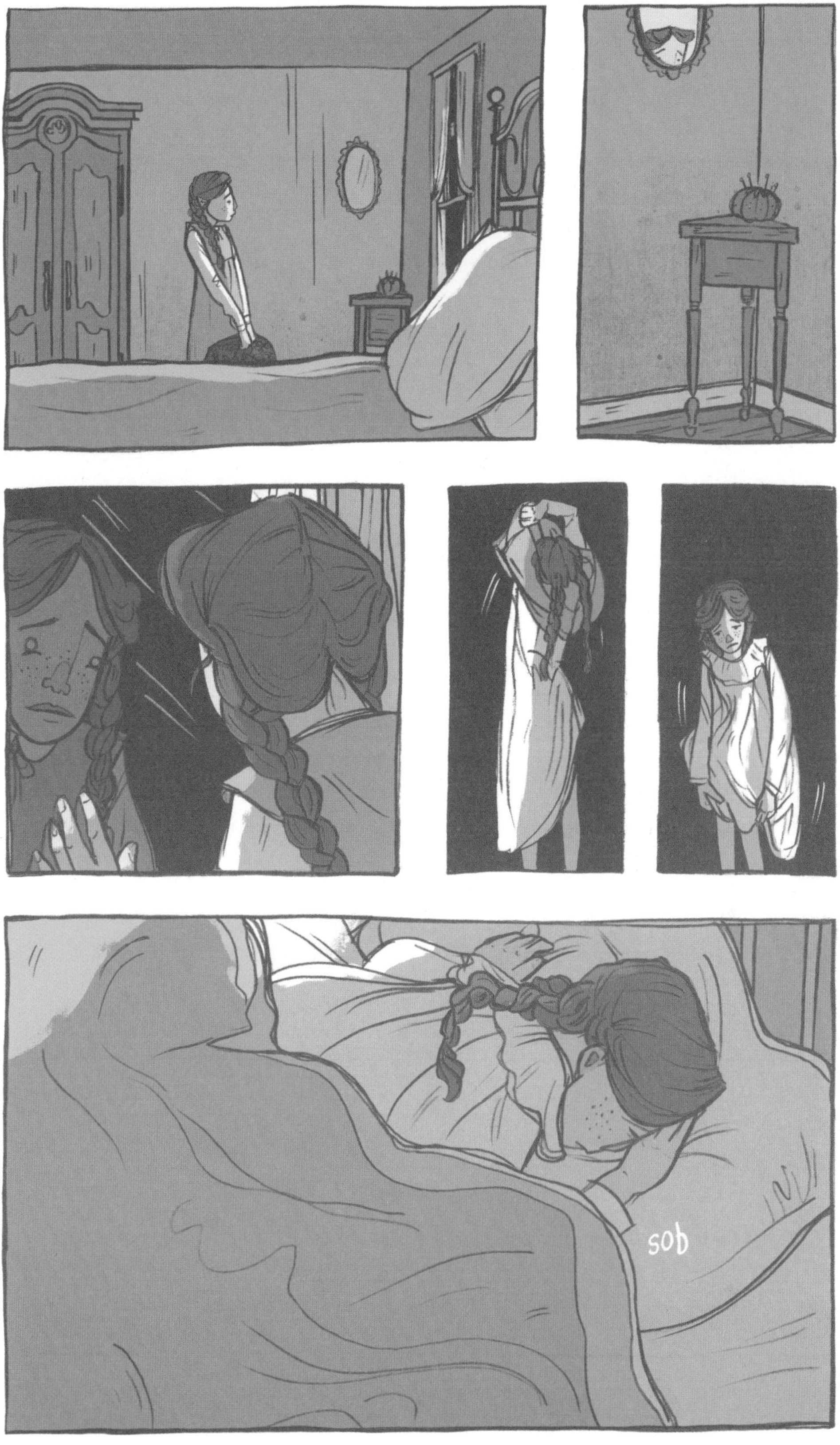
sob

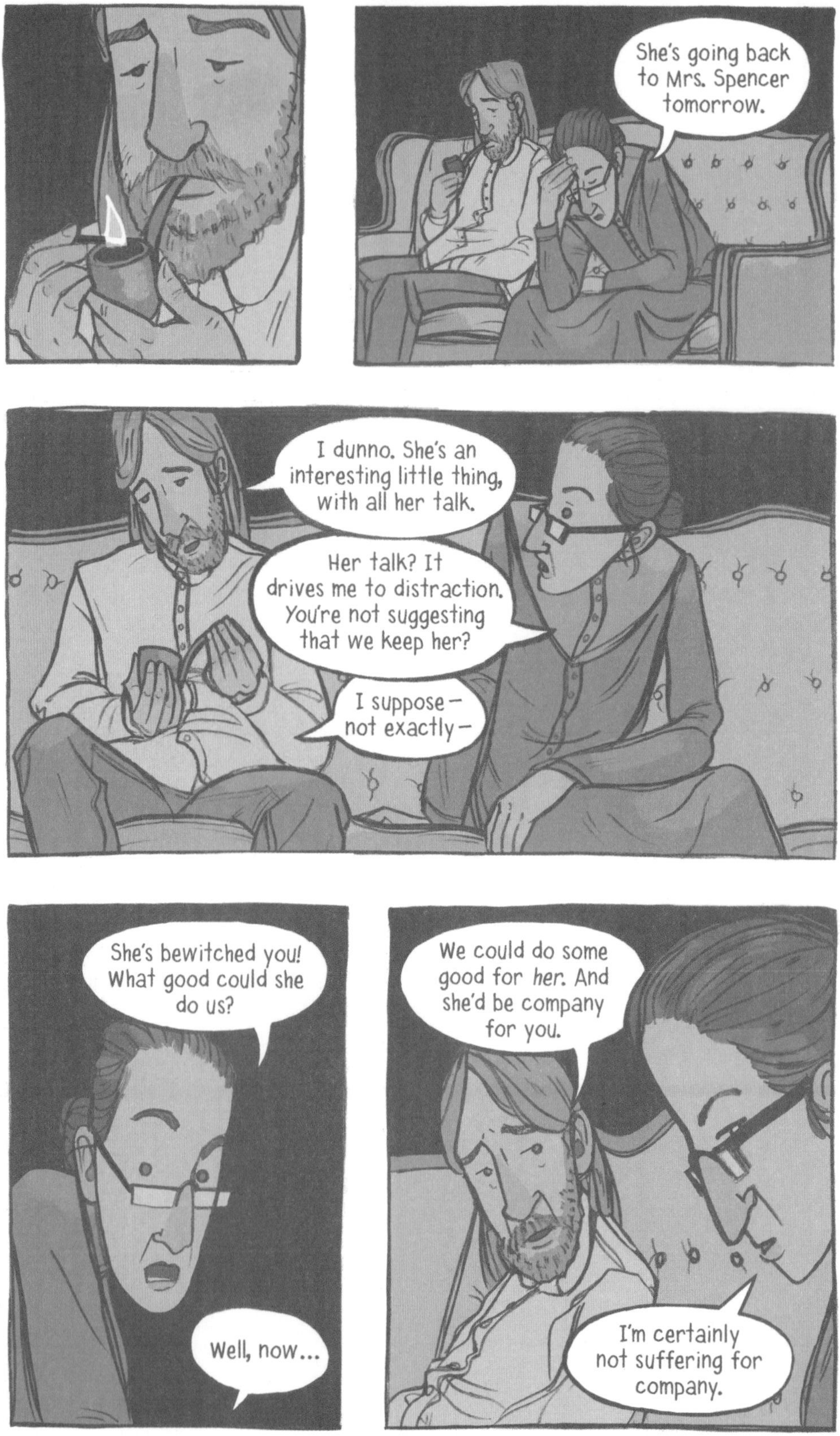
She's going back to Mrs. Spencer tomorrow.
I dunno. She's an interesting little thing, with all her talk.
Her talk? It drives me to distraction. You're not suggesting that we keep her?
I suppose— not exactly—
She's bewitched you! What good could she do us?
Well, now...
We could do some good for *her*. And she'd be company for you.
I'm certainly not suffering for company.

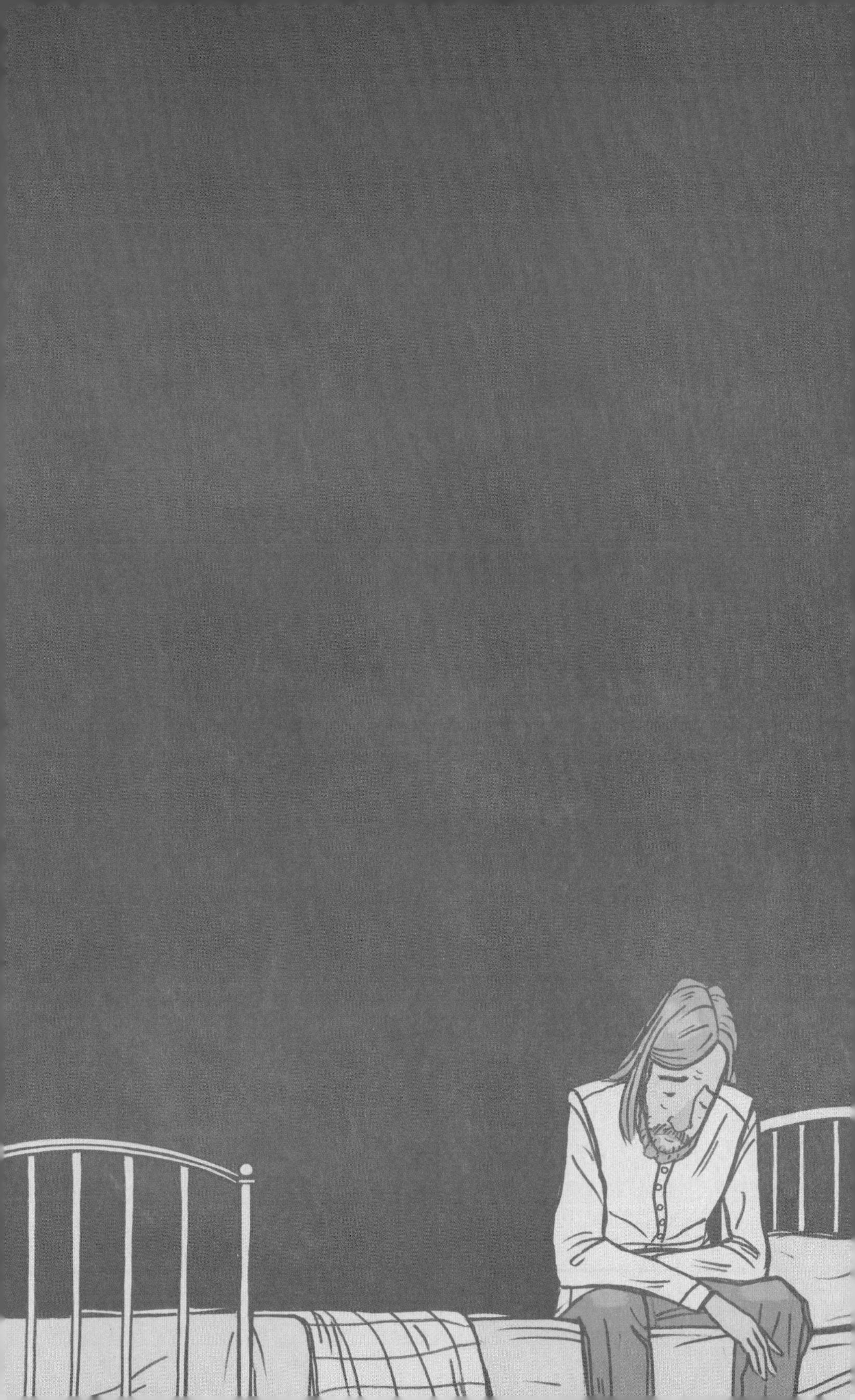

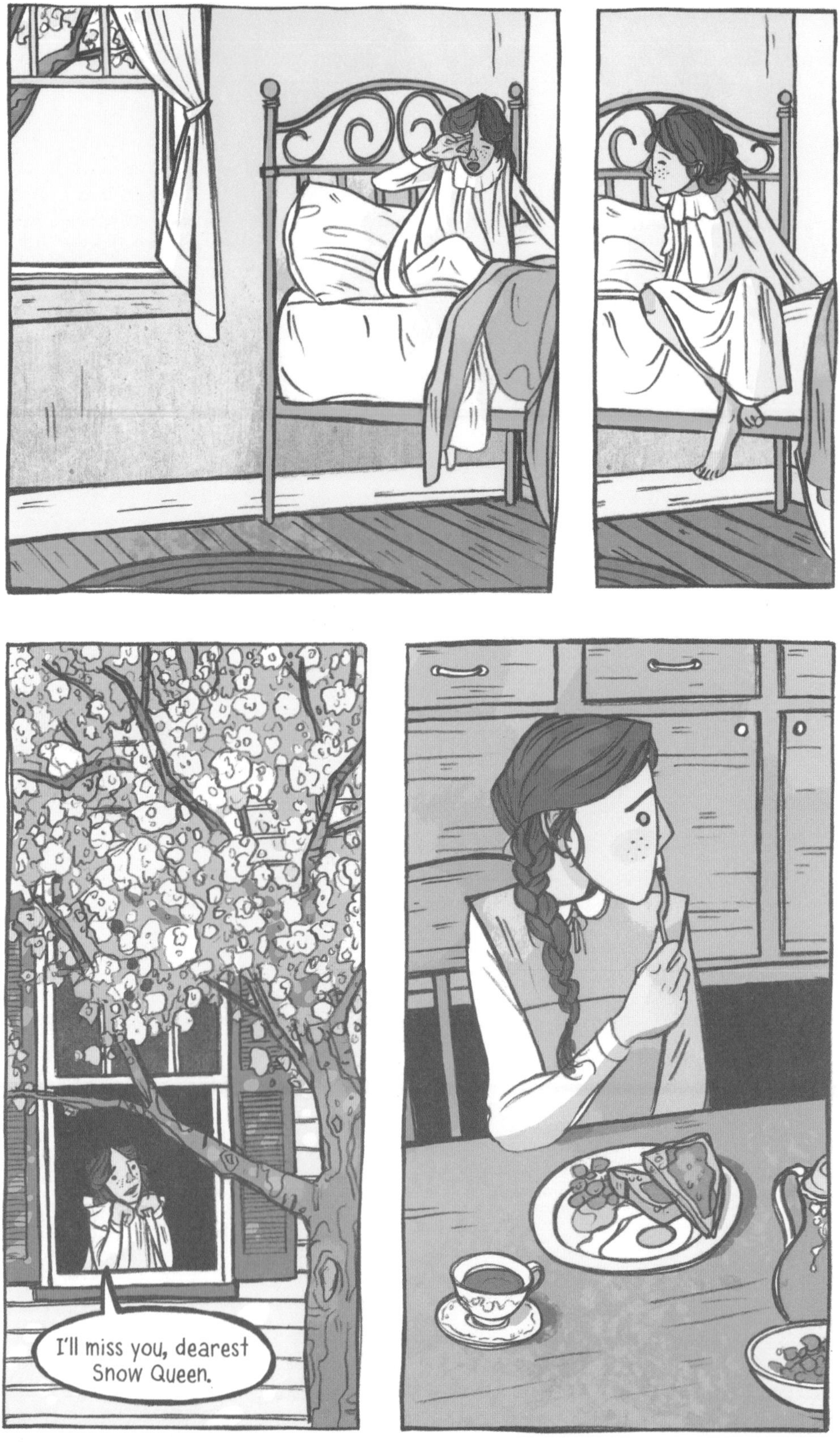
I'll miss you, dearest Snow Queen.

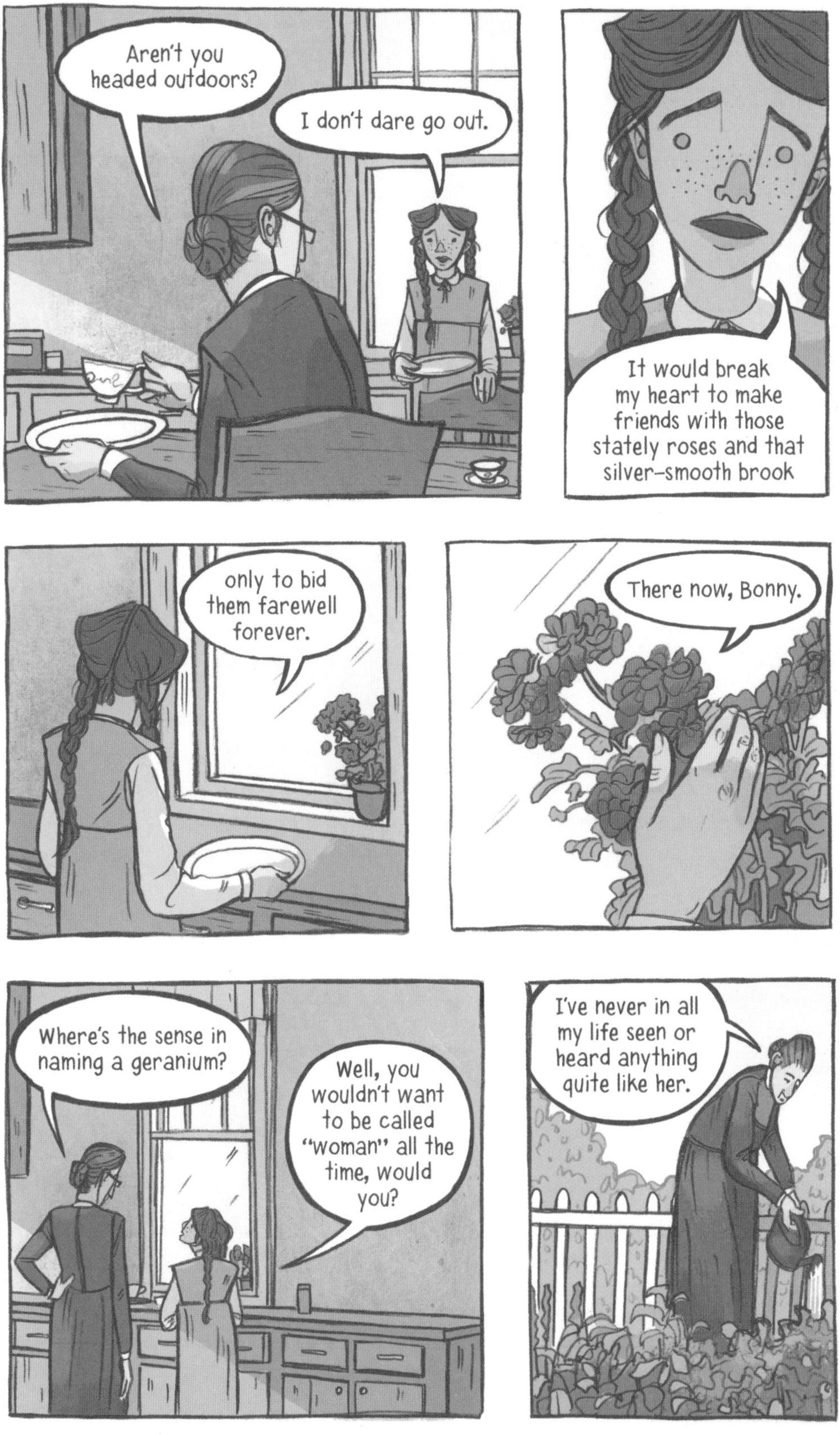
Aren't you headed outdoors?
I don't dare go out.
It would break my heart to make friends with those stately roses and that silver-smooth brook
only to bid them farewell forever.
There now, Bonny.
Where's the sense in naming a geranium?
Well, you wouldn't want to be called "woman" all the time, would you?
I've never in all my life seen or heard anything quite like her.

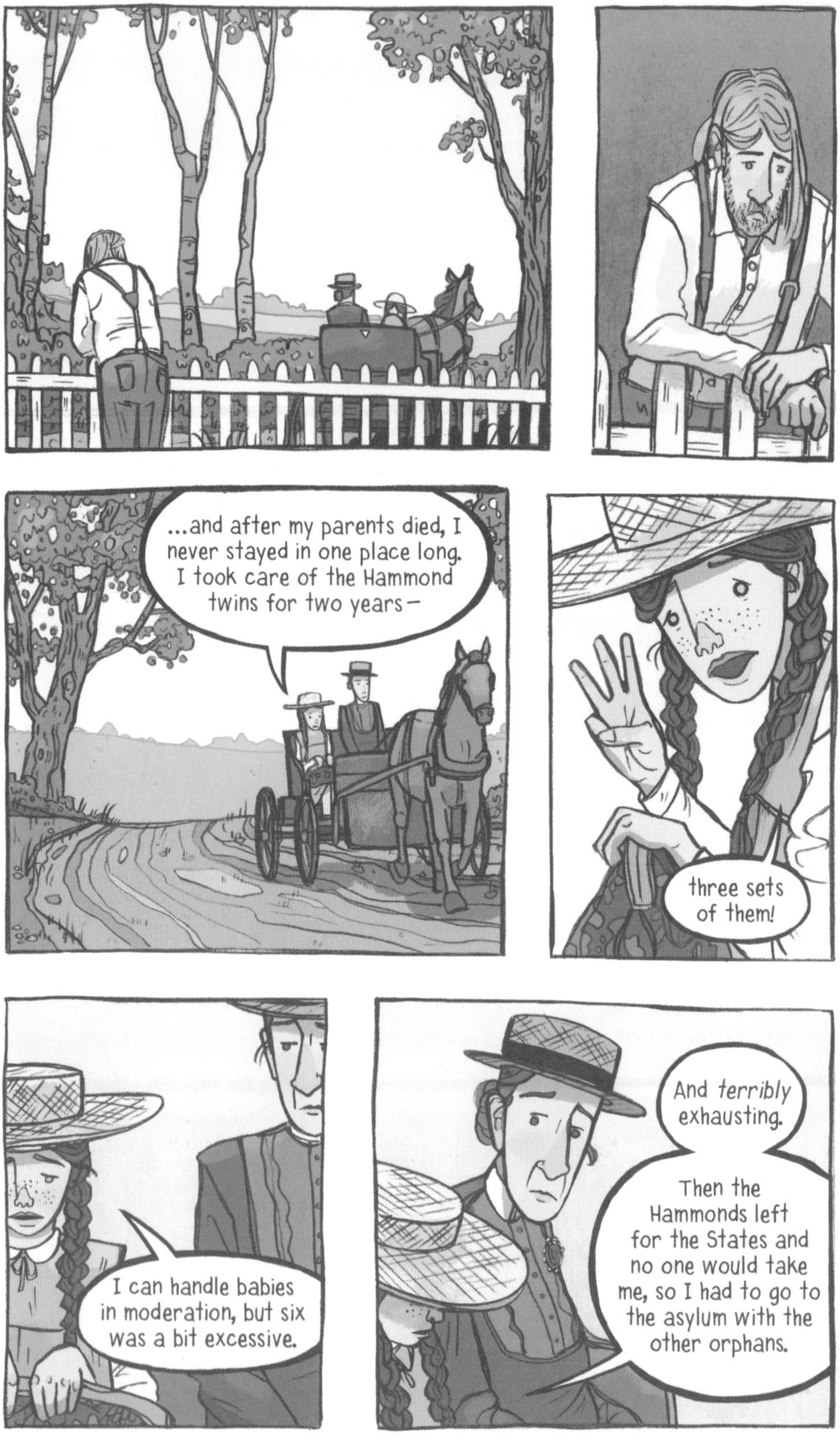
...and after my parents died, I never stayed in one place long. I took care of the Hammond twins for two years—
three sets of them!
I can handle babies in moderation, but six was a bit excessive.
And *terribly* exhausting.
Then the Hammonds left for the States and no one would take me, so I had to go to the asylum with the other orphans.

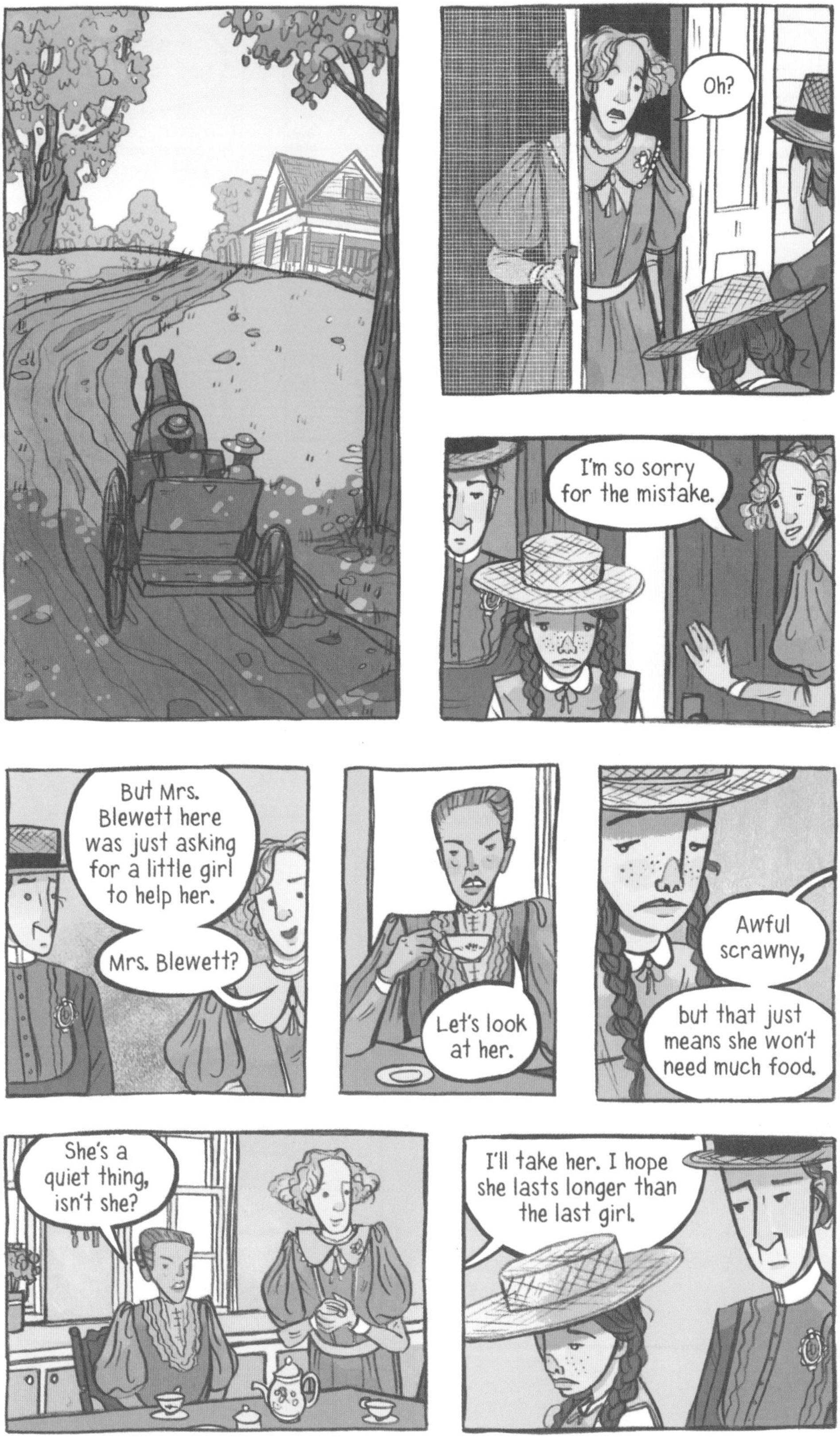
Oh?
I'm so sorry for the mistake.
But Mrs. Blewett here was just asking for a little girl to help her.
Mrs. Blewett?
Let's look at her.
Awful scrawny,
but that just means she won't need much food.
She's a quiet thing, isn't she?
I'll take her. I hope she lasts longer than the last girl.

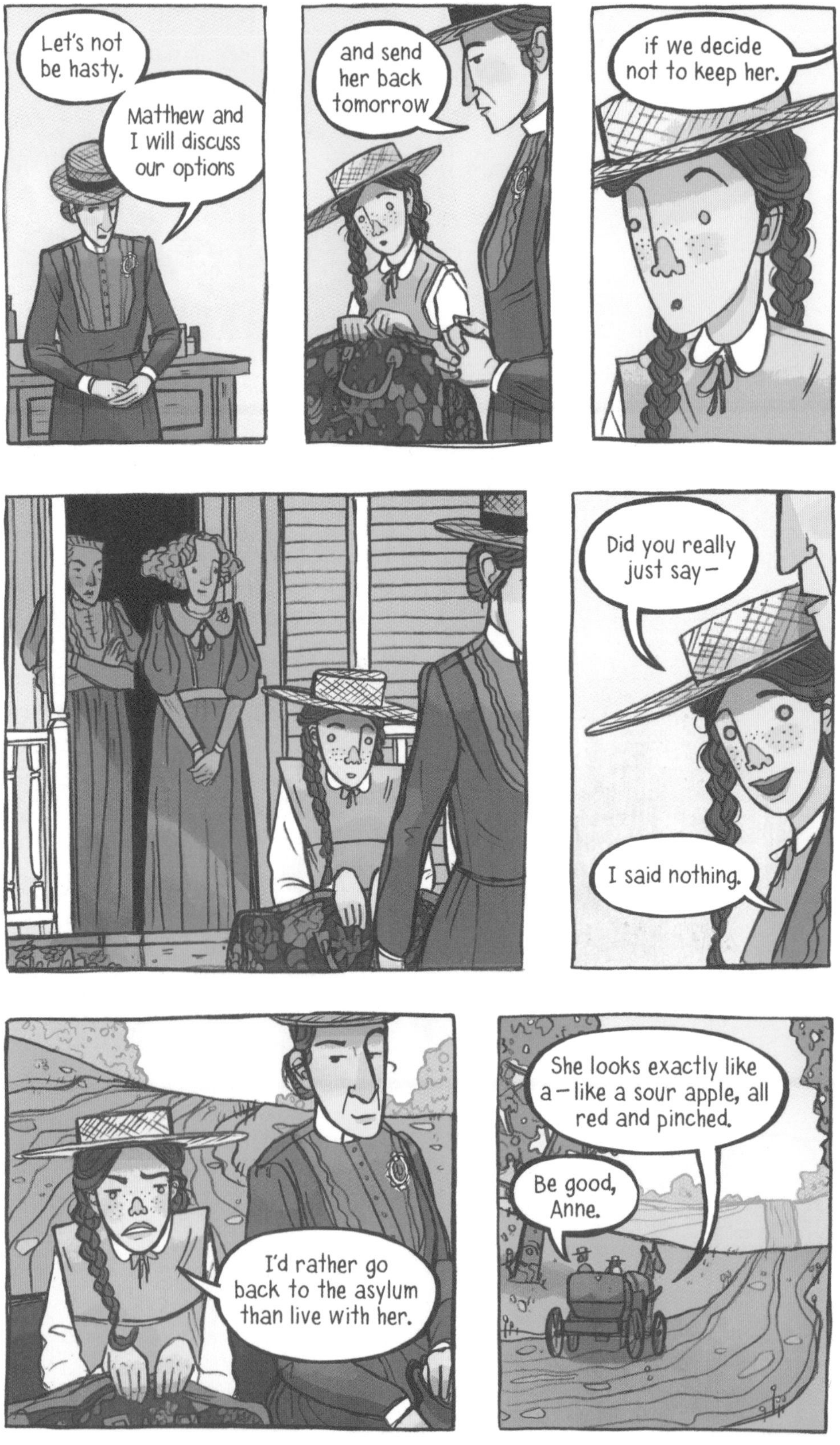
Let's not be hasty.
Matthew and I will discuss our options
and send her back tomorrow
if we decide not to keep her.
Did you really just say—
I said nothing.
I'd rather go back to the asylum than live with her.
She looks exactly like a—like a sour apple, all red and pinched.
Be good, Anne.

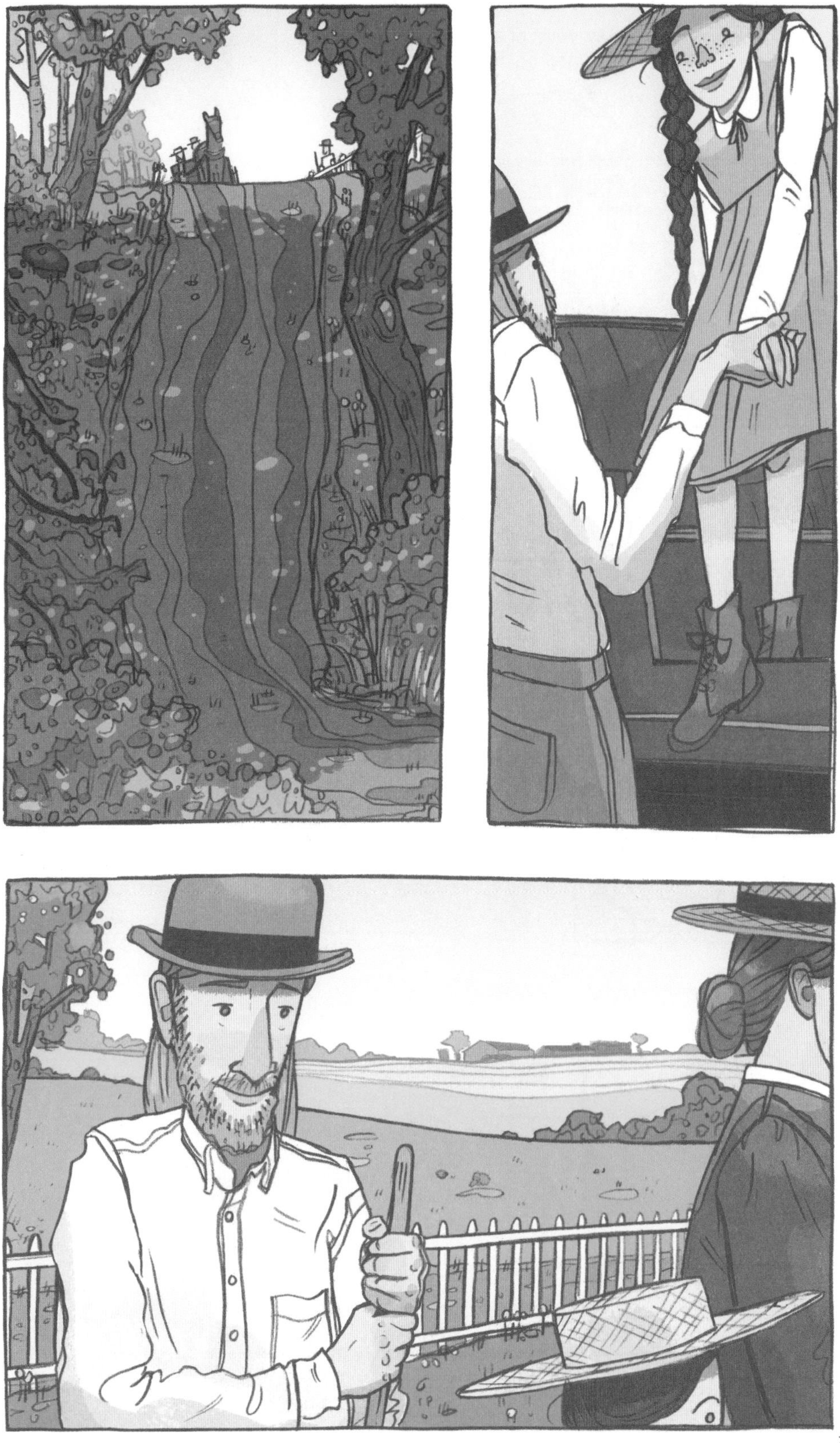

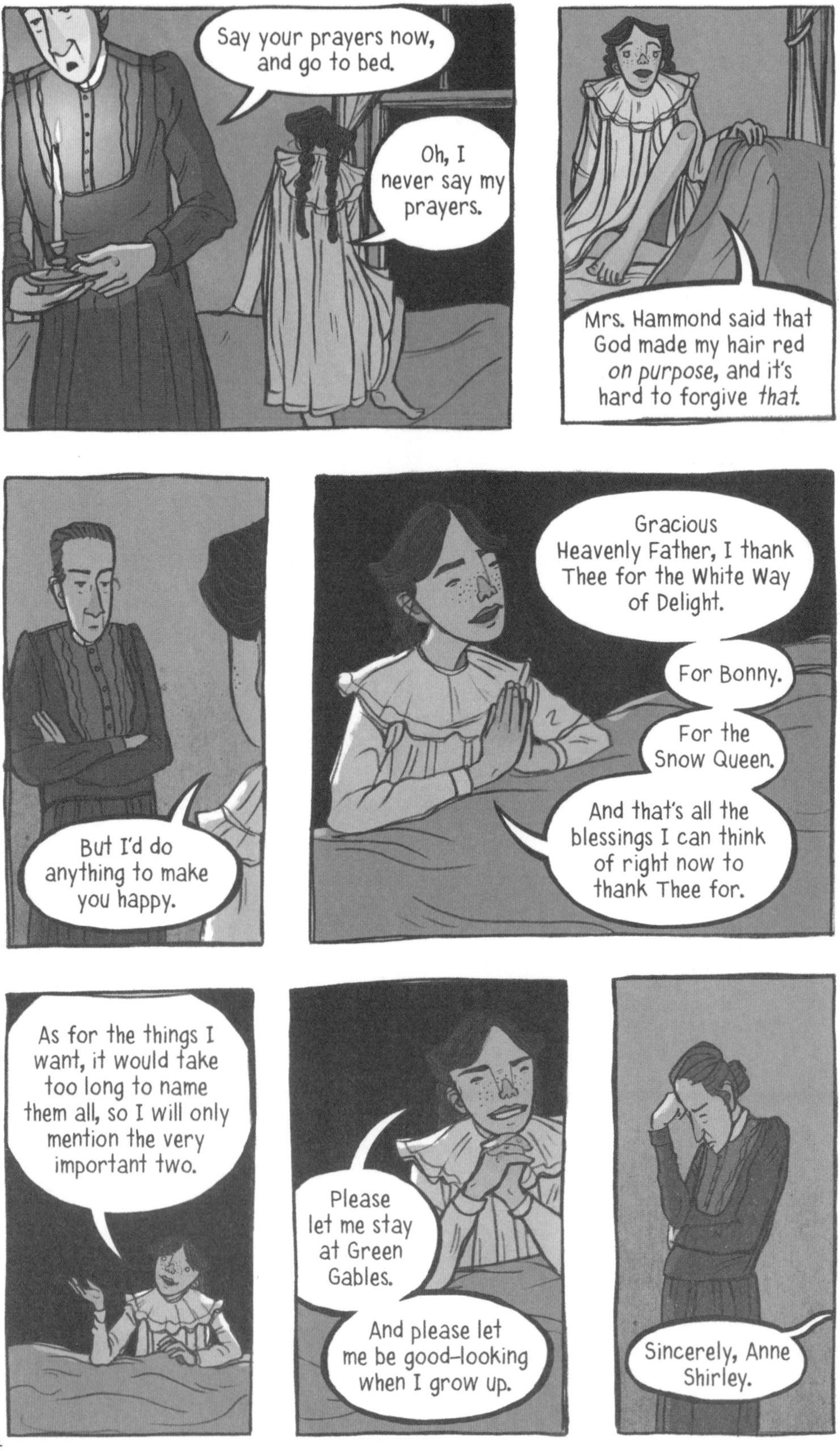

Say your prayers now, and go to bed.
Oh, I never say my prayers.
Mrs. Hammond said that God made my hair red *on purpose*, and it's hard to forgive *that*.
But I'd do anything to make you happy.
Gracious Heavenly Father, I thank Thee for the White Way of Delight.
For Bonny.
For the Snow Queen.
And that's all the blessings I can think of right now to thank Thee for.
As for the things I want, it would take too long to name them all, so I will only mention the very important two.
Please let me stay at Green Gables.
And please let me be good-looking when I grow up.
Sincerely, Anne Shirley.

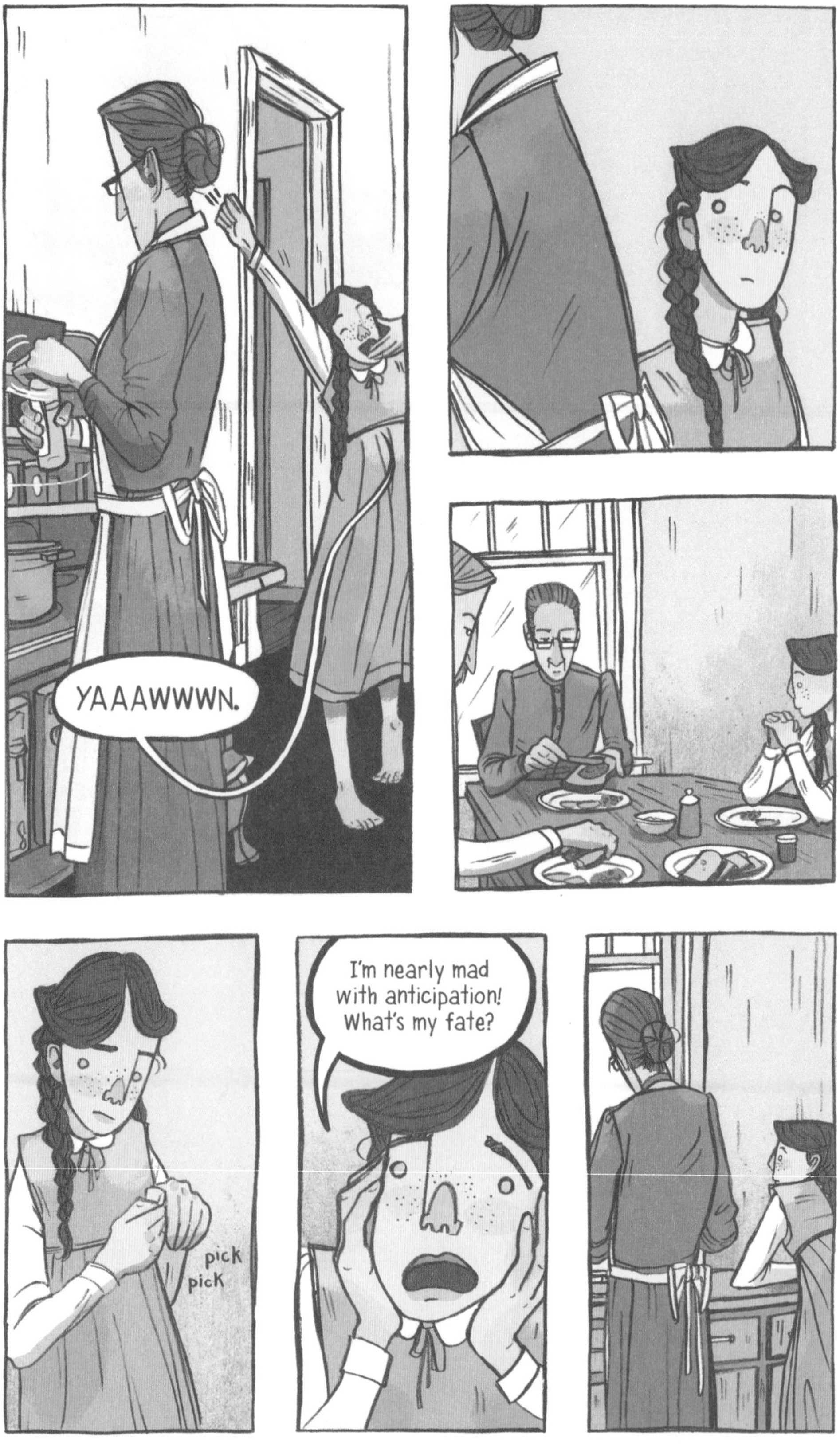
YAAAWWWN.
pick
pick
I'm nearly mad with anticipation! What's my fate?

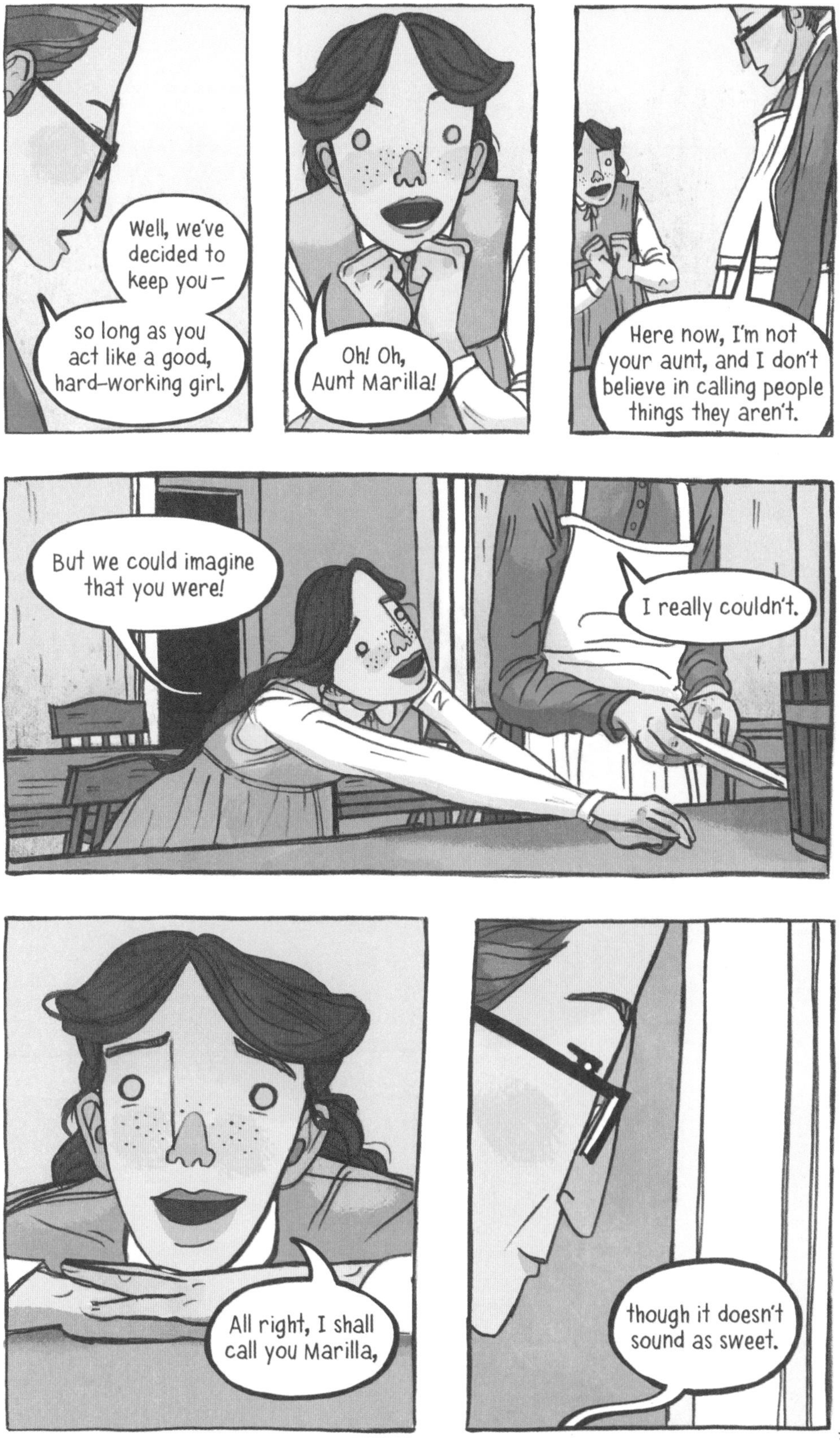

Well, we've decided to keep you—
so long as you act like a good, hard-working girl.
Oh! Oh, Aunt Marilla!
Here now, I'm not your aunt, and I don't believe in calling people things they aren't.
But we could imagine that you were!
I really couldn't.
All right, I shall call you Marilla,
though it doesn't sound as sweet.

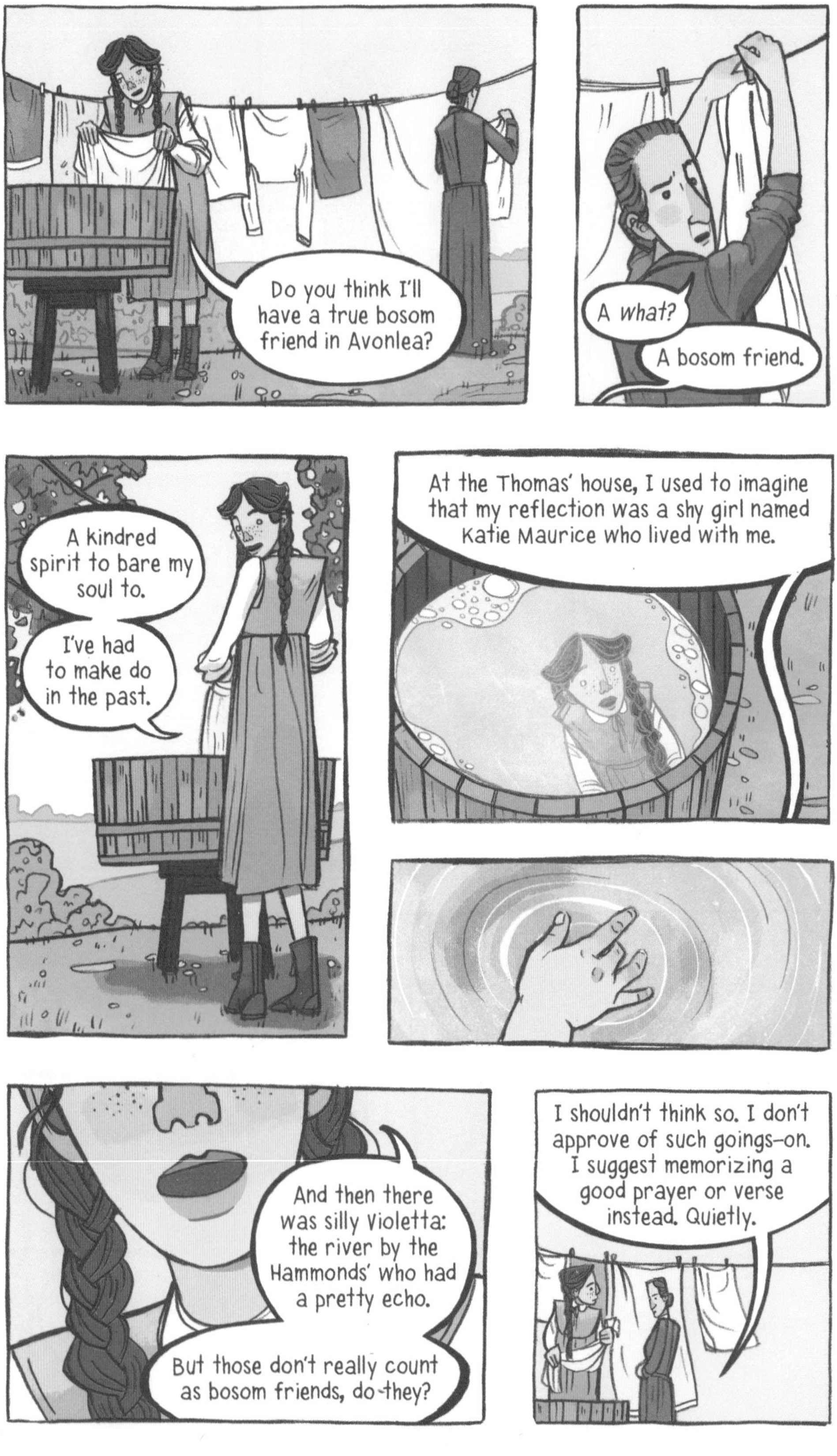

Do you think I'll have a true bosom friend in Avonlea?
A *what?*
A bosom friend.
A kindred spirit to bare my soul to.
I've had to make do in the past.
At the Thomas' house, I used to imagine that my reflection was a shy girl named Katie Maurice who lived with me.
And then there was silly Violetta: the river by the Hammonds' who had a pretty echo.
But those don't really count as bosom friends, do they?
I shouldn't think so. I don't approve of such goings-on. I suggest memorizing a good prayer or verse instead. Quietly.

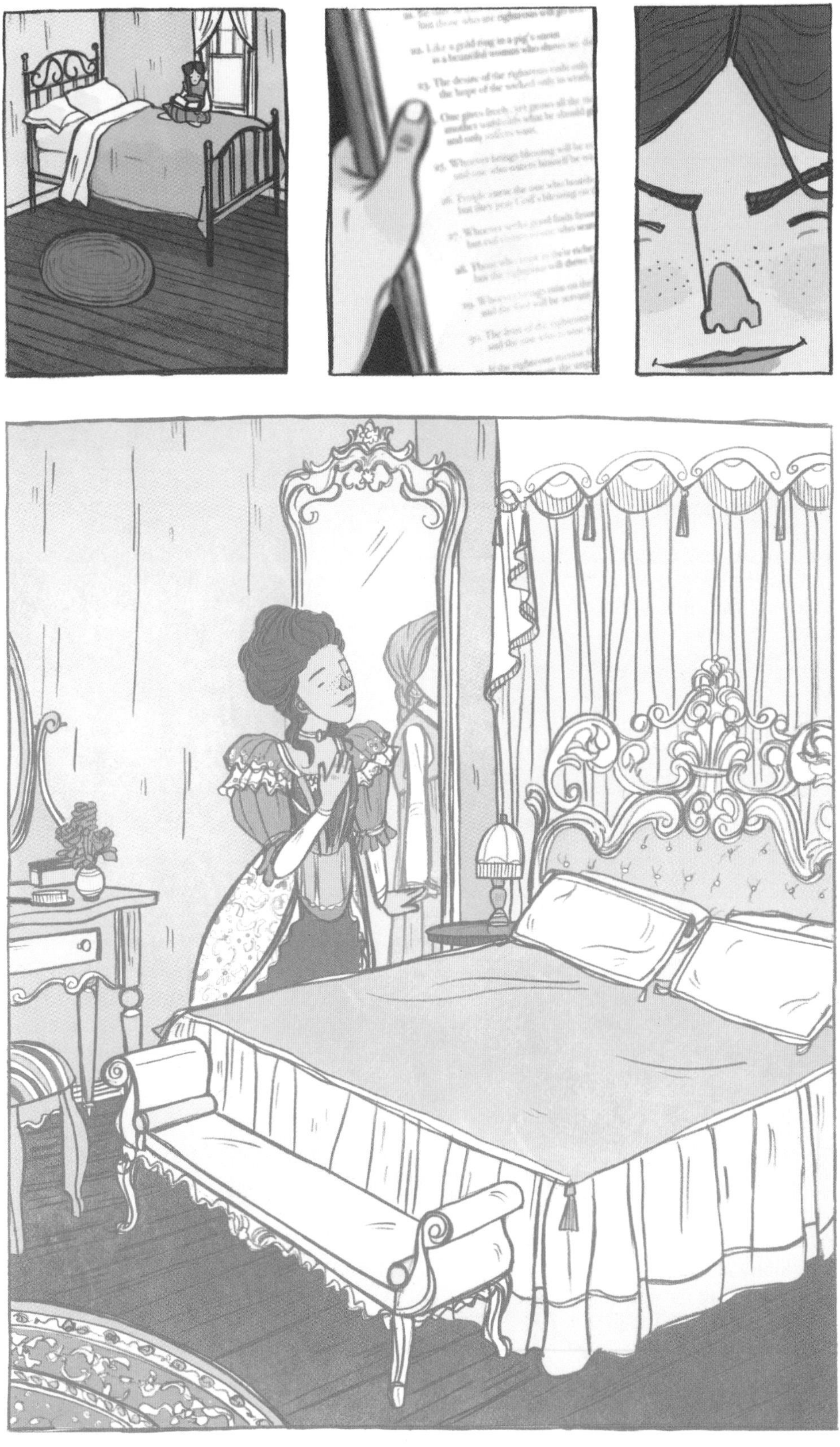

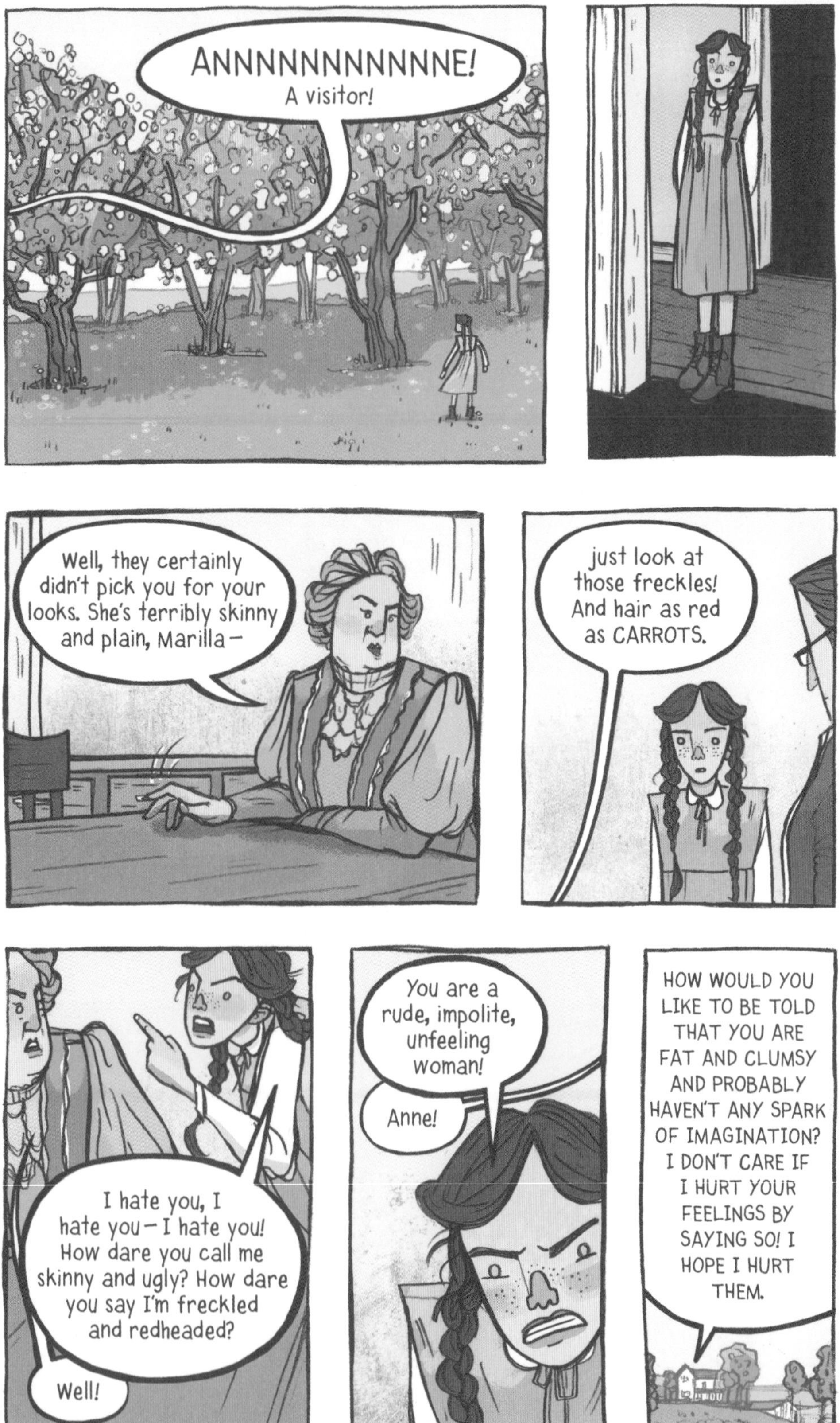
ANNNNNNNNNNNE!
A visitor!
Well, they certainly didn't pick you for your looks. She's terribly skinny and plain, Marilla—
just look at those freckles! And hair as red as CARROTS.
I hate you, I hate you—I hate you! How dare you call me skinny and ugly? How dare you say I'm freckled and redheaded?
Well!
You are a rude, impolite, unfeeling woman!
Anne!
HOW WOULD YOU LIKE TO BE TOLD THAT YOU ARE FAT AND CLUMSY AND PROBABLY HAVEN'T ANY SPARK OF IMAGINATION? I DON'T CARE IF I HURT YOUR FEELINGS BY SAYING SO! I HOPE I HURT THEM.

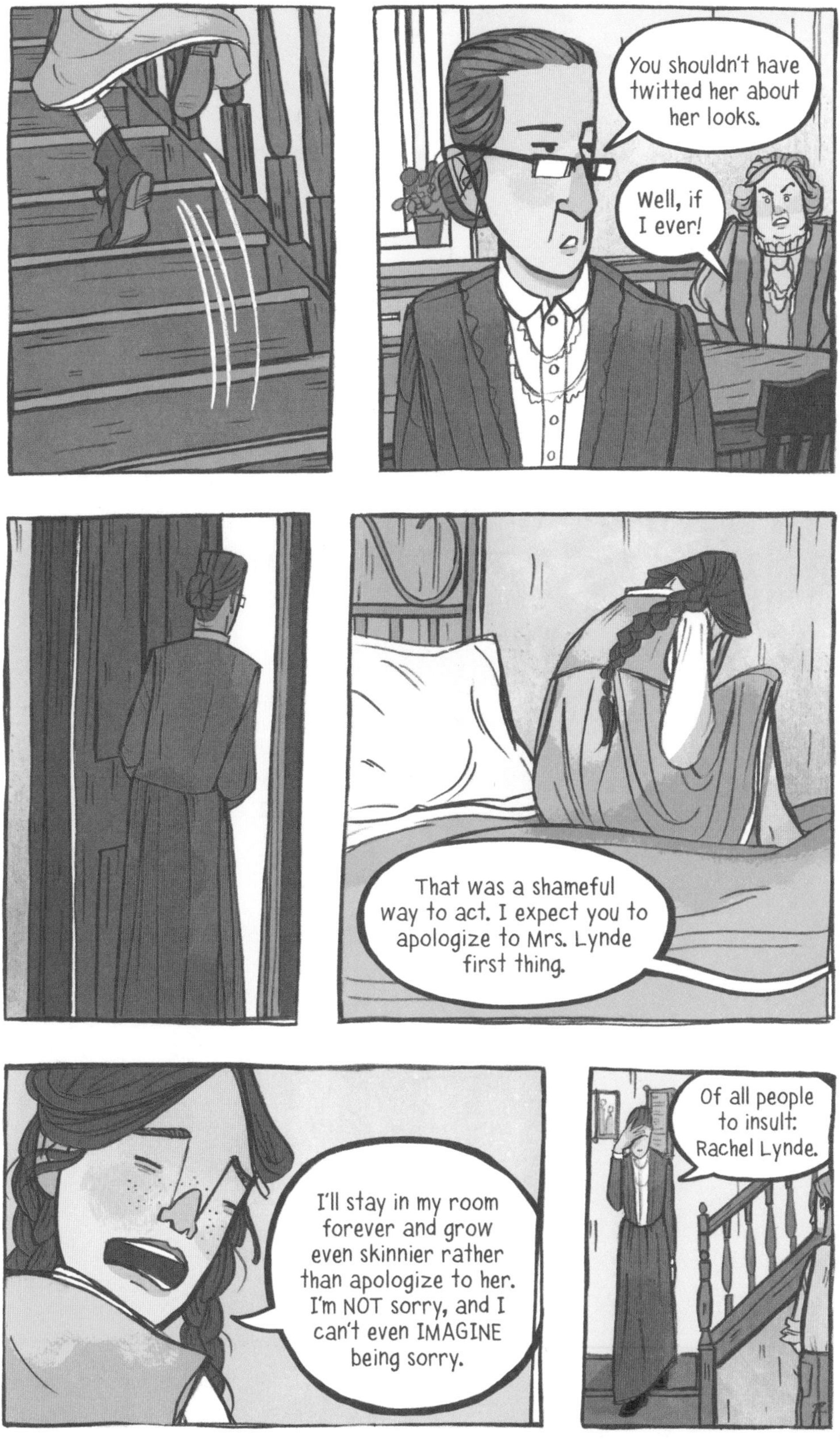
You shouldn't have twitted her about her looks.
Well, if I ever!
That was a shameful way to act. I expect you to apologize to Mrs. Lynde first thing.
I'll stay in my room forever and grow even skinnier rather than apologize to her. I'm NOT sorry, and I can't even IMAGINE being sorry.
Of all people to insult: Rachel Lynde.

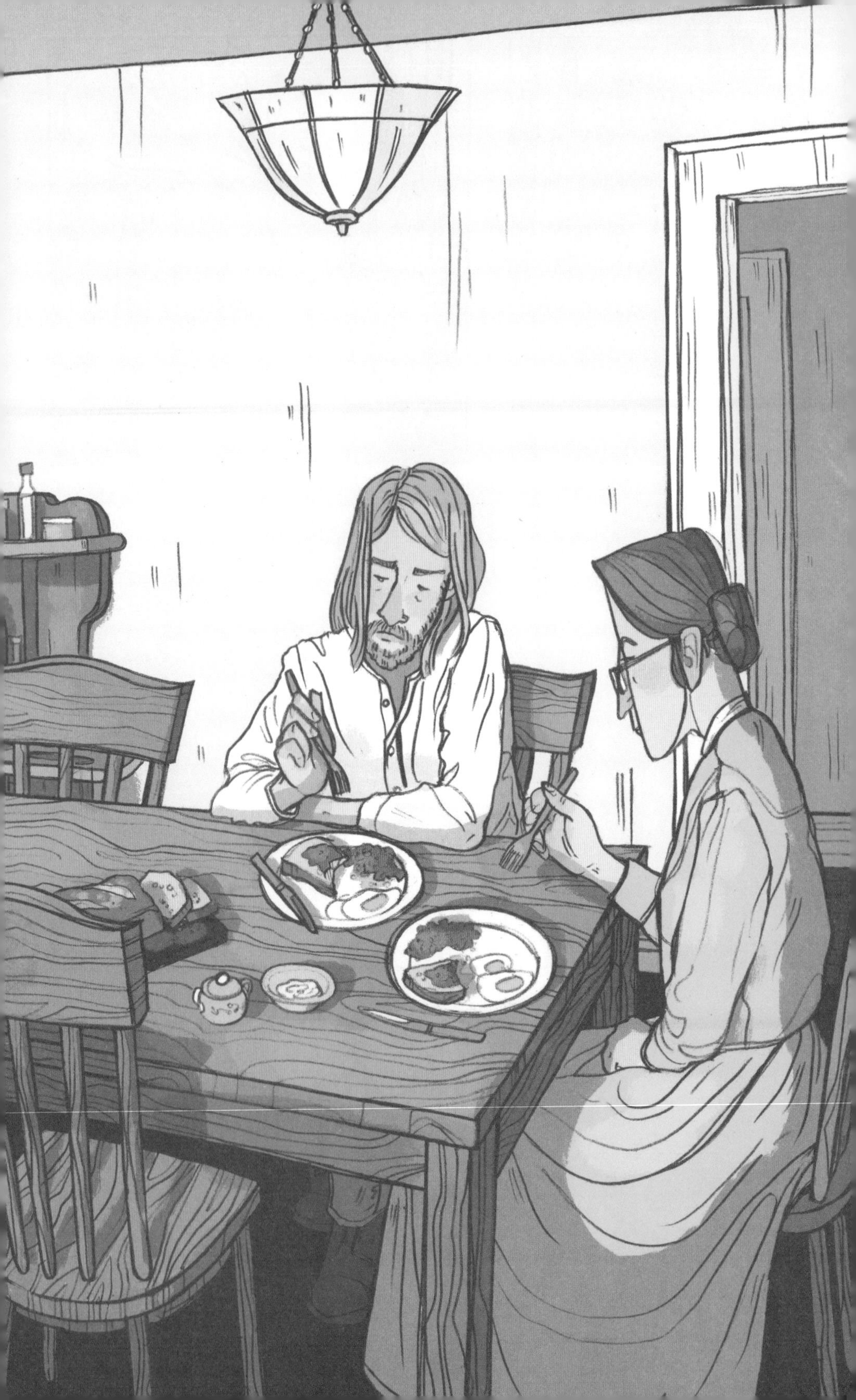

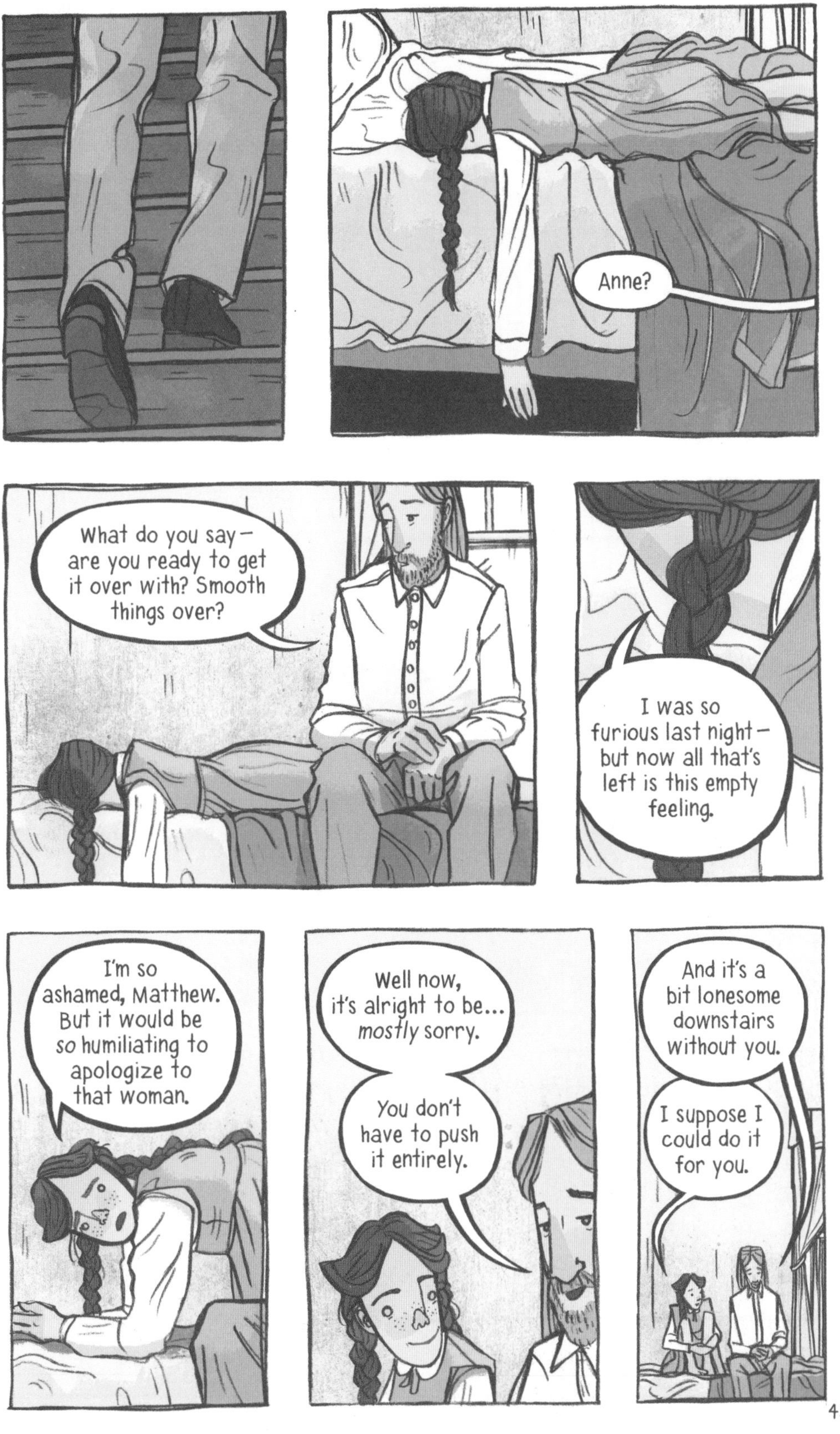
Anne?
What do you say— are you ready to get it over with? Smooth things over?
I was so furious last night— but now all that's left is this empty feeling.
I'm so ashamed, Matthew. But it would be *so* humiliating to apologize to that woman.
Well now, it's alright to be... *mostly* sorry.
You don't have to push it entirely.
And it's a bit lonesome downstairs without you.
I suppose I could do it for you.

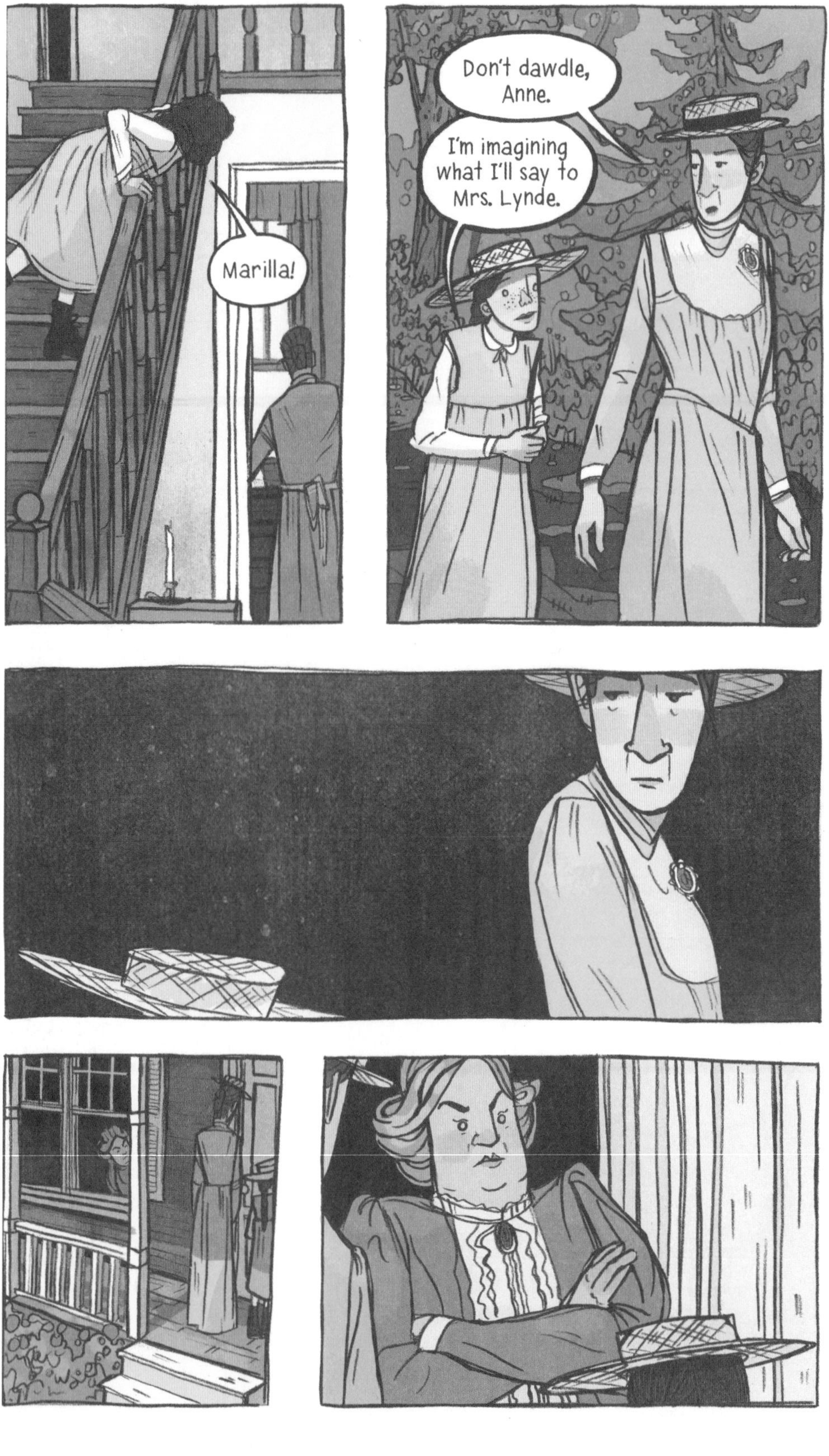
Marilla!
Don't dawdle, Anne.
I'm imagining what I'll say to Mrs. Lynde.

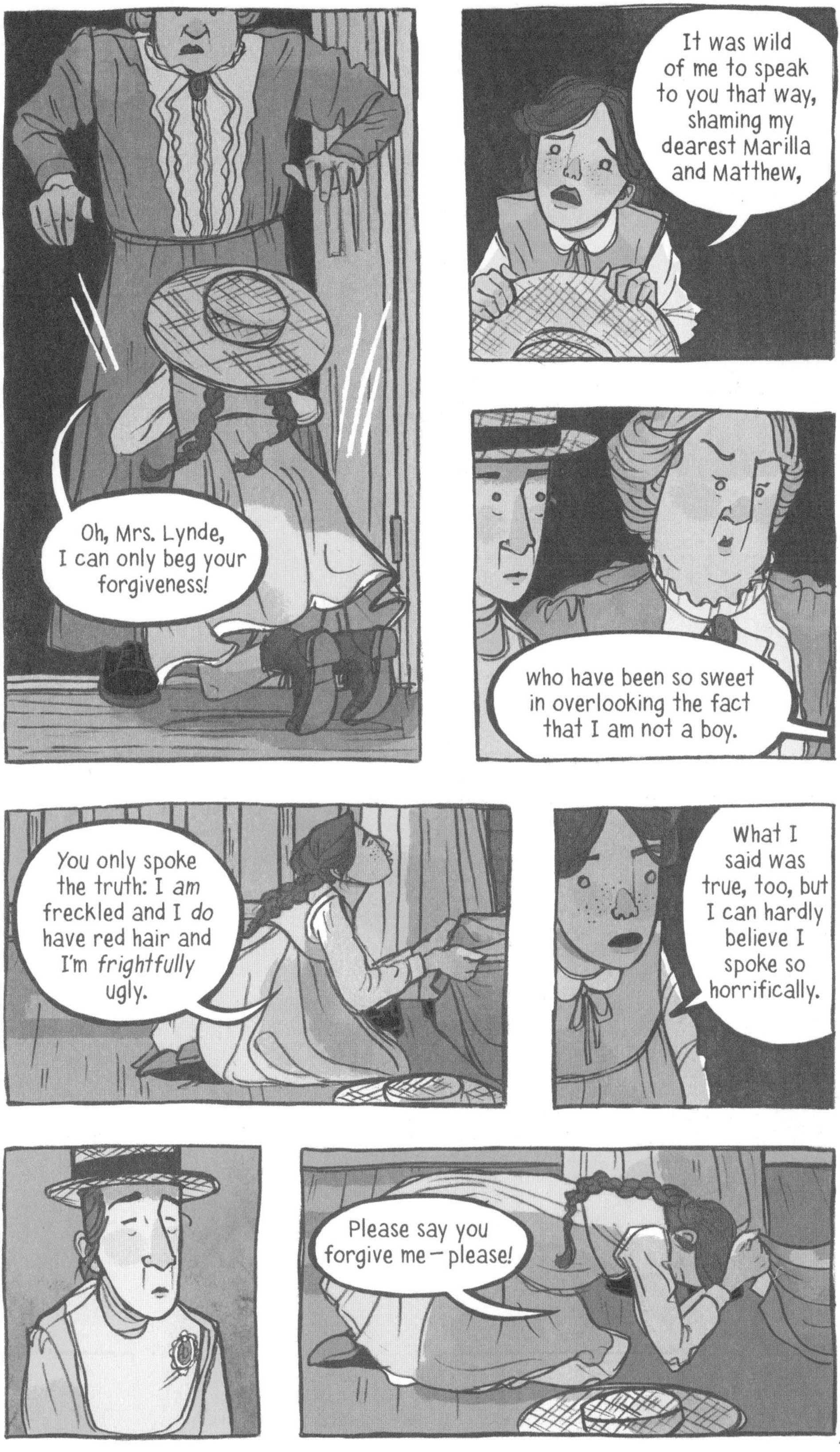
Oh, Mrs. Lynde, I can only beg your forgiveness!
It was wild of me to speak to you that way, shaming my dearest Marilla and Matthew,
who have been so sweet in overlooking the fact that I am not a boy.
You only spoke the truth: I *am* freckled and I *do* have red hair and I'm *frightfully* ugly.
What I said was true, too, but I can hardly believe I spoke so horrifically.
Please say you forgive me—please!

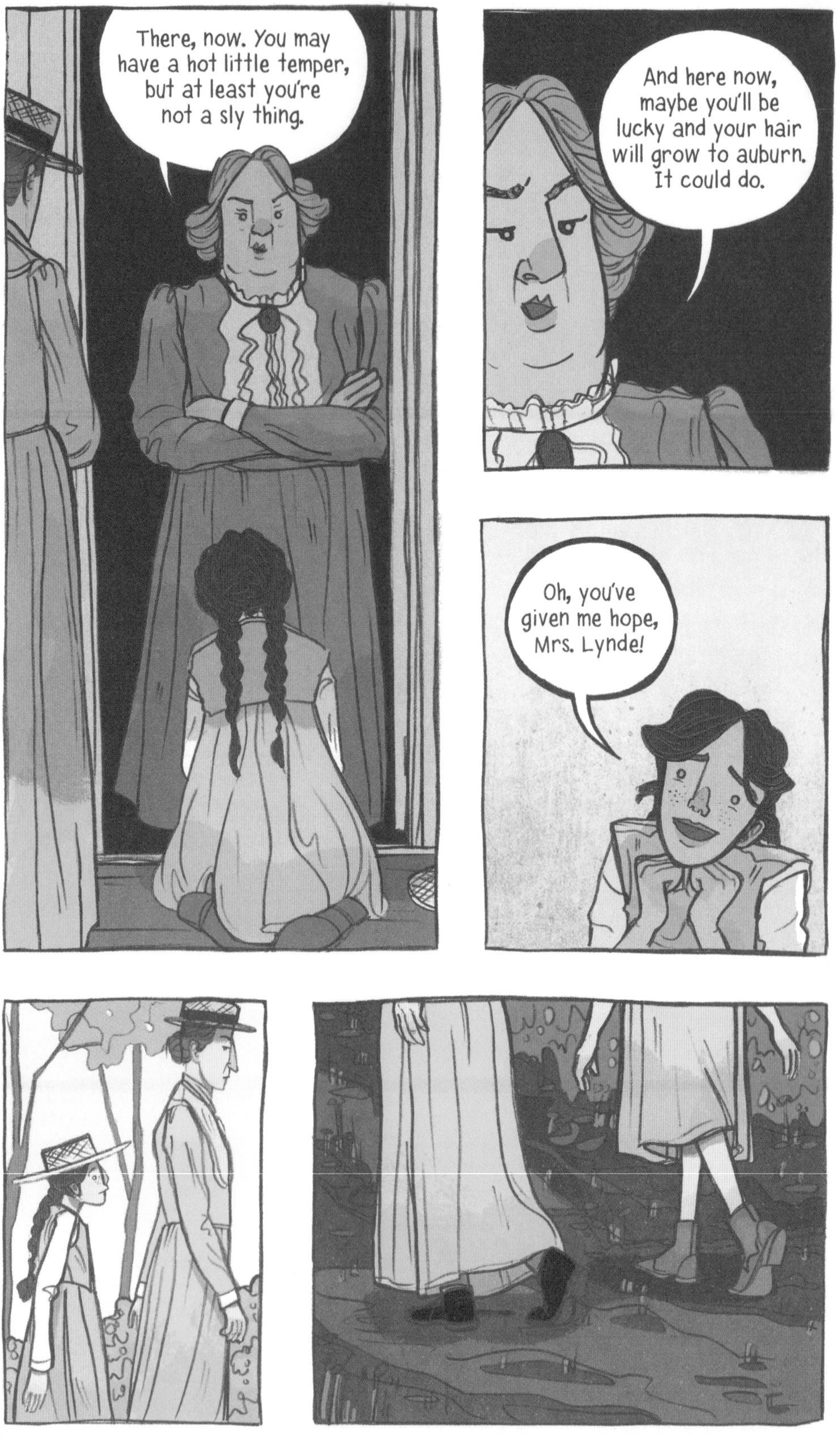
There, now. You may have a hot little temper, but at least you're not a sly thing.
And here now, maybe you'll be lucky and your hair will grow to auburn. It could do.
Oh, you've given me hope, Mrs. Lynde!

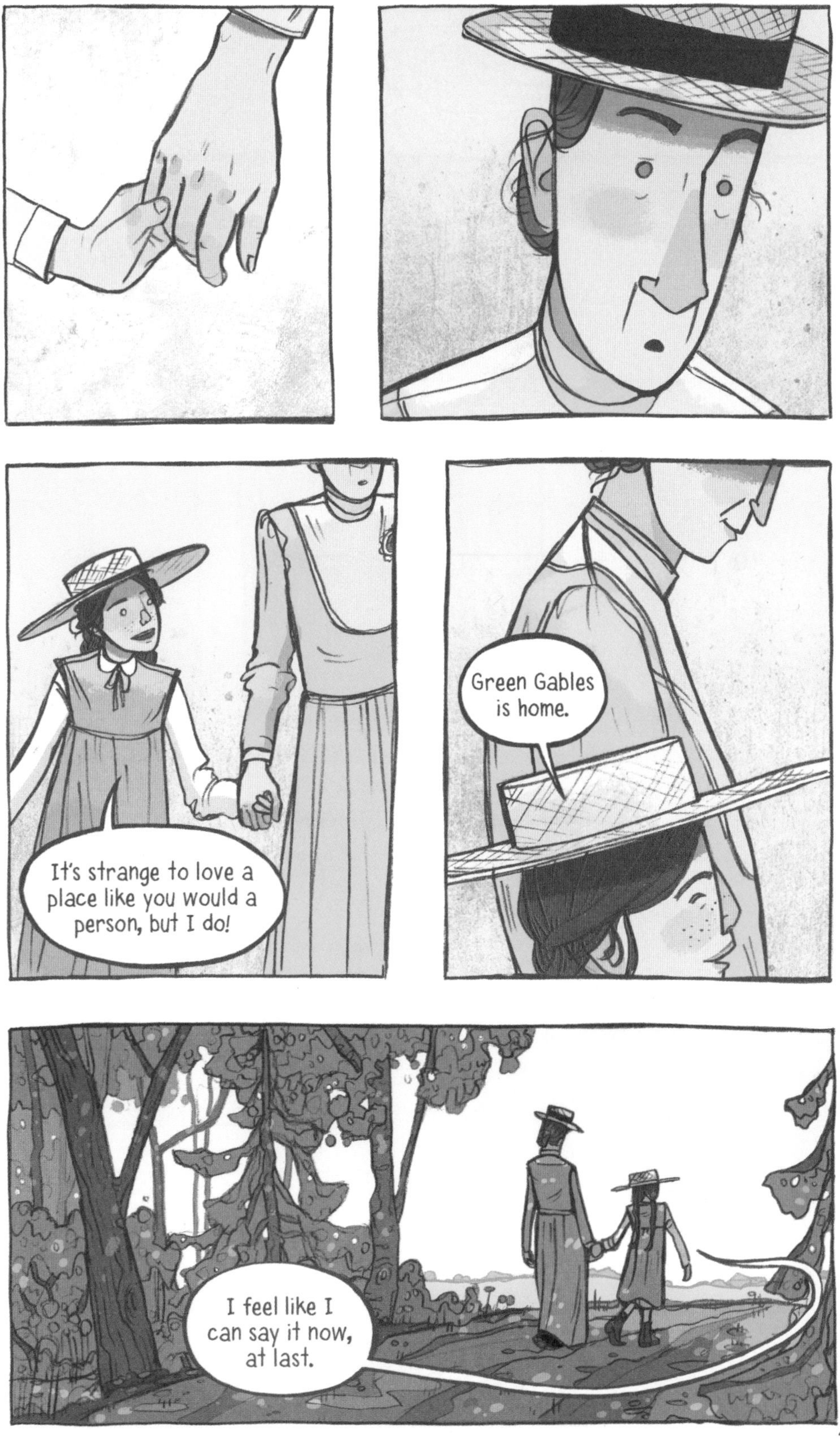
It's strange to love a place like you would a person, but I do!
Green Gables is home.
I feel like I can say it now, at last.

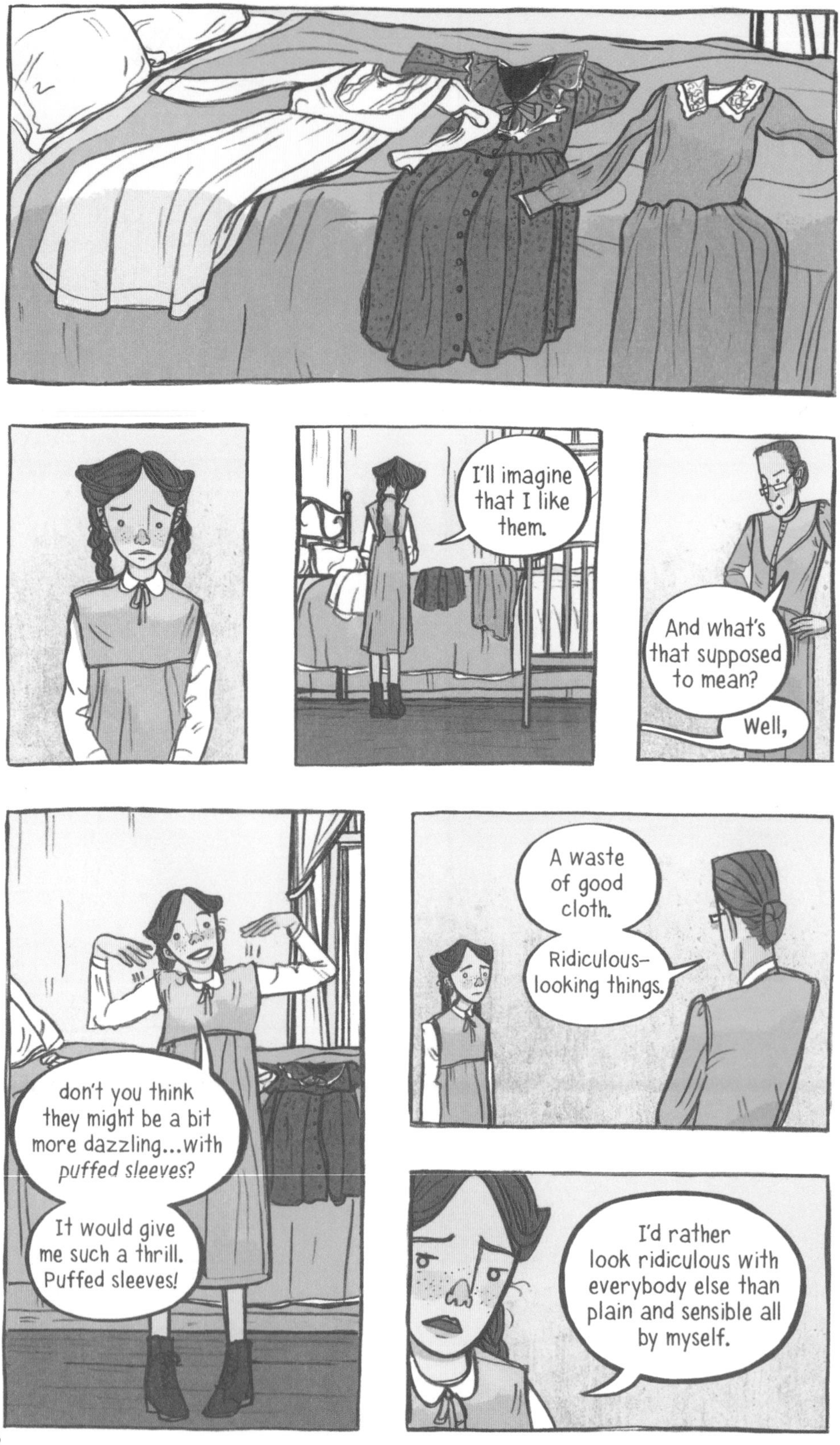

I'll imagine that I like them.
And what's that supposed to mean?
Well,
don't you think they might be a bit more dazzling...with *puffed sleeves*?
It would give me such a thrill. Puffed sleeves!
A waste of good cloth.
Ridiculous-looking things.
I'd rather look ridiculous with everybody else than plain and sensible all by myself.

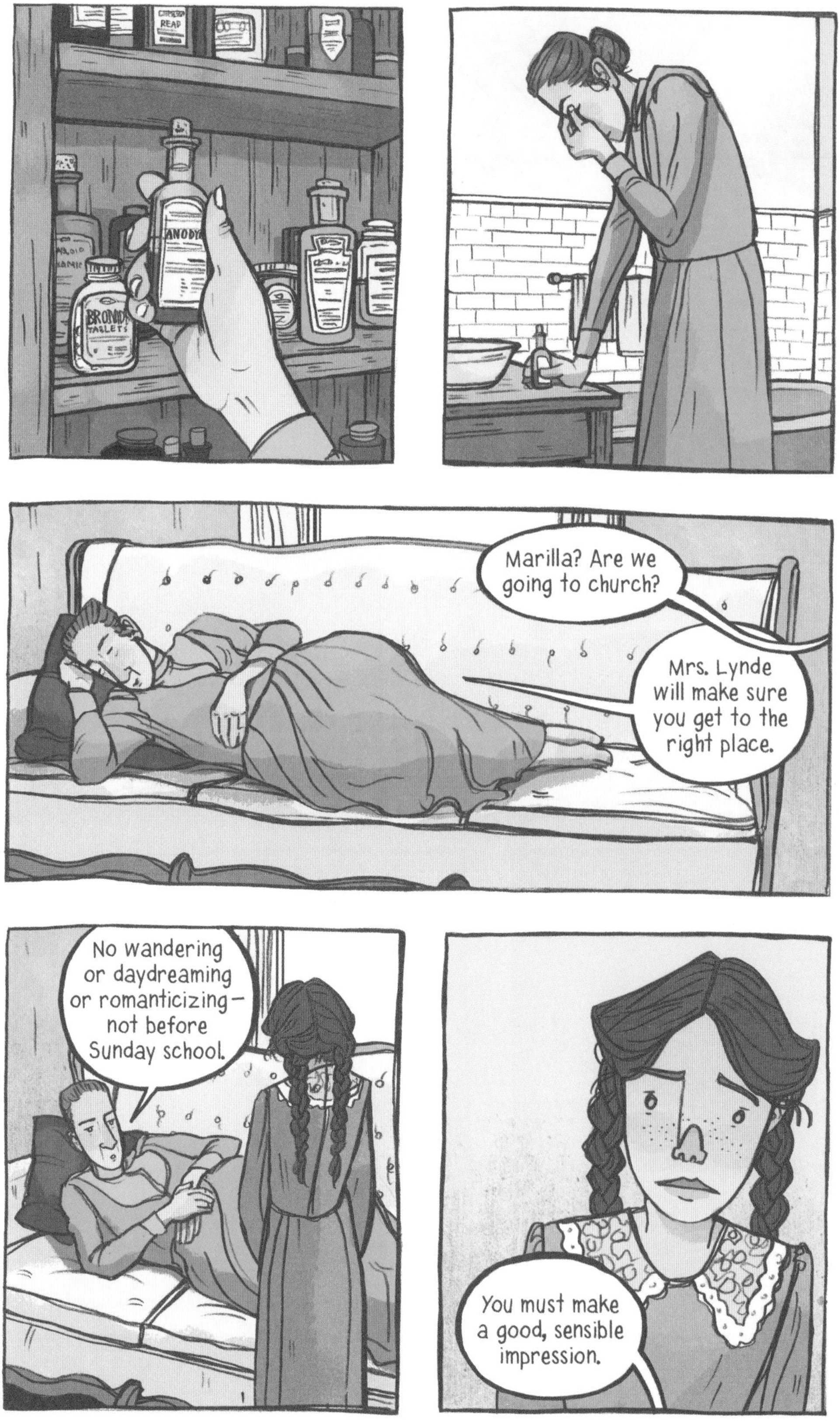
Marilla? Are we going to church?
Mrs. Lynde will make sure you get to the right place.
No wandering or daydreaming or romanticizing— not before Sunday school.
You must make a good, sensible impression.

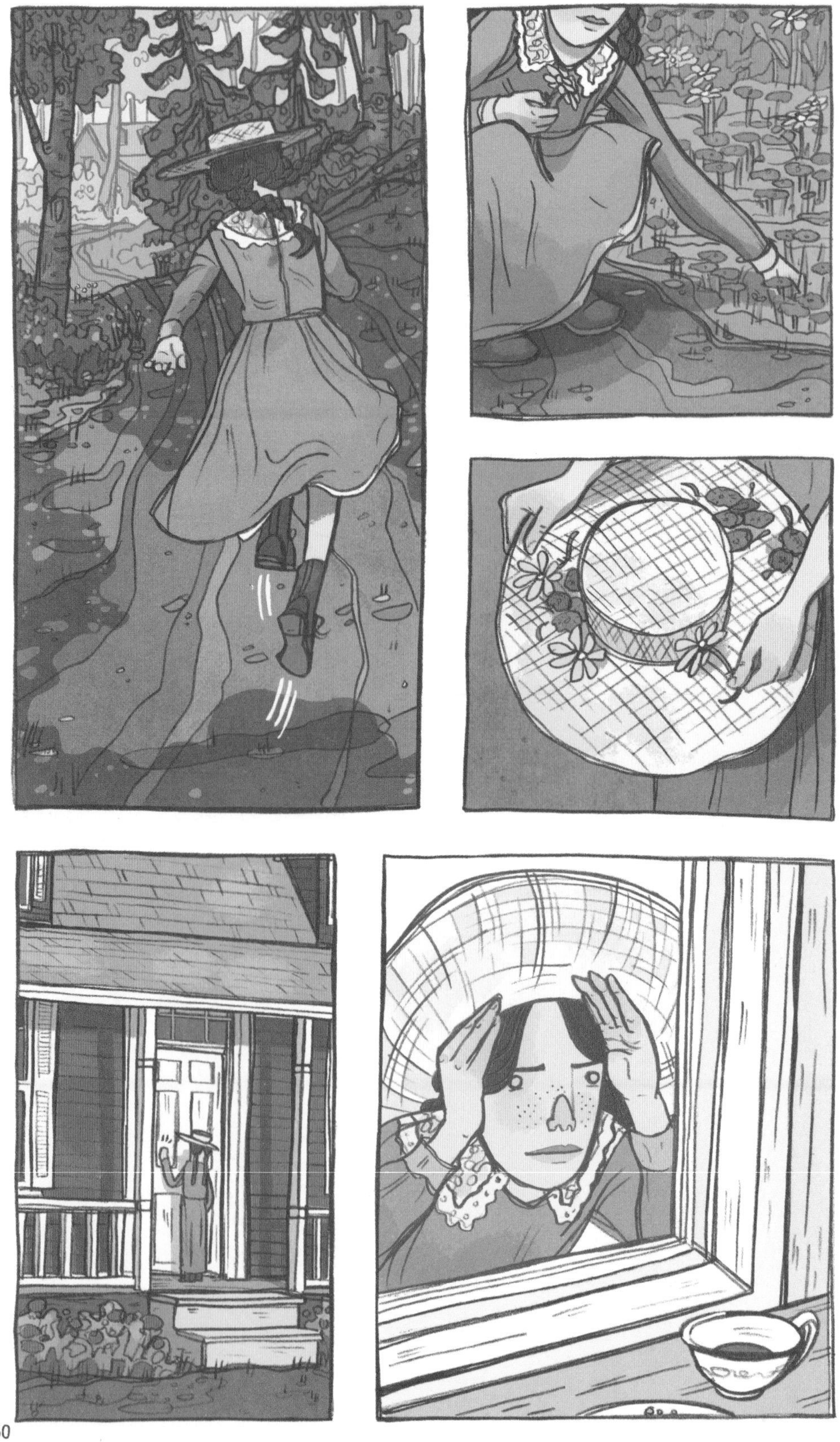

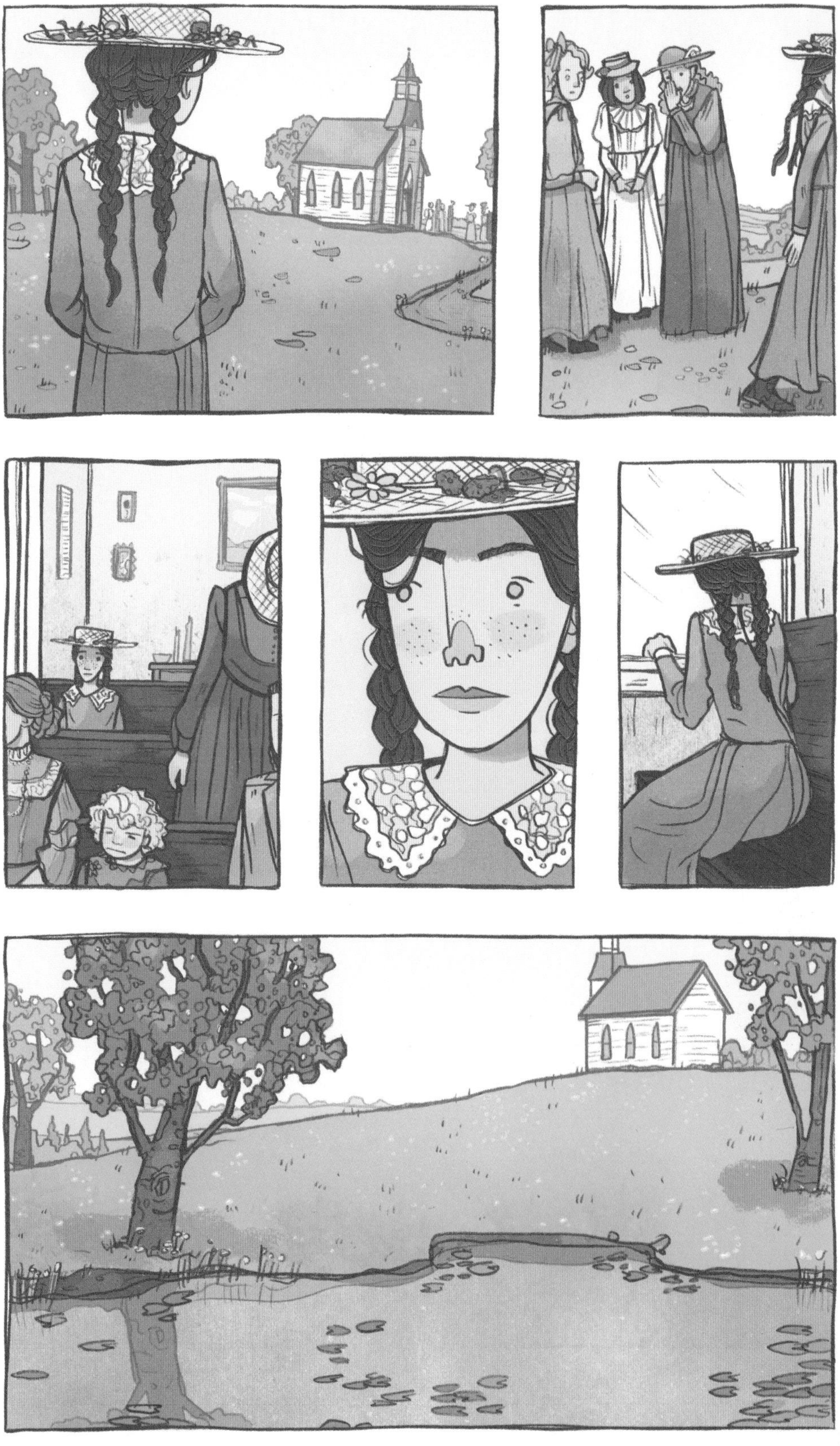

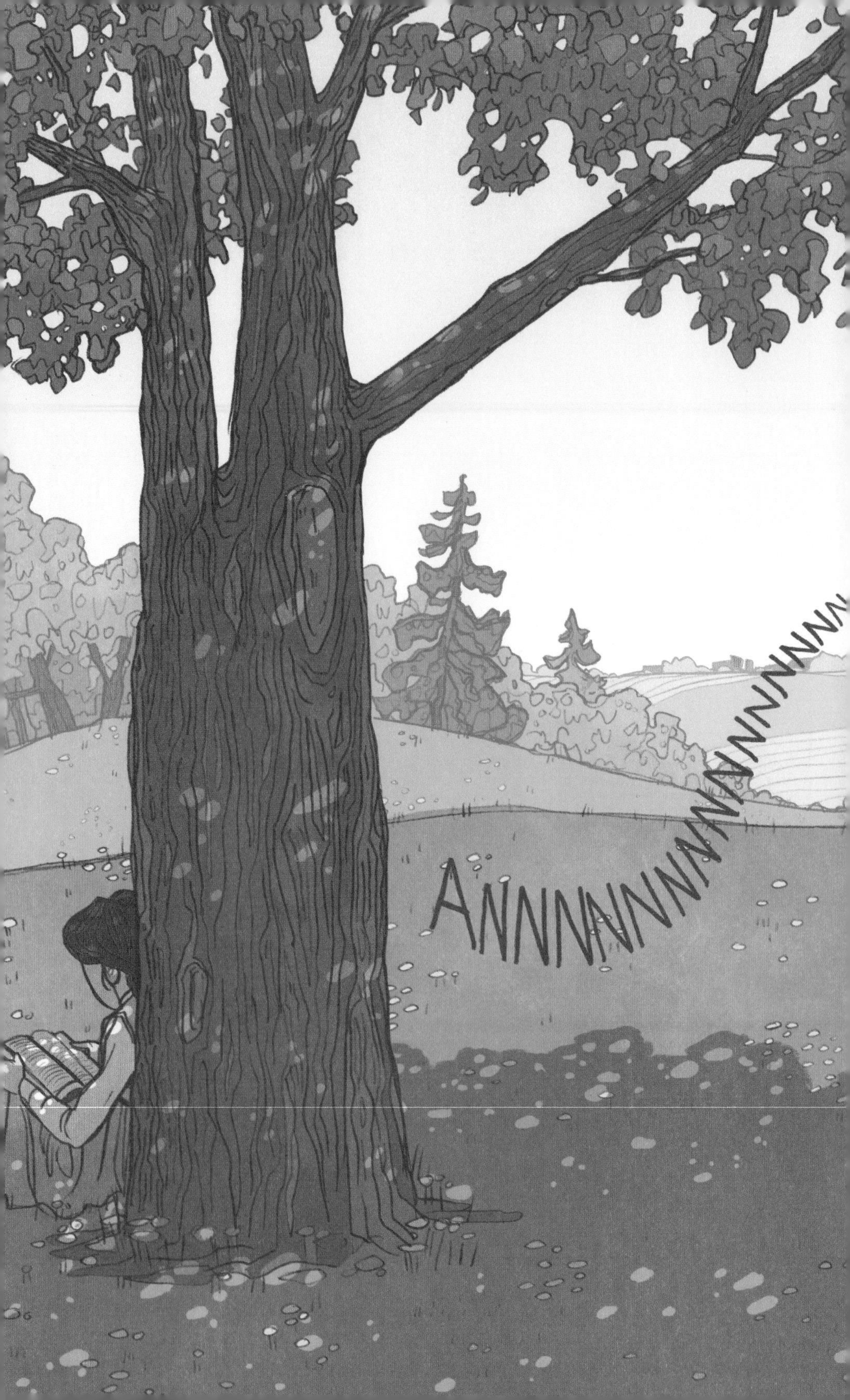
ANNNNNNNNNNNNNNNNNNNNNNNN

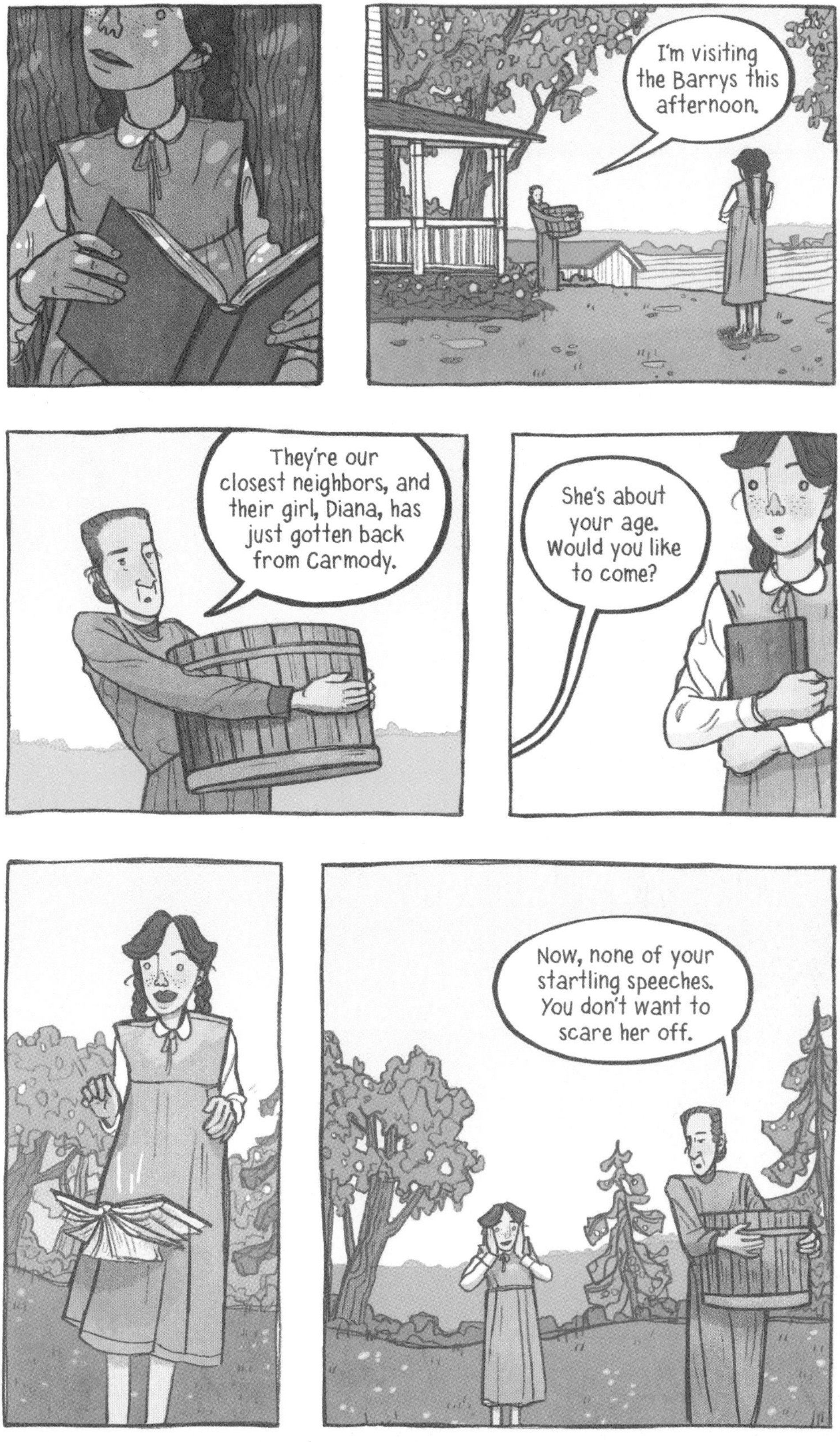
I'm visiting the Barrys this afternoon.
They're our closest neighbors, and their girl, Diana, has just gotten back from Carmody.
She's about your age. Would you like to come?
Now, none of your startling speeches. You don't want to scare her off.

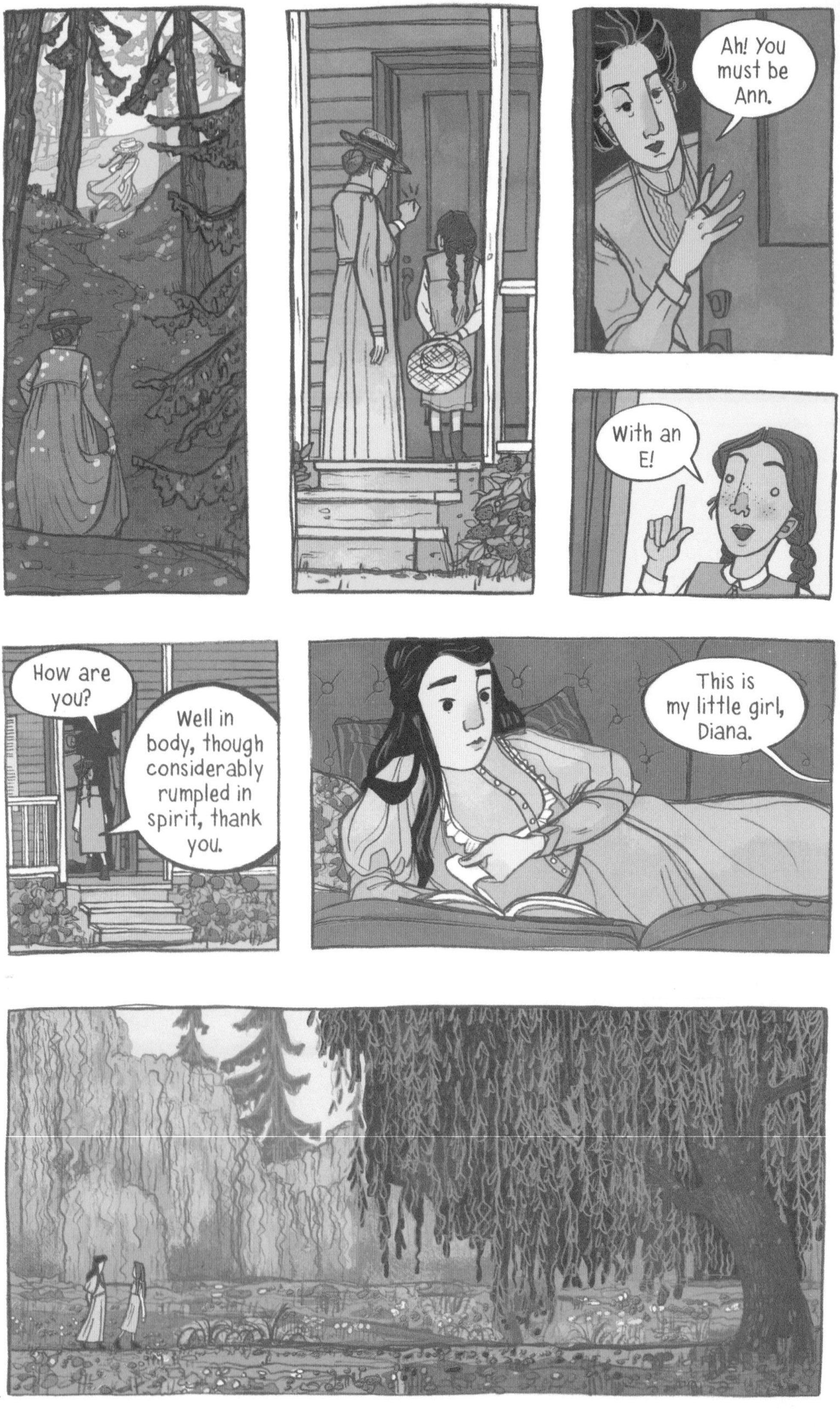
Ah! You must be Ann.
With an E!
How are you?
Well in body, though considerably rumpled in spirit, thank you.
This is my little girl, Diana.

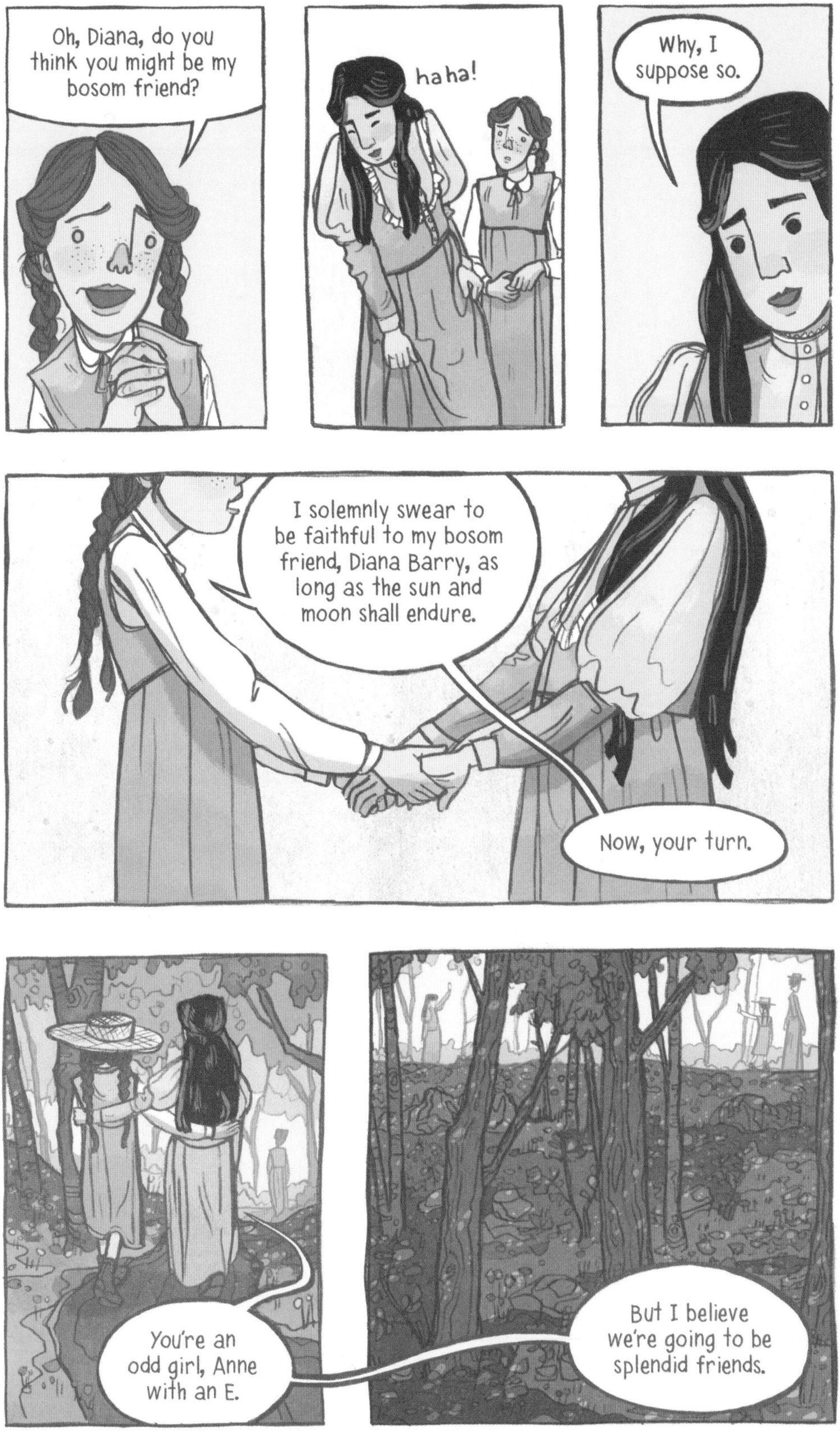
Oh, Diana, do you think you might be my bosom friend?
haha!
Why, I suppose so.
I solemnly swear to be faithful to my bosom friend, Diana Barry, as long as the sun and moon shall endure.
Now, your turn.
You're an odd girl, Anne with an E.
But I believe we're going to be splendid friends.

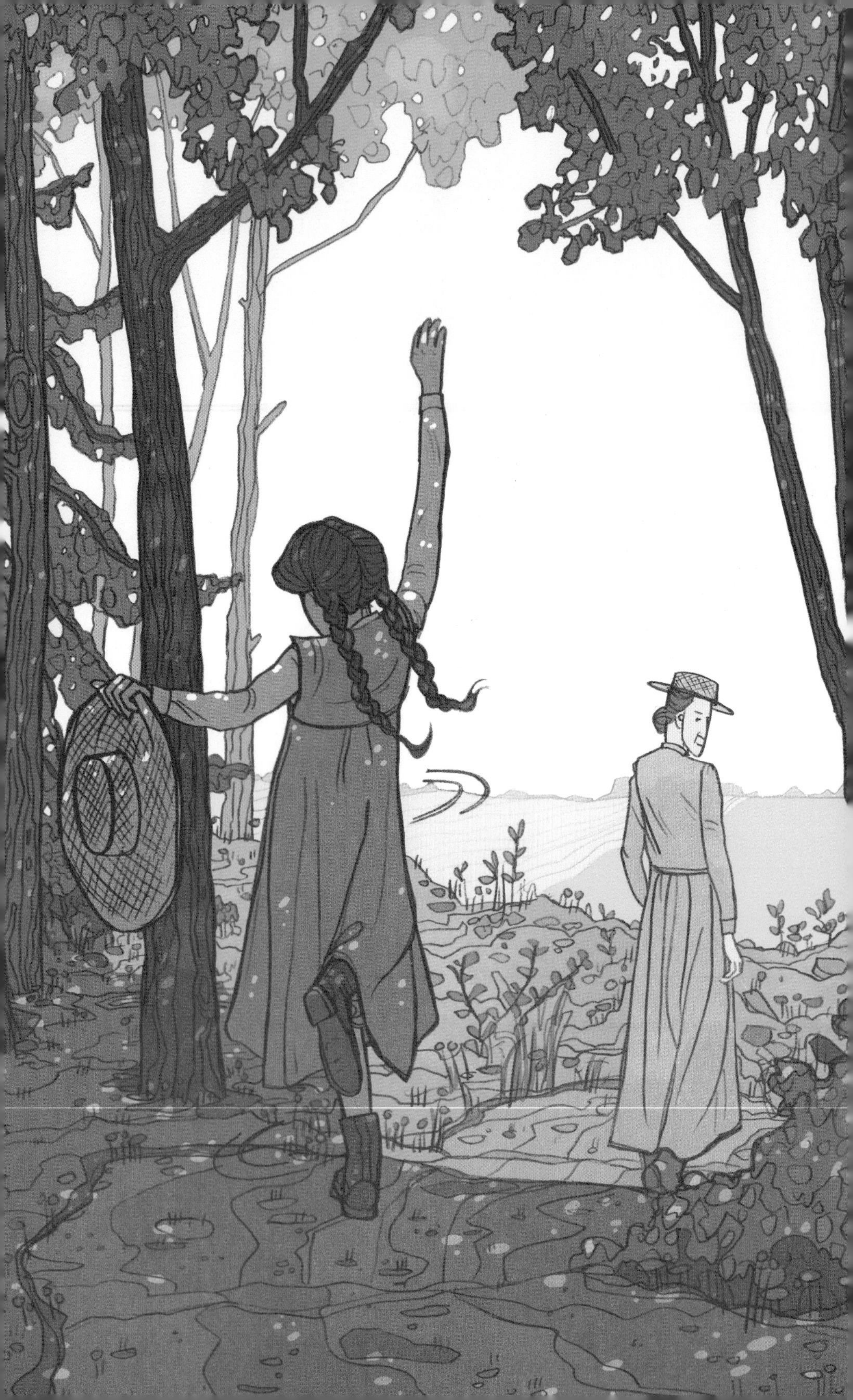

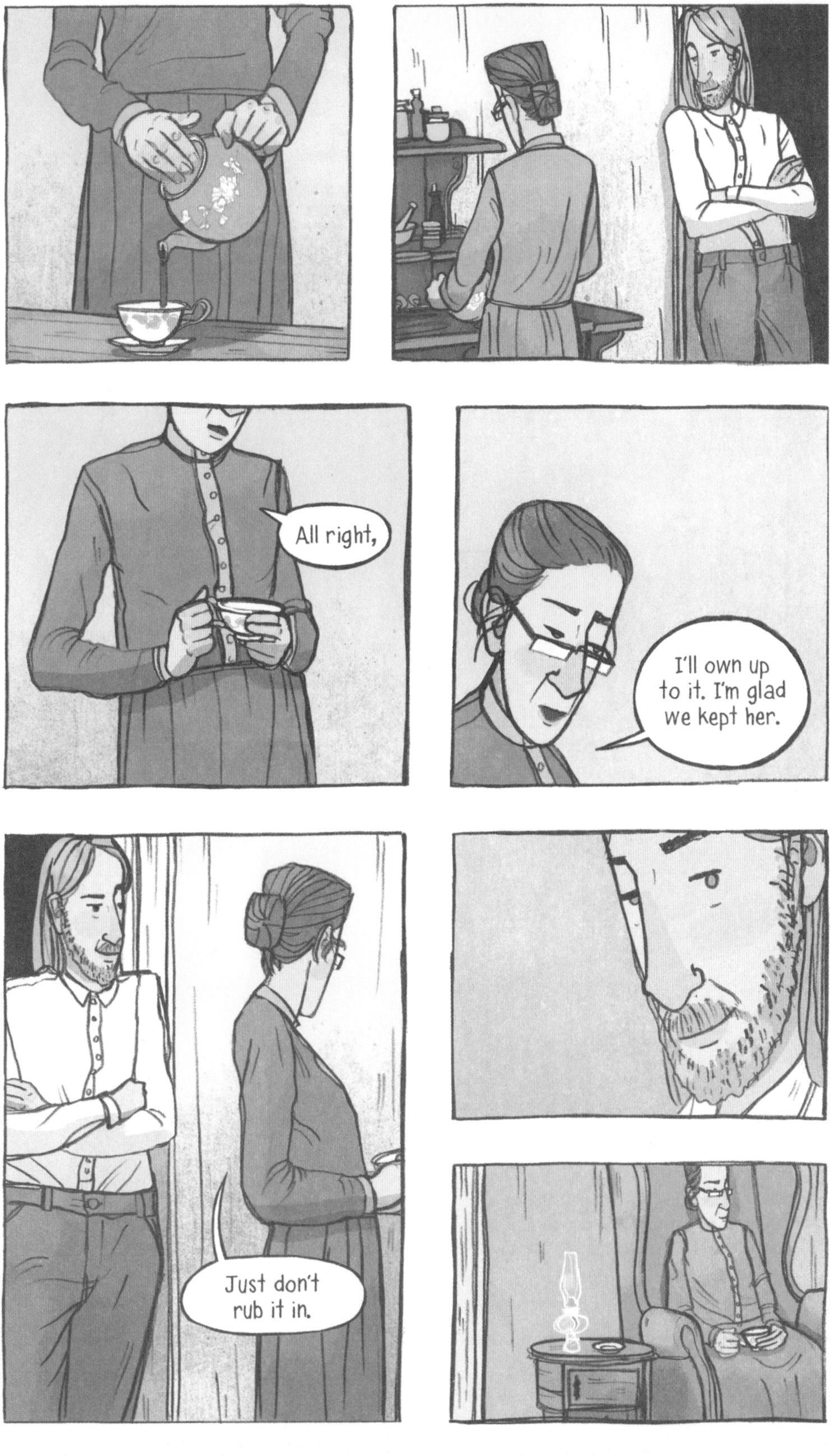
All right,
I'll own up to it. I'm glad we kept her.
Just don't rub it in.

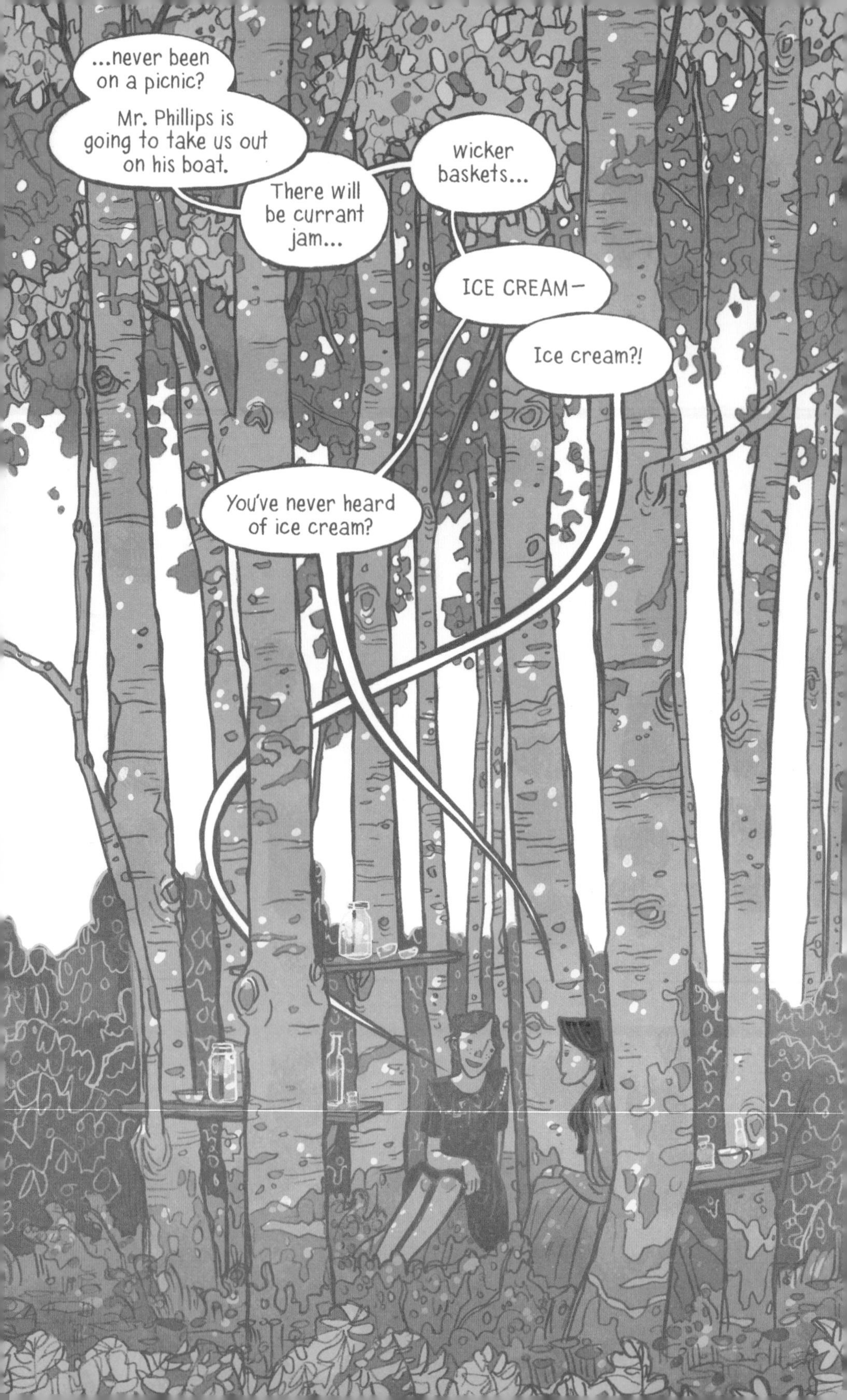
...never been on a picnic?
Mr. Phillips is going to take us out on his boat.
There will be currant jam...
wicker baskets...
ICE CREAM—
Ice cream?!
You've never heard of ice cream?

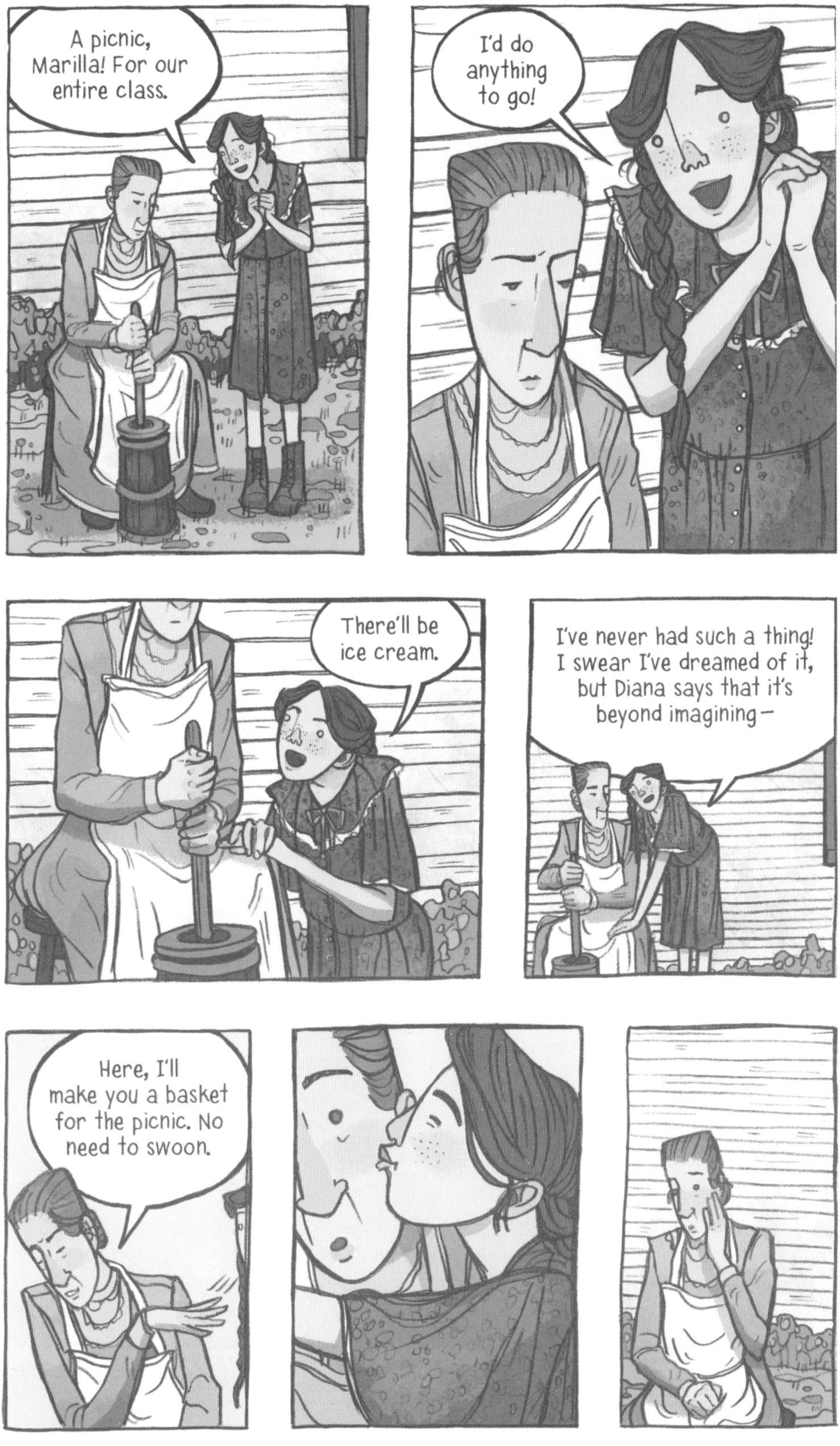
A picnic, Marilla! For our entire class.
I'd do anything to go!
There'll be ice cream.
I've never had such a thing! I swear I've dreamed of it, but Diana says that it's beyond imagining—
Here, I'll make you a basket for the picnic. No need to swoon.

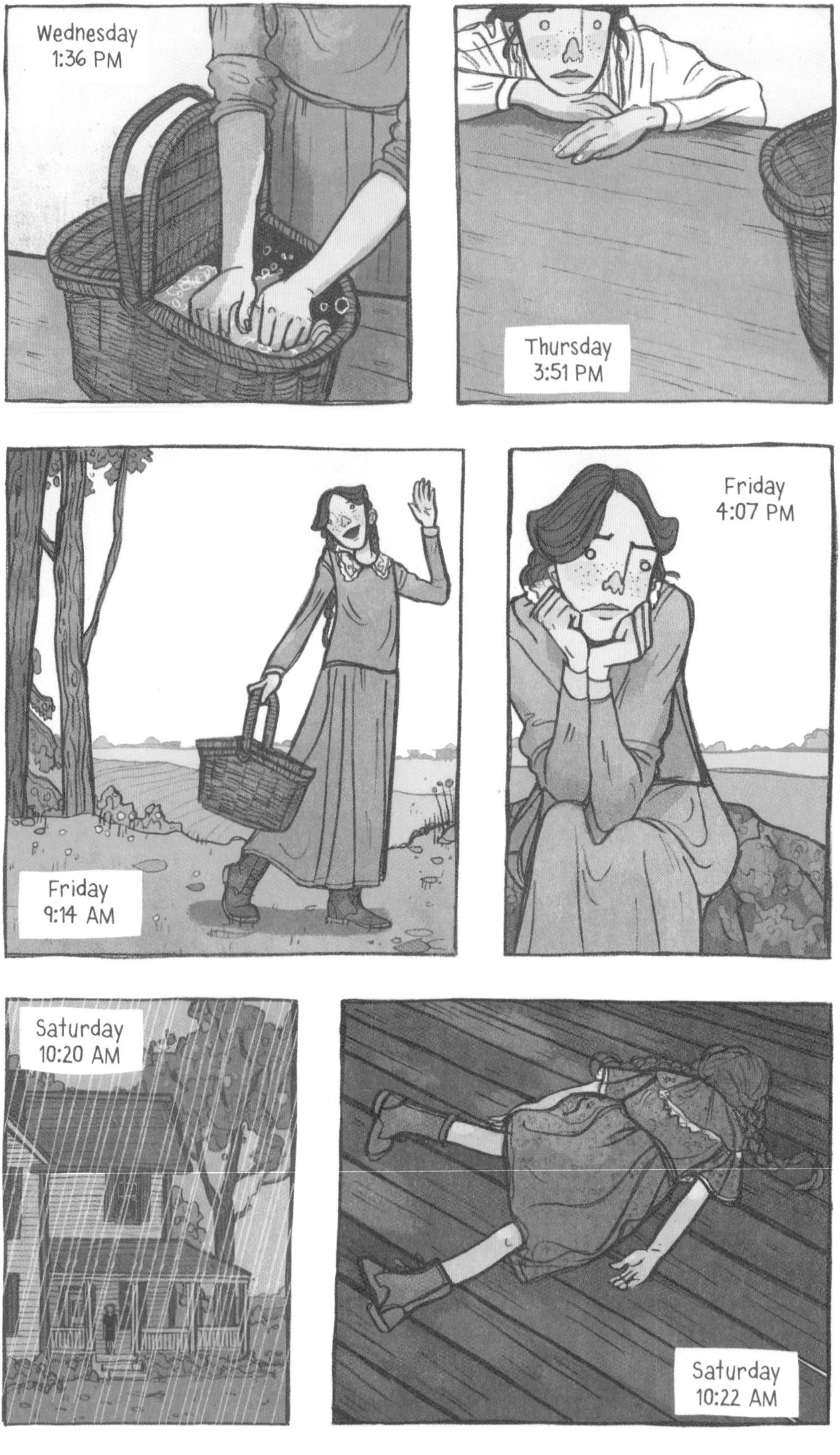
Wednesday
1:36 PM
Thursday
3:51 PM
Friday
9:14 AM
Friday
4:07 PM
Saturday
10:20 AM
Saturday
10:22 AM

Sunday
7:48 AM

Oh, that brooch!

Do you think I might hold it for a moment?

I read somewhere that amethysts must be the souls of good violet flowers.

Doesn't that sound *poetical?*

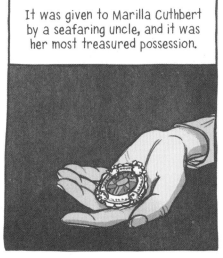

It was given to Marilla Cuthbert by a seafaring uncle, and it was her most treasured possession.

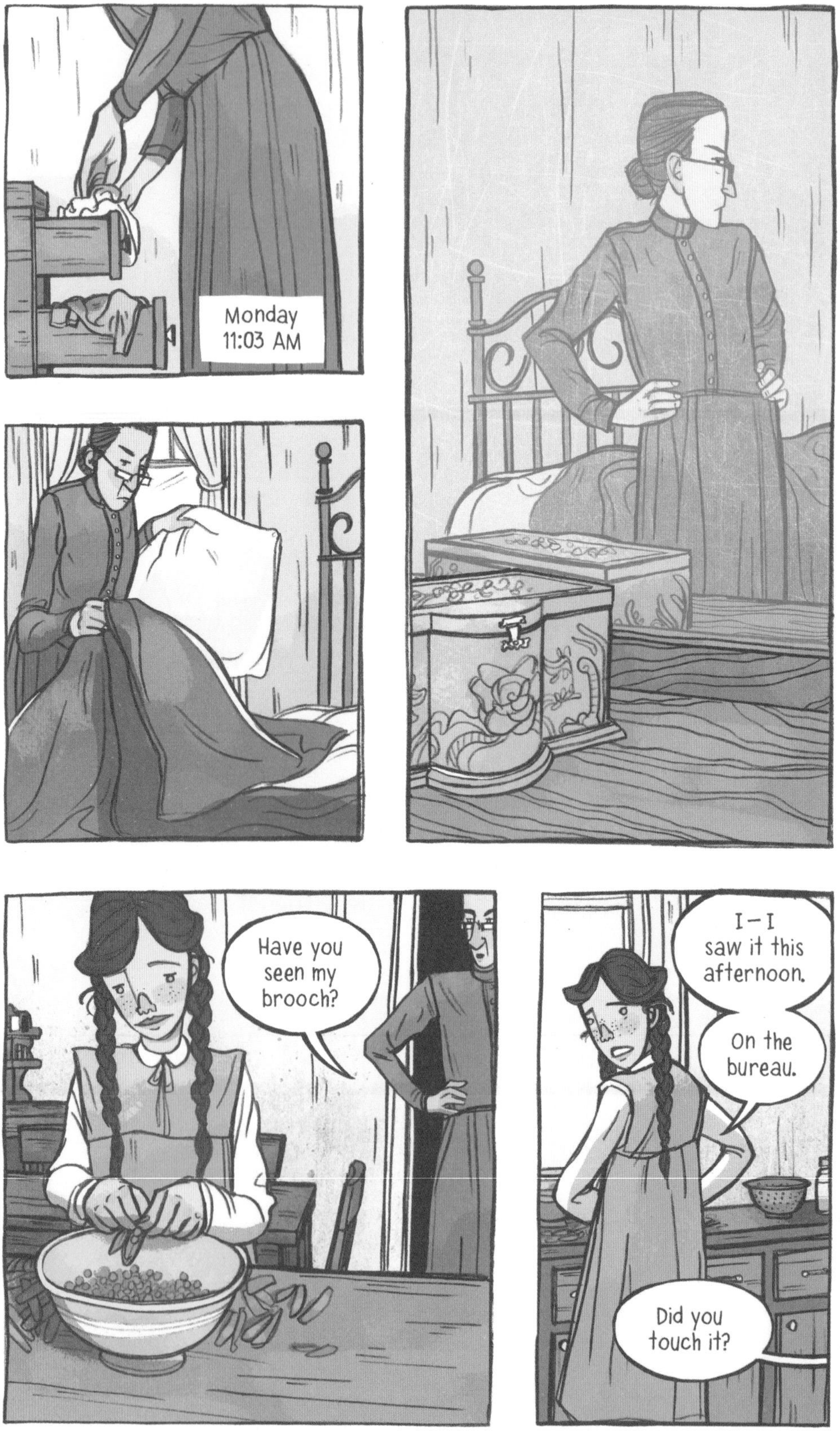
Monday
11:03 AM
Have you seen my brooch?
I—I saw it this afternoon.
On the bureau.
Did you touch it?

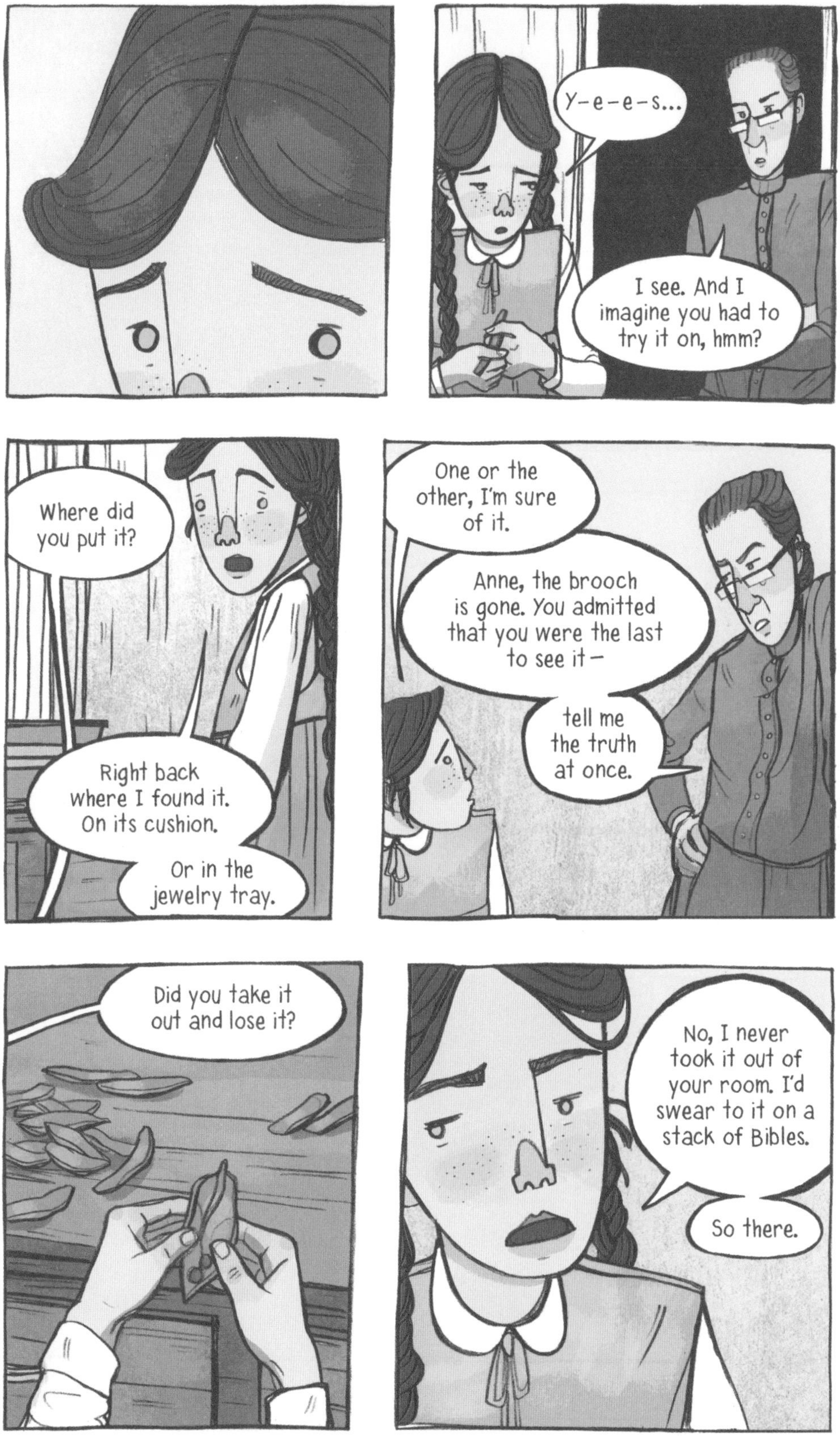
Y-e-e-s...
I see. And I imagine you had to try it on, hmm?
Where did you put it?
Right back where I found it. On its cushion.
Or in the jewelry tray.
One or the other, I'm sure of it.
Anne, the brooch is gone. You admitted that you were the last to see it—
tell me the truth at once.
Did you take it out and lose it?
No, I never took it out of your room. I'd swear to it on a stack of Bibles.
So there.

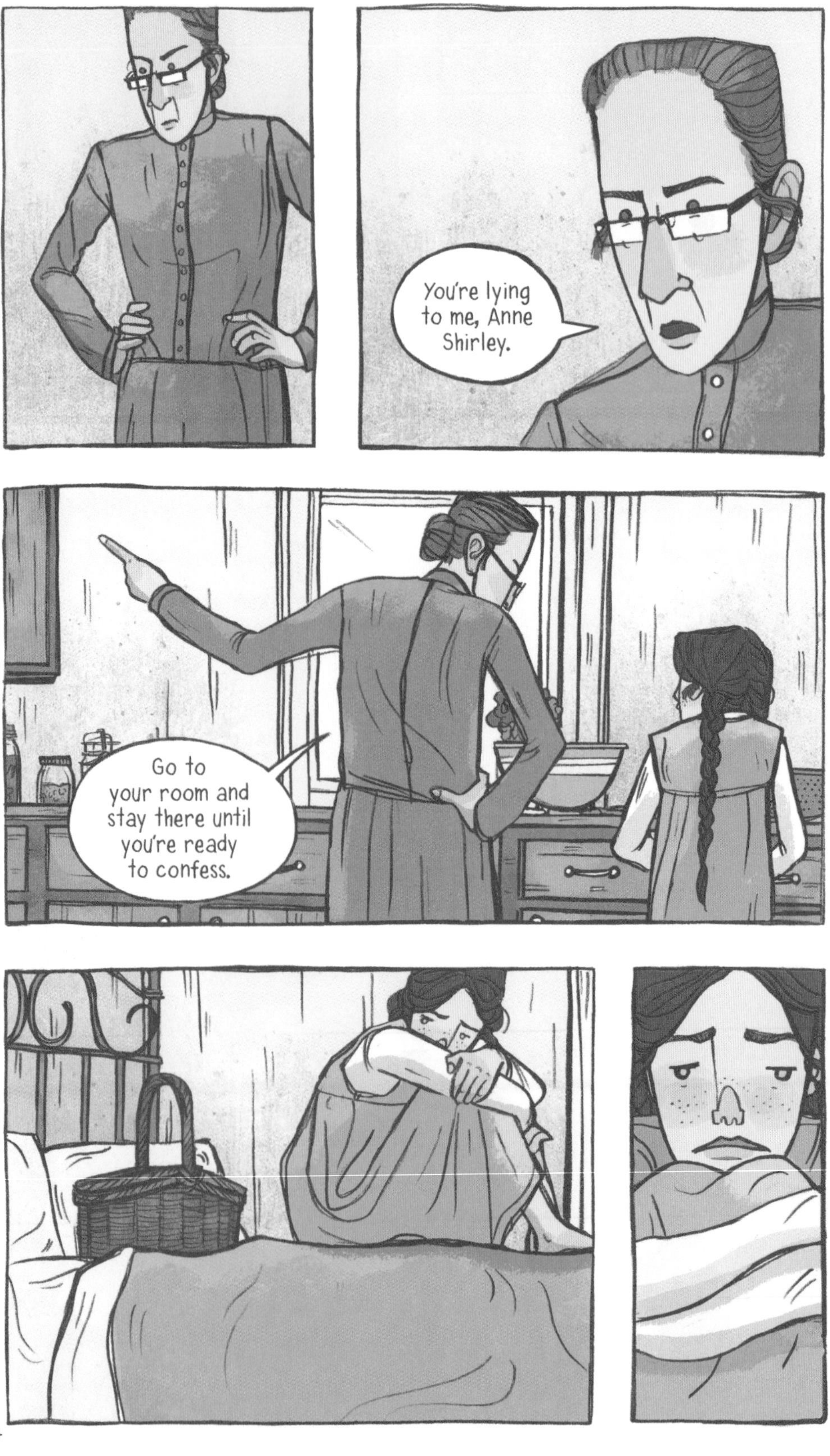
You're lying to me, Anne Shirley.
Go to your room and stay there until you're ready to confess.

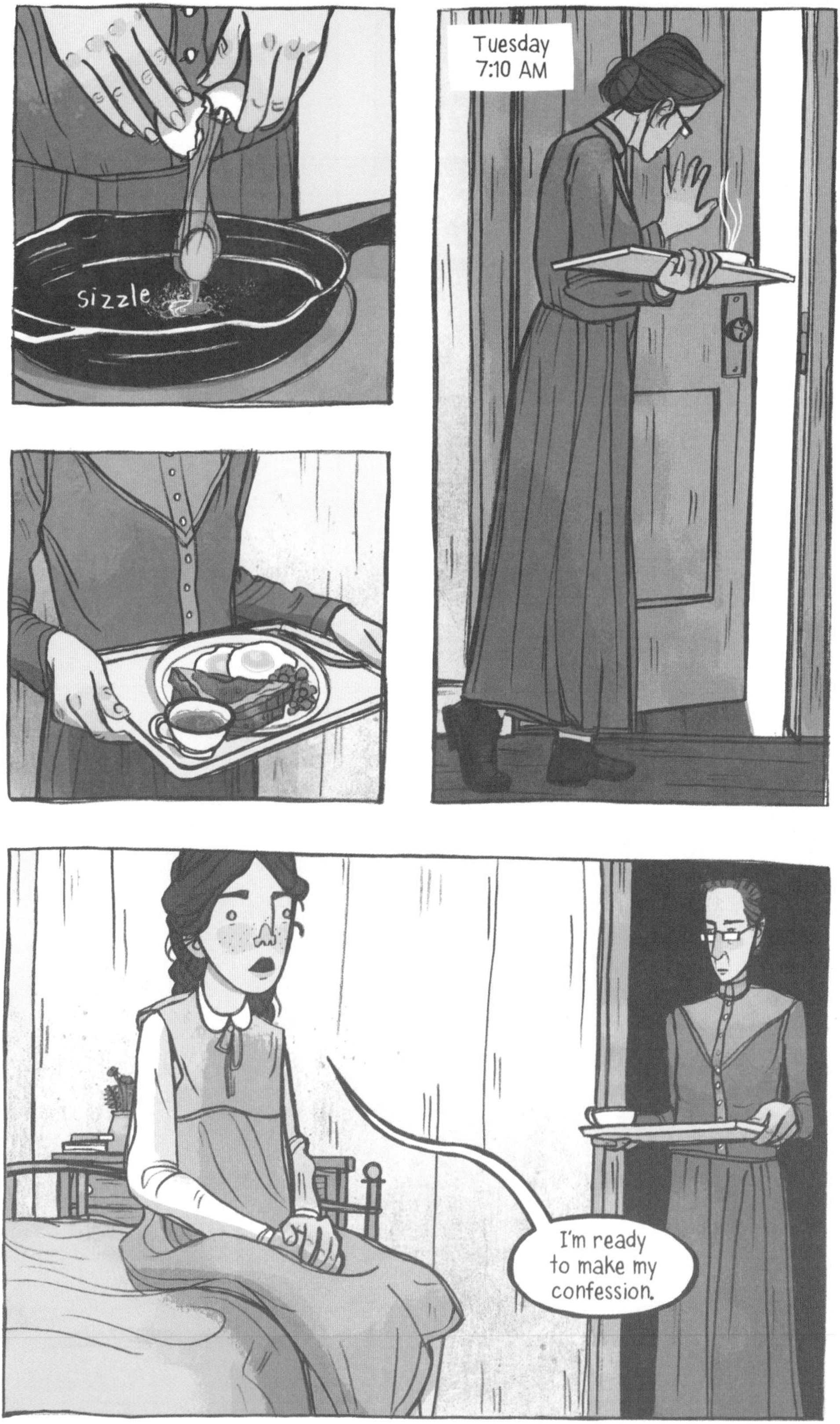
sizzle
Tuesday
7:10 AM
I'm ready
to make my
confession.

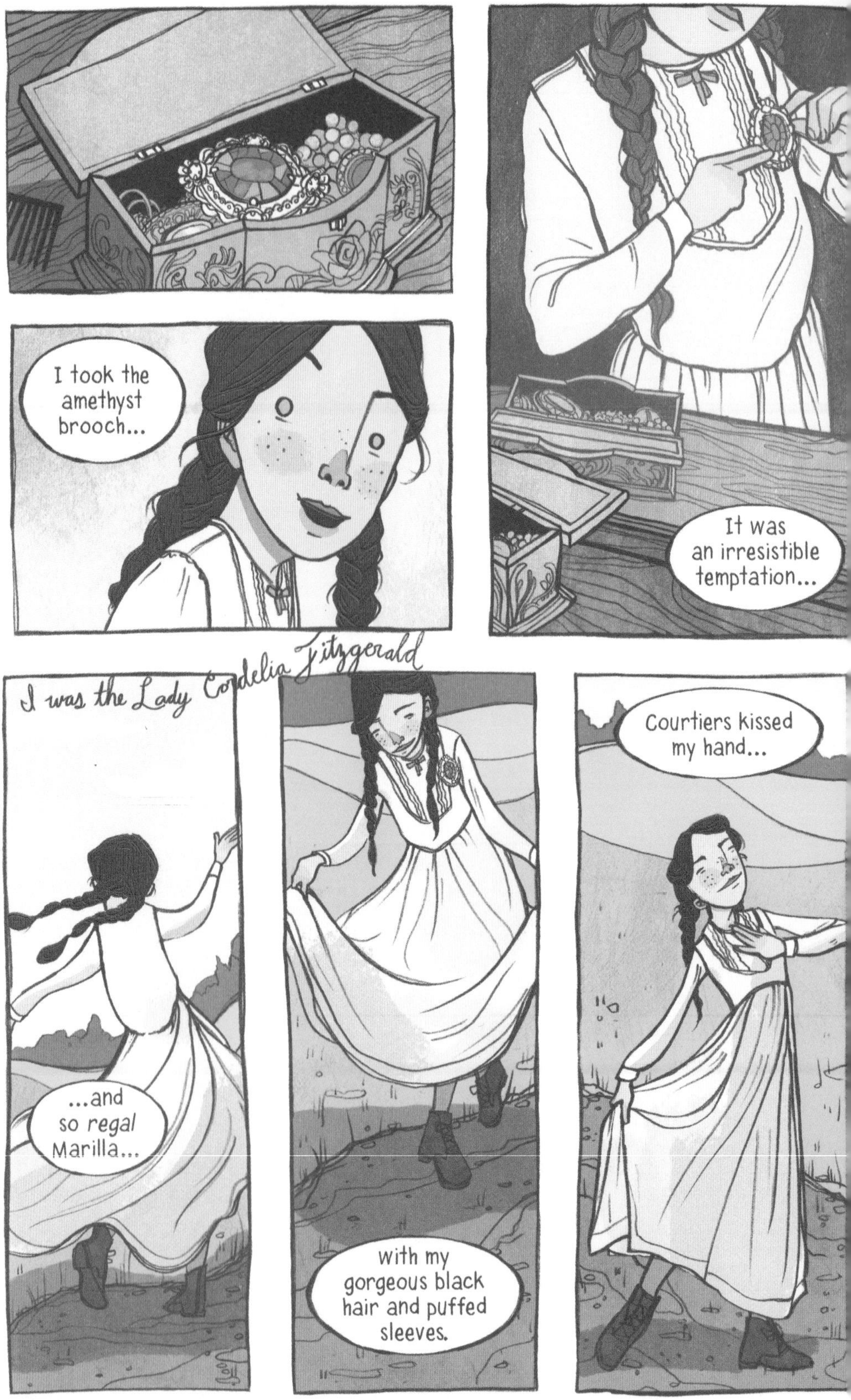

I took the amethyst brooch...
It was an irresistible temptation...
I was the Lady Cordelia Fitzgerald
...and so regal Marilla...
with my gorgeous black hair and puffed sleeves.
Courtiers kissed my hand...

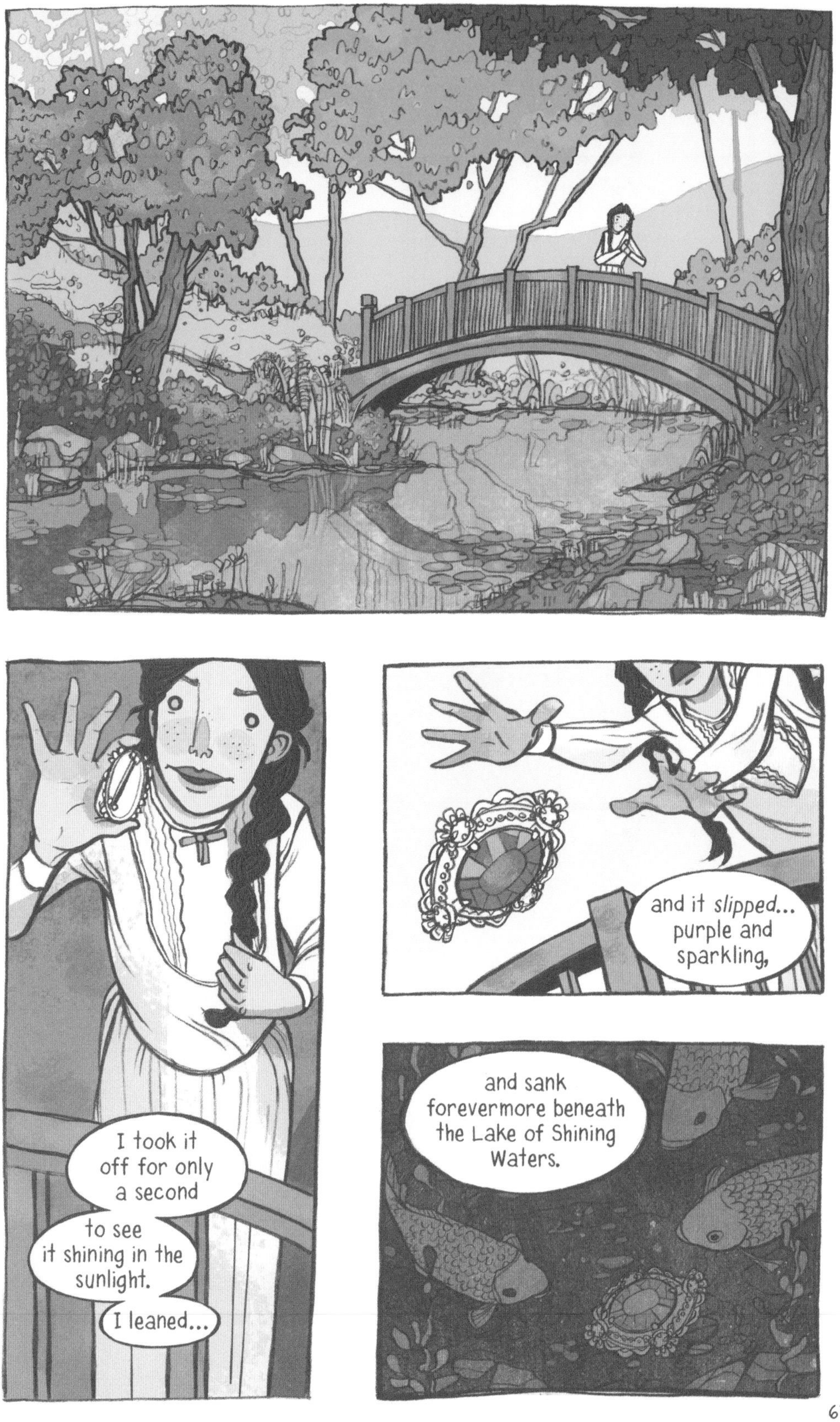
I took it off for only a second
to see it shining in the sunlight.
I leaned...
and it *slipped*... purple and sparkling,
and sank forevermore beneath the Lake of Shining Waters.

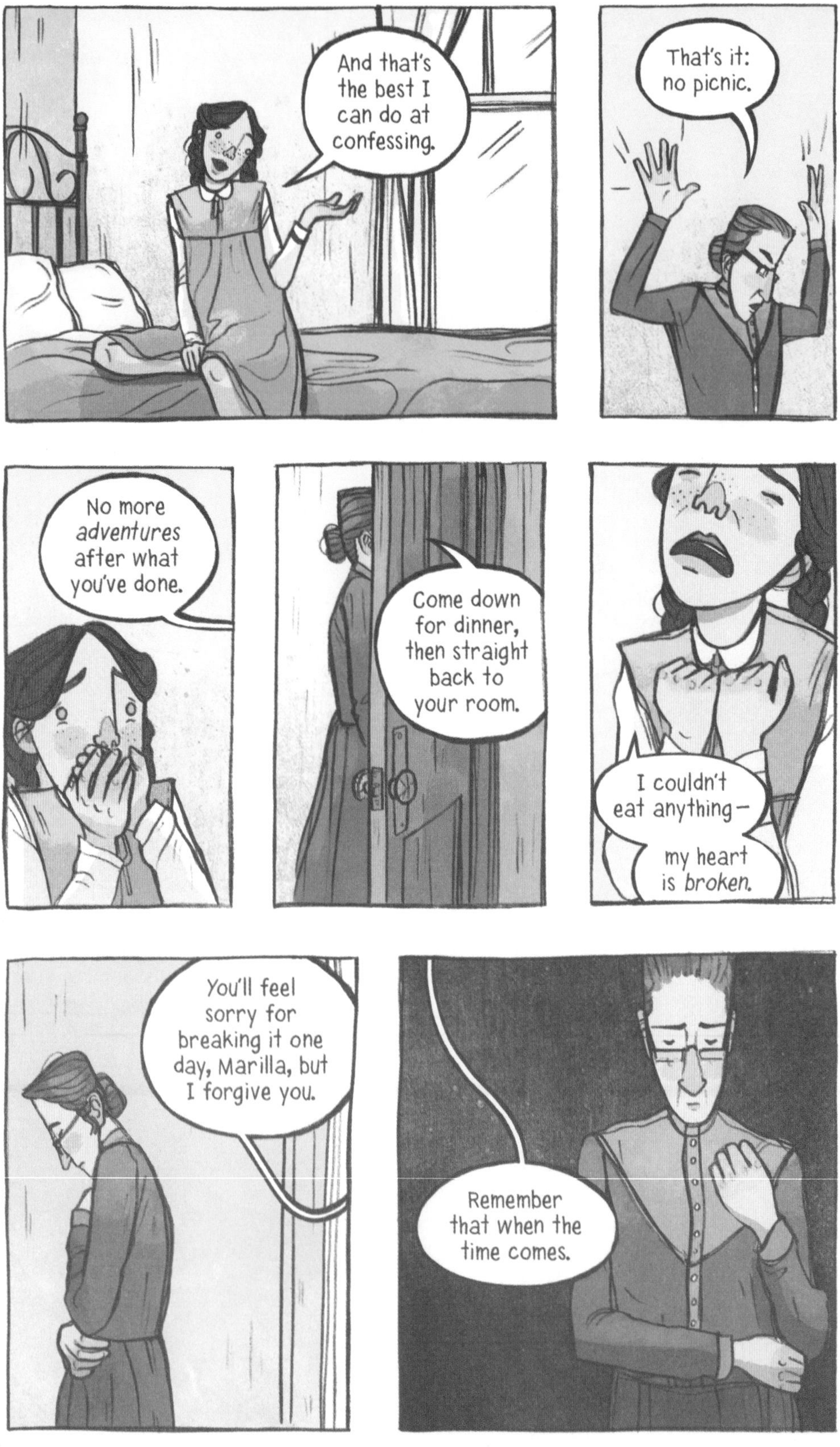
And that's the best I can do at confessing.
That's it: no picnic.
No more *adventures* after what you've done.
Come down for dinner, then straight back to your room.
I couldn't eat anything—
my heart is *broken*.
You'll feel sorry for breaking it one day, Marilla, but I forgive you.
Remember that when the time comes.

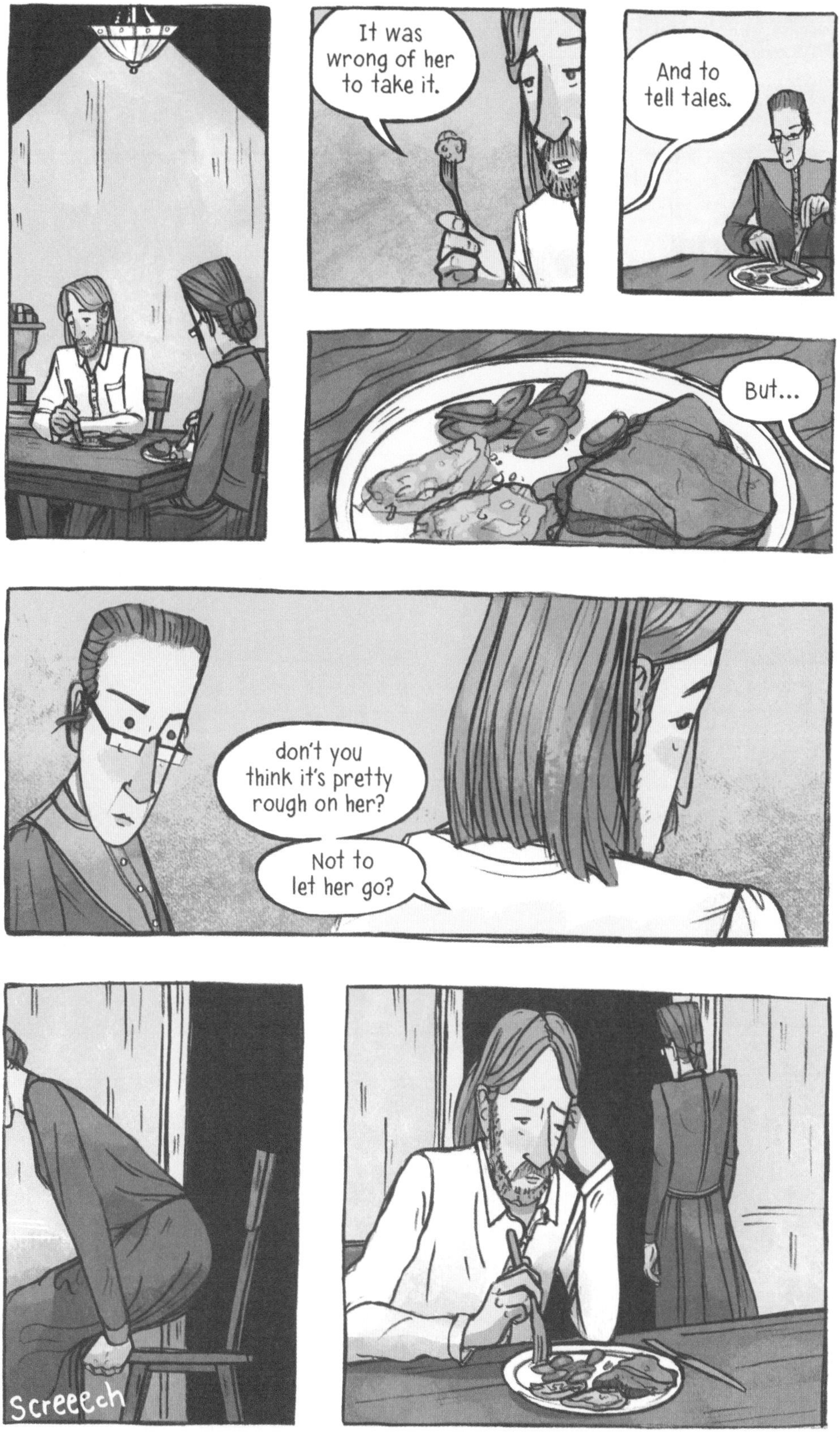
It was wrong of her to take it.
And to tell tales.
But...
don't you think it's pretty rough on her?
Not to let her go?
Screeech

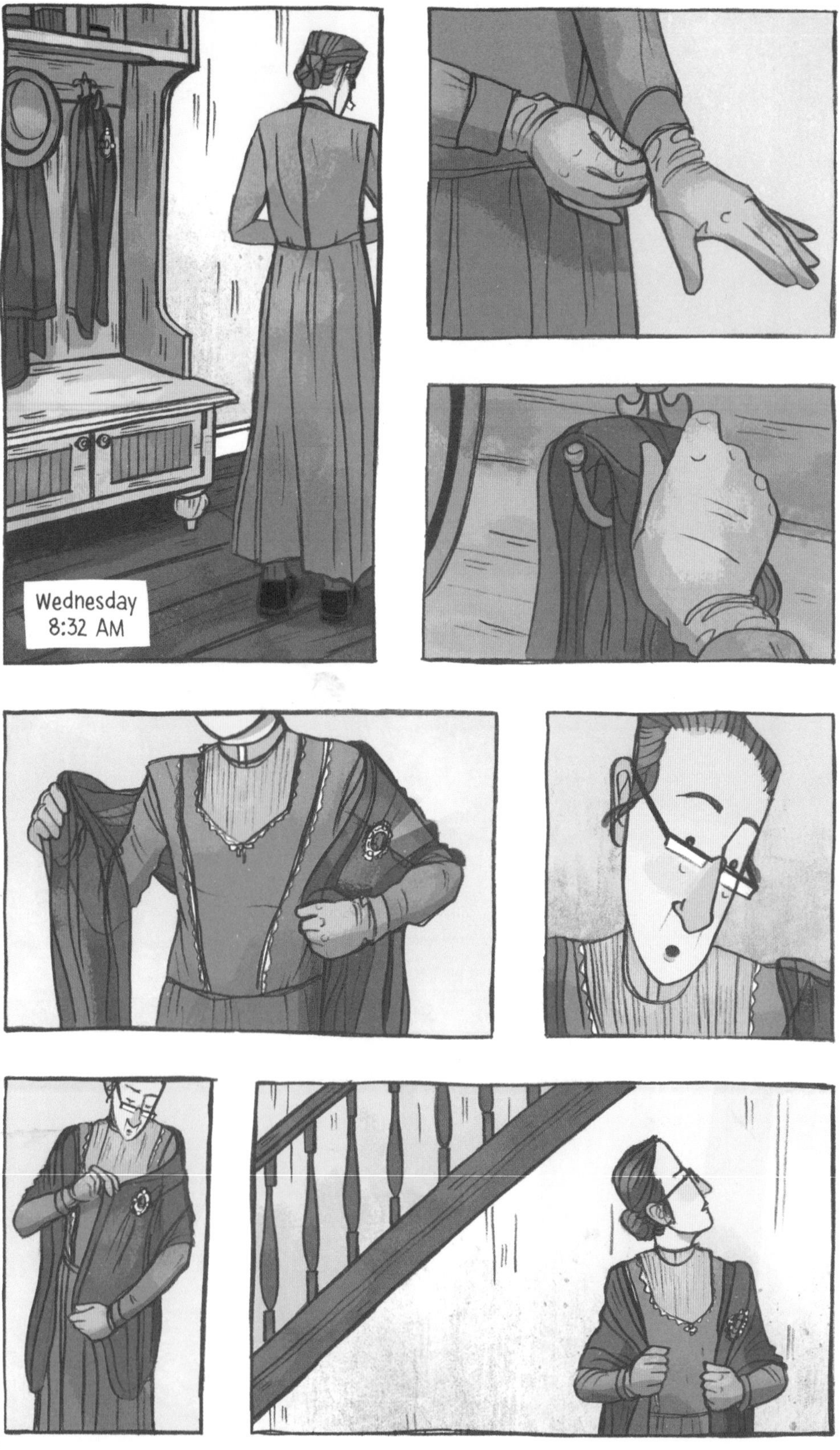
Wednesday
8:32 AM

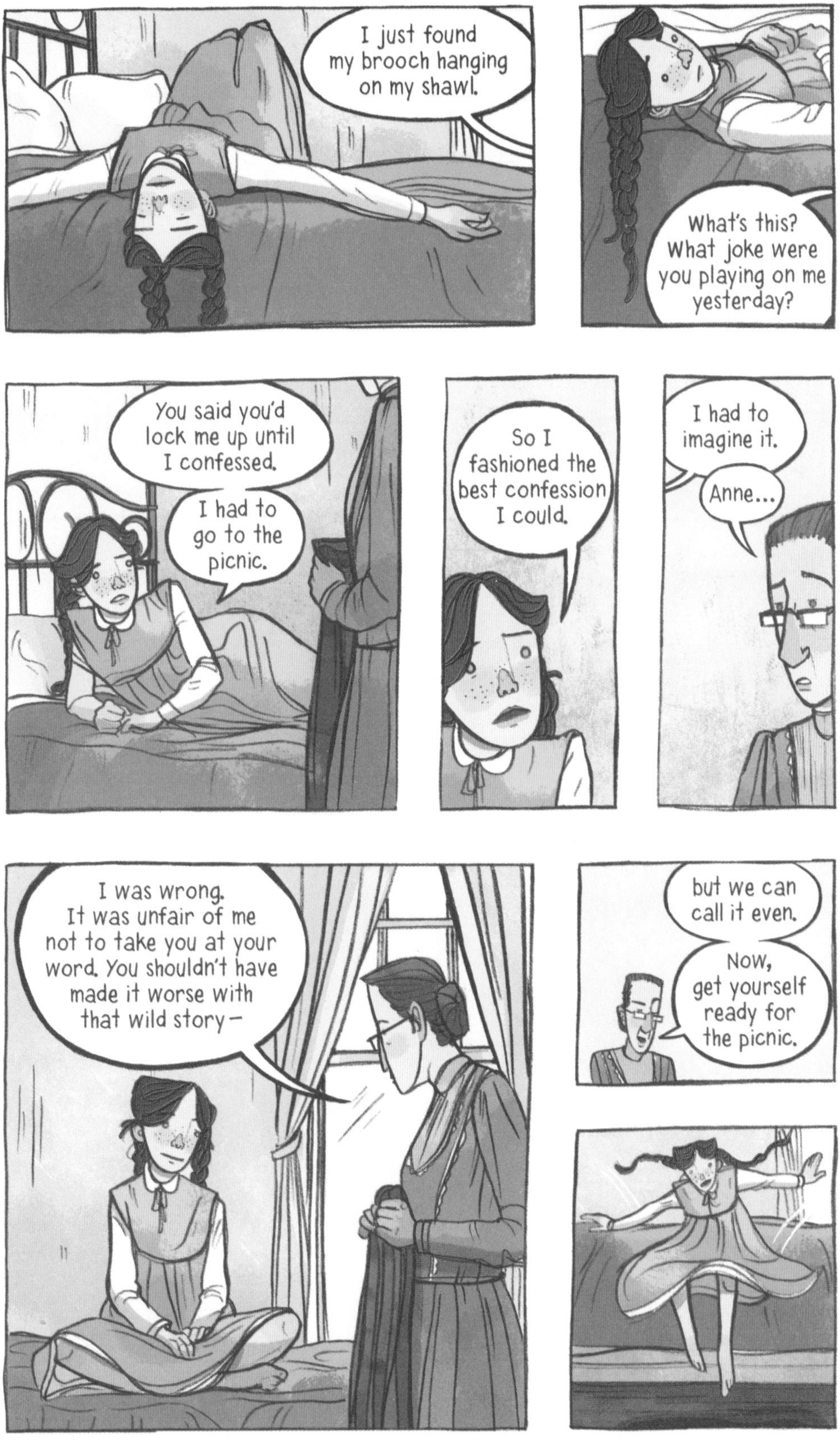
I just found my brooch hanging on my shawl.
What's this? What joke were you playing on me yesterday?
You said you'd lock me up until I confessed.
I had to go to the picnic.
So I fashioned the best confession I could.
I had to imagine it.
Anne...
I was wrong. It was unfair of me not to take you at your word. You shouldn't have made it worse with that wild story—
but we can call it even.
Now, get yourself ready for the picnic.

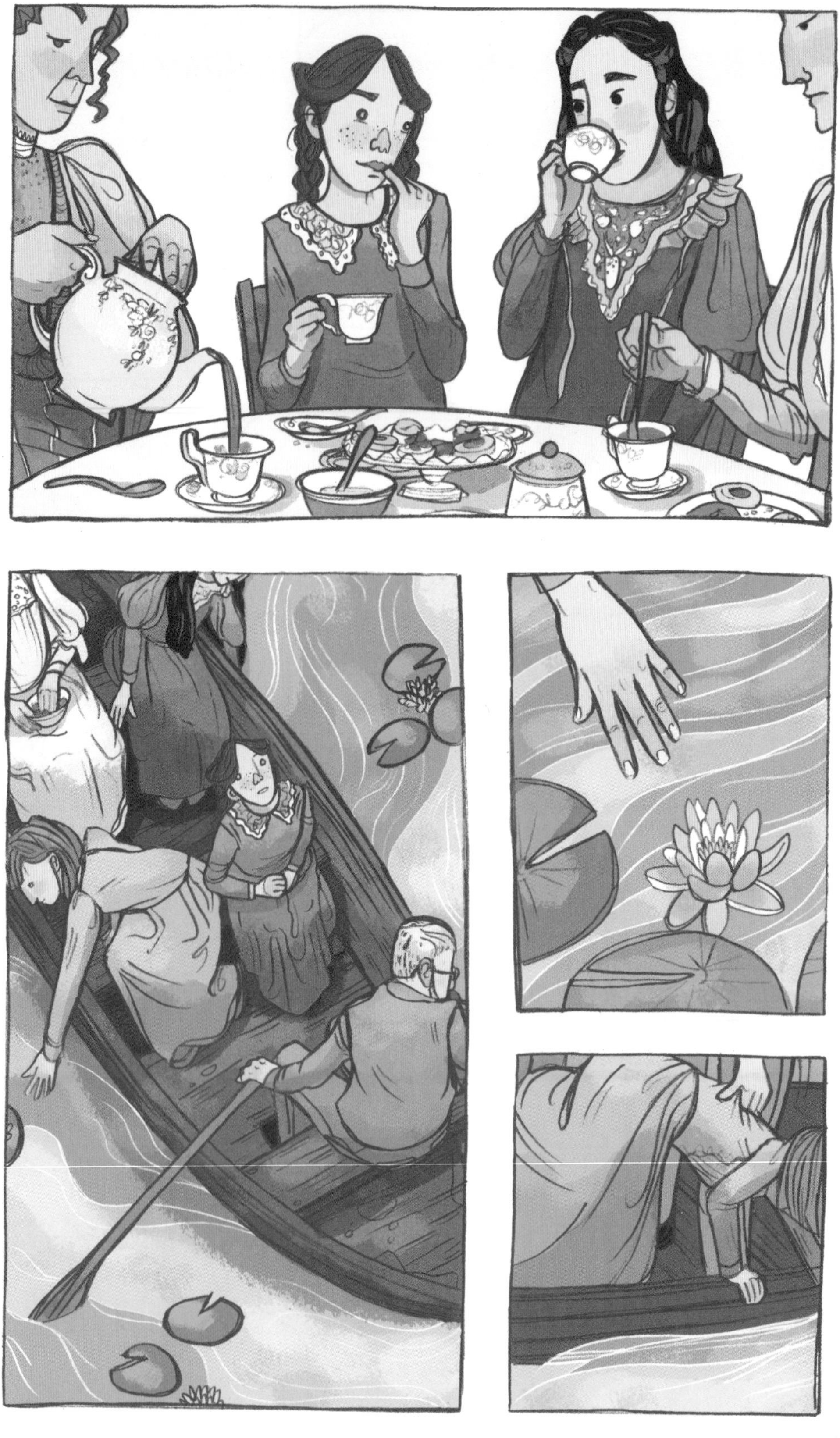

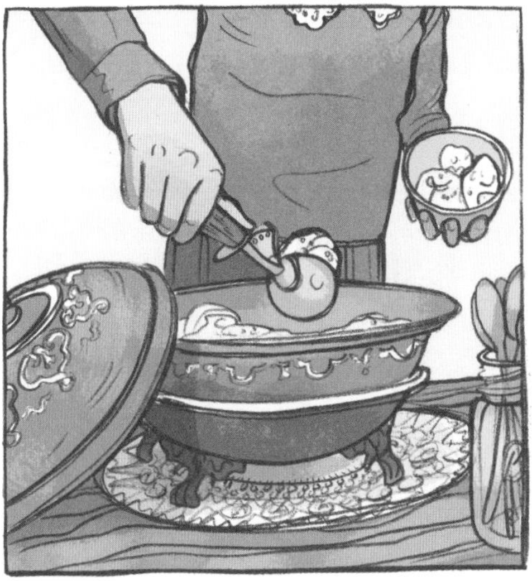

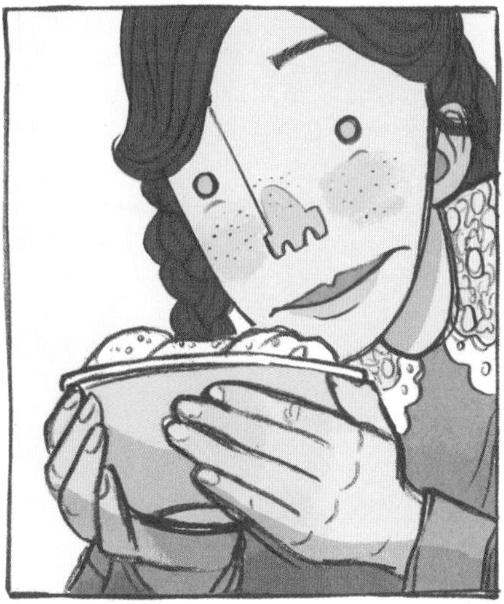

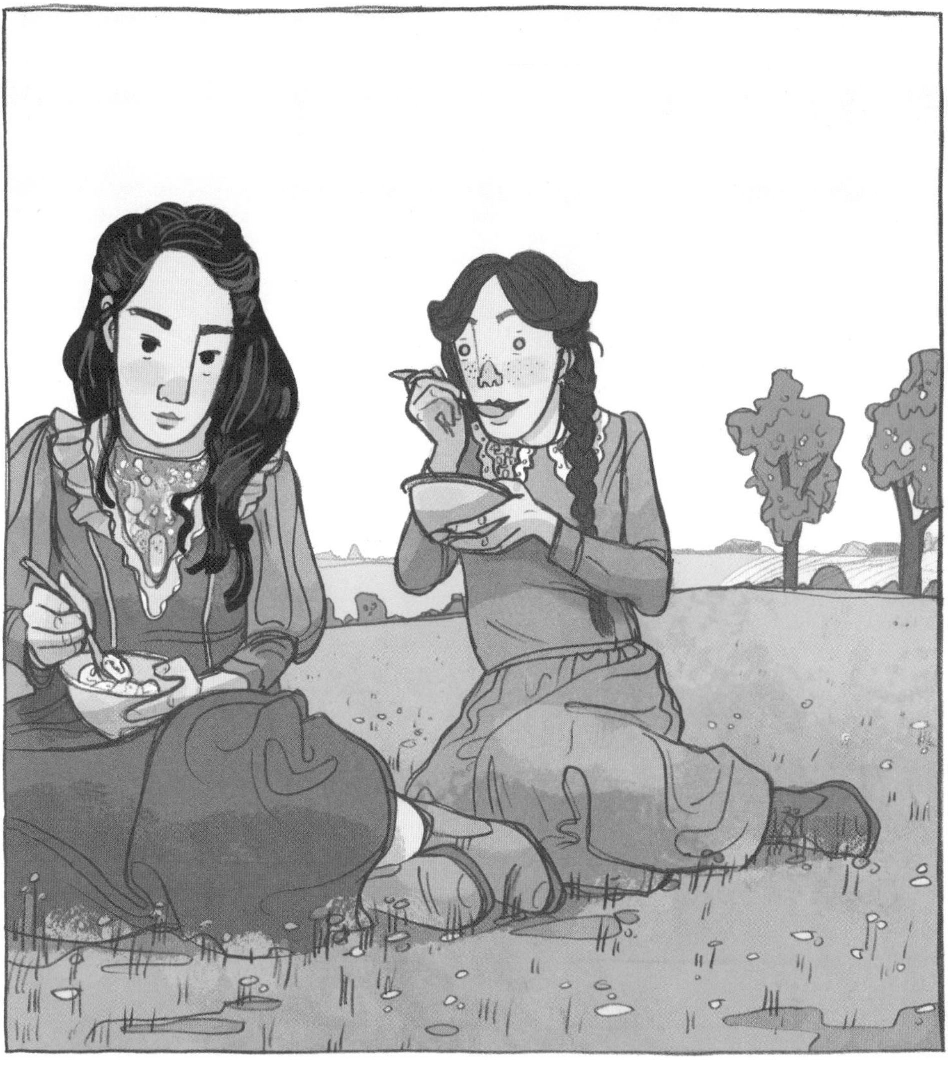

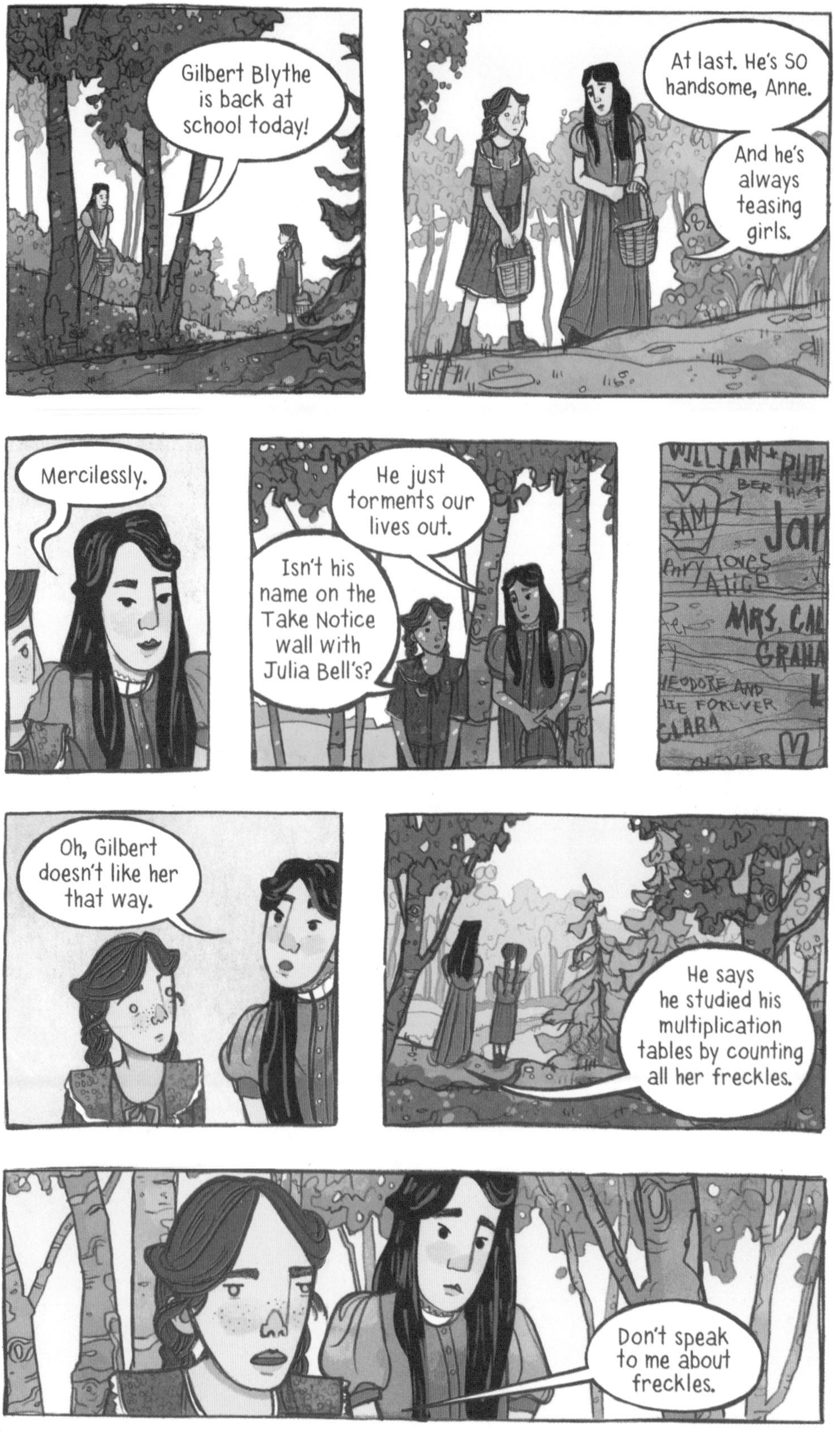
Gilbert Blythe is back at school today!
At last. He's SO handsome, Anne.
And he's always teasing girls.
Mercilessly.
He just torments our lives out.
Isn't his name on the Take Notice wall with Julia Bell's?
WILLIAM +
BERTHA
SAM
loves
ALICE
MRS.
FOREVER
CLARA
Oh, Gilbert doesn't like her that way.
He says he studied his multiplication tables by counting all her freckles.
Don't speak to me about freckles.

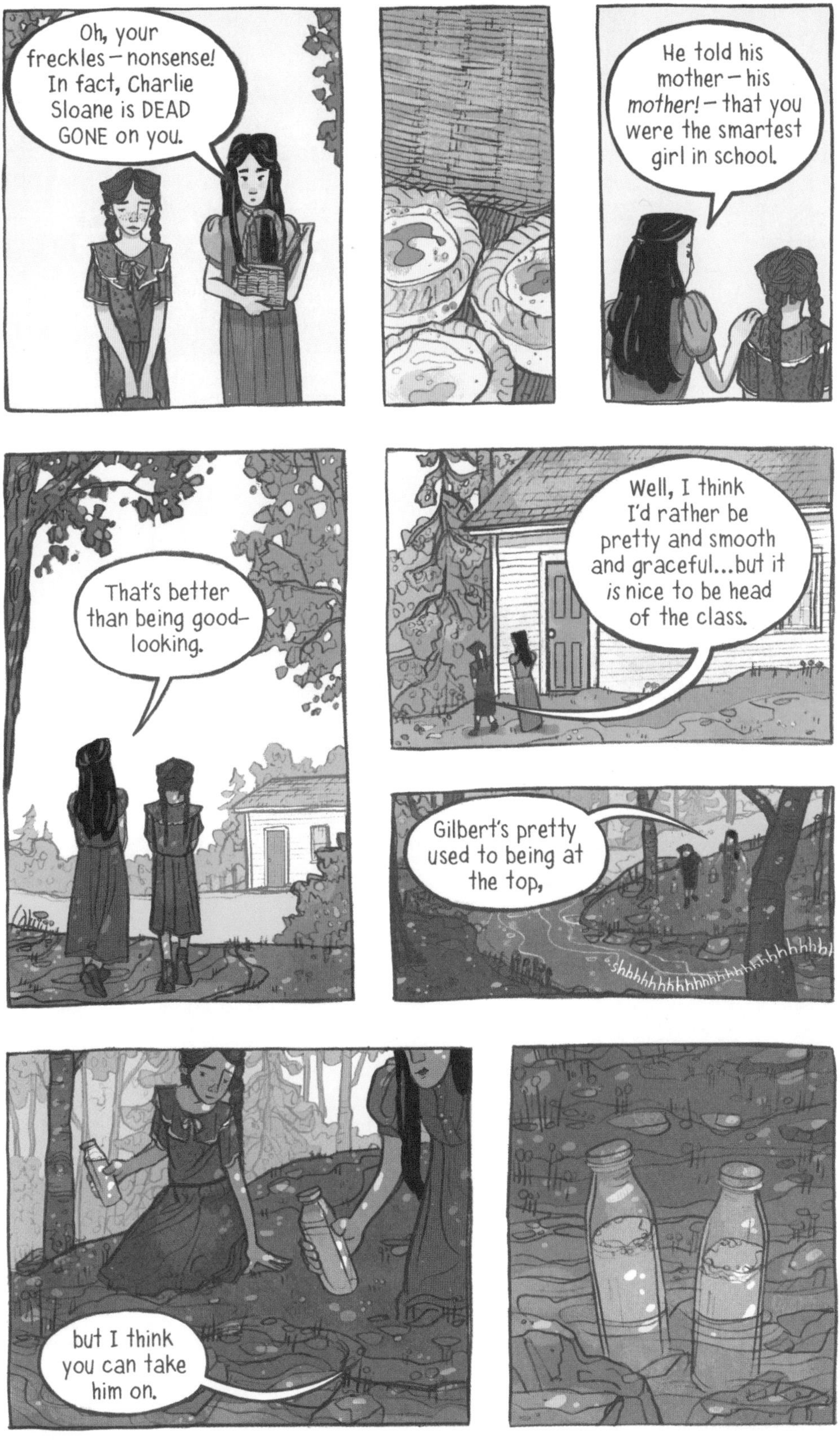
Oh, your freckles—nonsense! In fact, Charlie Sloane is DEAD GONE on you.
He told his mother—his *mother!*—that you were the smartest girl in school.
That's better than being good-looking.
Well, I think I'd rather be pretty and smooth and graceful...but it *is* nice to be head of the class.
Gilbert's pretty used to being at the top,
shhhhhhhhhhhhhhhhhhhhhhhh
but I think you can take him on.

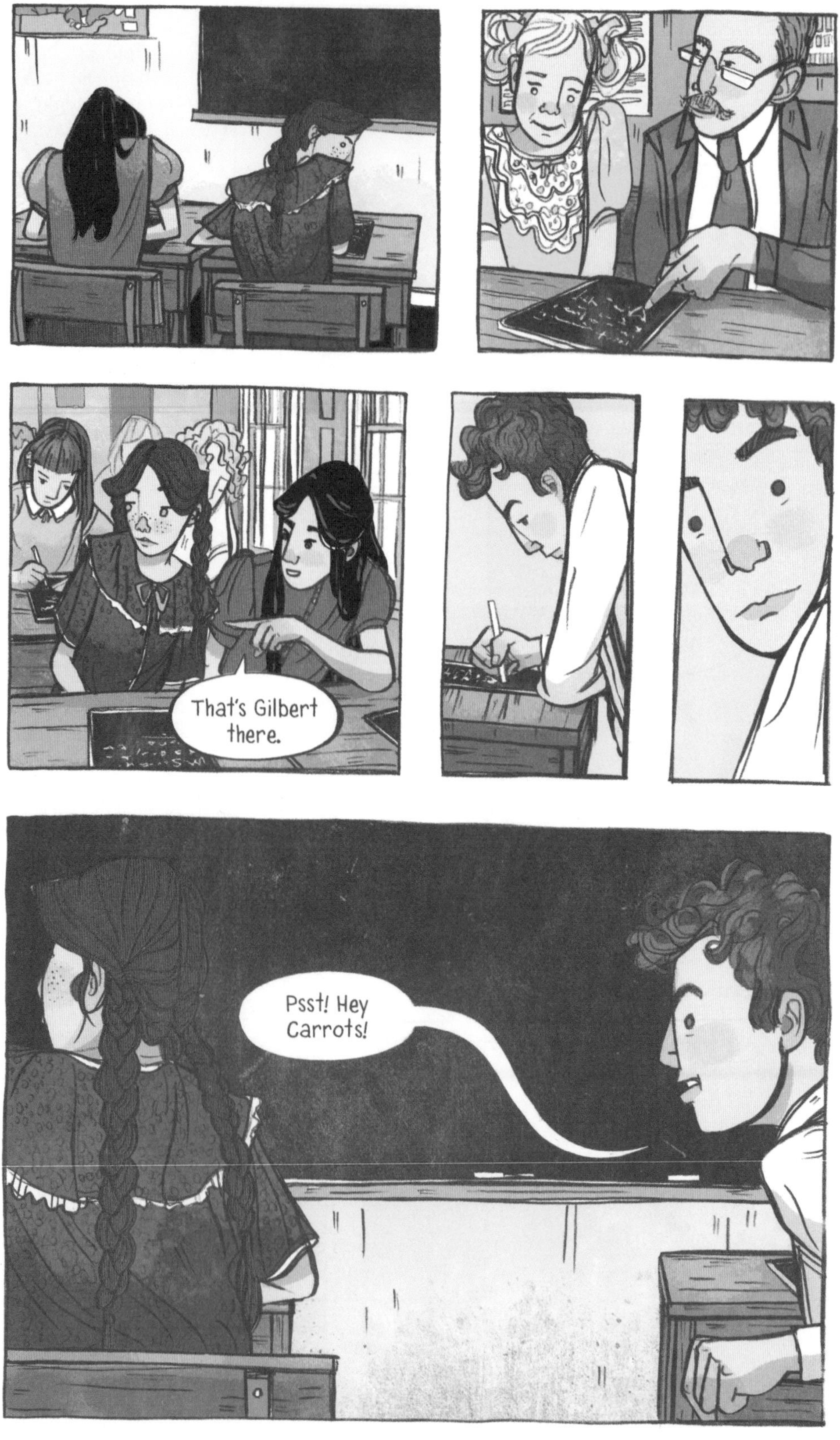
That's Gilbert there.
Psst! Hey Carrots!

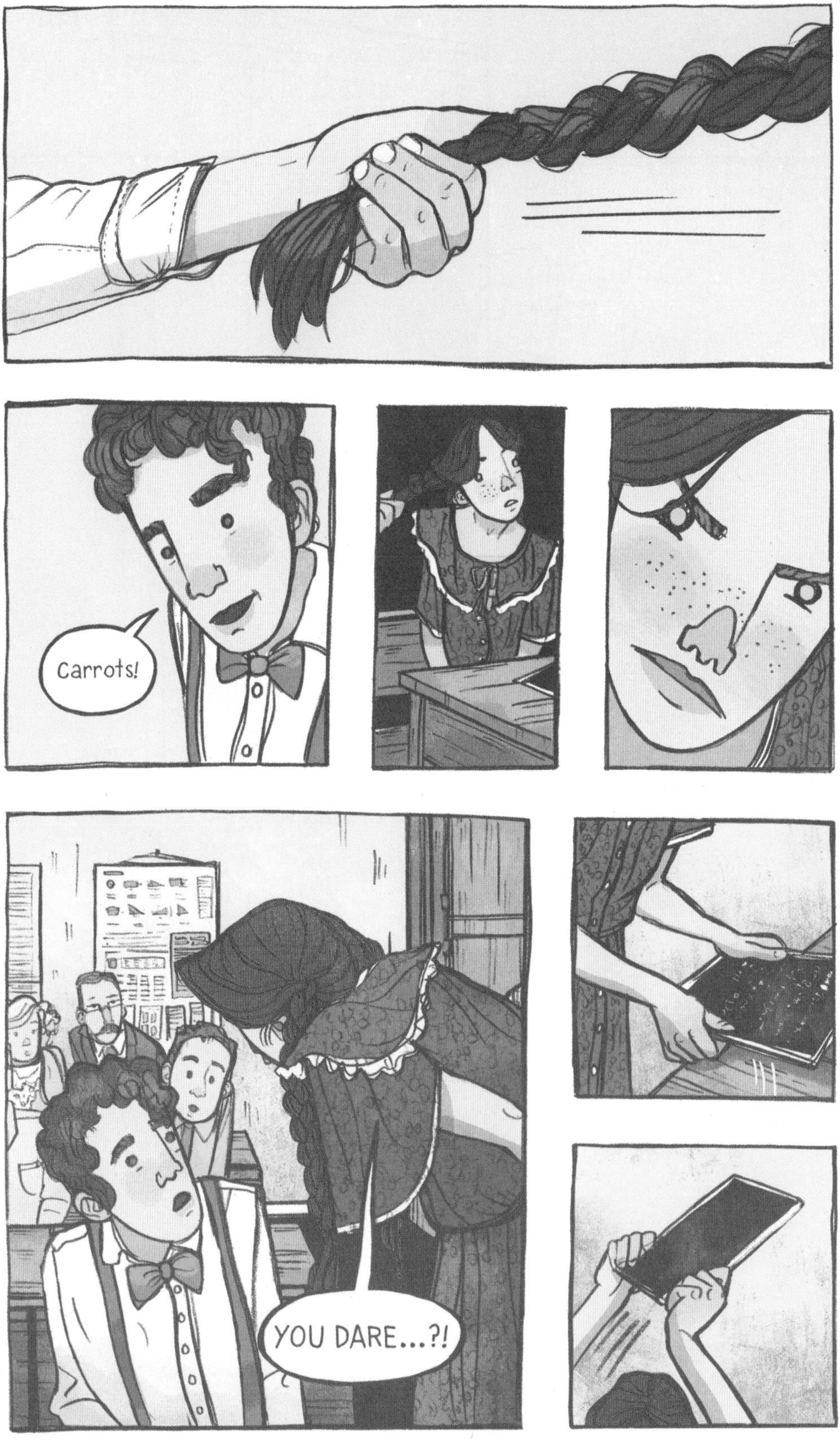
Carrots!
YOU DARE...?!

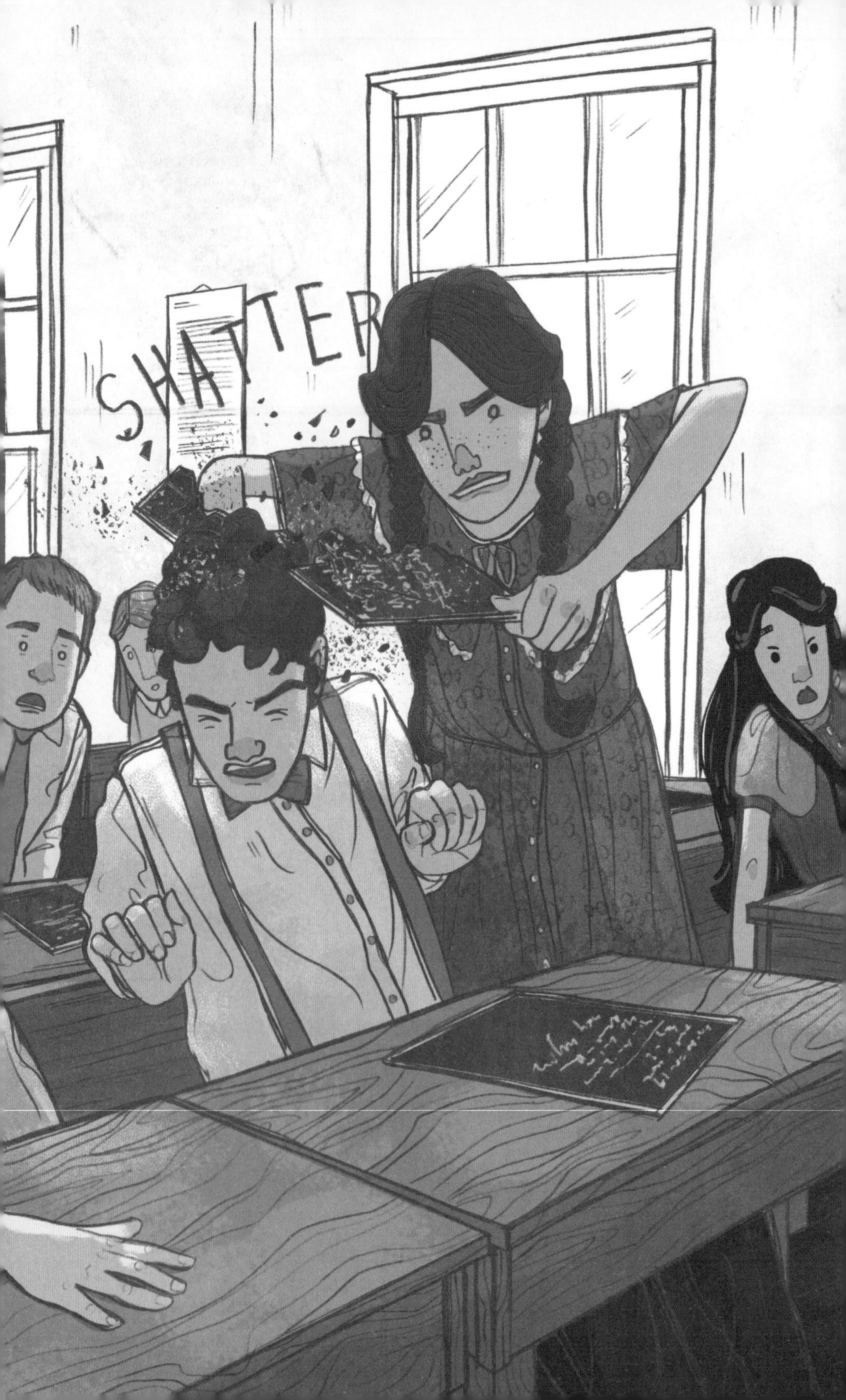
SHATTER

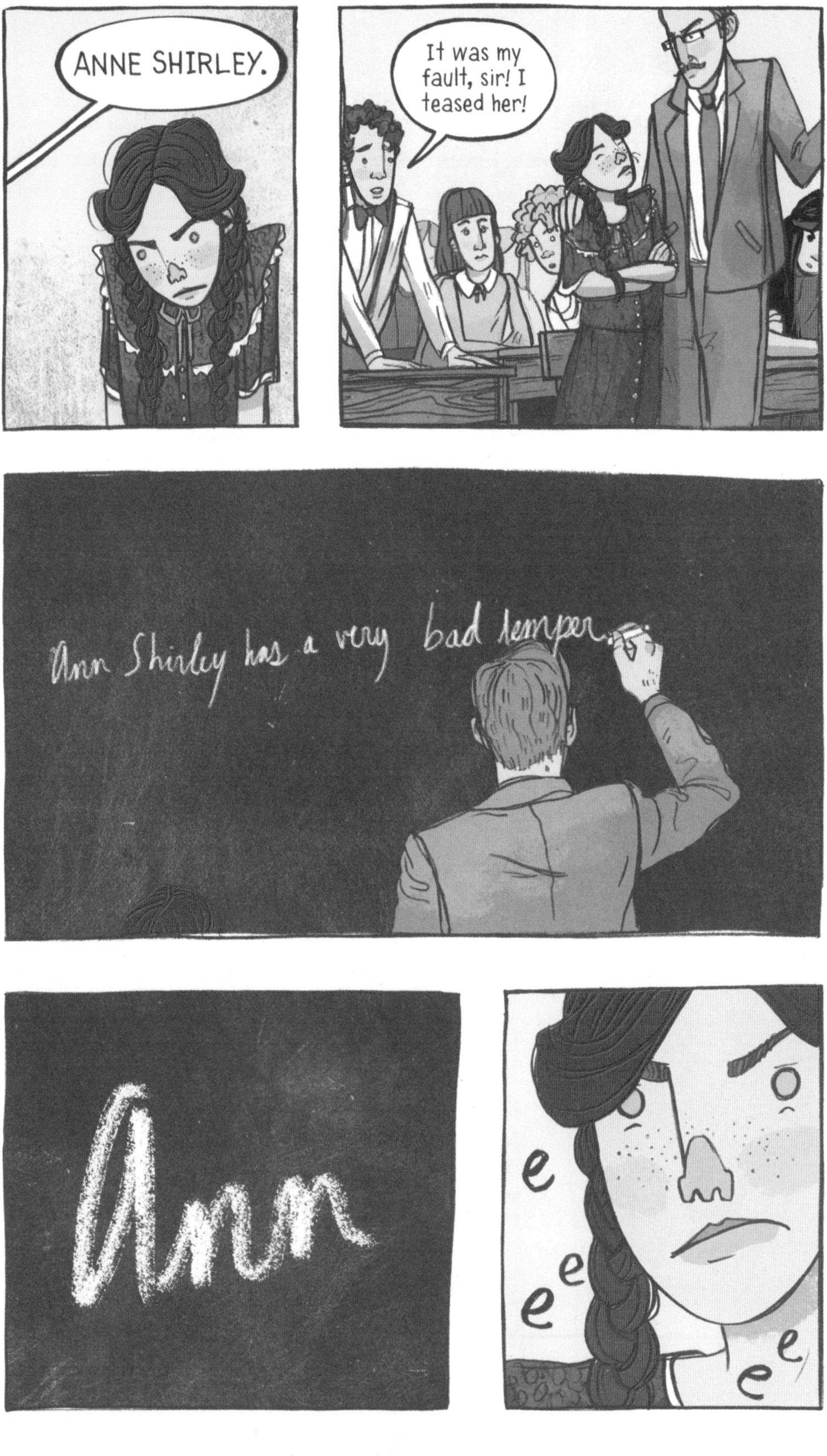
ANNE SHIRLEY.
It was my fault, sir! I teased her!
Ann Shirley has a very bad temper.
Ann
e
e e
e e
e

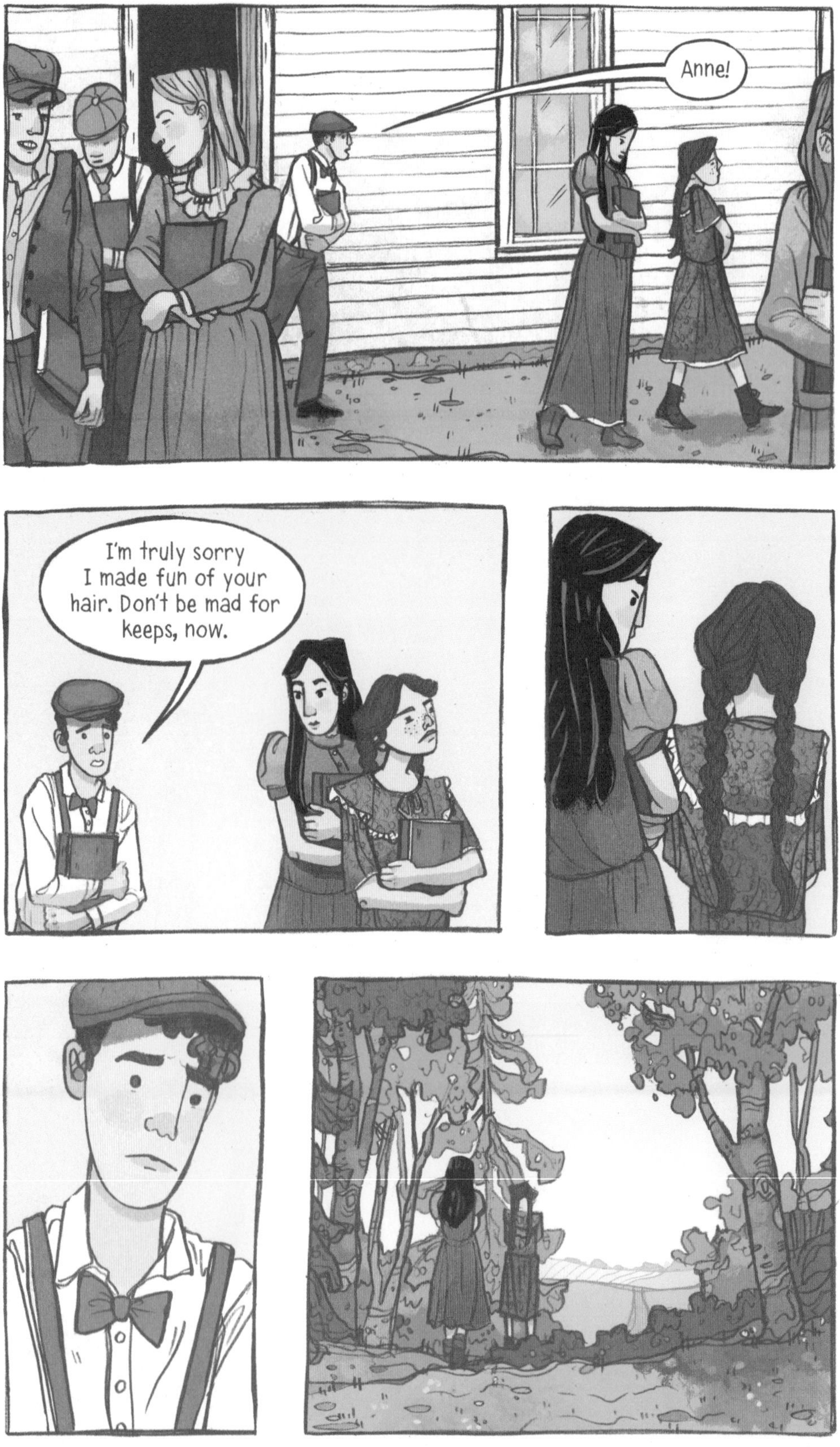
Anne!
I'm truly sorry I made fun of your hair. Don't be mad for keeps, now.

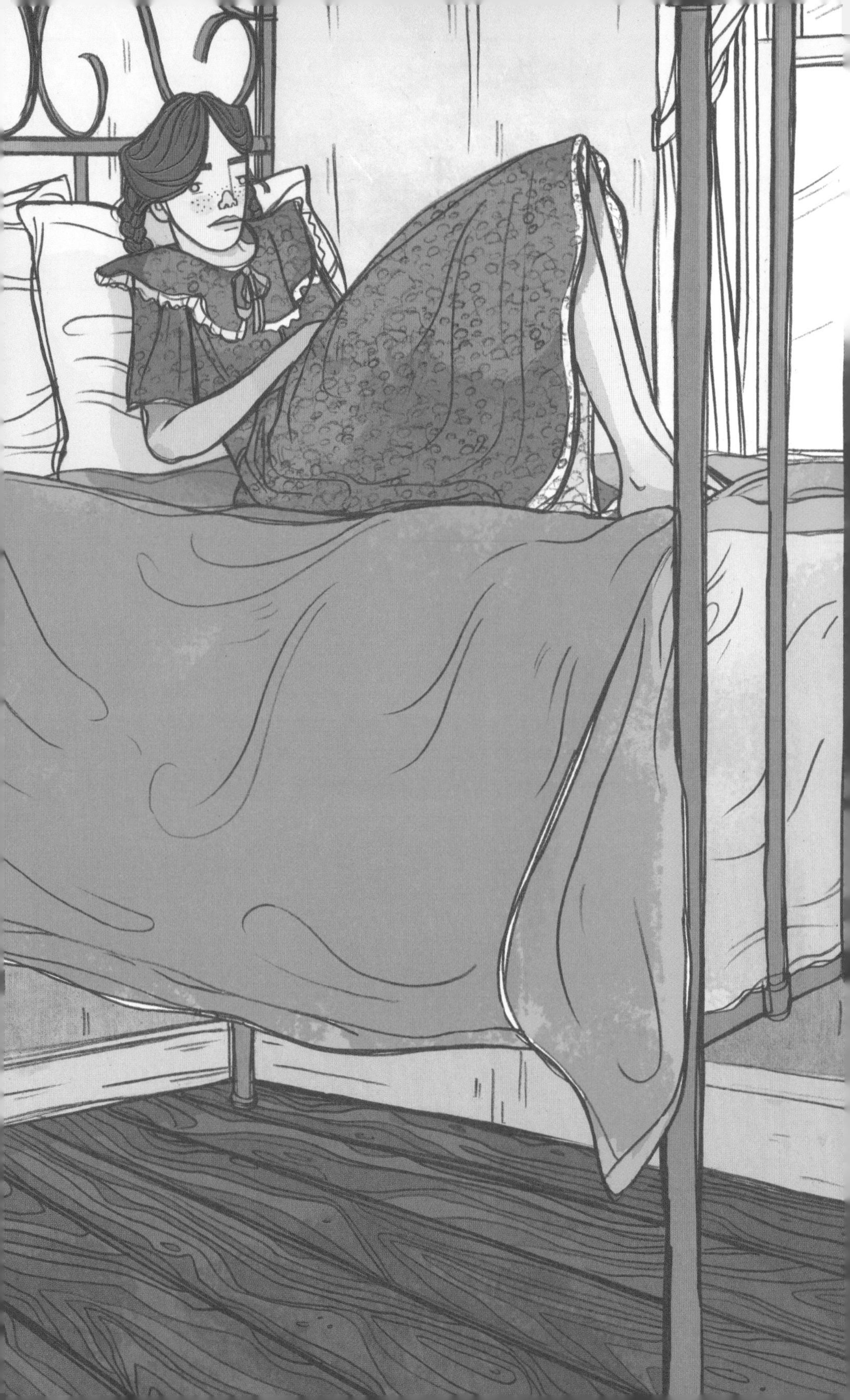

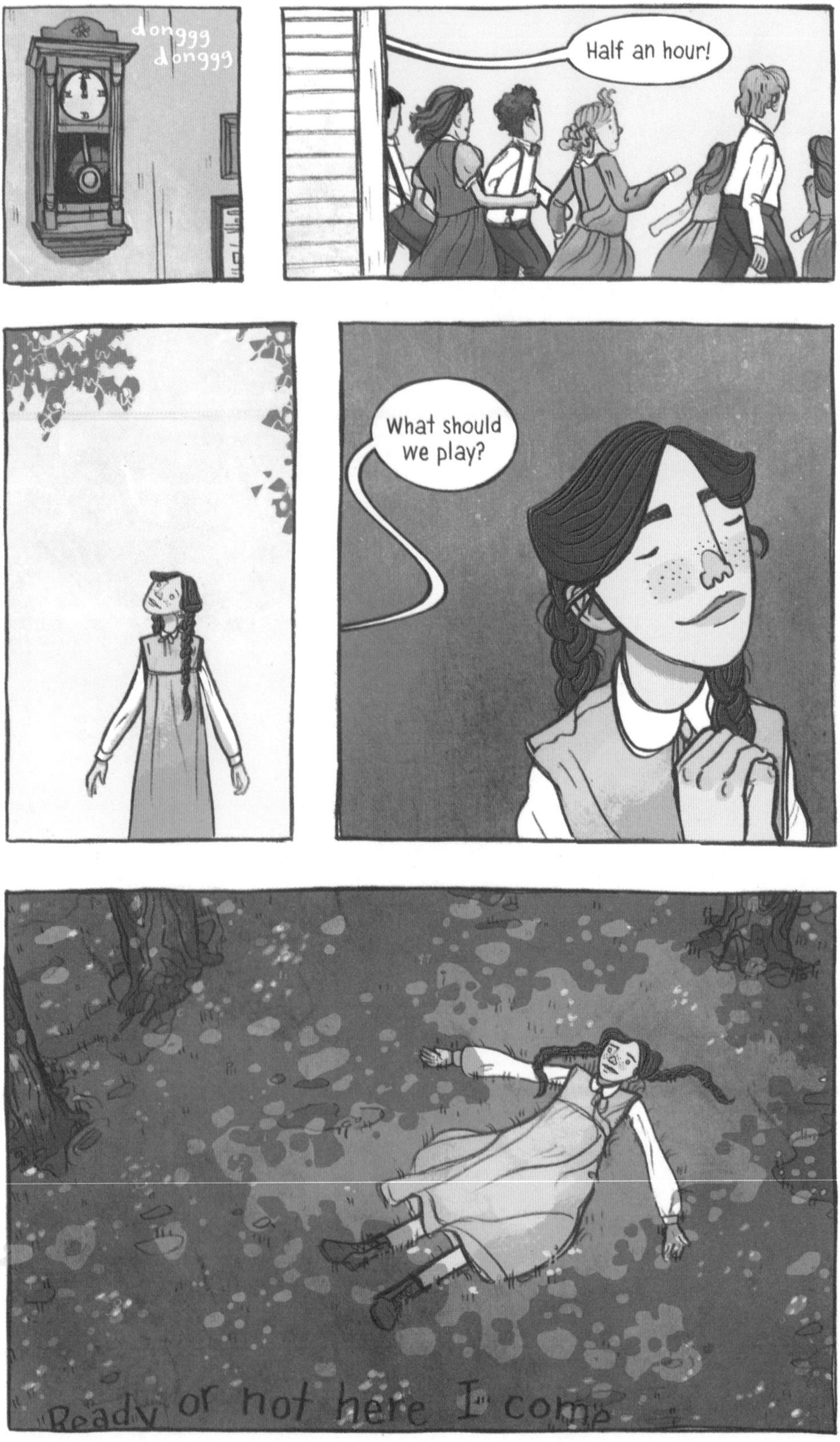

dongggg
dongggg
Half an hour!
What should we play?
Ready or not here I come

I see you!
Found you!

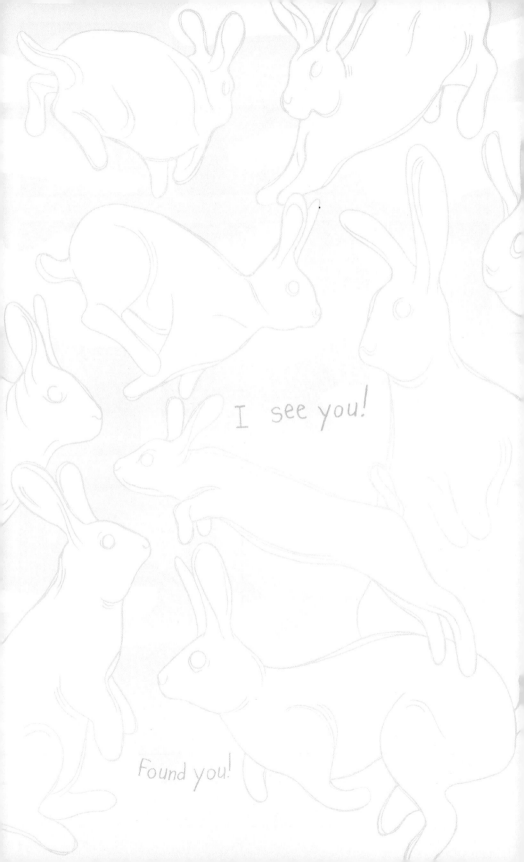

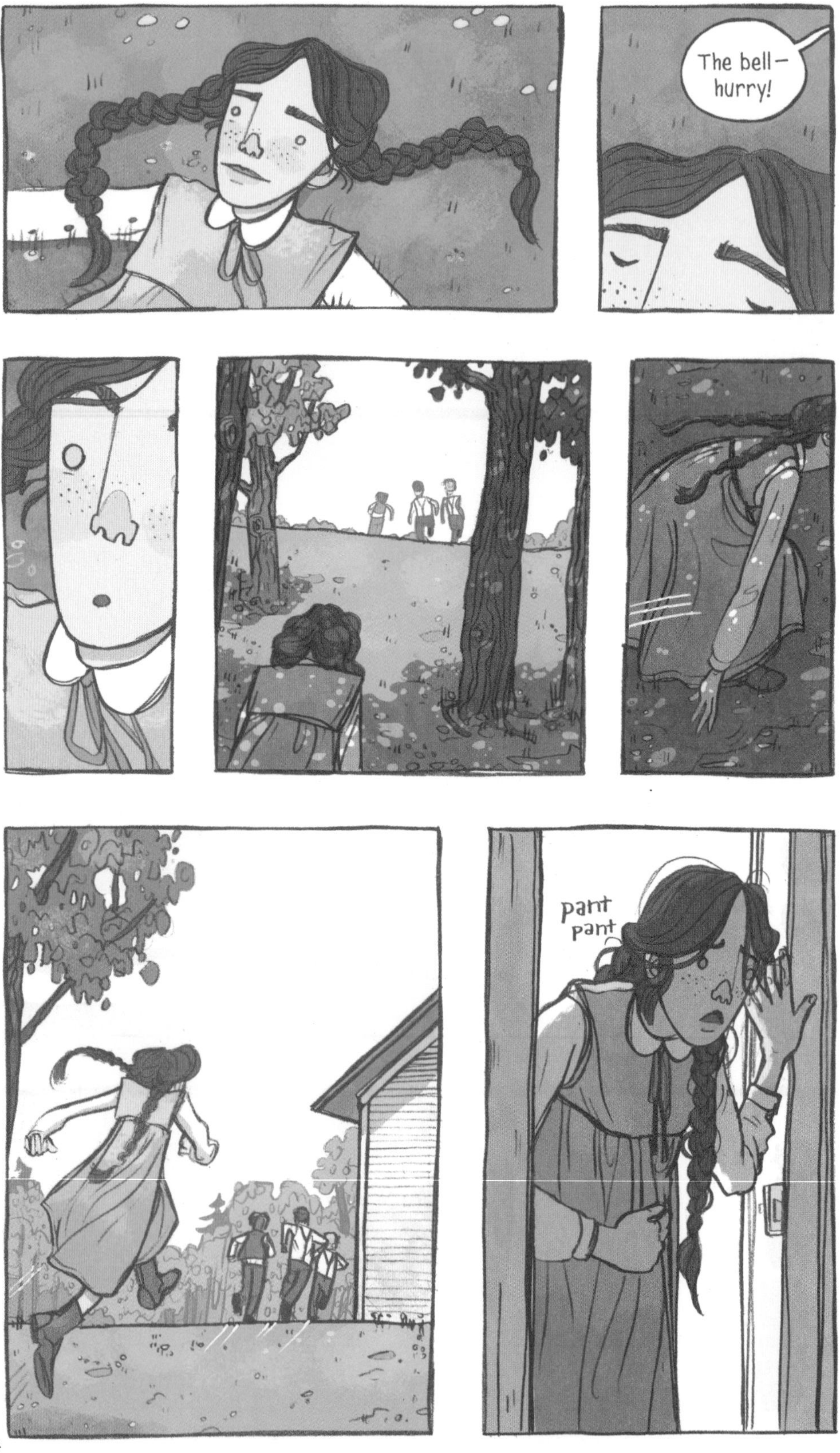
The bell—
hurry!
pant
pant

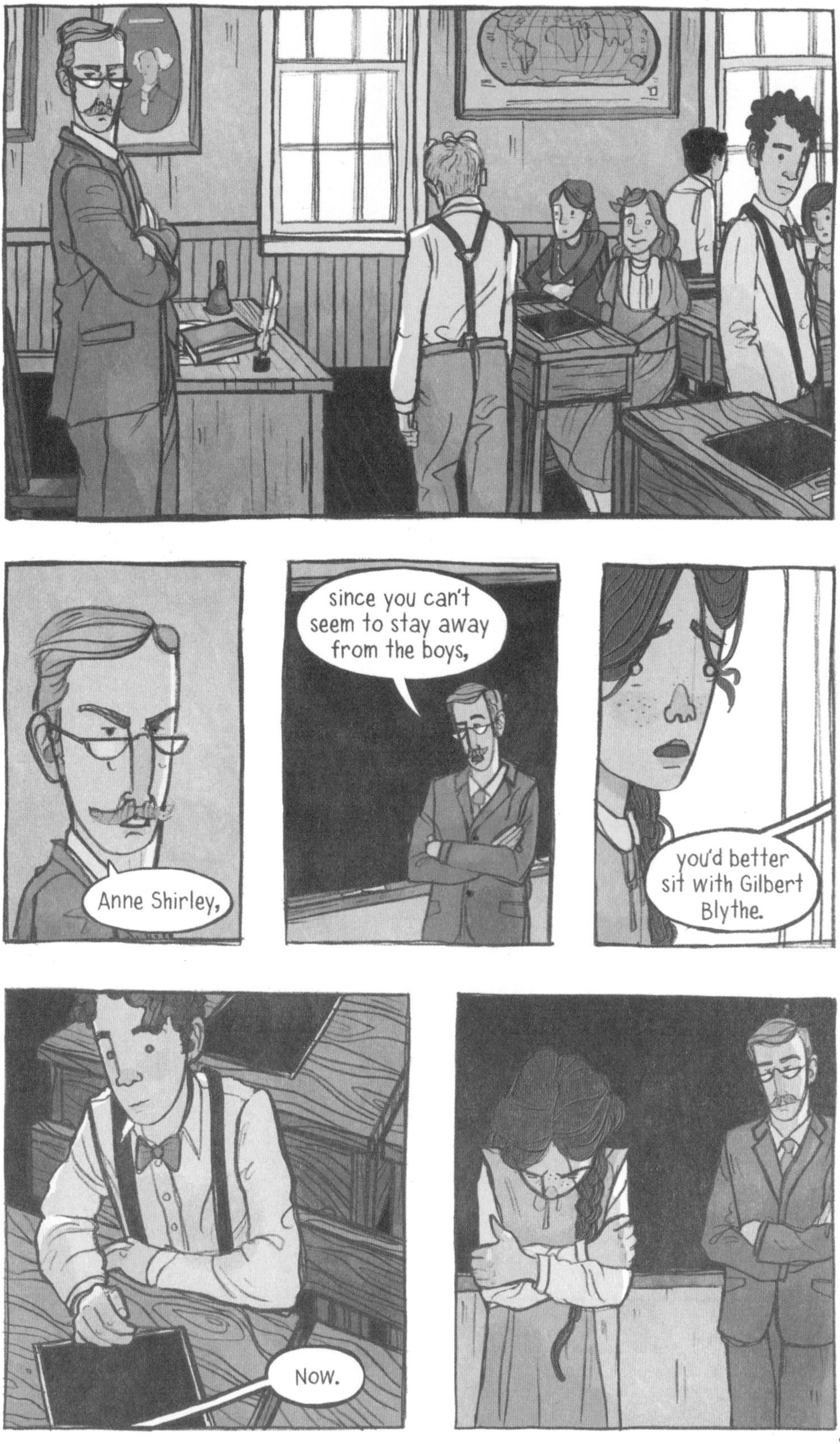
Anne Shirley,
since you can't seem to stay away from the boys,
you'd better sit with Gilbert Blythe.
Now.

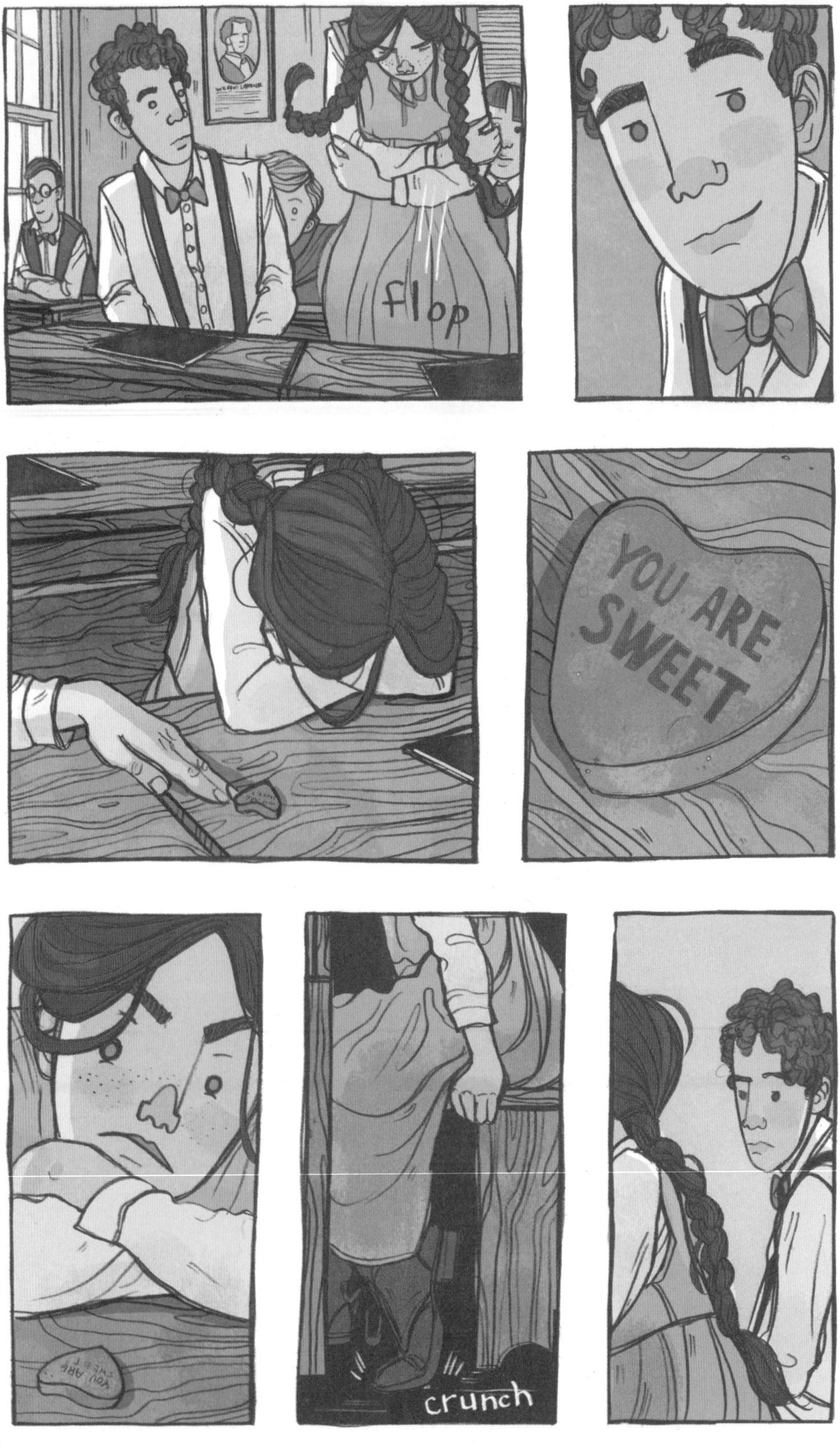
flop
YOU ARE SWEET
crunch

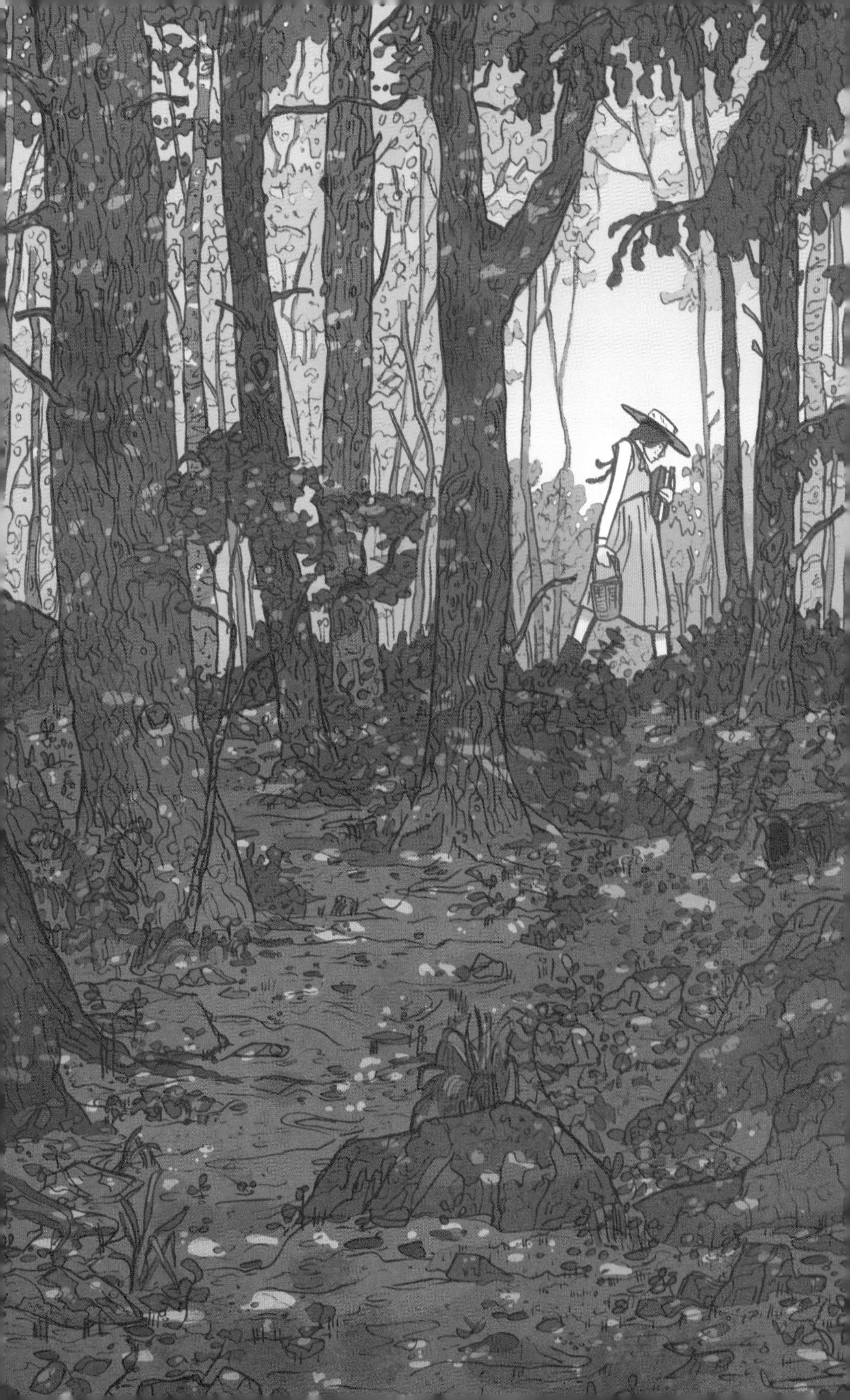

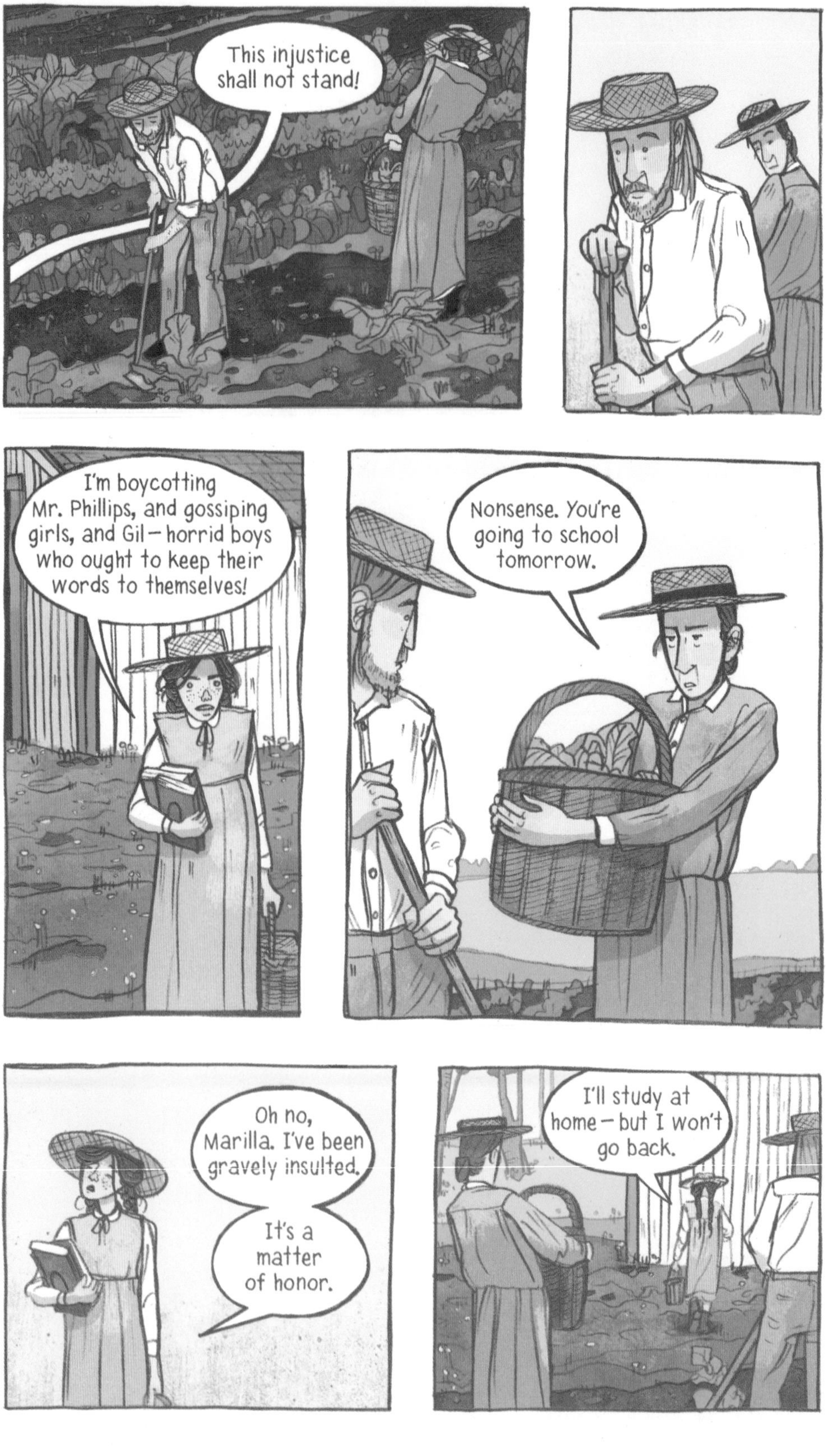
This injustice shall not stand!
I'm boycotting Mr. Phillips, and gossiping girls, and Gil—horrid boys who ought to keep their words to themselves!
Nonsense. *You're* going to school tomorrow.
Oh no, Marilla. I've been gravely insulted.
It's a matter of honor.
I'll study at home—but I won't go back.

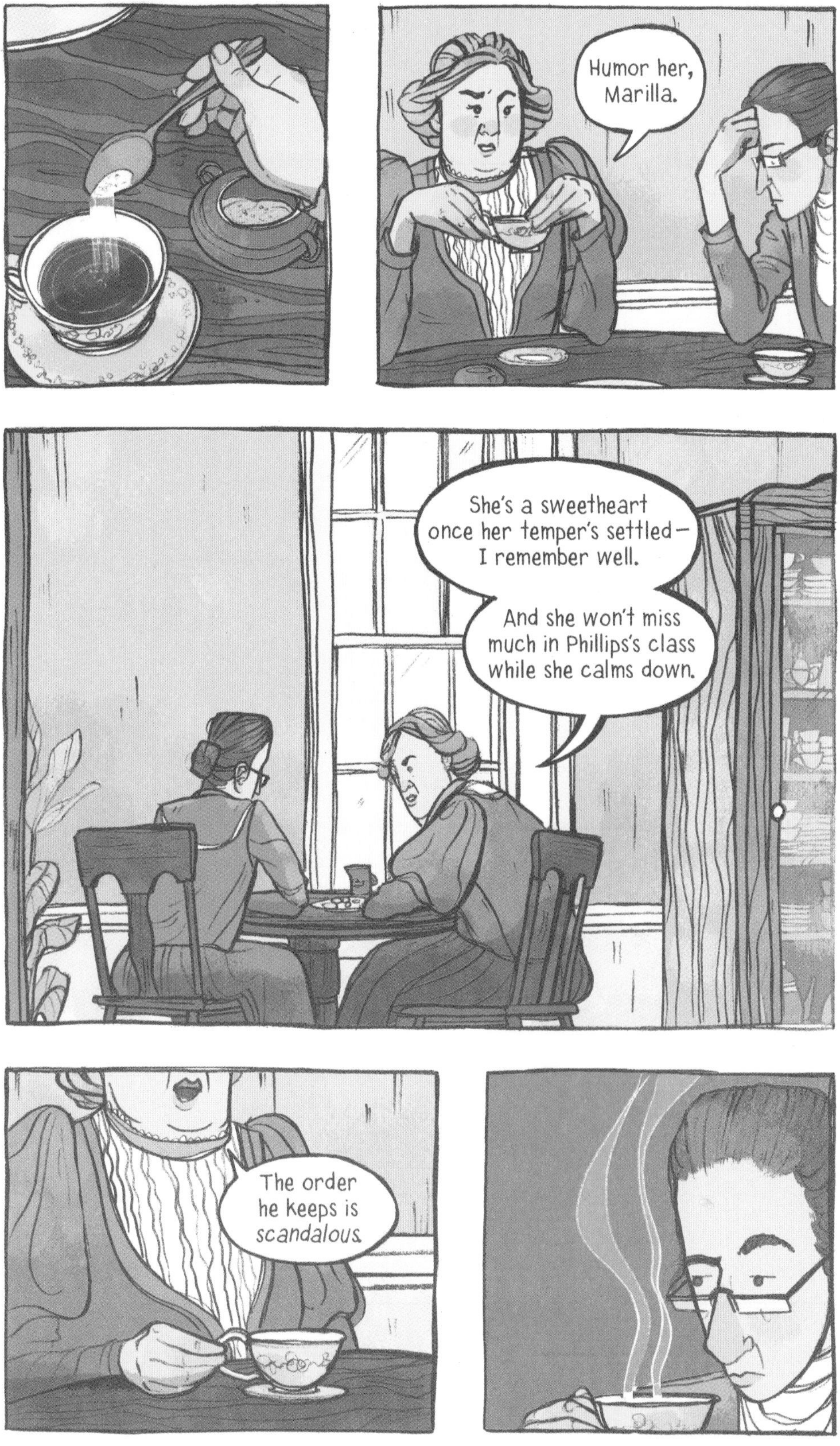
Humor her, Marilla.
She's a sweetheart once her temper's settled— I remember well.
And she won't miss much in Phillips's class while she calms down.
The order he keeps is *scandalous*.

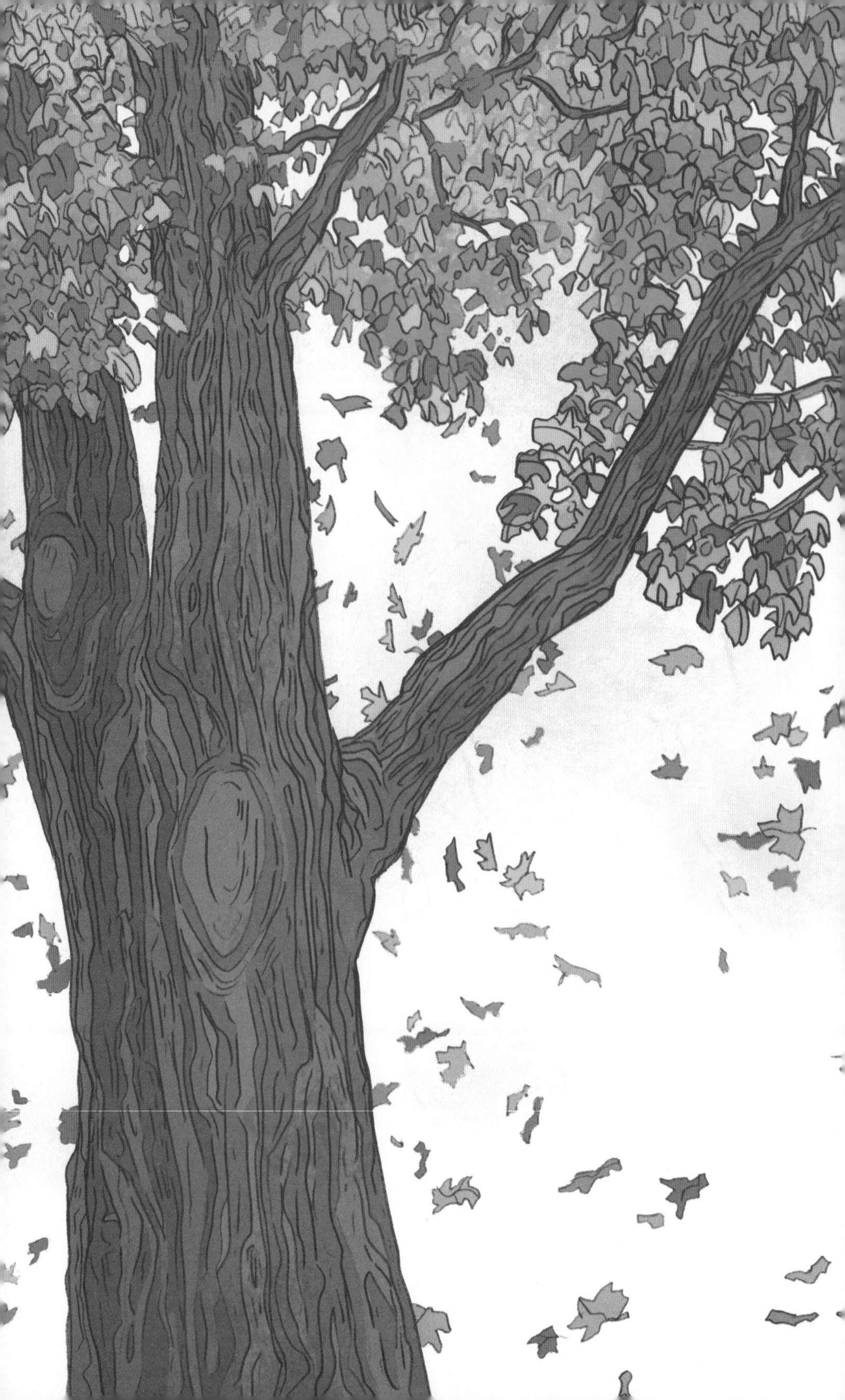

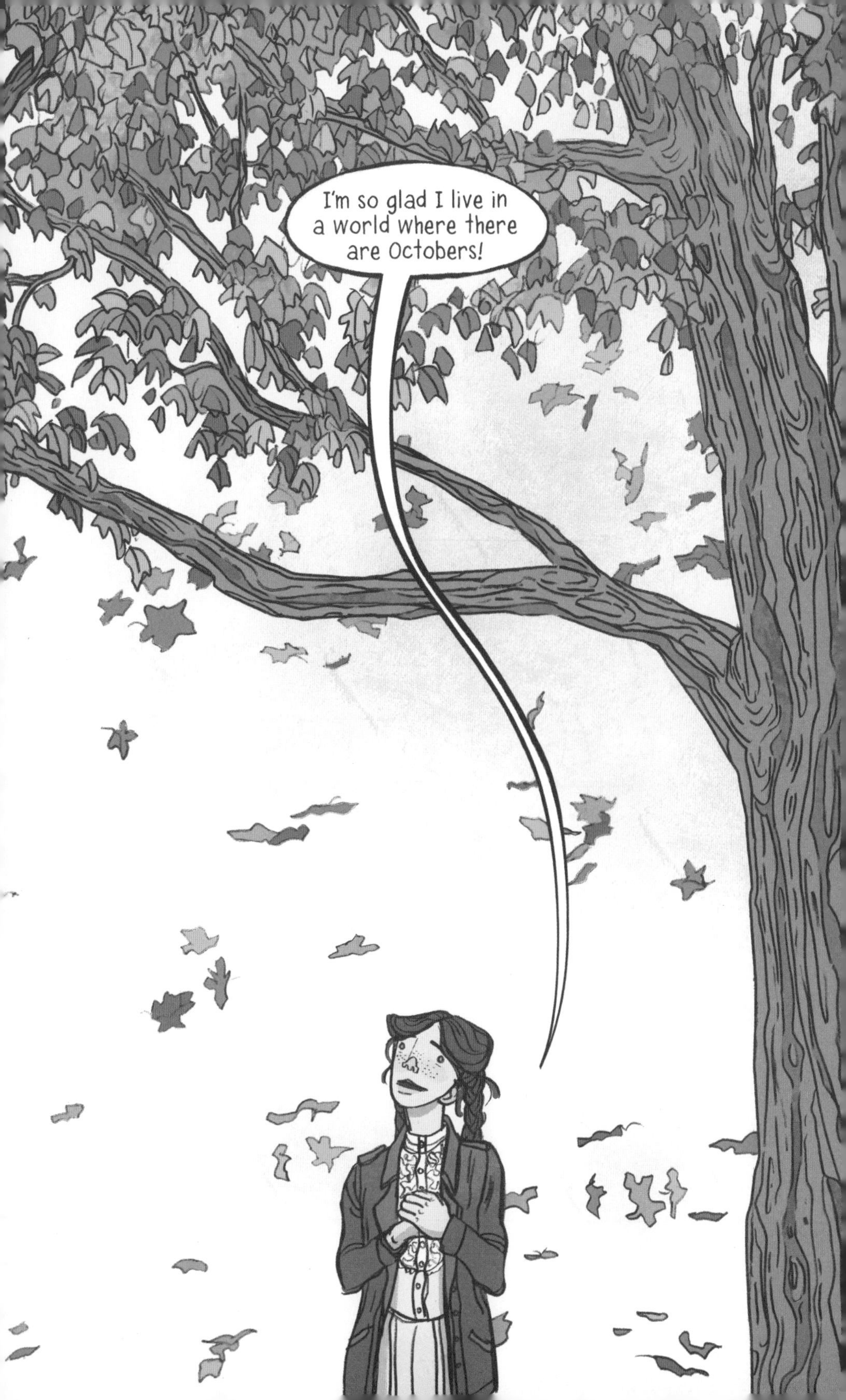
I'm so glad I live in a world where there are Octobers!

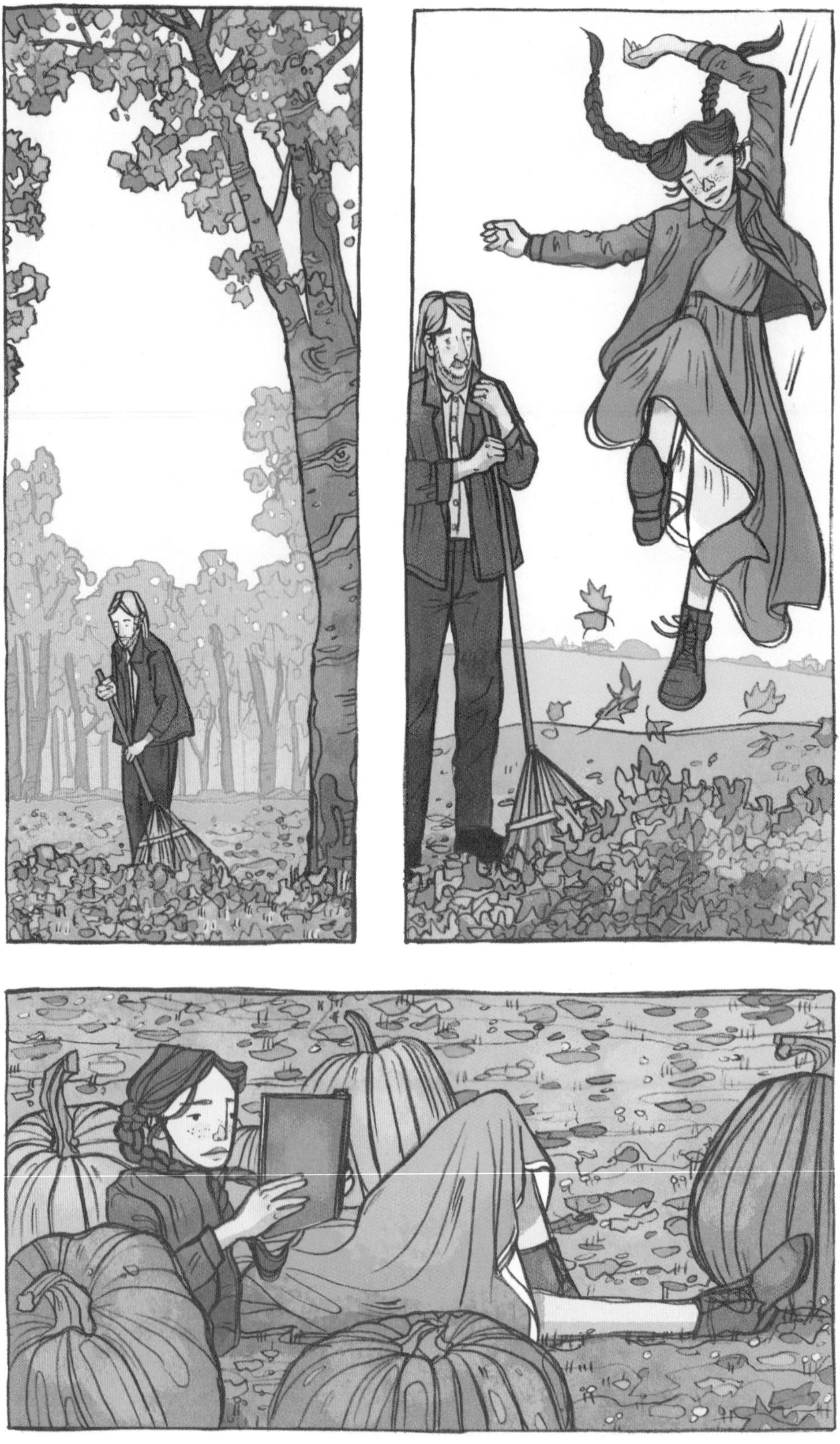

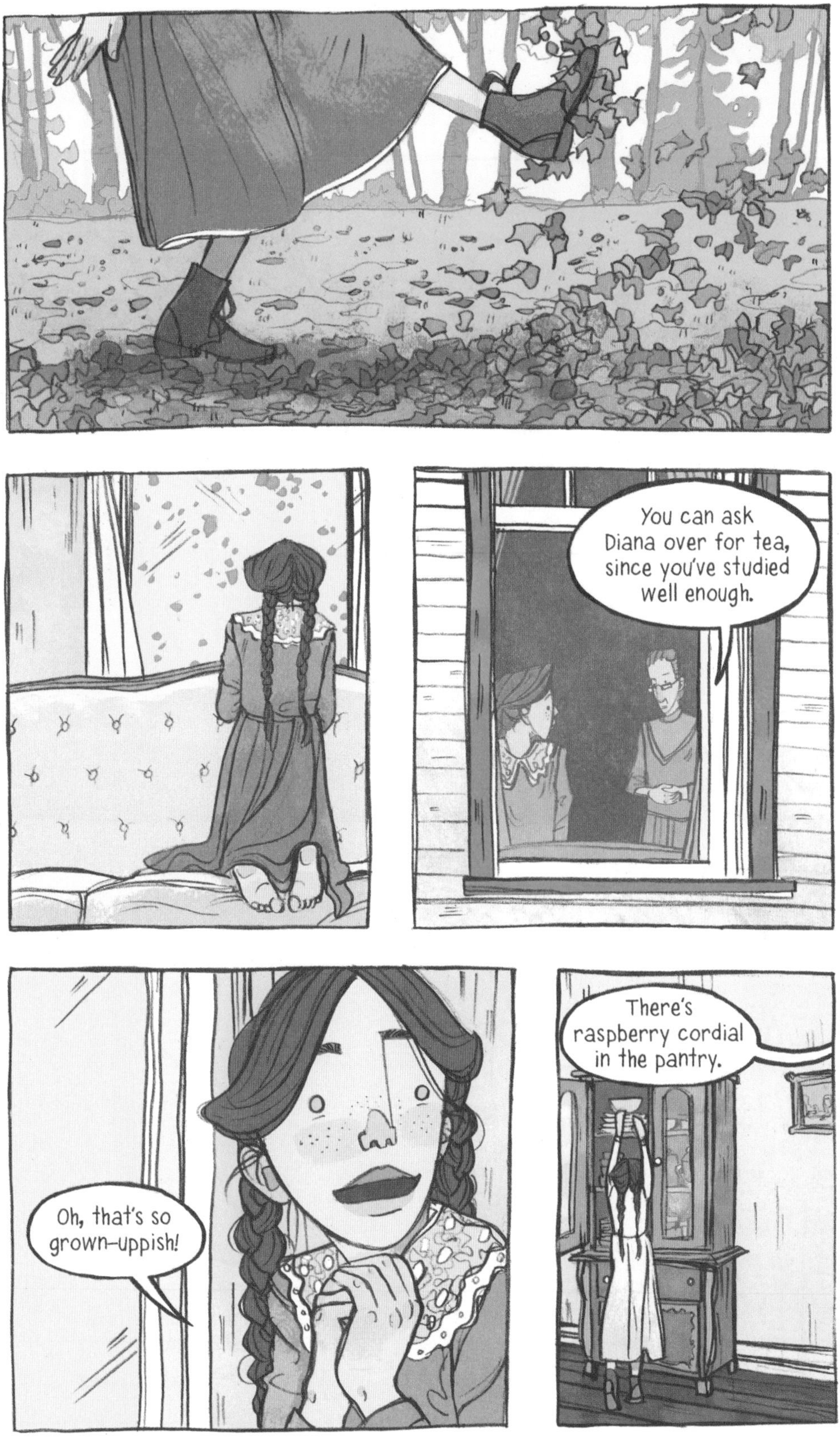
You can ask Diana over for tea, since you've studied well enough.
Oh, that's so grown-uppish!
There's raspberry cordial in the pantry.

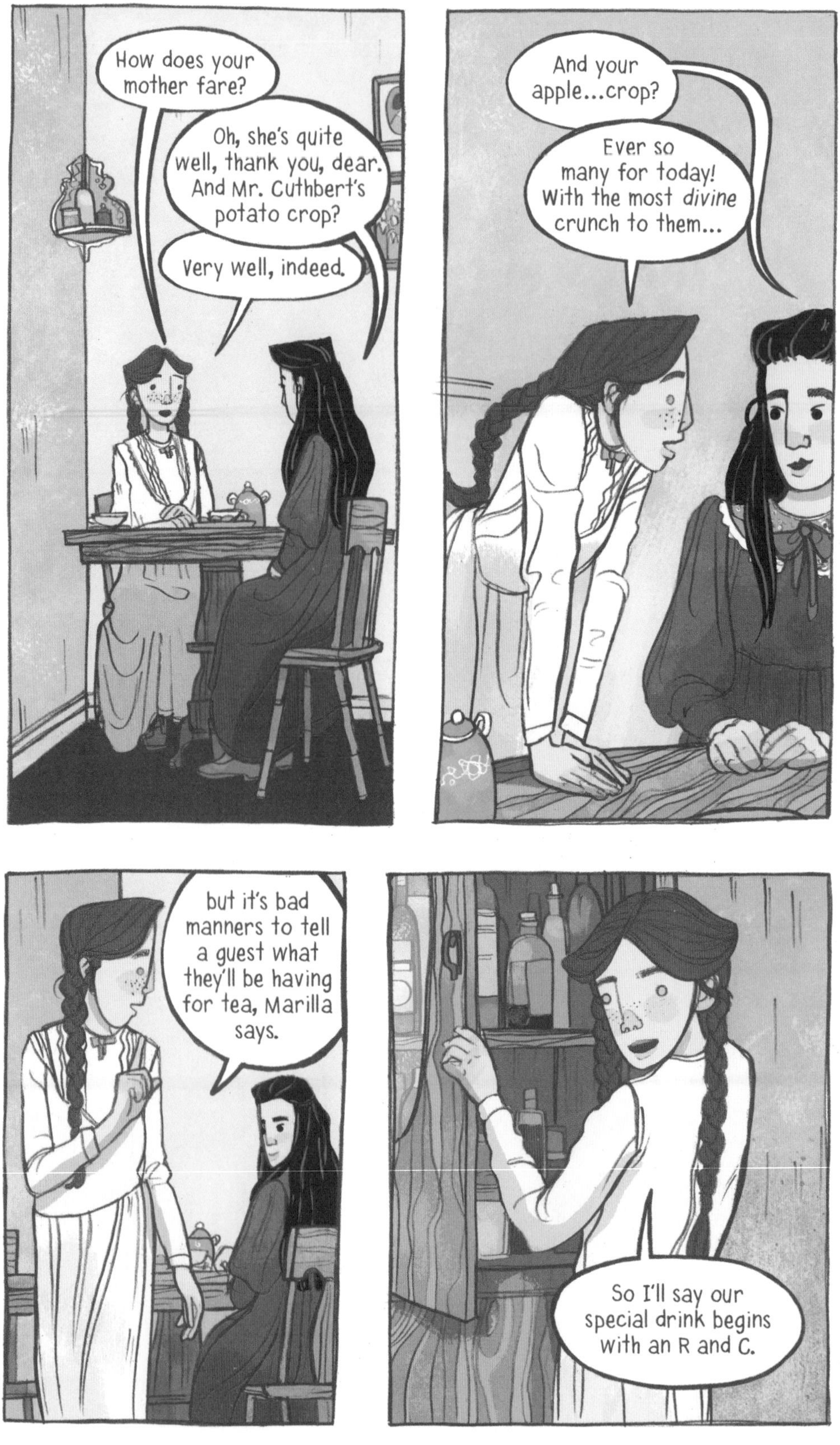
How does your mother fare?
Oh, she's quite well, thank you, dear. And Mr. Cuthbert's potato crop?
Very well, indeed.
And your apple...crop?
Ever so many for today! With the most *divine* crunch to them...
but it's bad manners to tell a guest what they'll be having for tea, Marilla says.
So I'll say our special drink begins with an R and C.

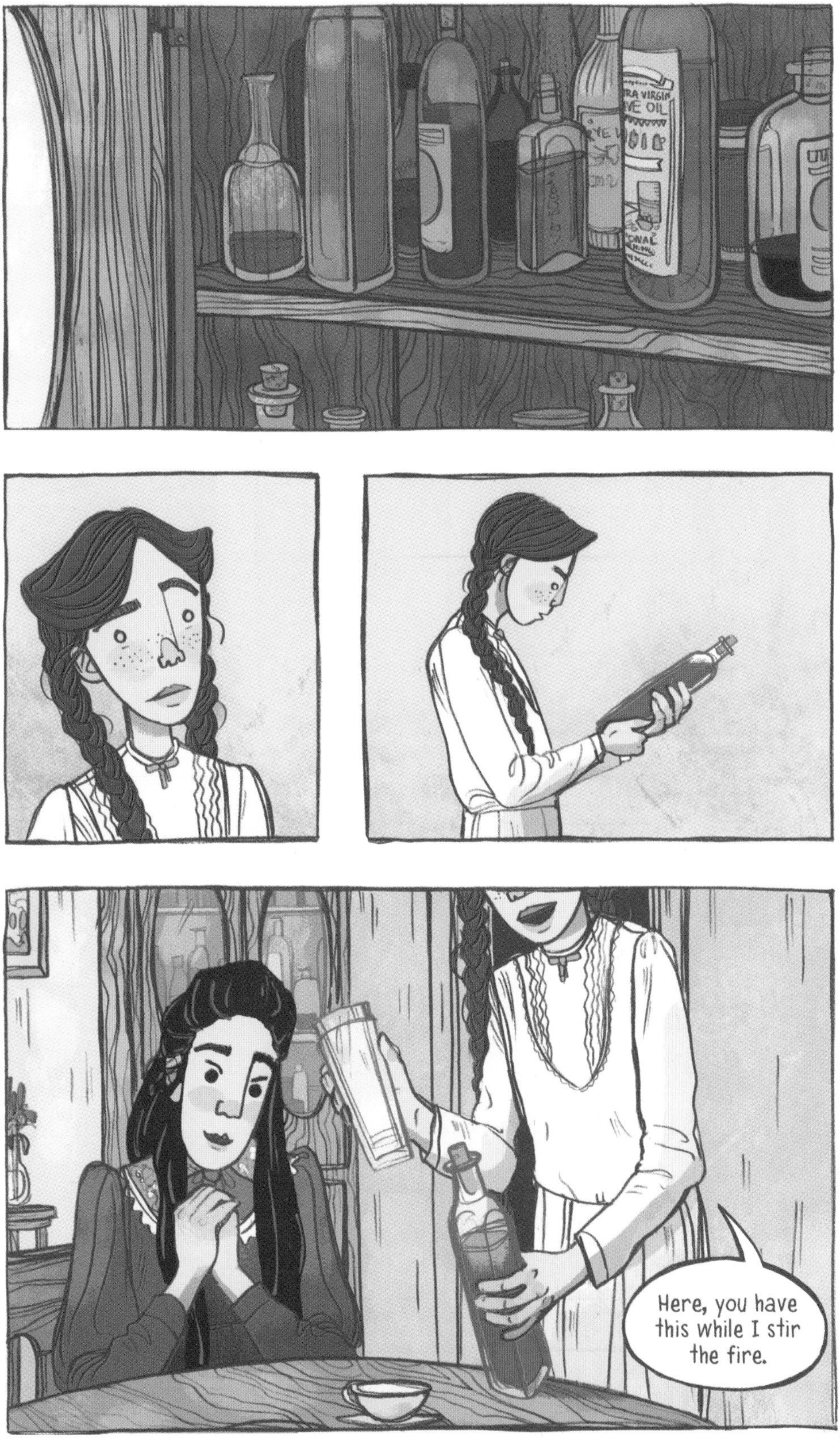
Here, you have this while I stir the fire.

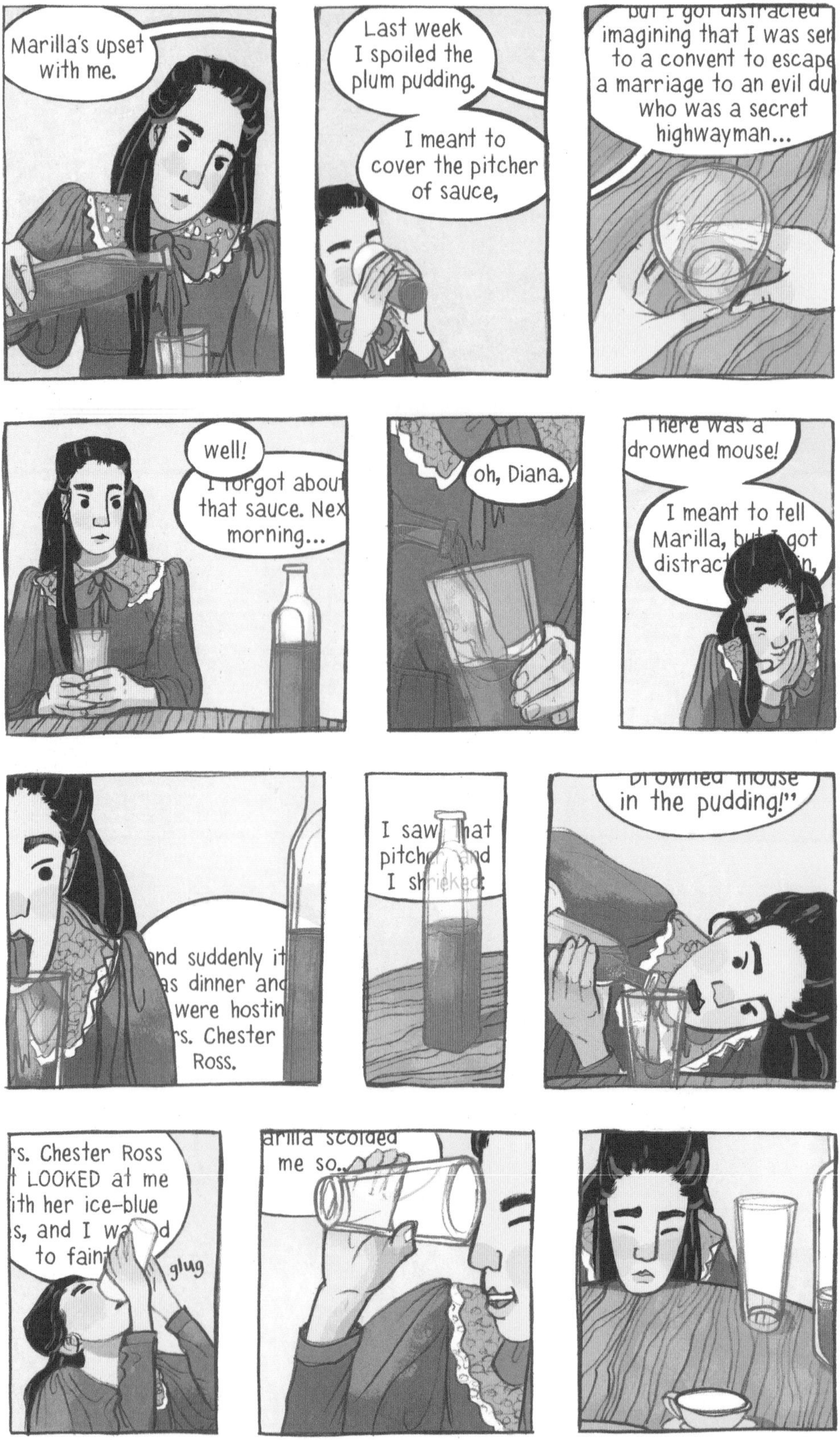

Marilla's upset with me.
Last week I spoiled the plum pudding.
I meant to cover the pitcher of sauce,
imagining that I was sen
to a convent to escape
a marriage to an evil du
who was a secret
highwayman...
well!
I forgot about that sauce. Nex morning...
oh, Diana.
drowned mouse!
I meant to tell Marilla, but I got distract
nd suddenly it
as dinner and
were hostin
rs. Chester
Ross.
I saw that pitcher and I shrieked:
in the pudding!"
rs. Chester Ross
LOOKED at me
ith her ice-blue
s, and I wa d
to faint
glug
me so...

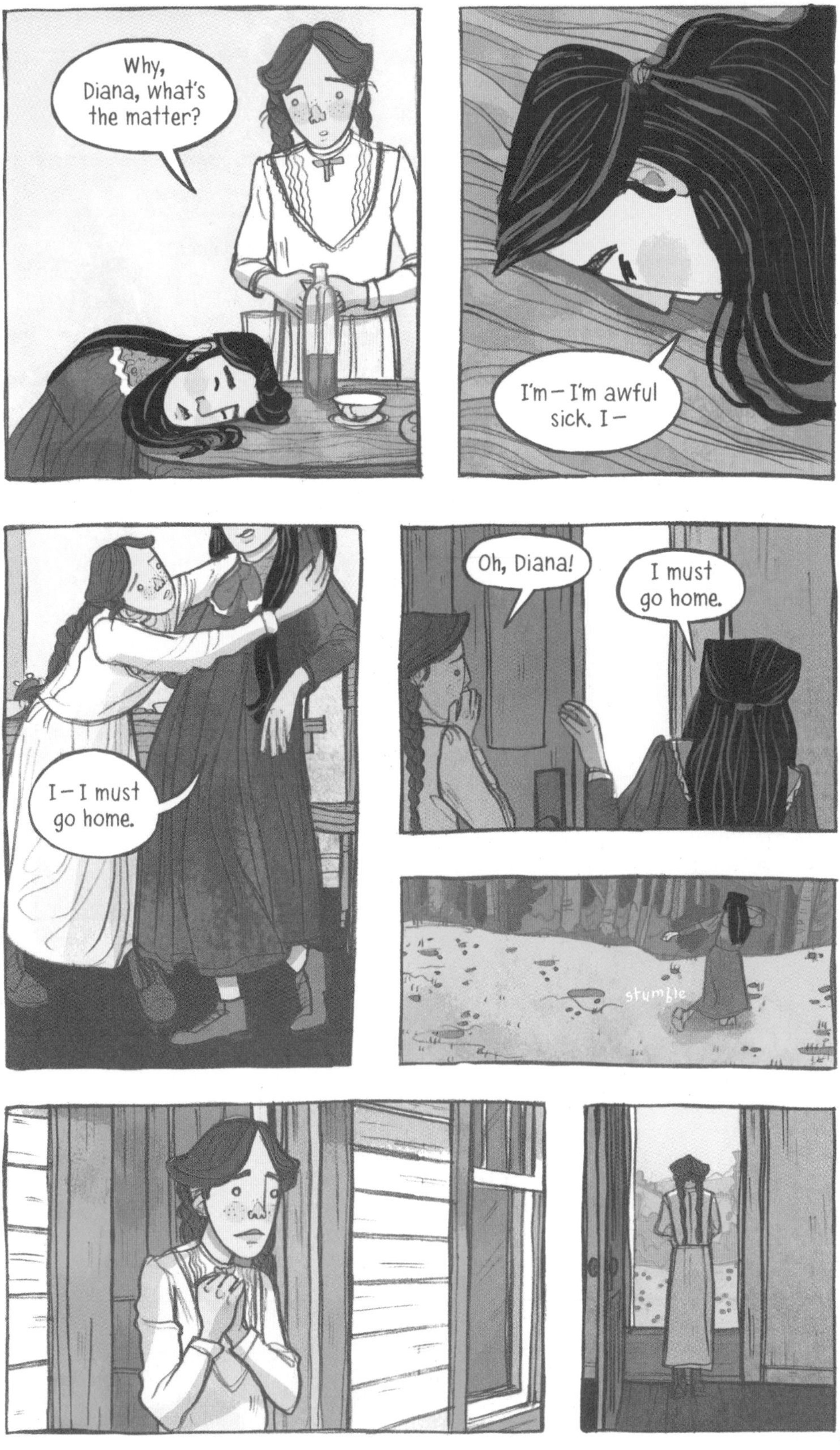
Why, Diana, what's the matter?
I'm — I'm awful sick. I —
I — I must go home.
Oh, Diana!
I must go home.
stumble

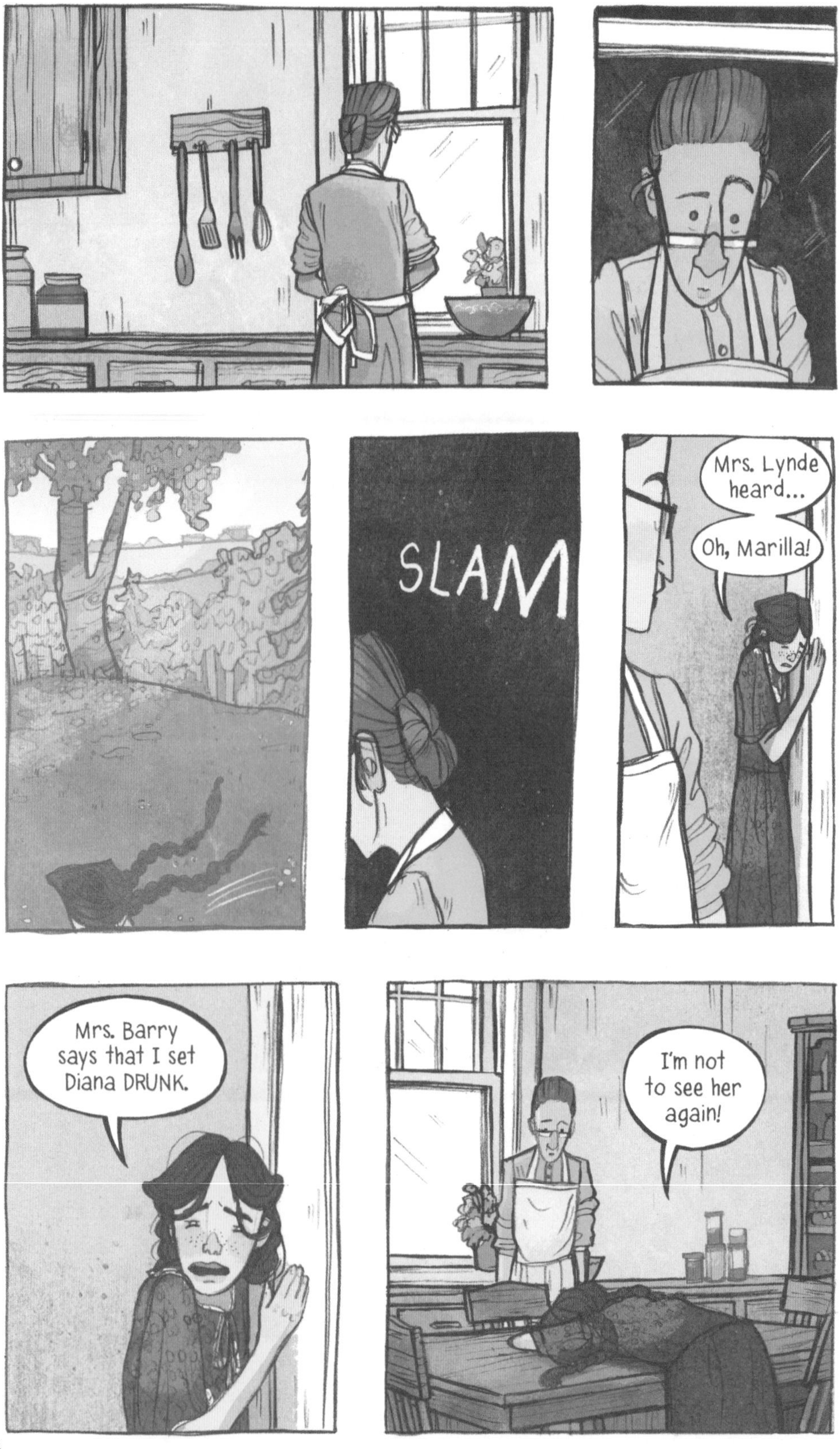
SLAM
Mrs. Lynde heard...
Oh, Marilla!
Mrs. Barry says that I set Diana DRUNK.
I'm not to see her again!

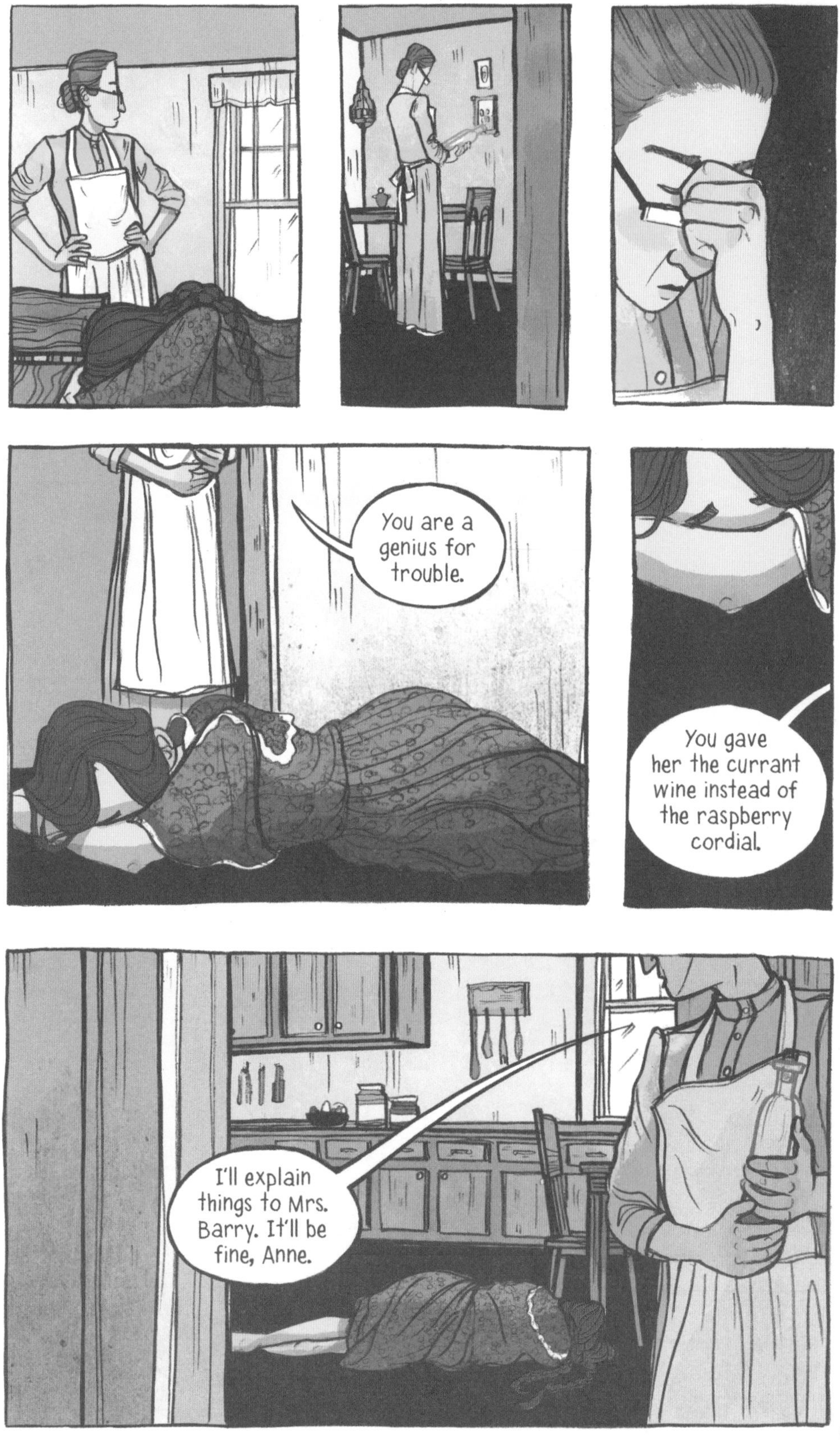
You are a genius for trouble.
You gave her the currant wine instead of the raspberry cordial.
I'll explain things to Mrs. Barry. It'll be fine, Anne.

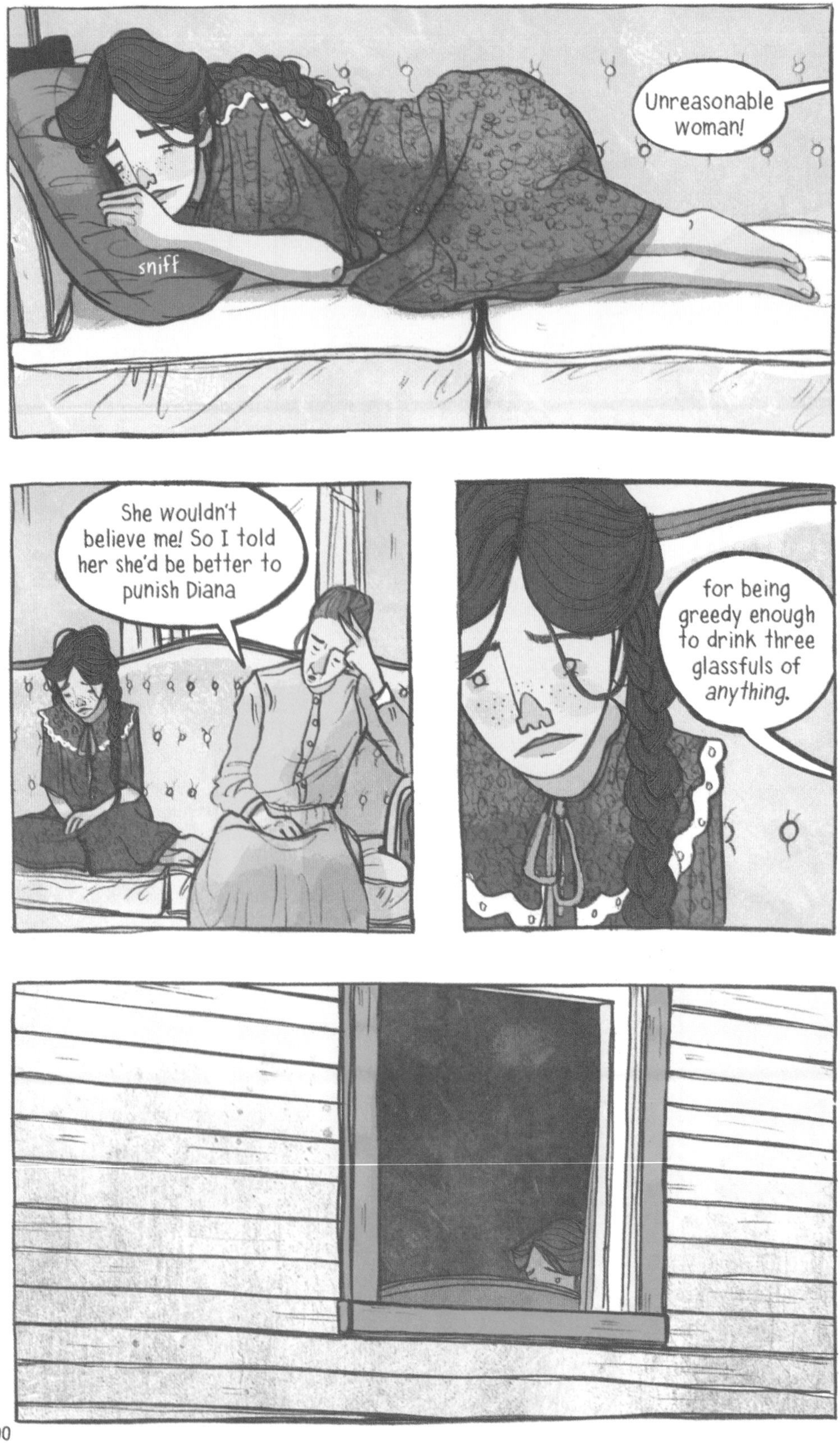
Unreasonable woman!
sniff
She wouldn't believe me! So I told her she'd be better to punish Diana
for being greedy enough to drink three glassfuls of *anything*.

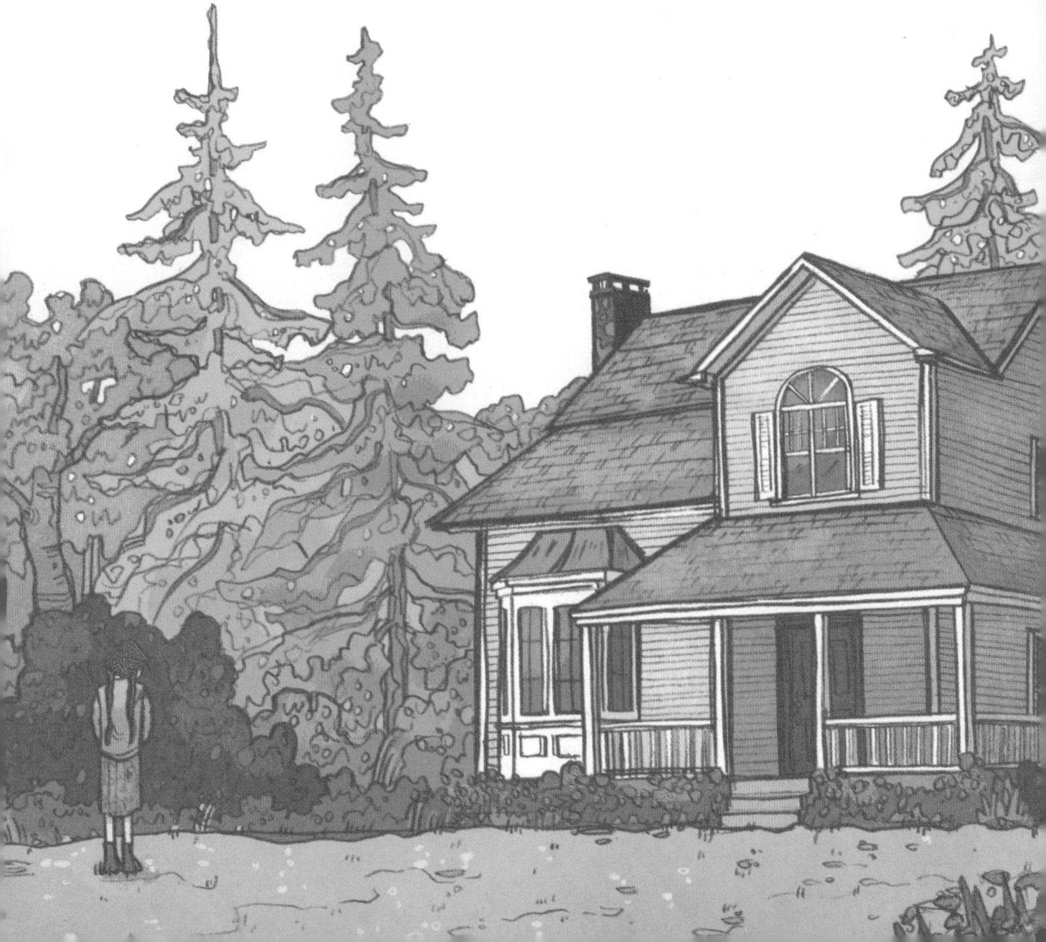

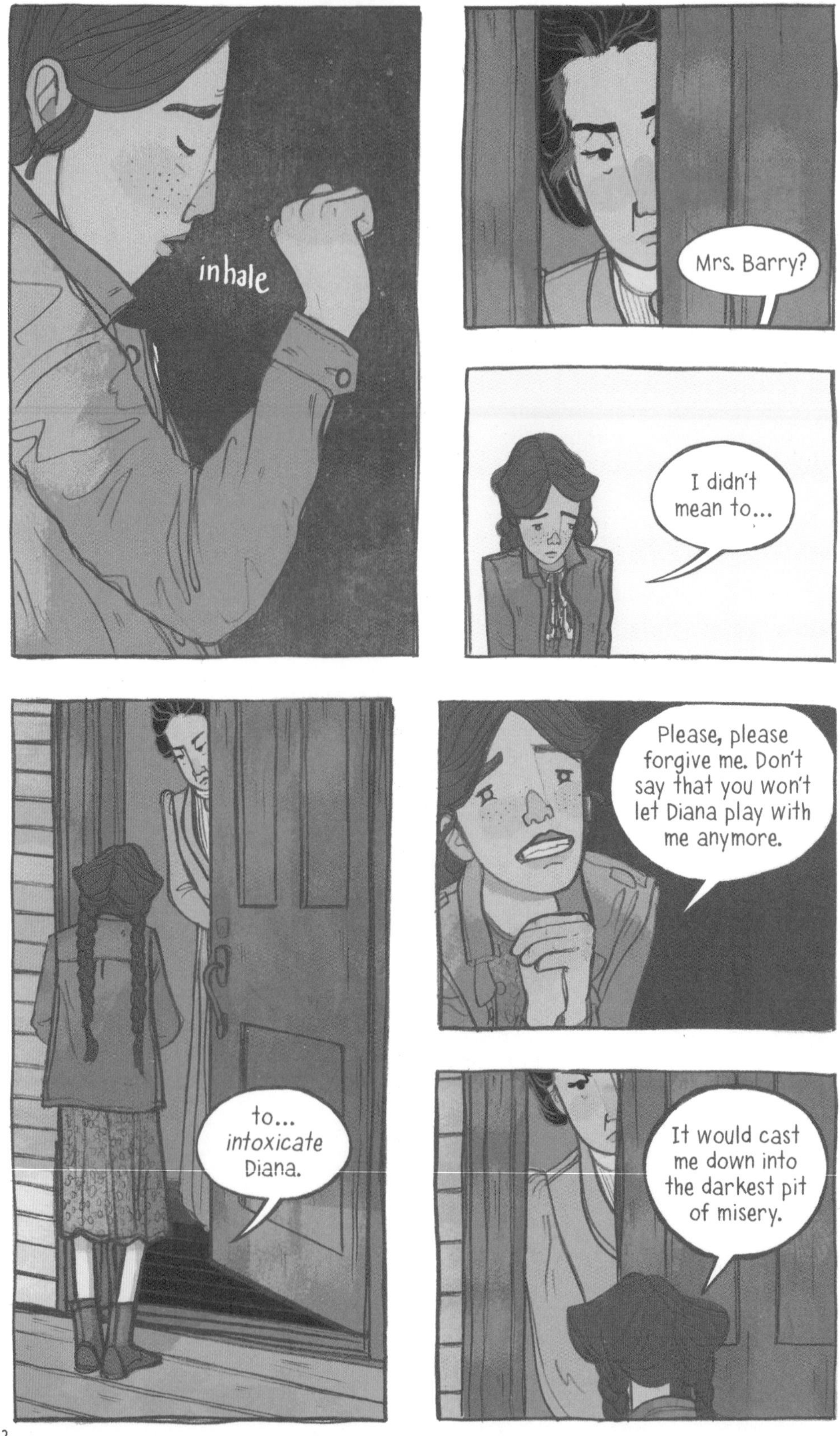
inhale
Mrs. Barry?
I didn't mean to...
to... intoxicate Diana.
Please, please forgive me. Don't say that you won't let Diana play with me anymore.
It would cast me down into the darkest pit of misery.

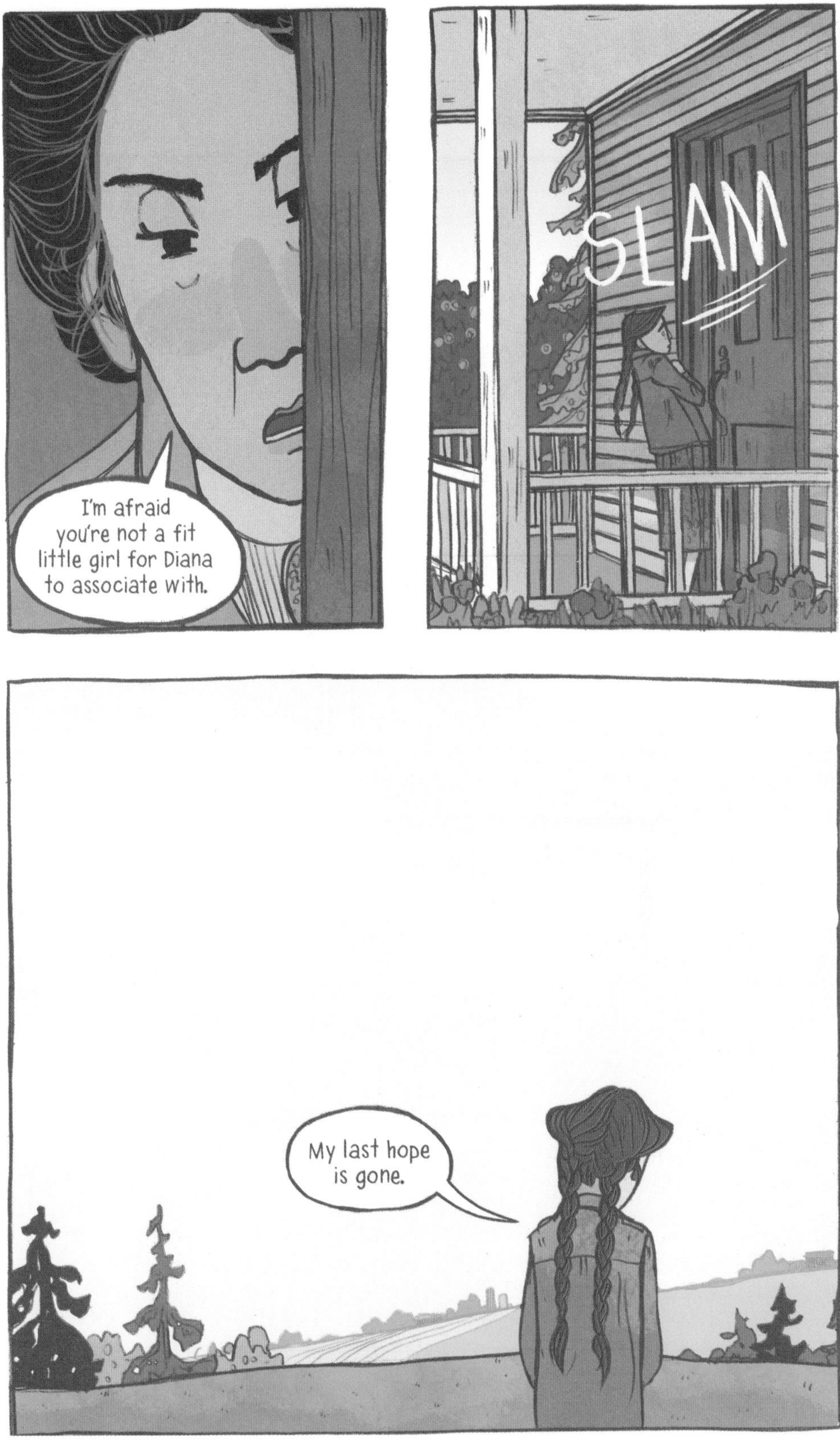
I'm afraid you're not a fit little girl for Diana to associate with.
SLAM
My last hope is gone.

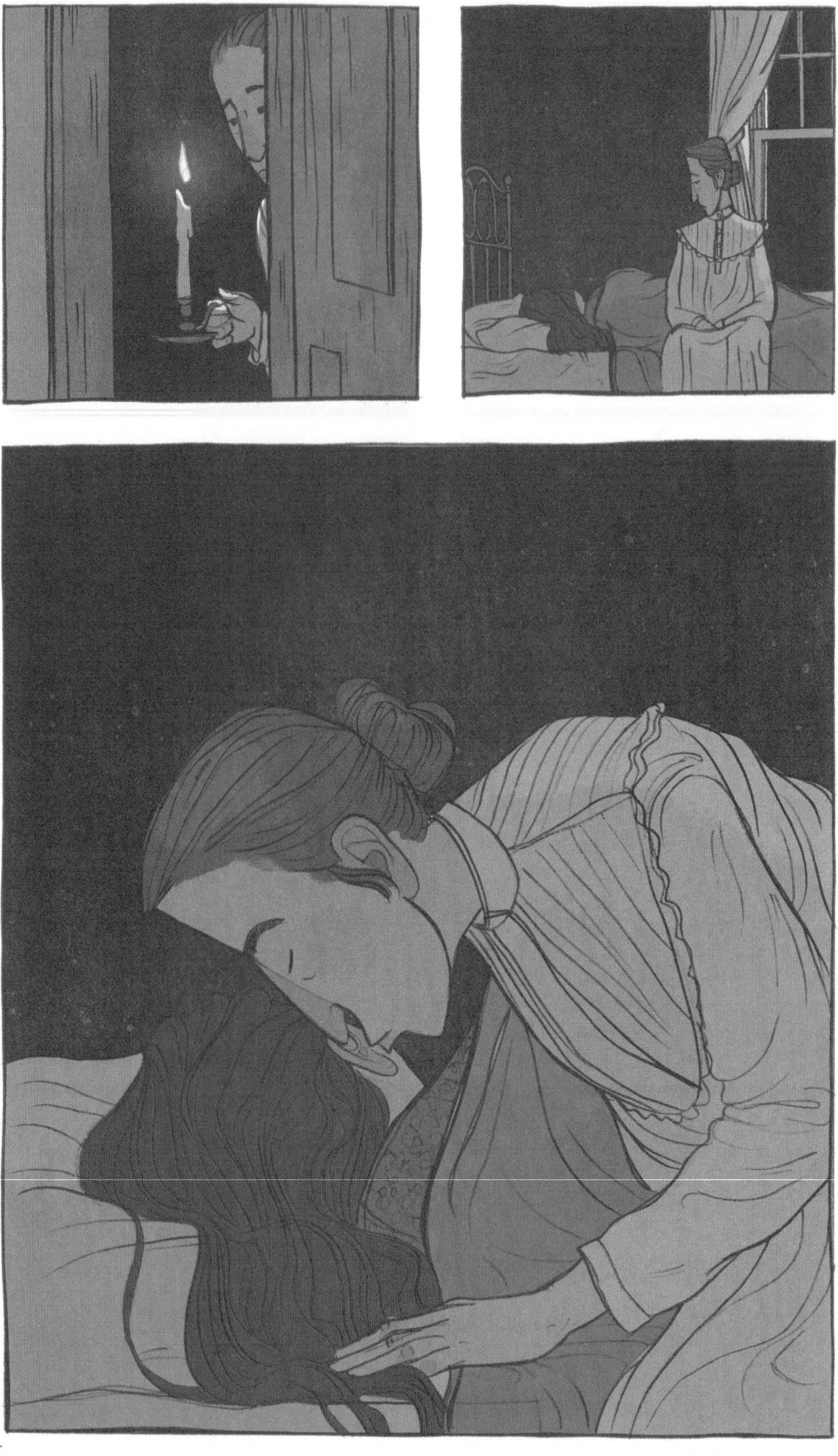

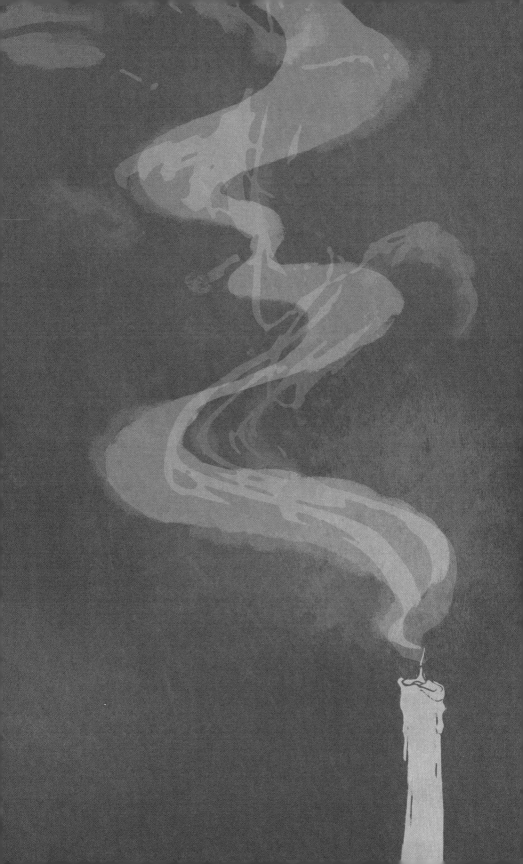

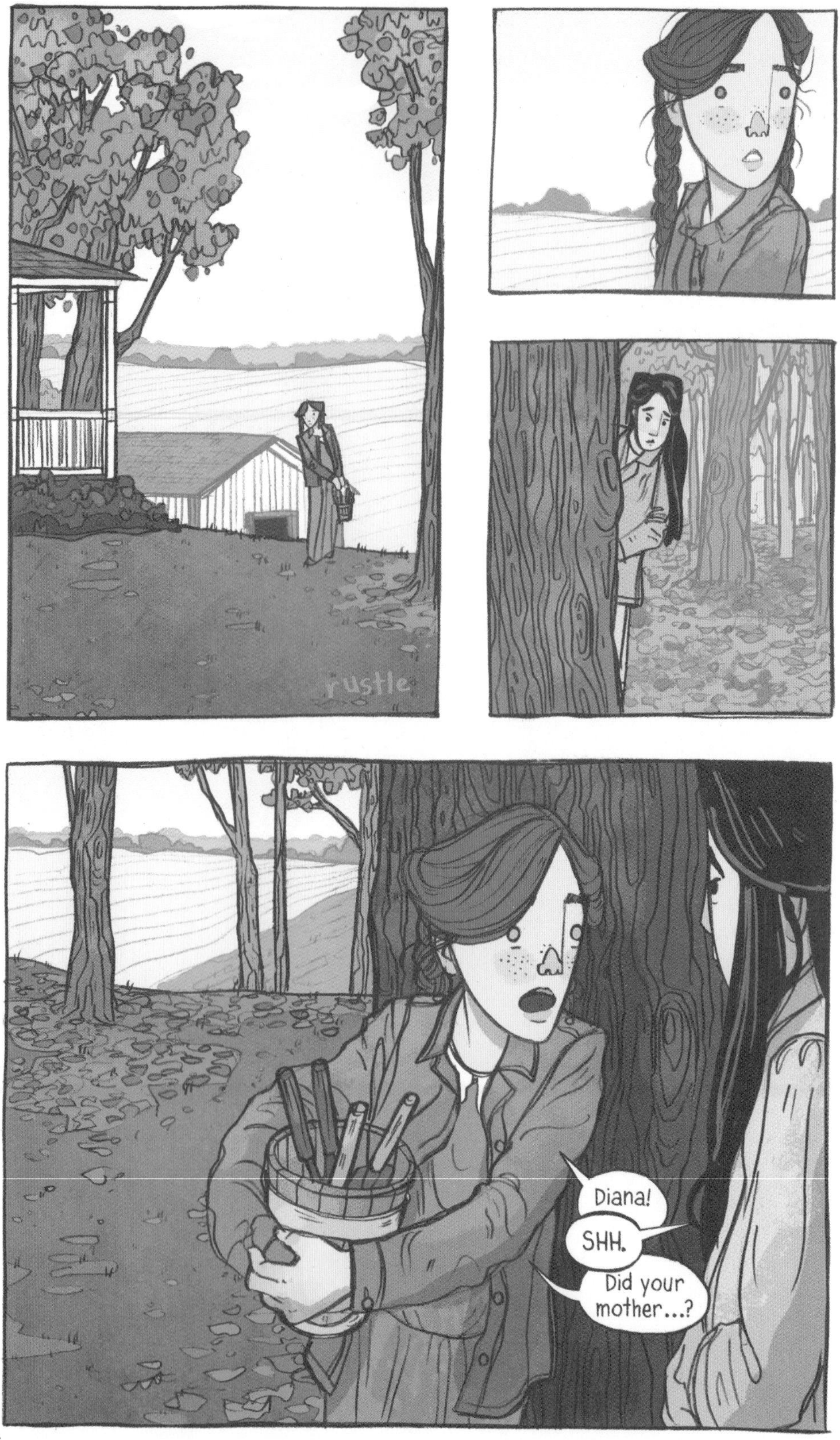
rustle
Diana!
SHH.
Did your mother...?

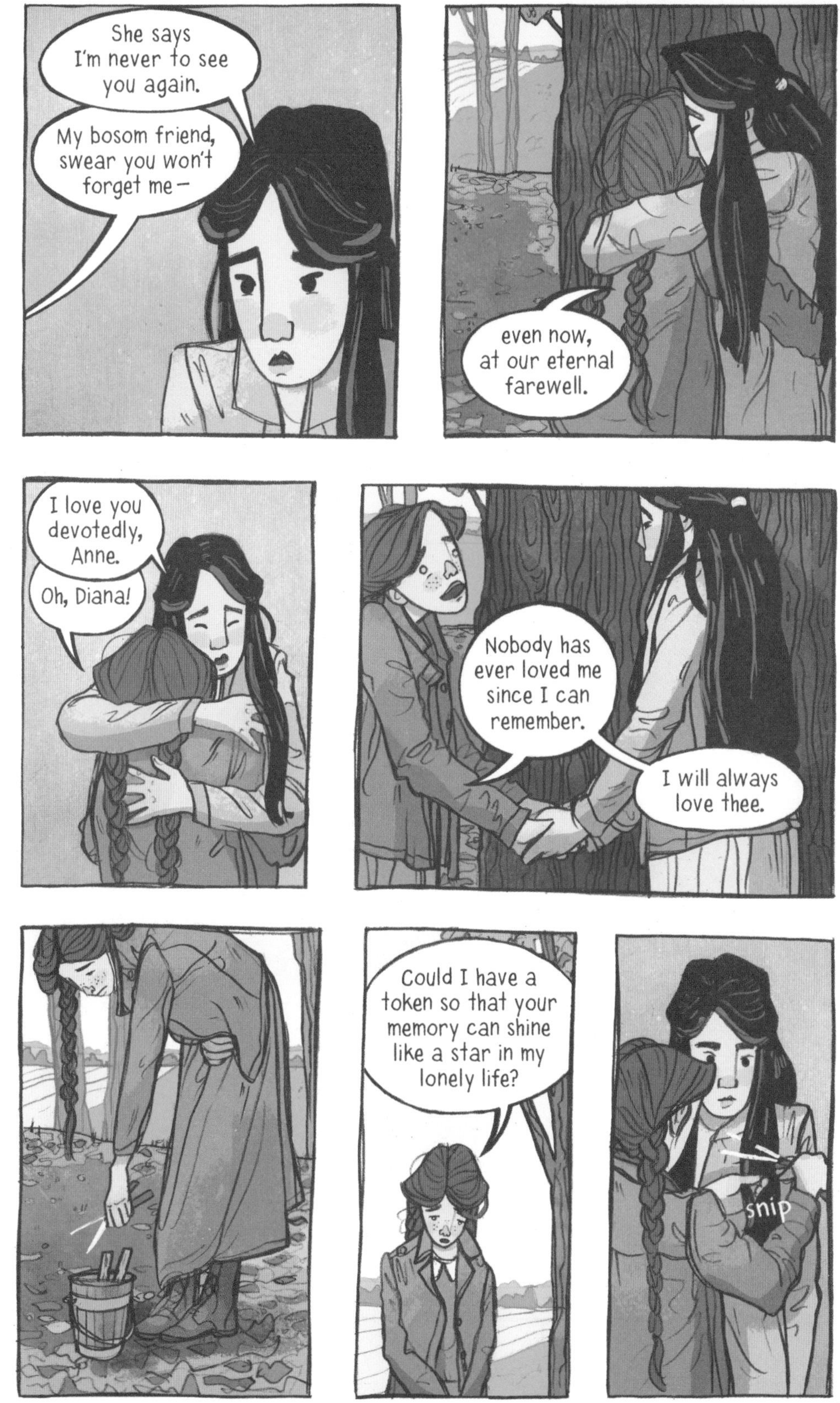

She says I'm never to see you again.
My bosom friend, swear you won't forget me—
even now, at our eternal farewell.
I love you devotedly, Anne.
Oh, Diana!
Nobody has ever loved me since I can remember.
I will always love thee.
Could I have a token so that your memory can shine like a star in my lonely life?
snip

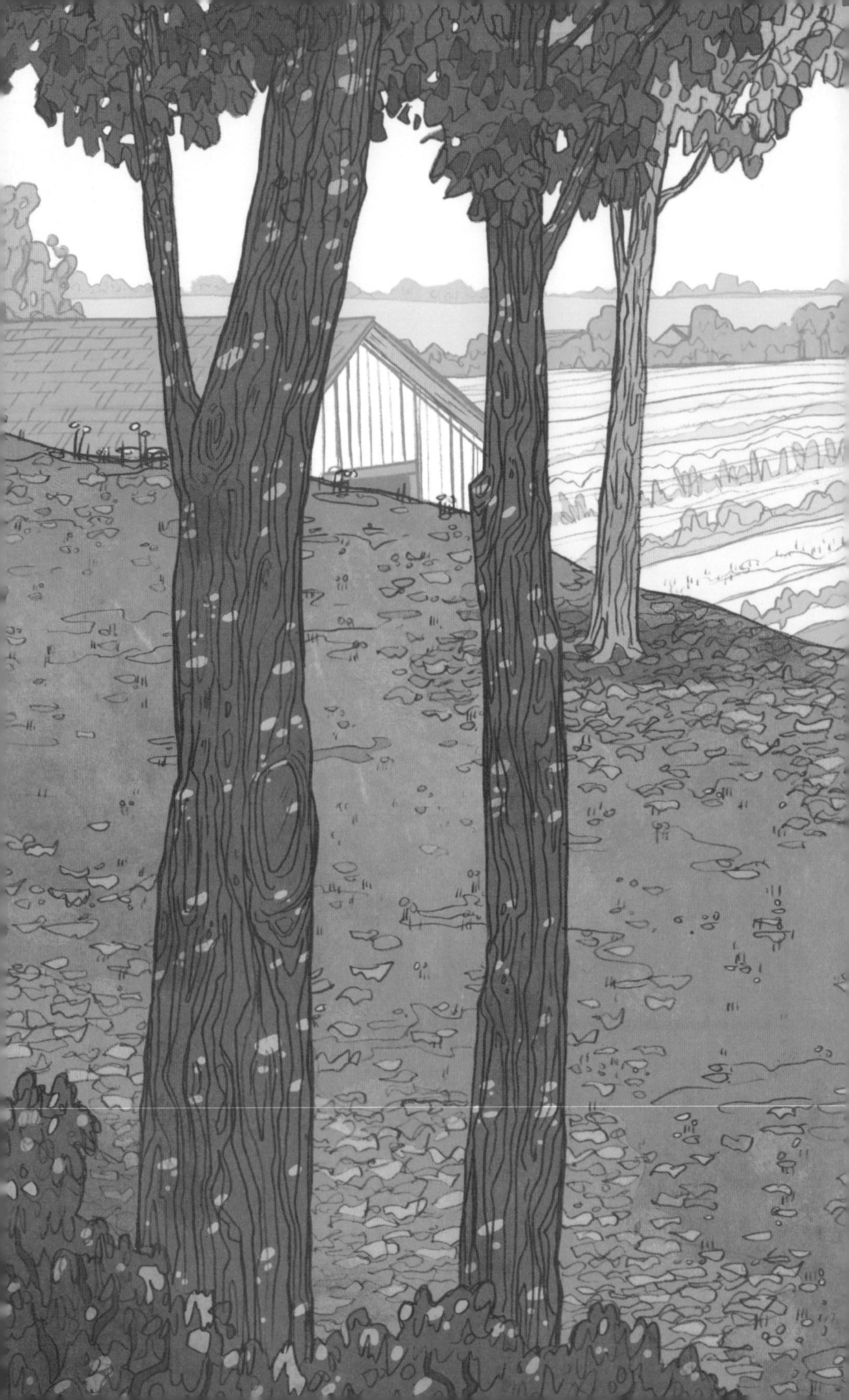

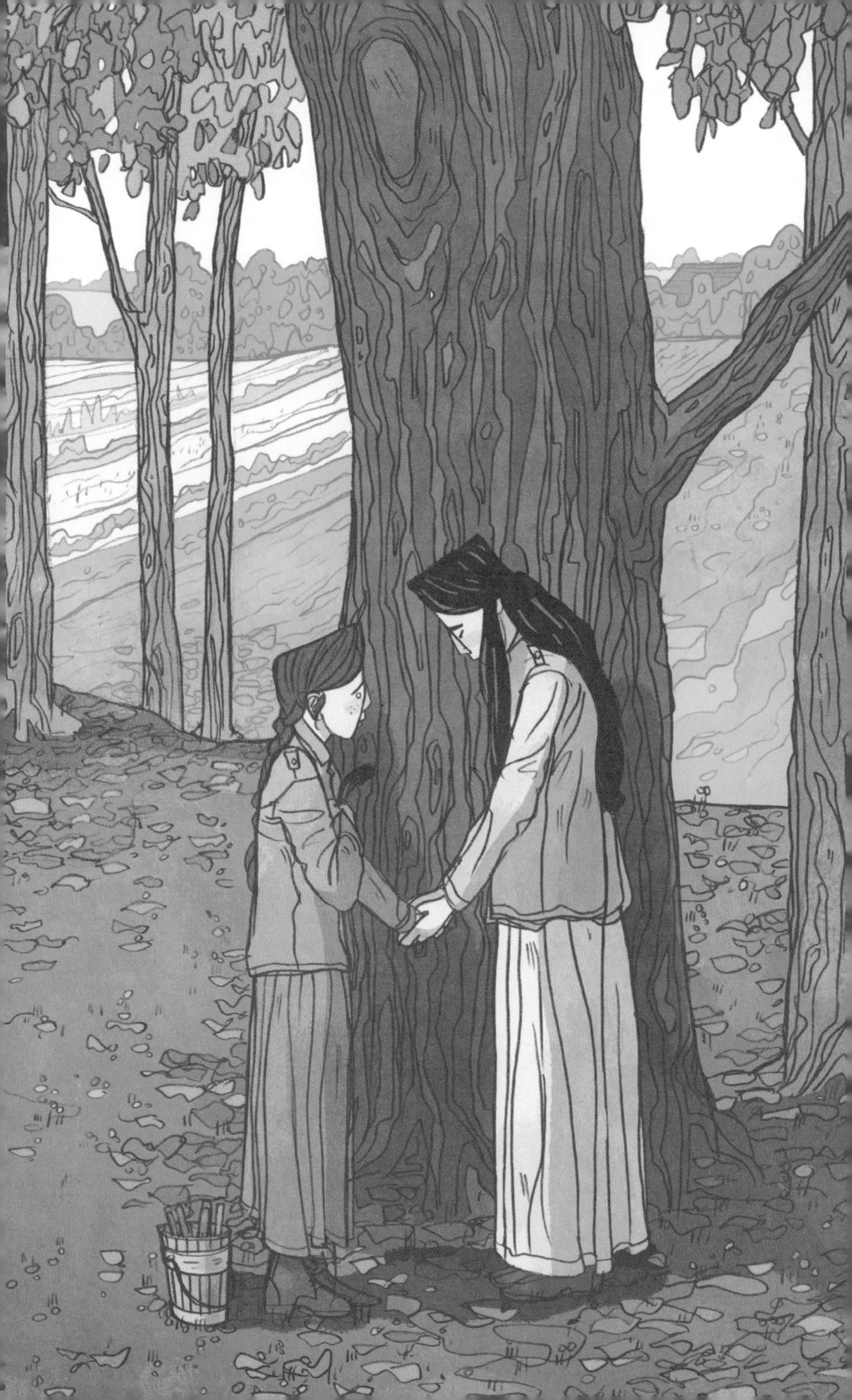

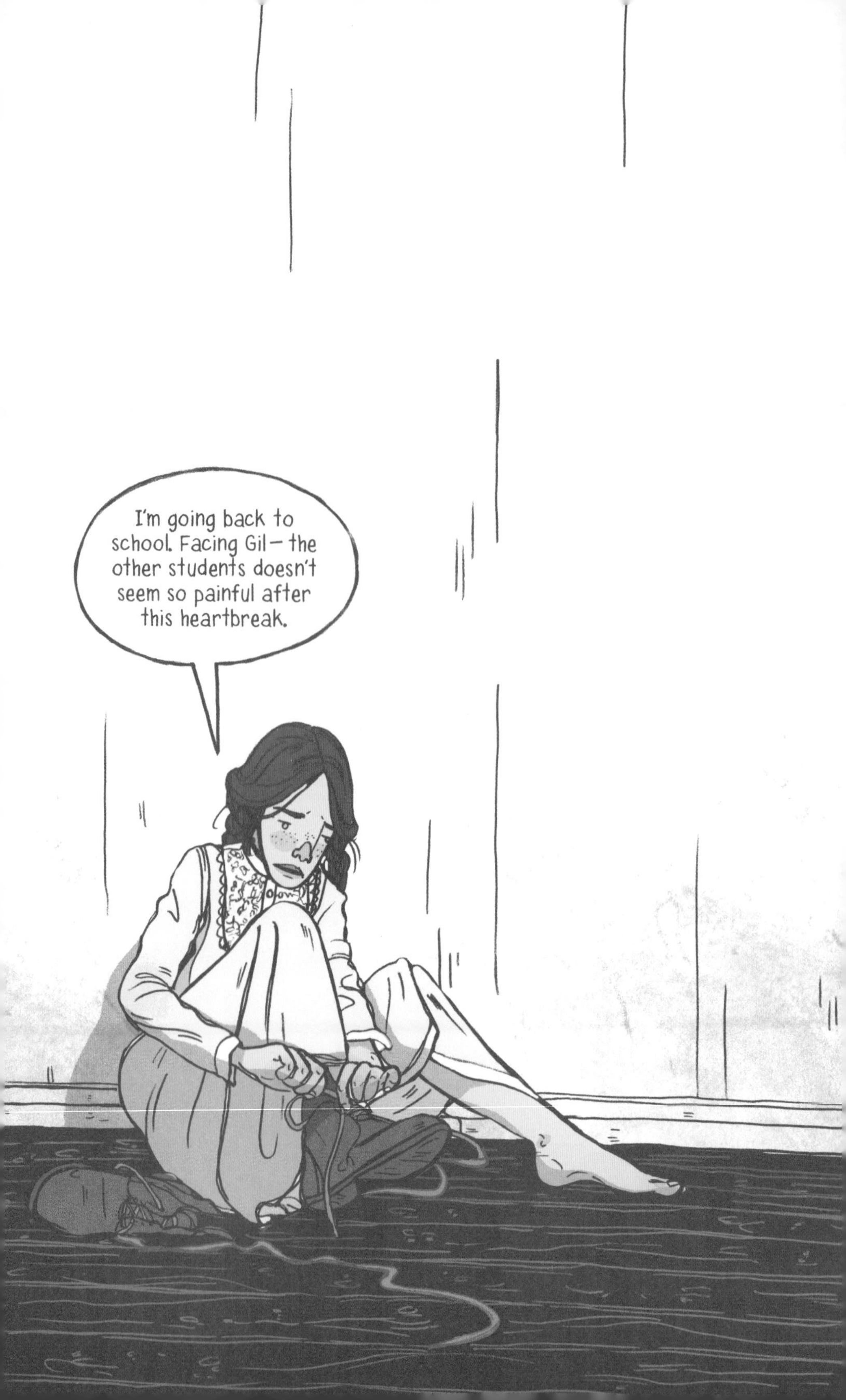
I'm going back to school. Facing Gil—the other students doesn't seem so painful after this heartbreak.

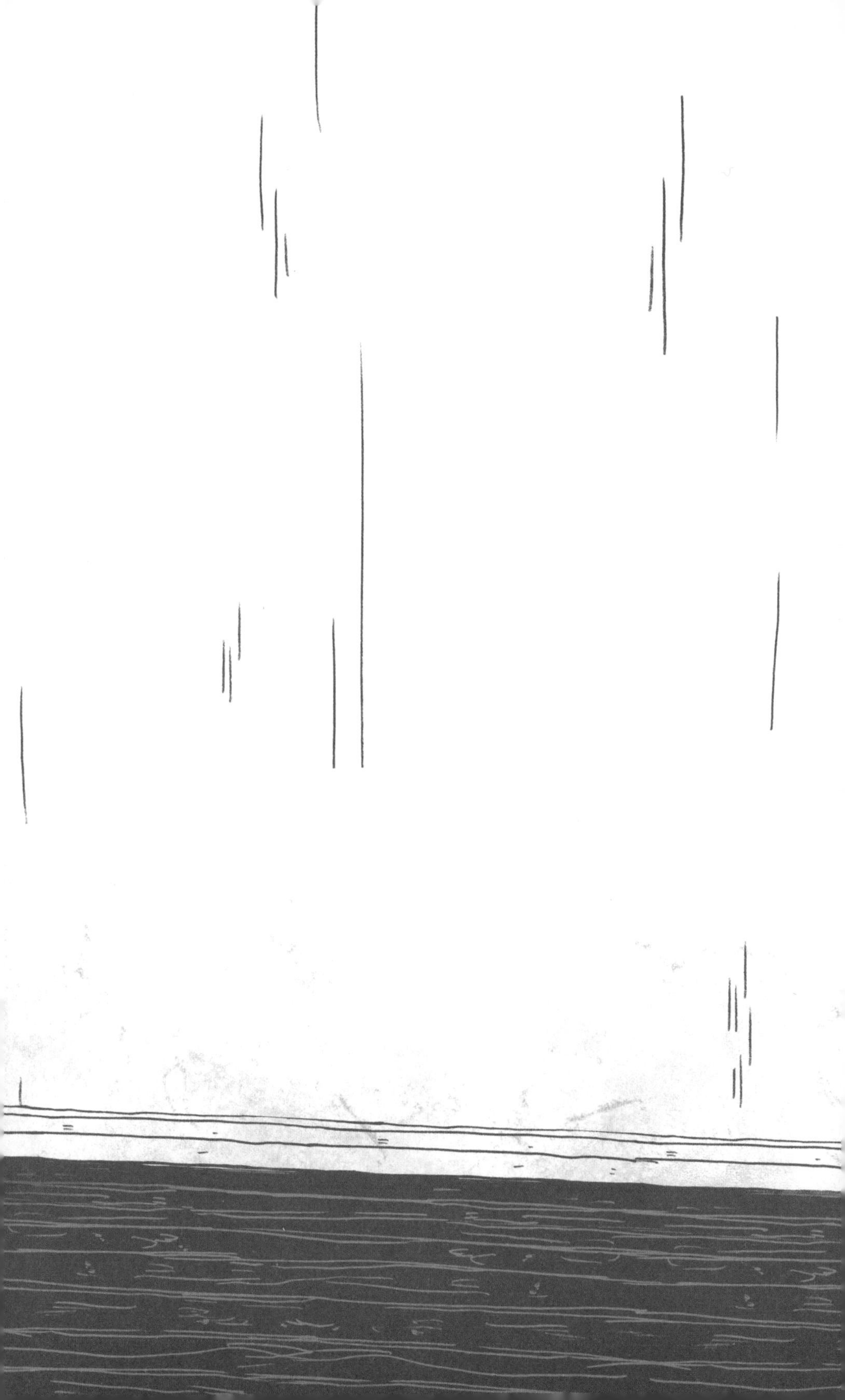

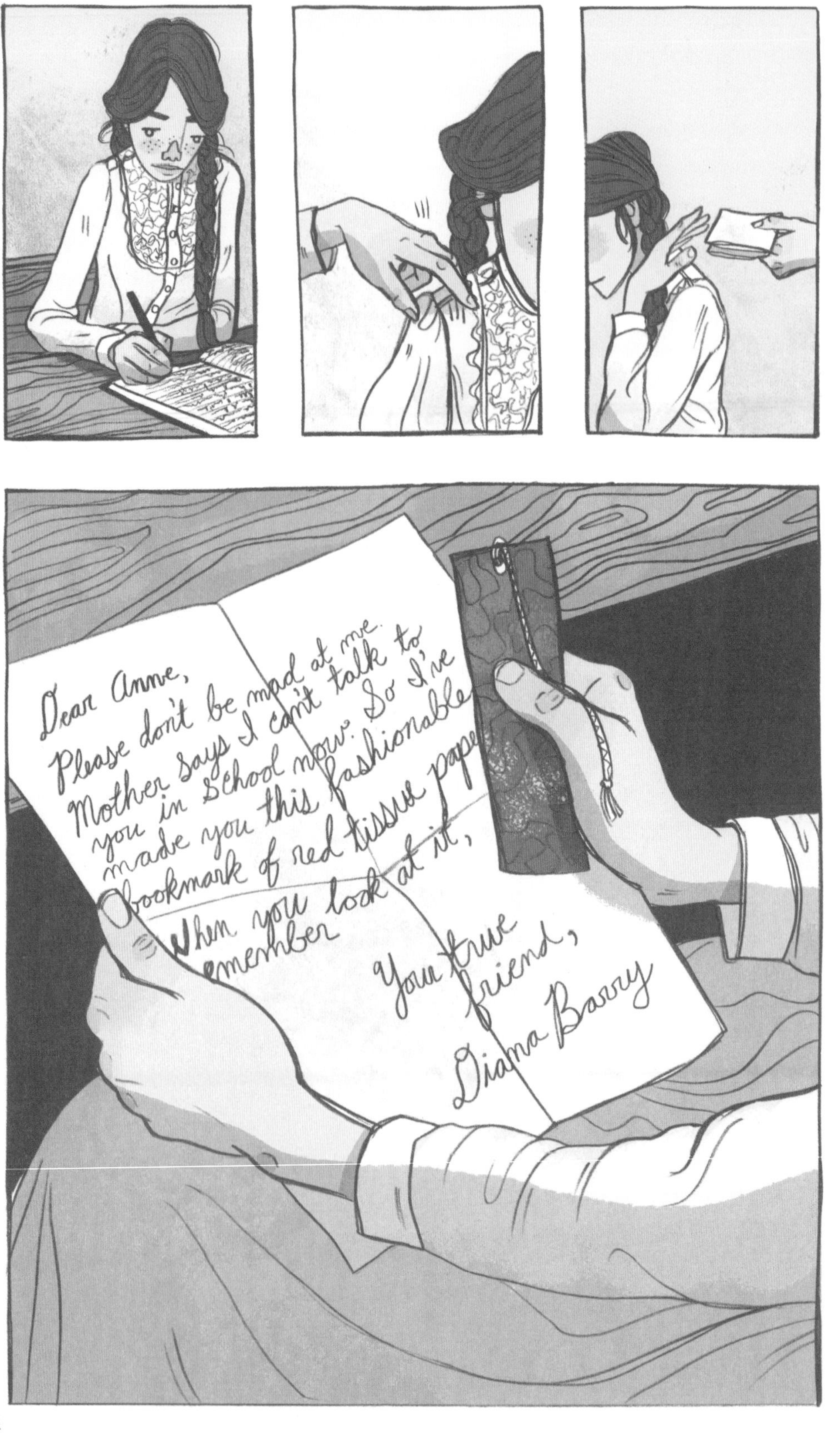
Dear Anne,
Please don't be mad at me.
Mother says I can't talk to
you in School now. So I've
made you this fashionable
bookmark of red tissue pape
When you look at it,
emember
Your true friend,
Diana Barry

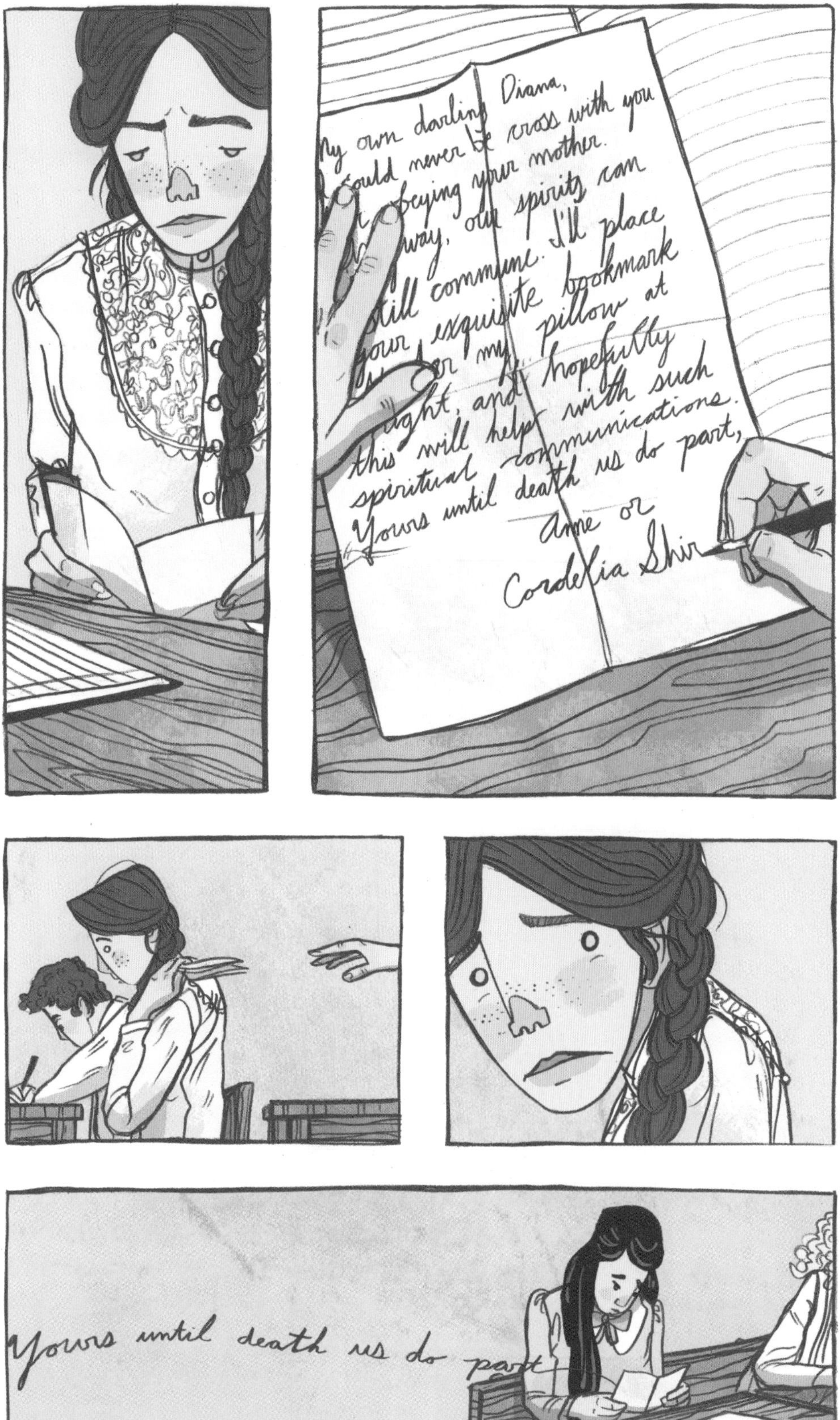

My own darling Diana,
could never be cross with you
obeying your mother.
way, our spirits can
still commune. I'll place
your exquisite bookmark
my pillow at
night, and hopefully
this will help with such
spiritual communications.
Yours until death us do part,
Anne or
Cordelia Shir
Yours until death us do part

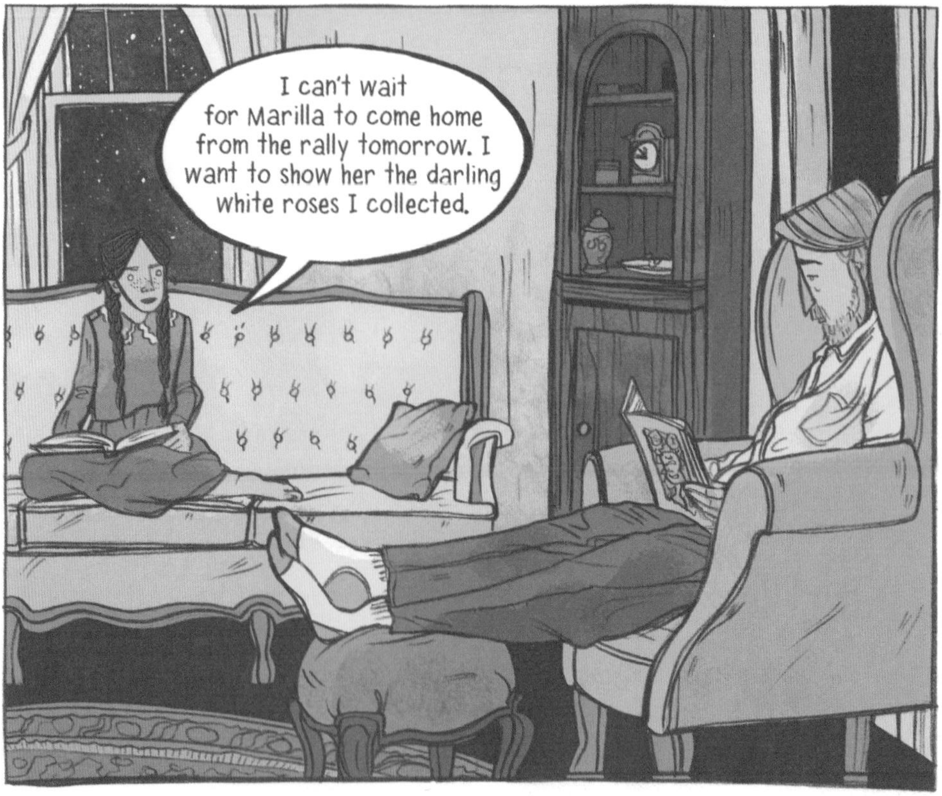
I can't wait for Marilla to come home from the rally tomorrow. I want to show her the darling white roses I collected.

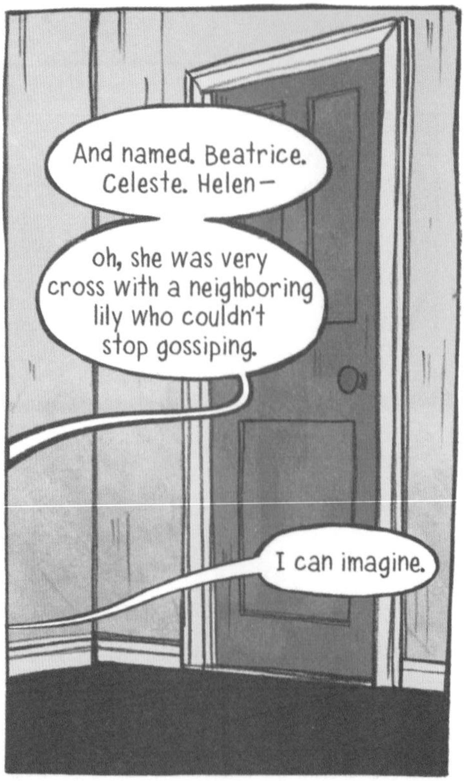
And named. Beatrice. Celeste. Helen—
oh, she was very cross with a neighboring lily who couldn't stop gossiping.
I can imagine.

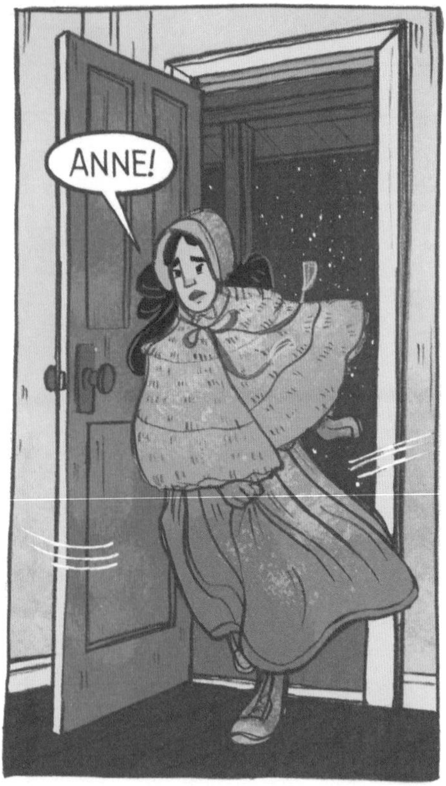
ANNE!

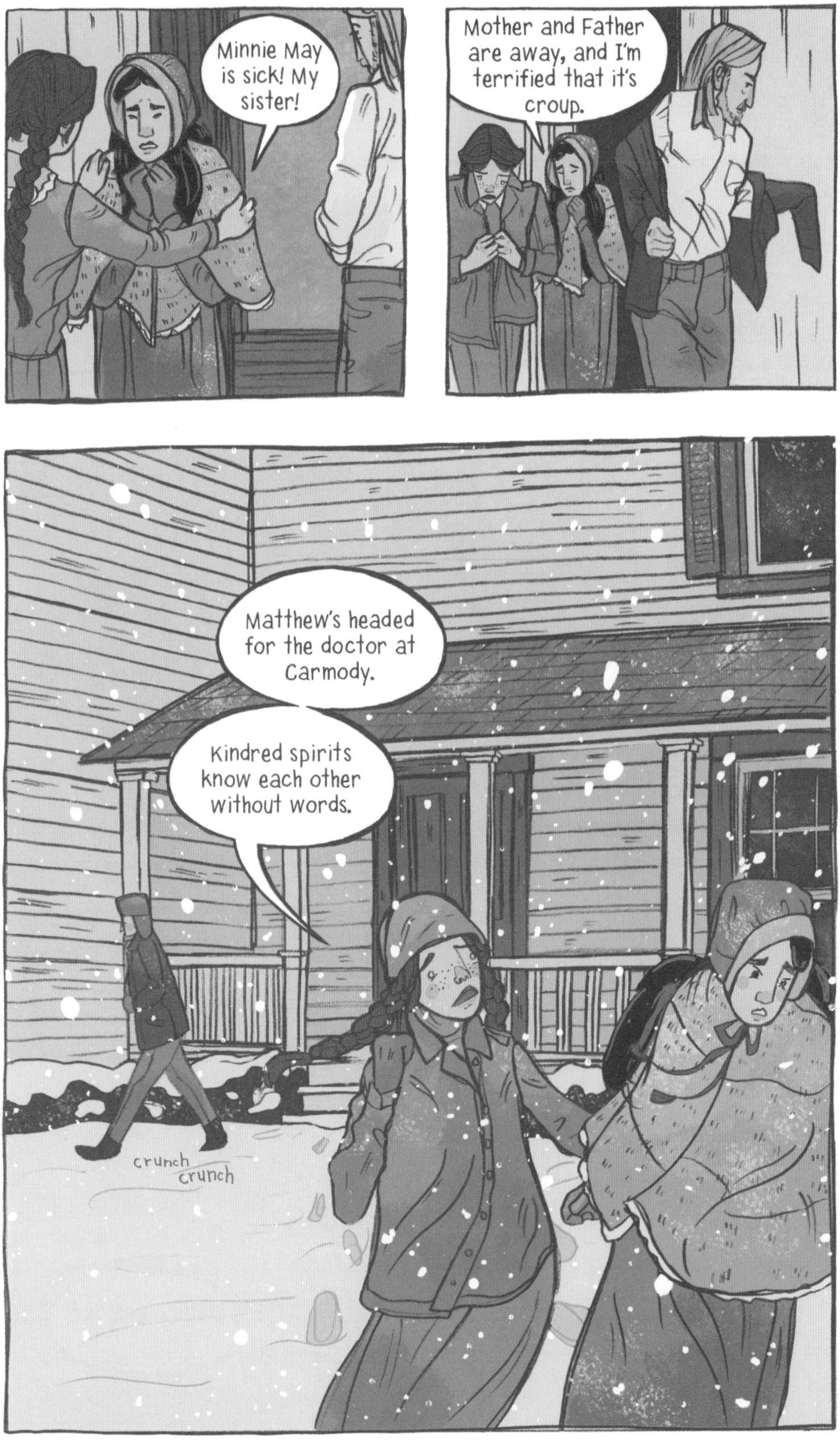
Minnie May is sick! My sister!
Mother and Father are away, and I'm terrified that it's croup.
Matthew's headed for the doctor at Carmody.
Kindred spirits know each other without words.
crunch crunch

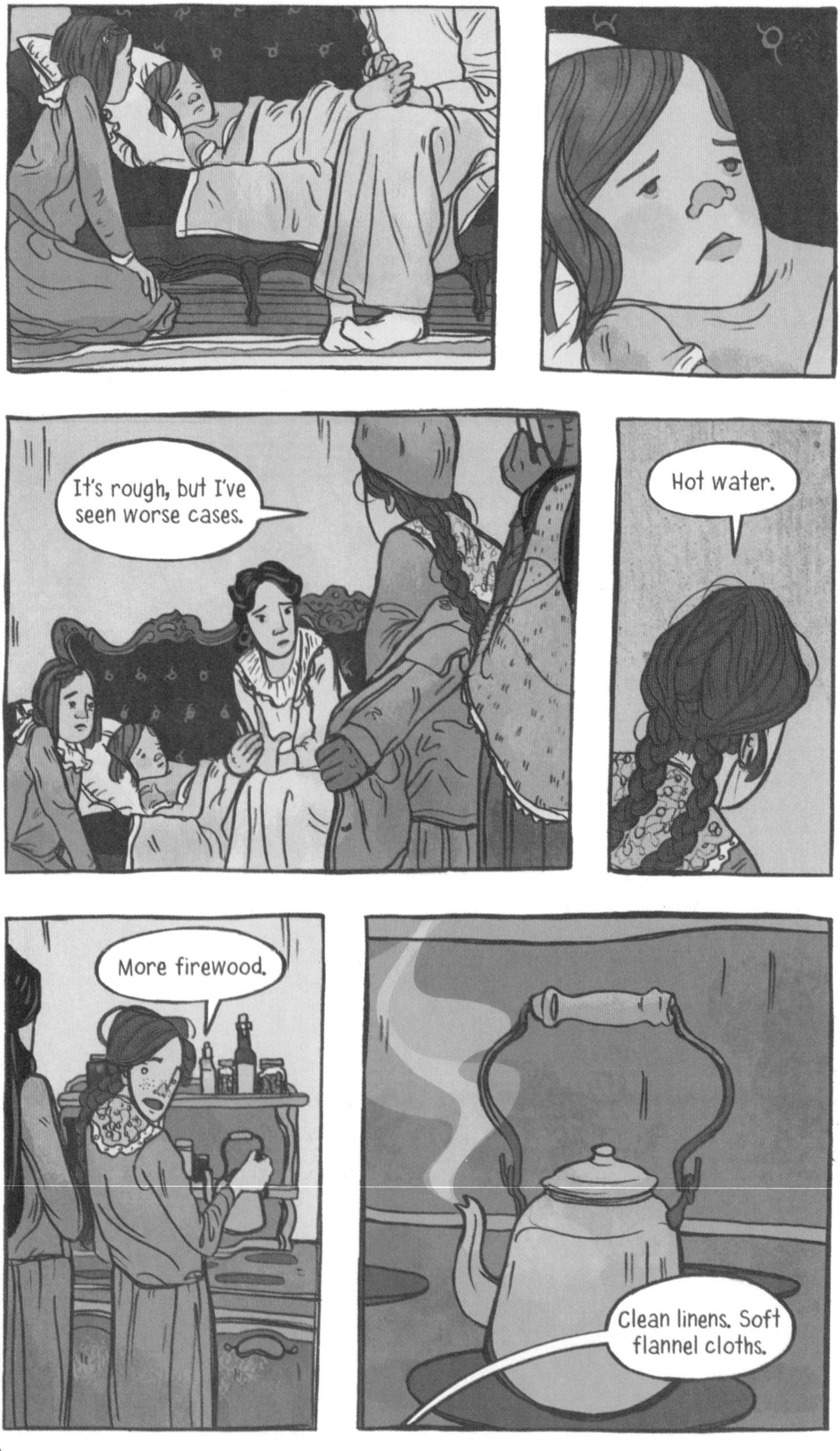
It's rough, but I've seen worse cases.
Hot water.
More firewood.
Clean linens. Soft flannel cloths.

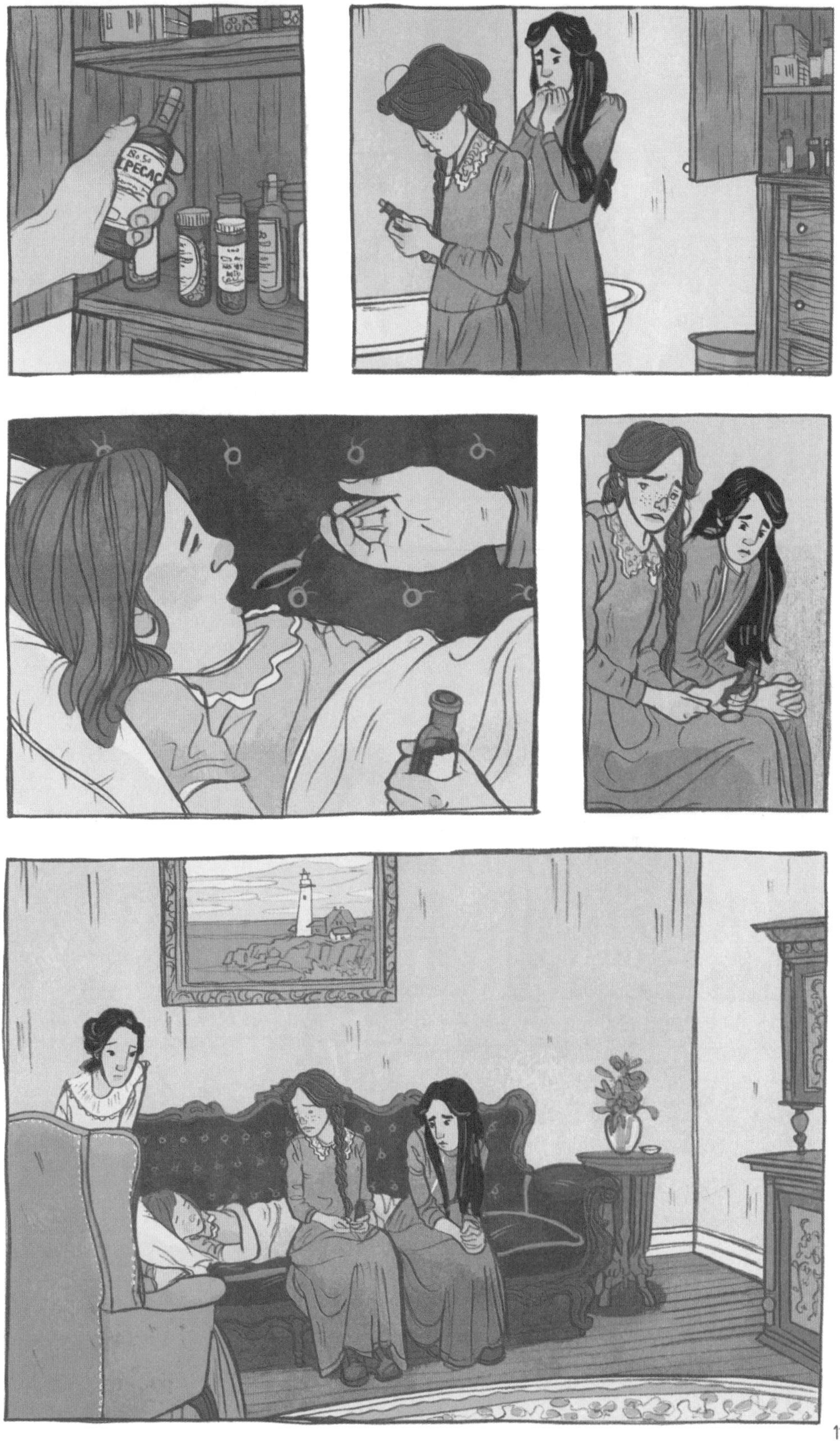
No. 50
IPECAC

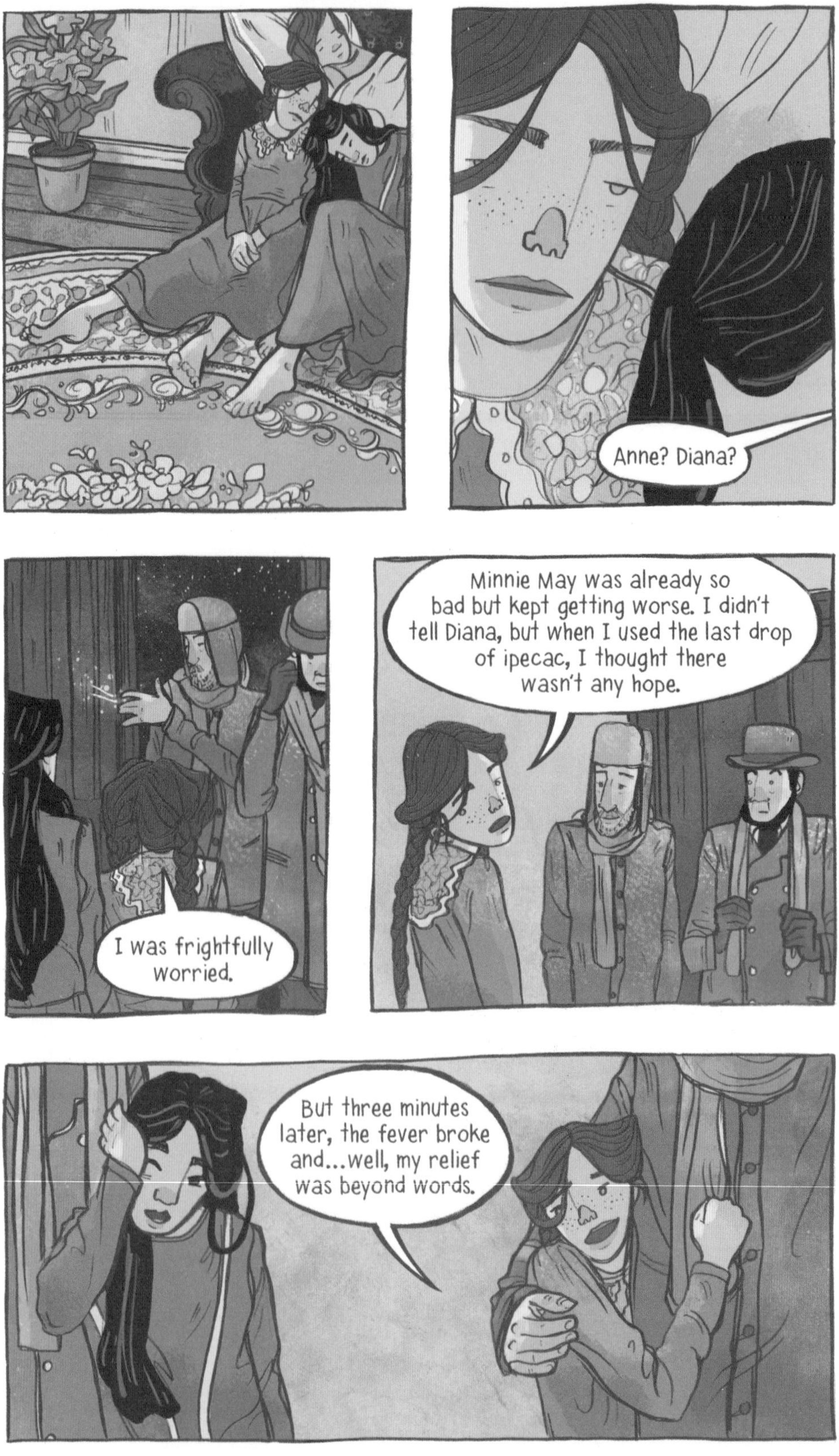
Anne? Diana?
I was frightfully worried.
Minnie May was already so bad but kept getting worse. I didn't tell Diana, but when I used the last drop of ipecac, I thought there wasn't any hope.
But three minutes later, the fever broke and...well, my relief was beyond words.

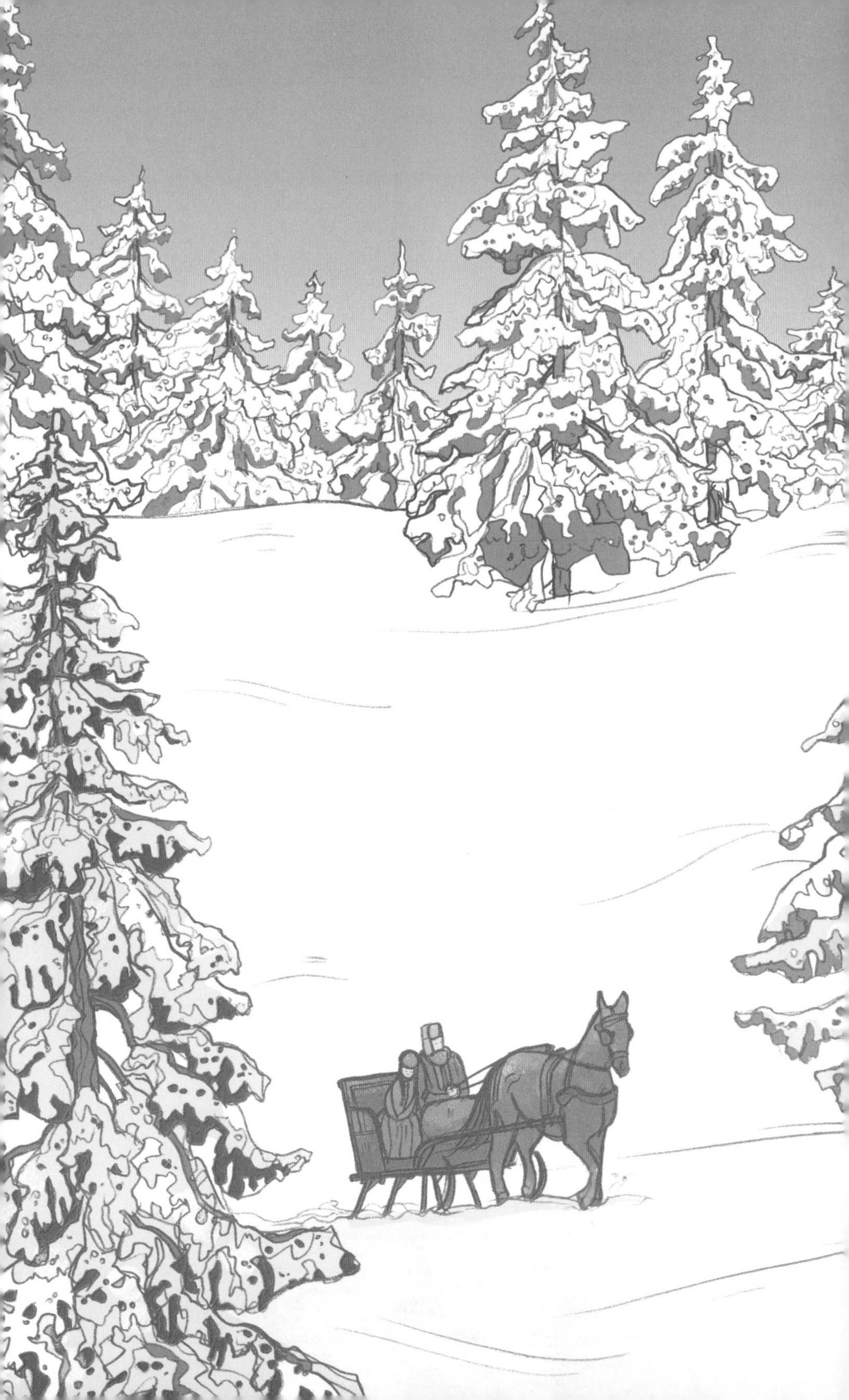

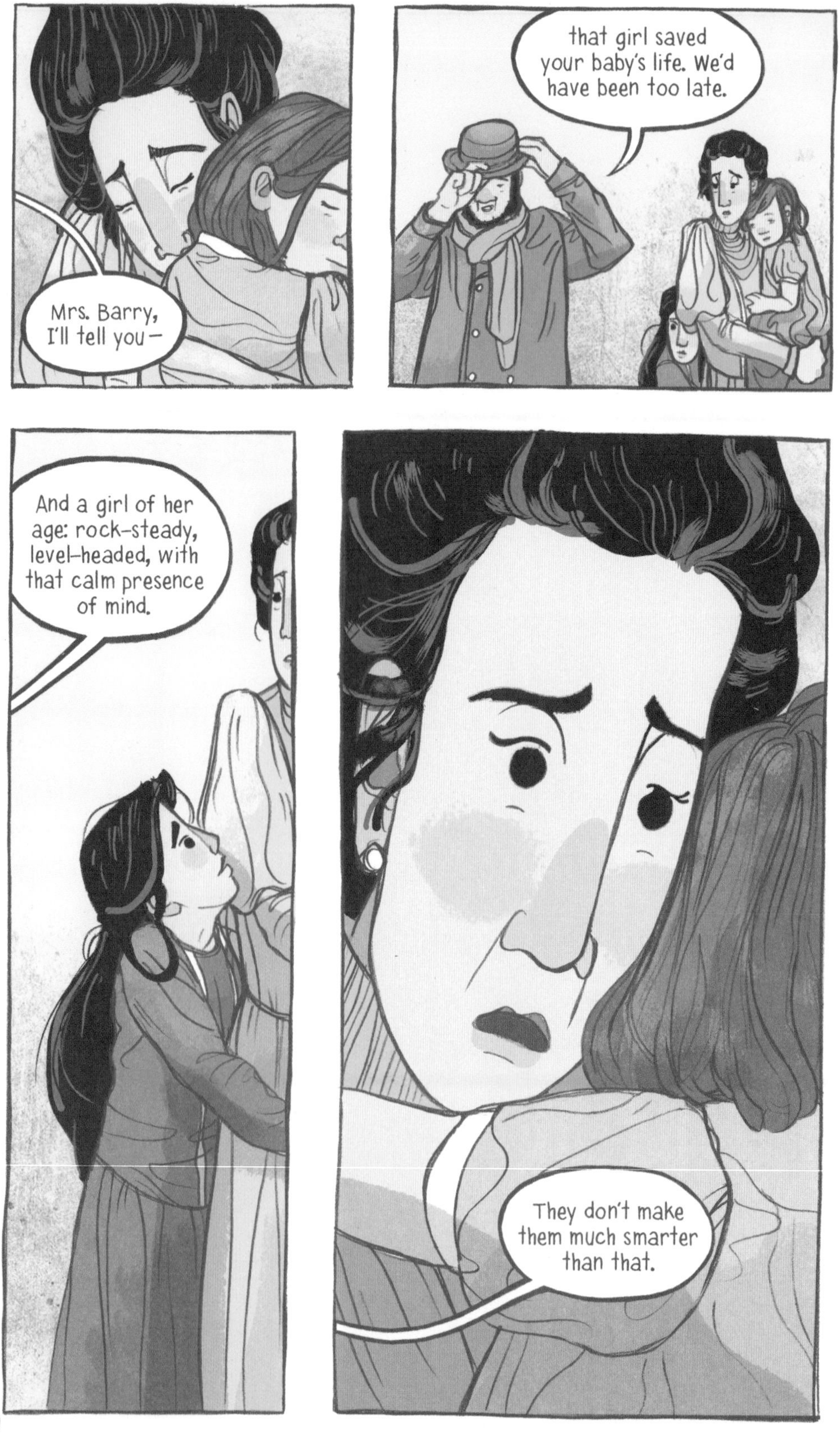
Mrs. Barry,
I'll tell you—
that girl saved your baby's life. We'd have been too late.
And a girl of her age: rock-steady, level-headed, with that calm presence of mind.
They don't make them much smarter than that.

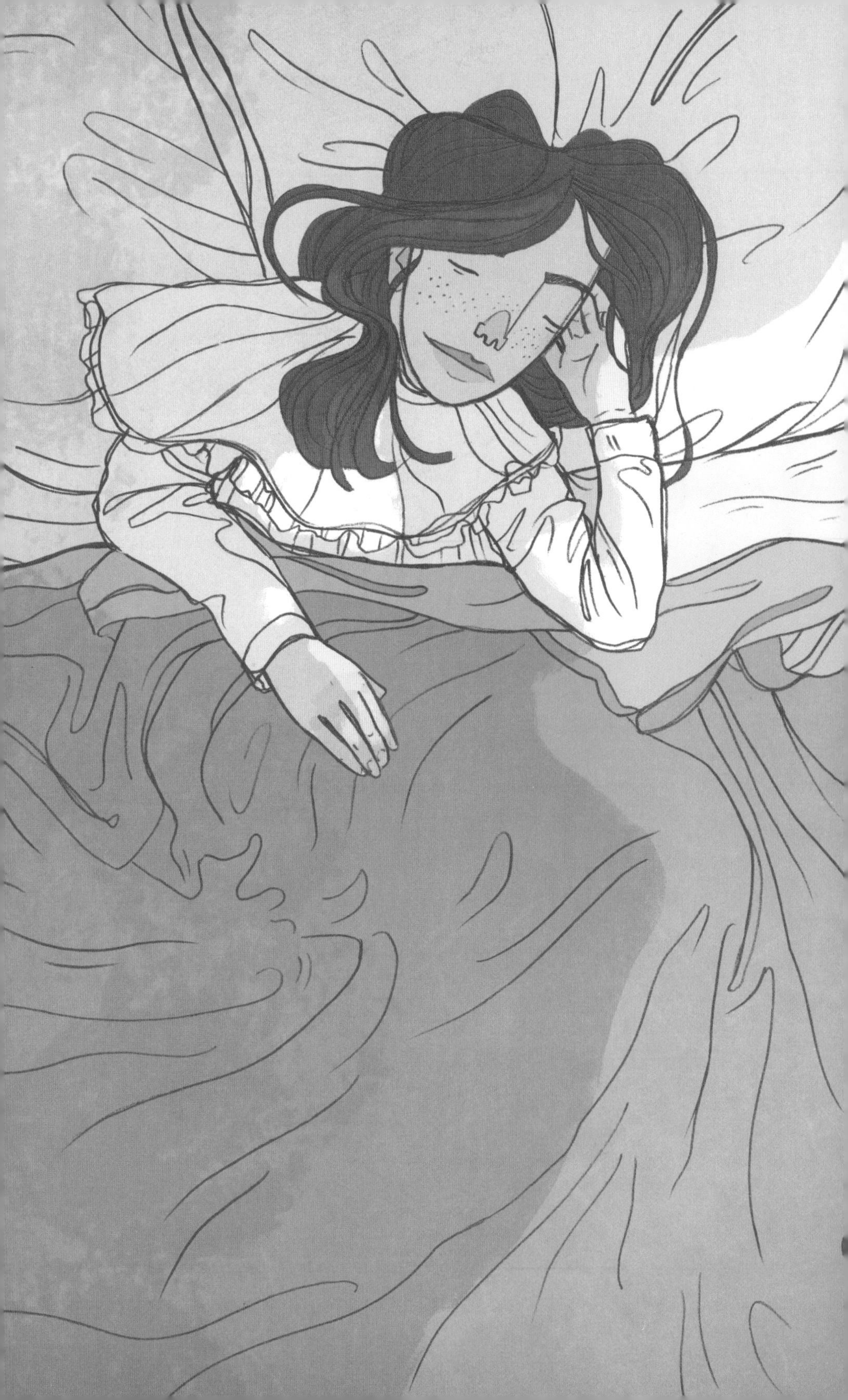

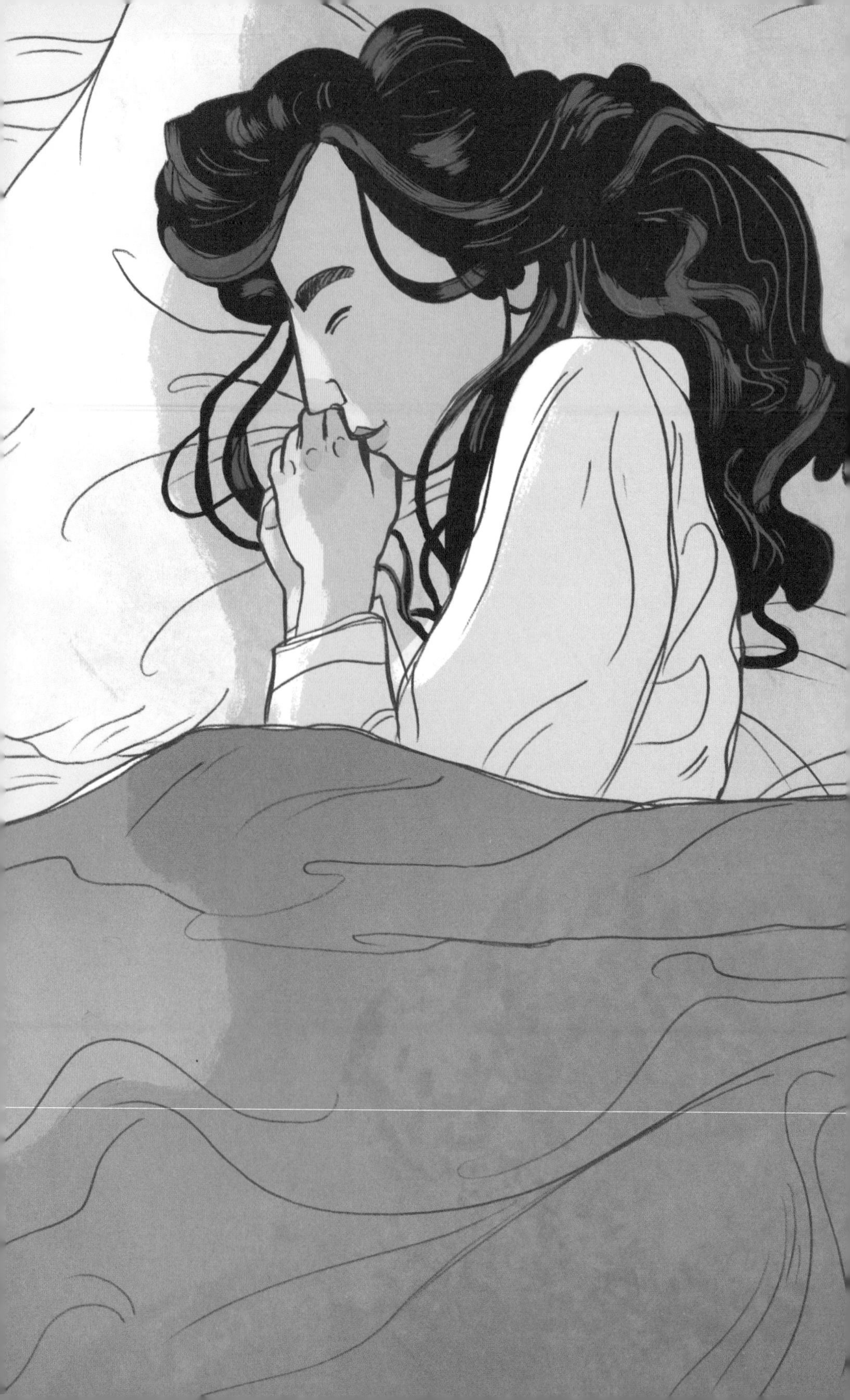

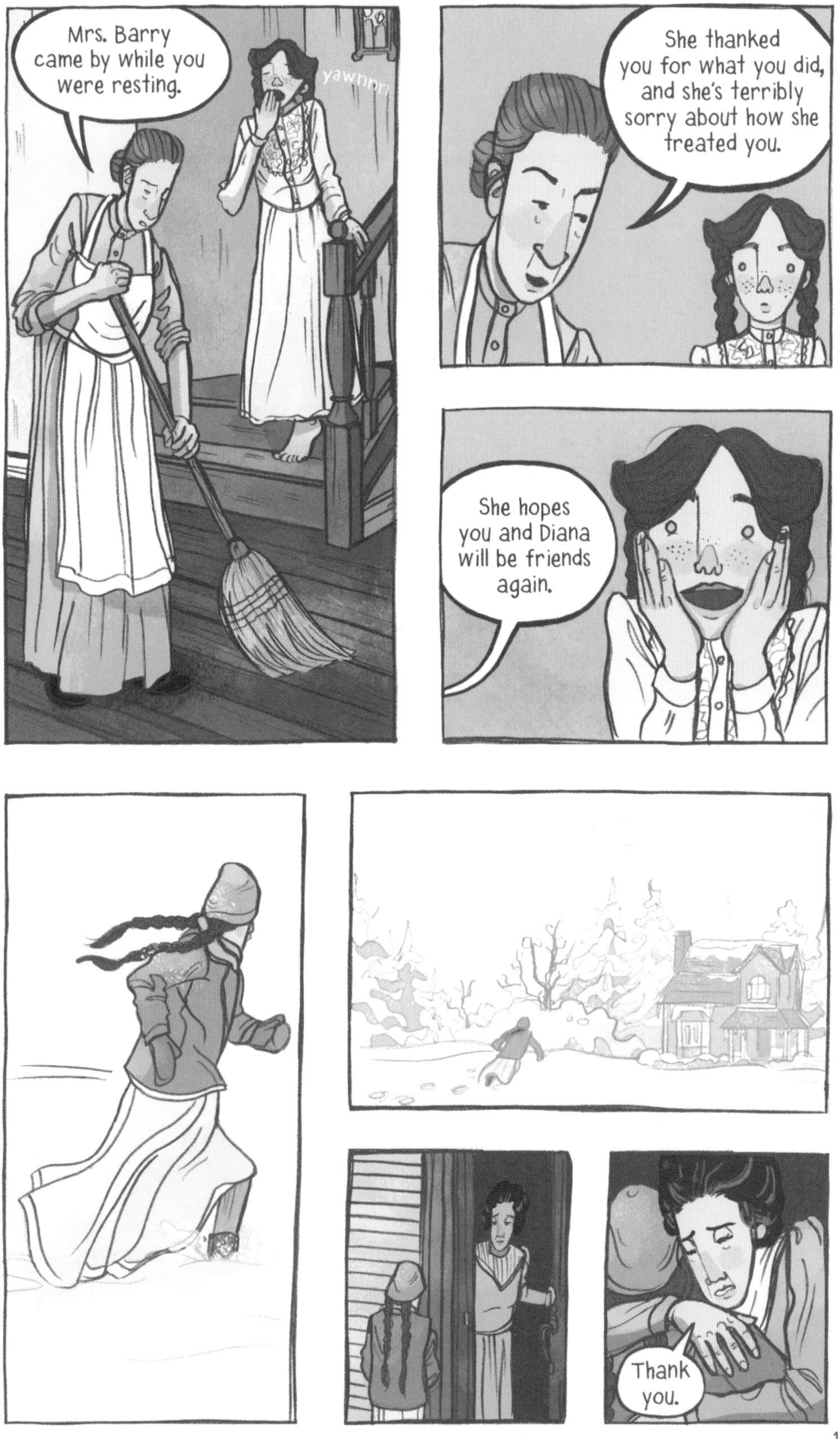
Mrs. Barry came by while you were resting.
yawhnn
She thanked you for what you did, and she's terribly sorry about how she treated you.
She hopes you and Diana will be friends again.
Thank you.

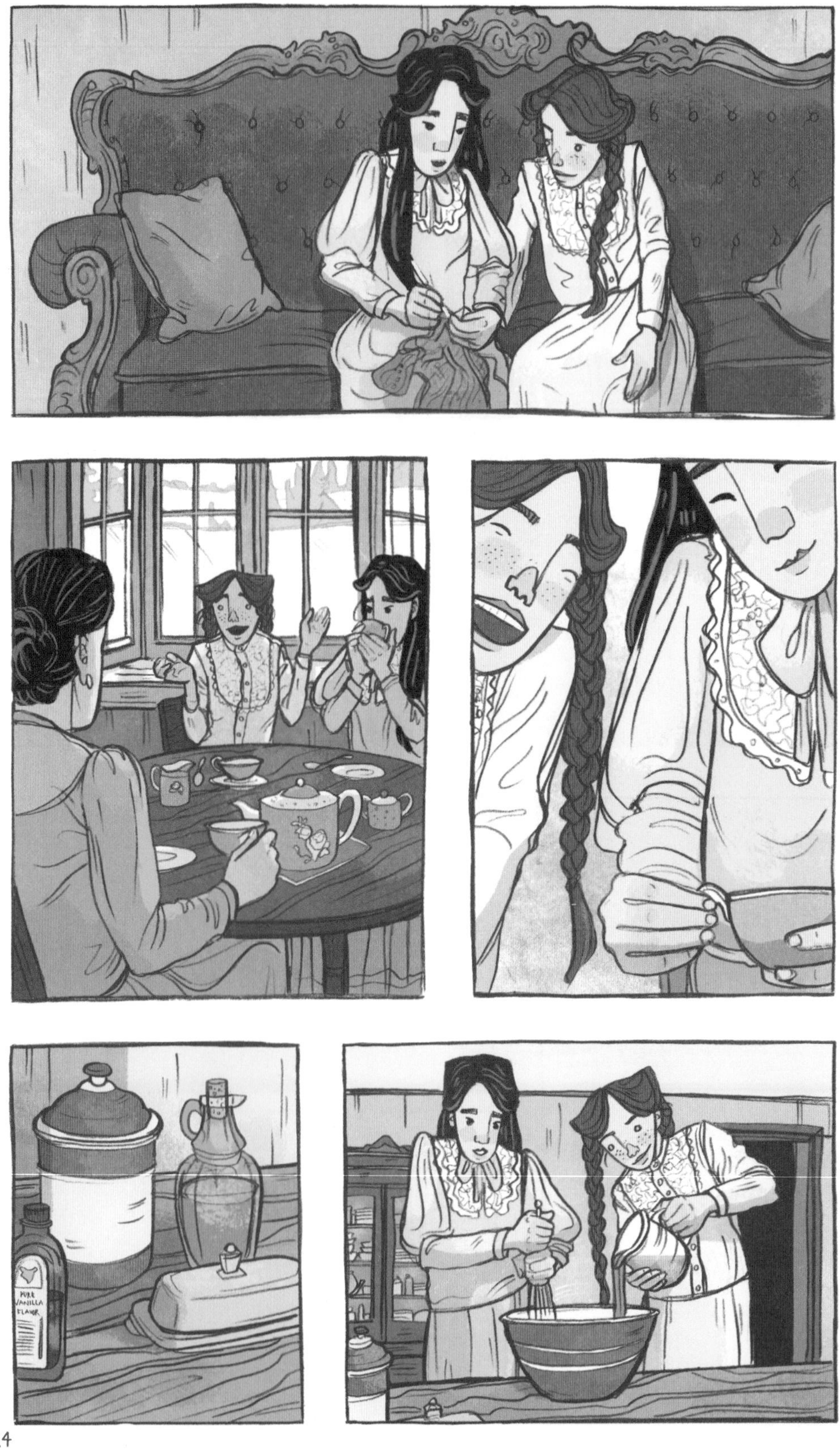
PURE VANILLA FLAVOR

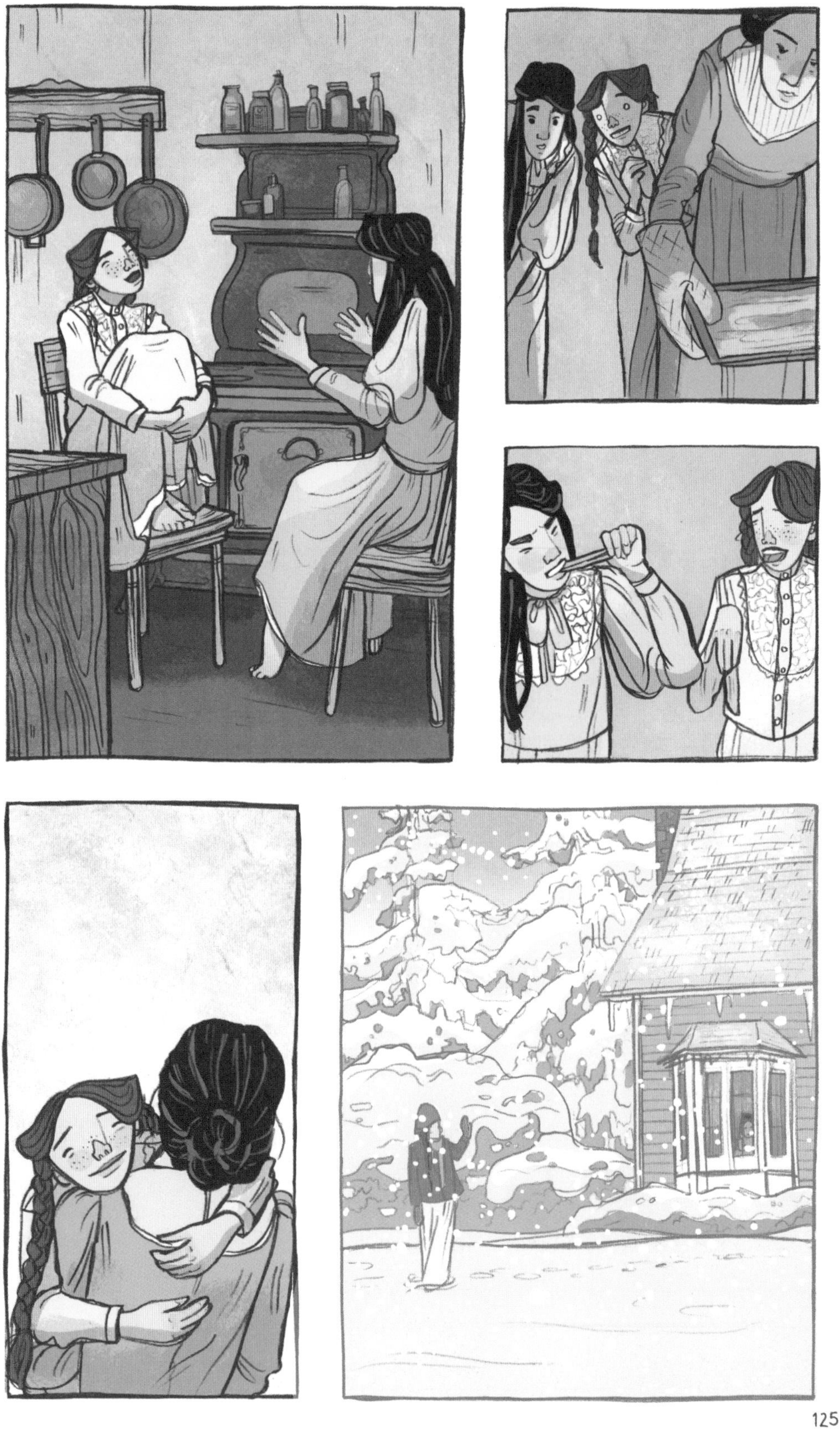

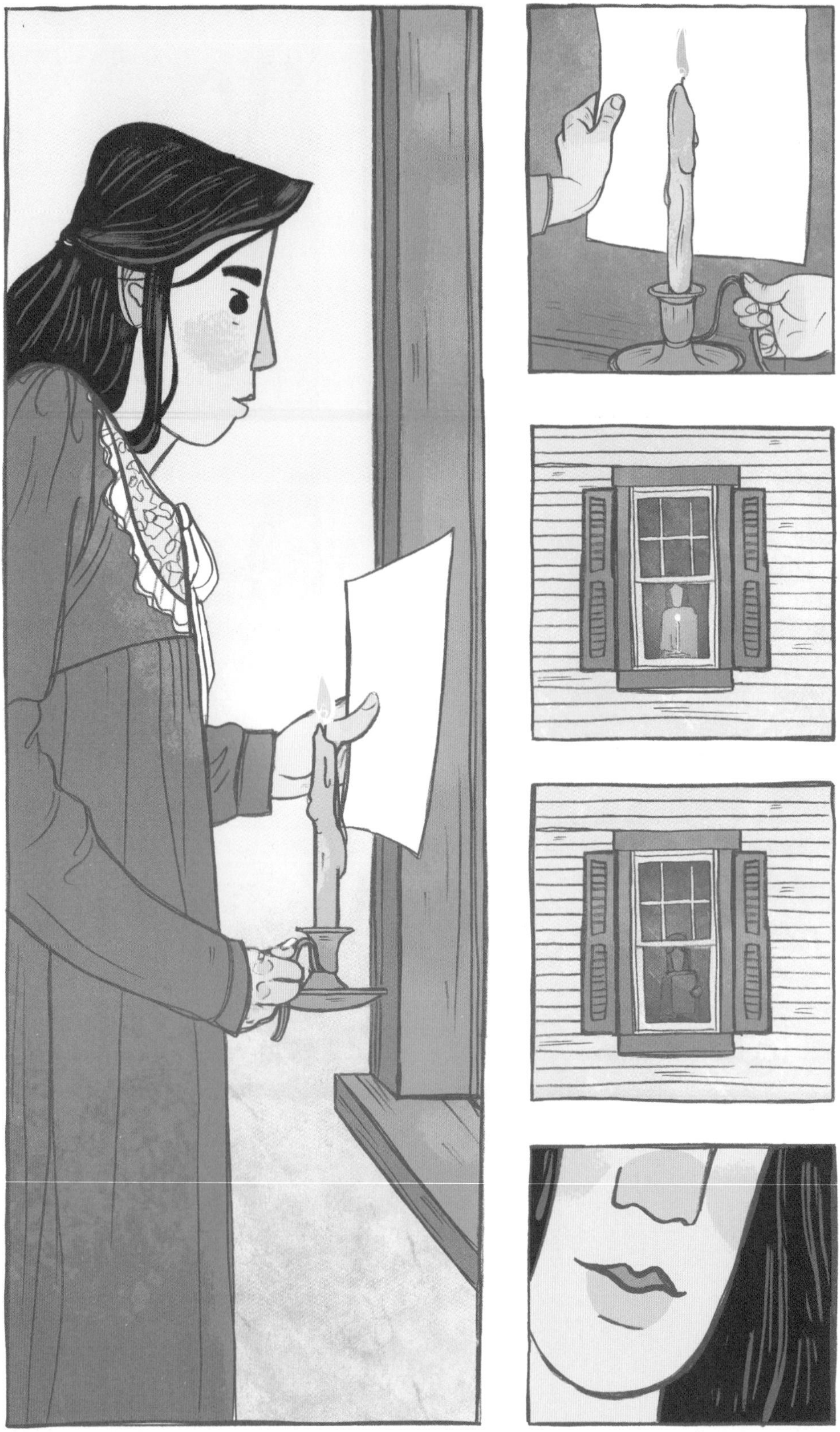

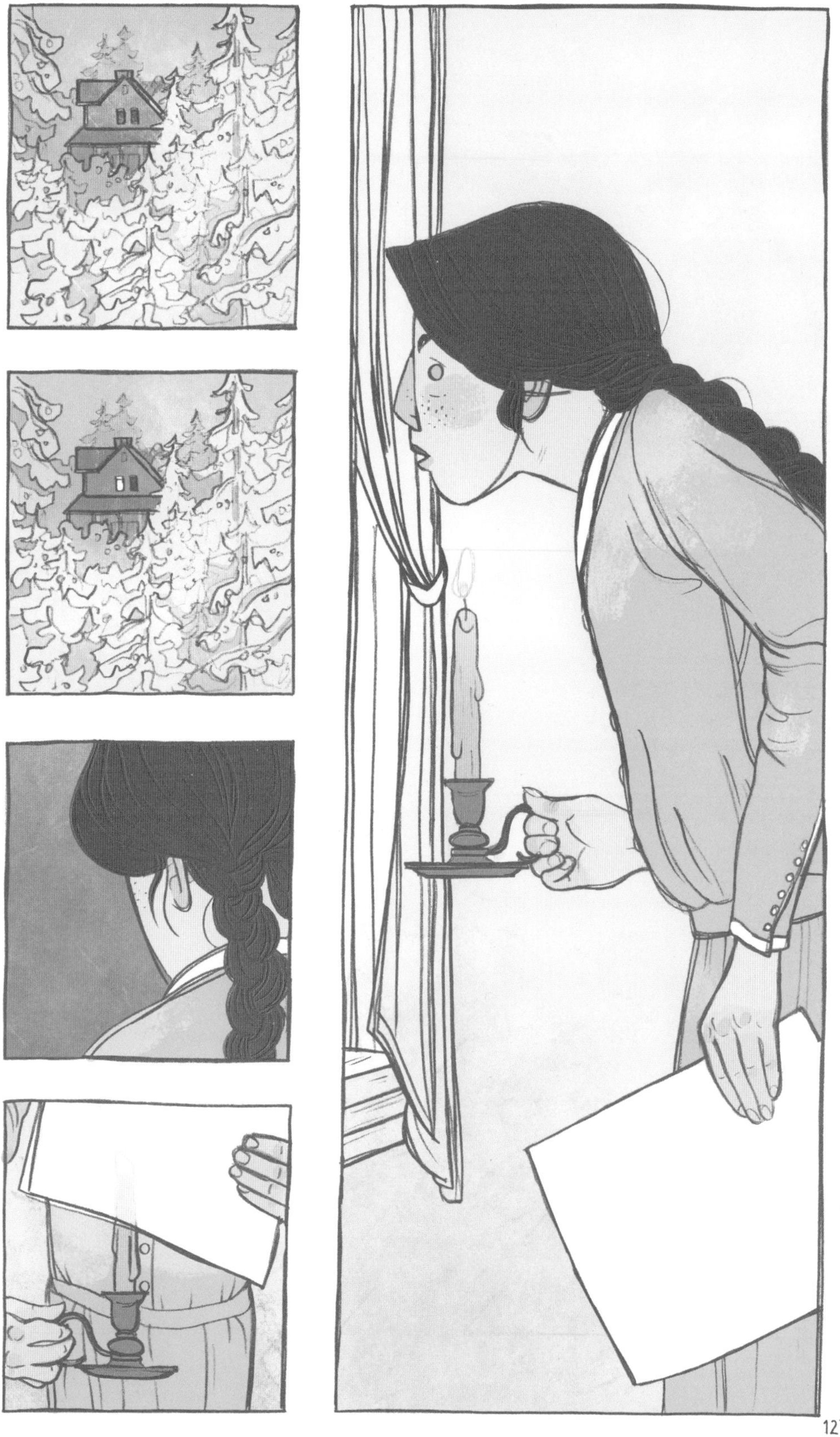

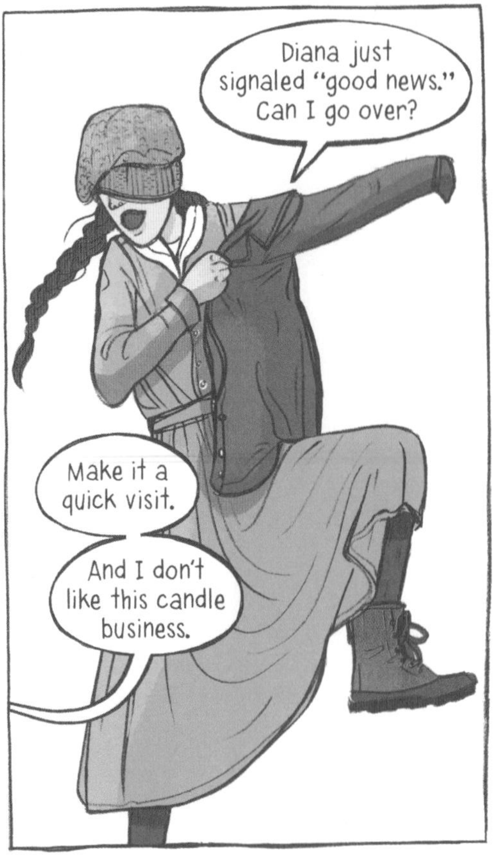
Diana just signaled "good news." Can I go over?
Make it a quick visit.
And I don't like this candle business.

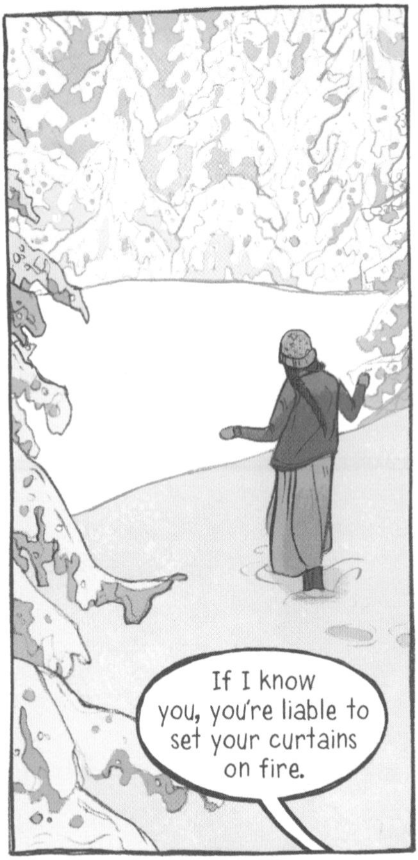
If I know you, you're liable to set your curtains on fire.

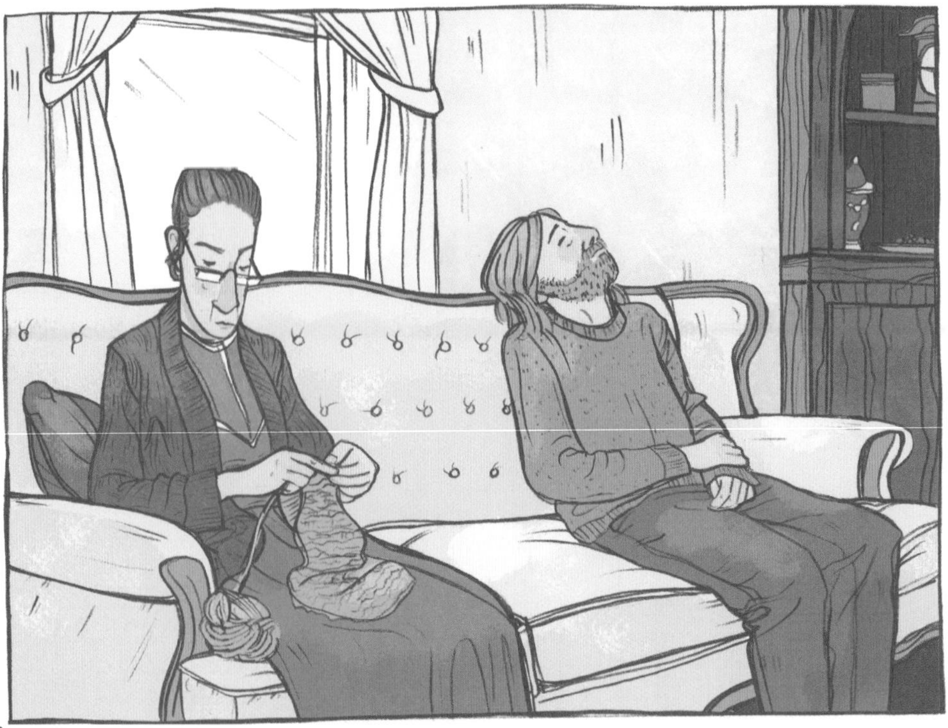

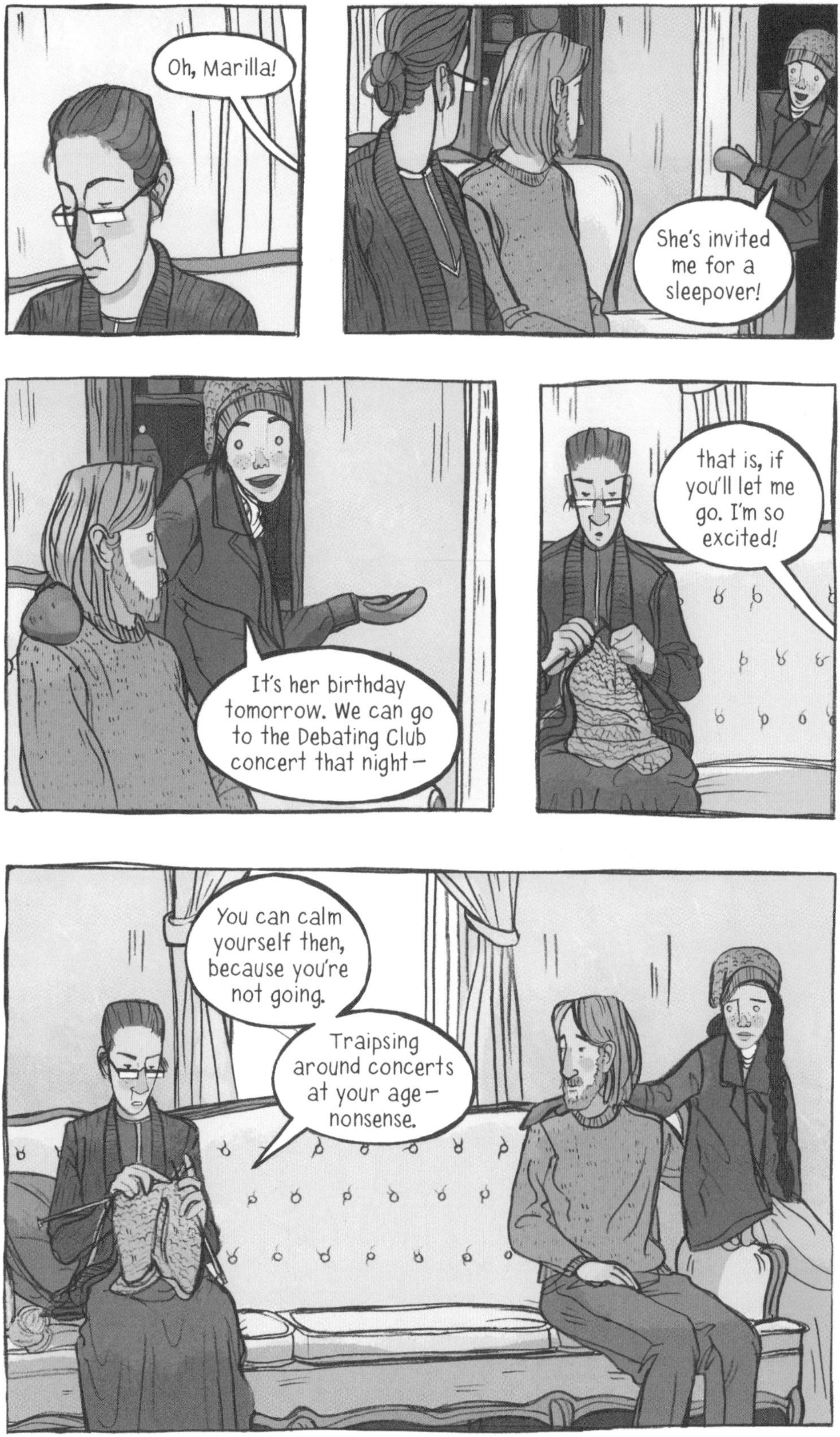

Oh, Marilla!
She's invited me for a sleepover!
It's her birthday tomorrow. We can go to the Debating Club concert that night—
that is, if you'll let me go. I'm so excited!
You can calm yourself then, because you're not going.
Traipsing around concerts at your age—nonsense.

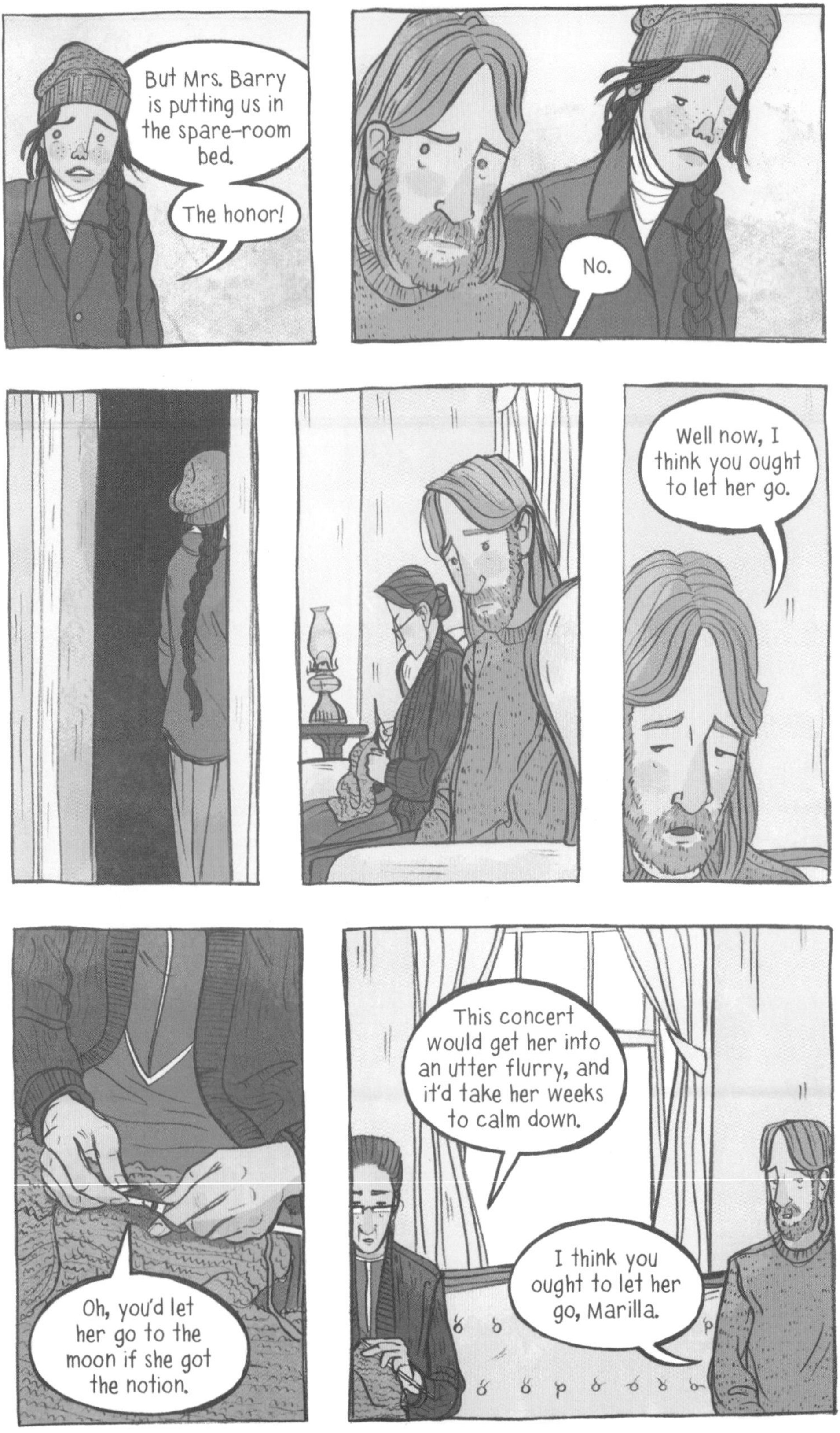
But Mrs. Barry is putting us in the spare-room bed.
The honor!
No.
Well now, I think you ought to let her go.
Oh, you'd let her go to the moon if she got the notion.
This concert would get her into an utter flurry, and it'd take her weeks to calm down.
I think you ought to let her go, Marilla.

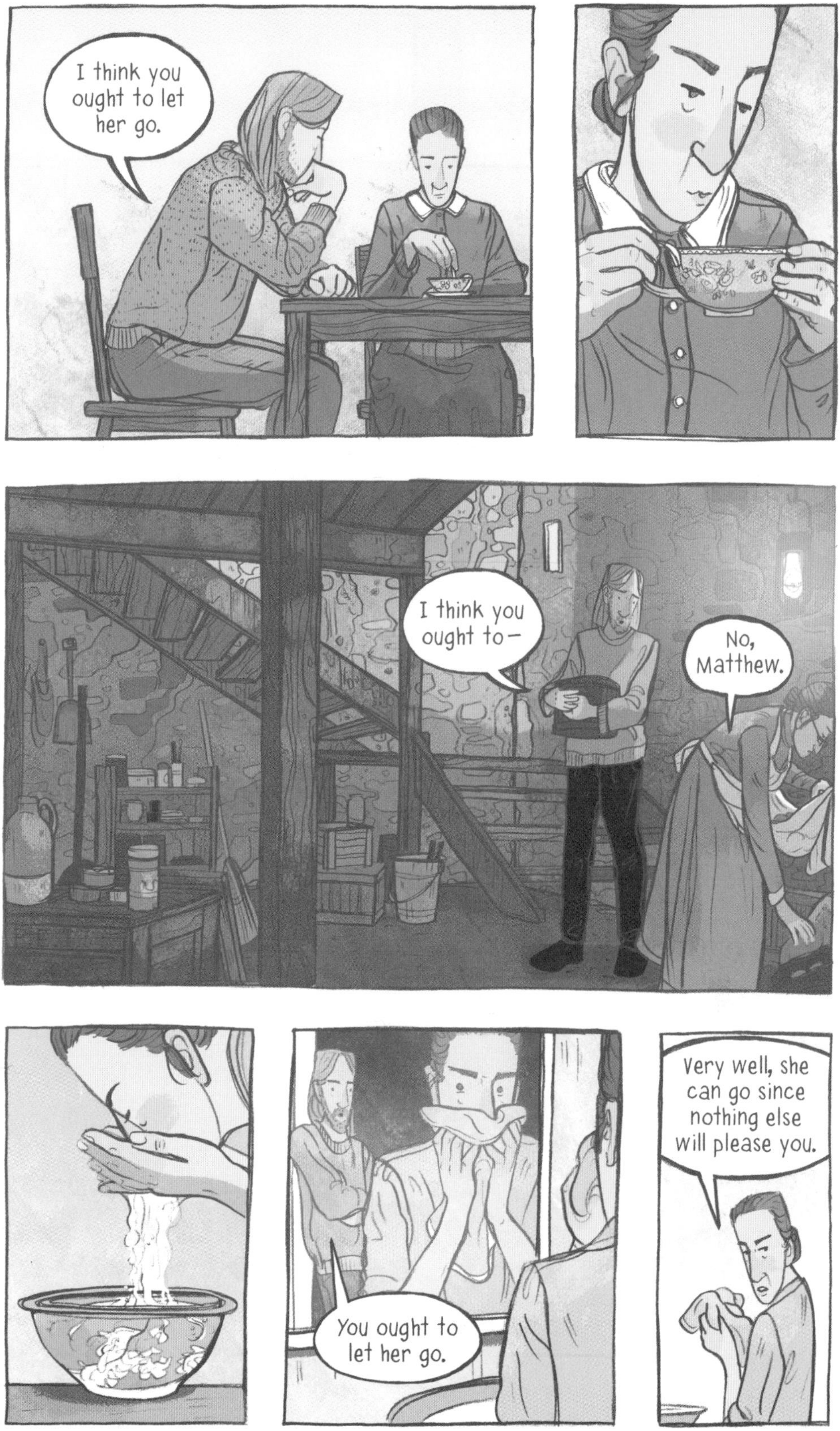
I think you ought to let her go.
I think you ought to—
No, Matthew.
You ought to let her go.
Very well, she can go since nothing else will please you.

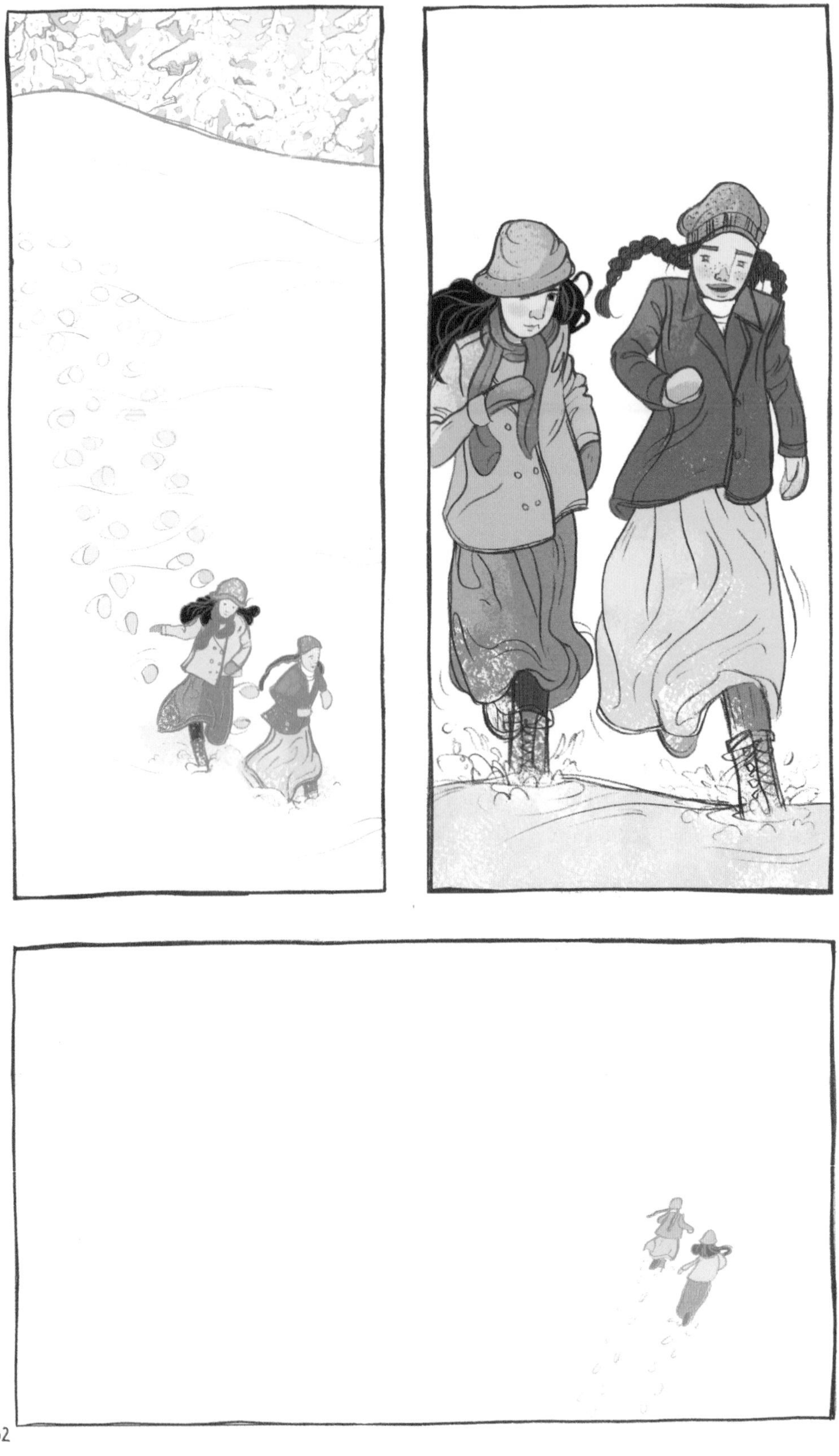

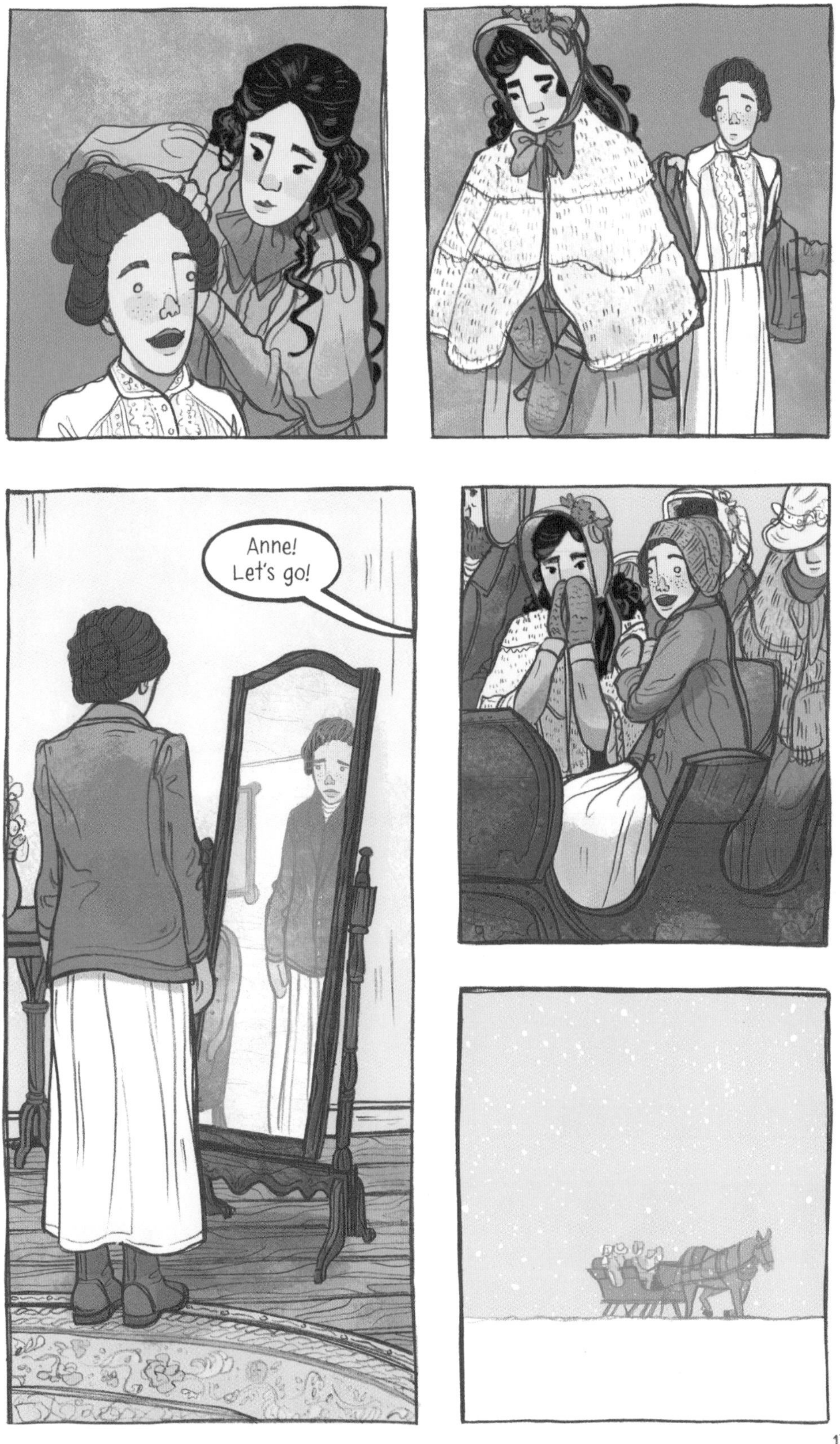
Anne!
Let's go!

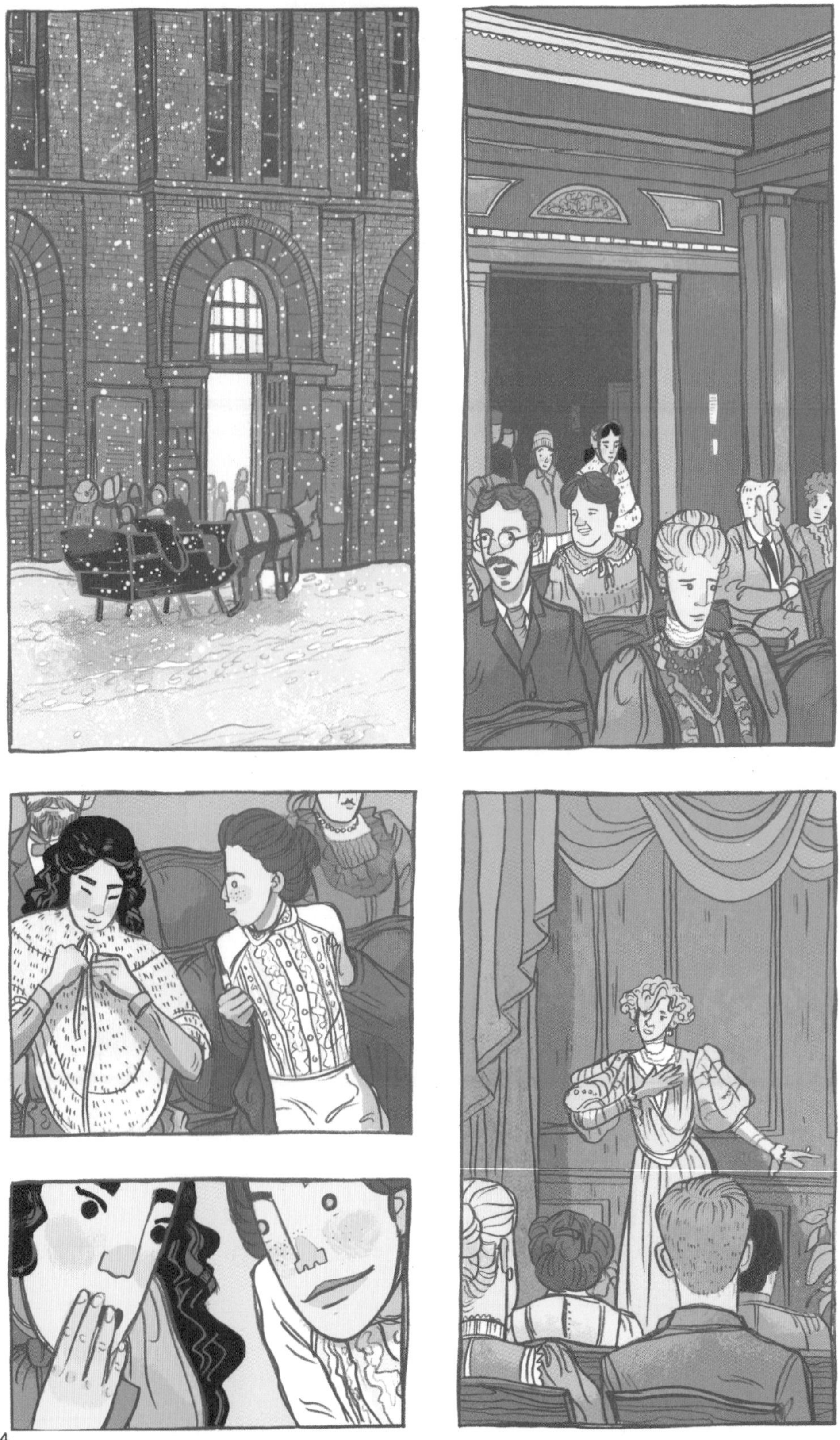

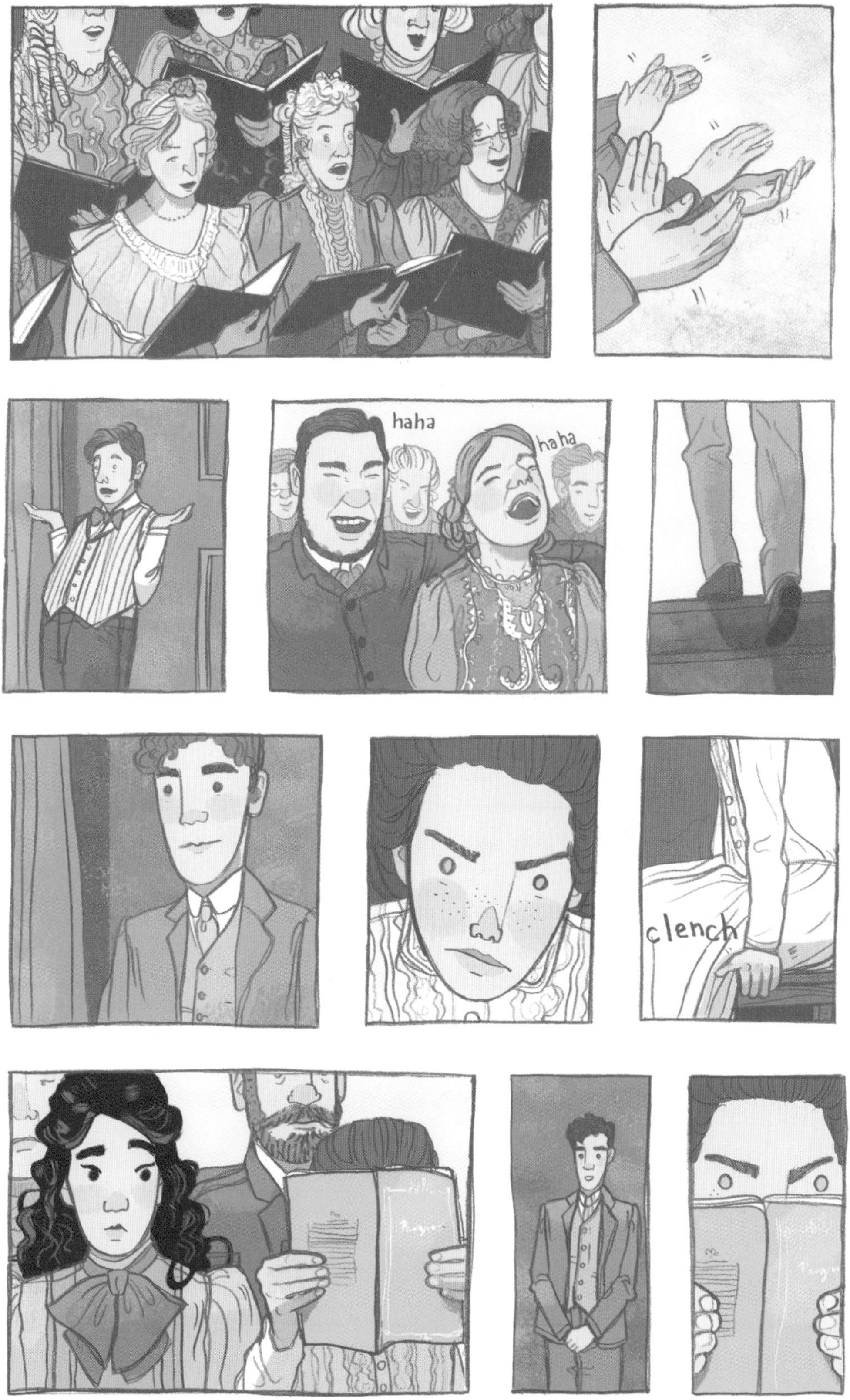
haha
haha
clench

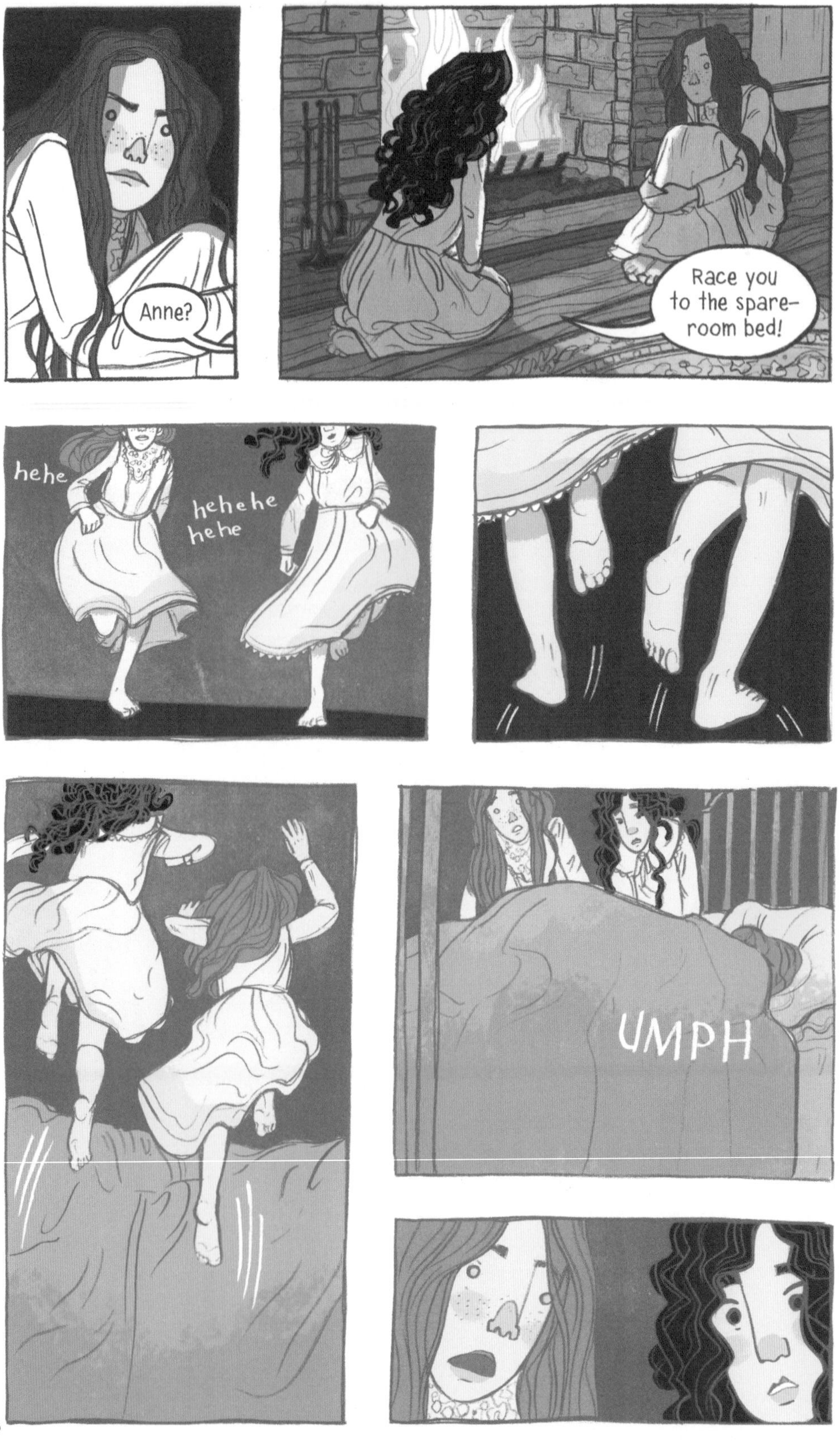
Anne?
Race you to the spare-room bed!
hehe
hehehe hehe
UMPH

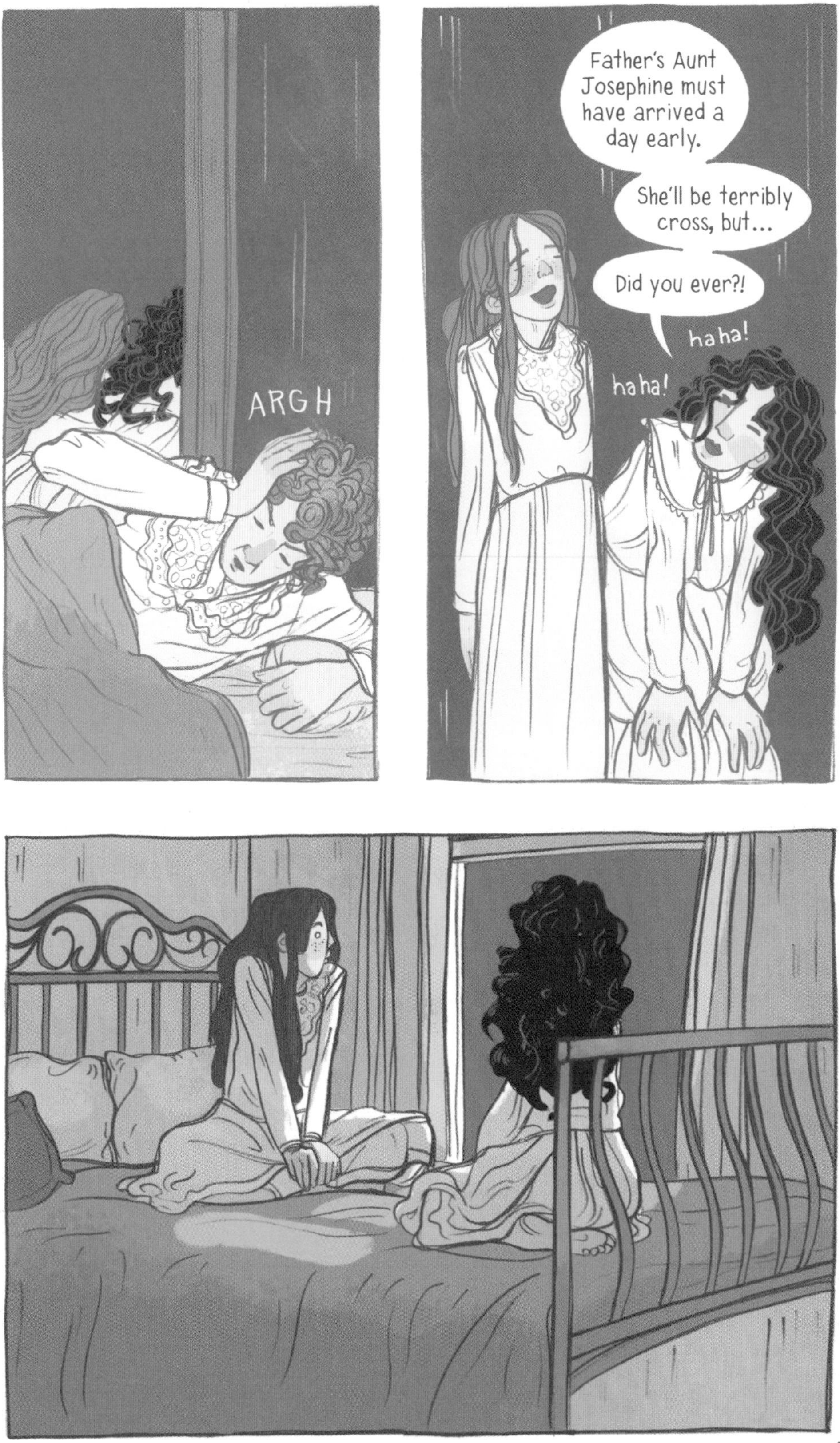
ARGH
Father's Aunt Josephine must have arrived a day early.
She'll be terribly cross, but...
Did you ever?!
ha ha!
ha ha!

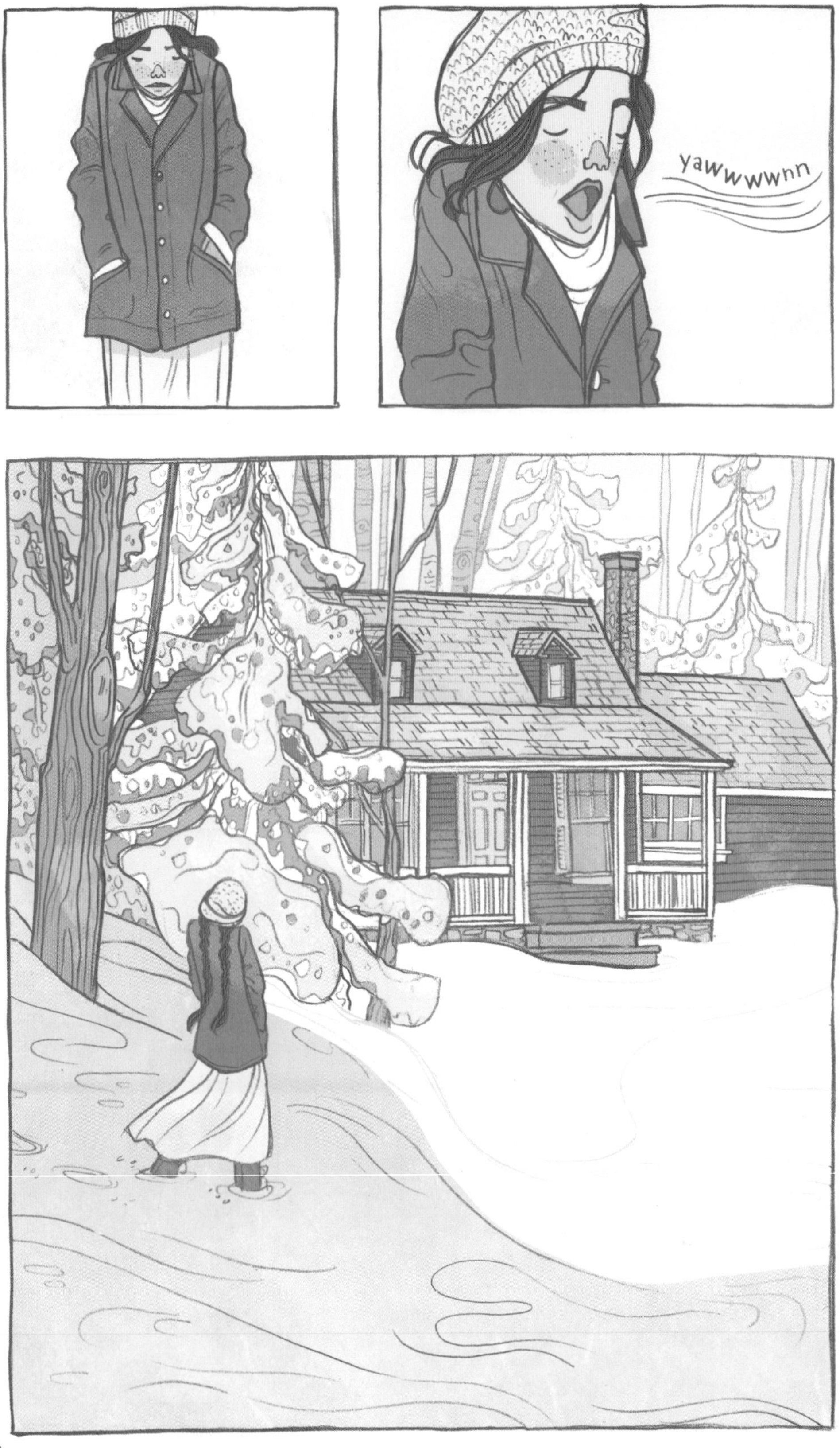
yawwwwnn

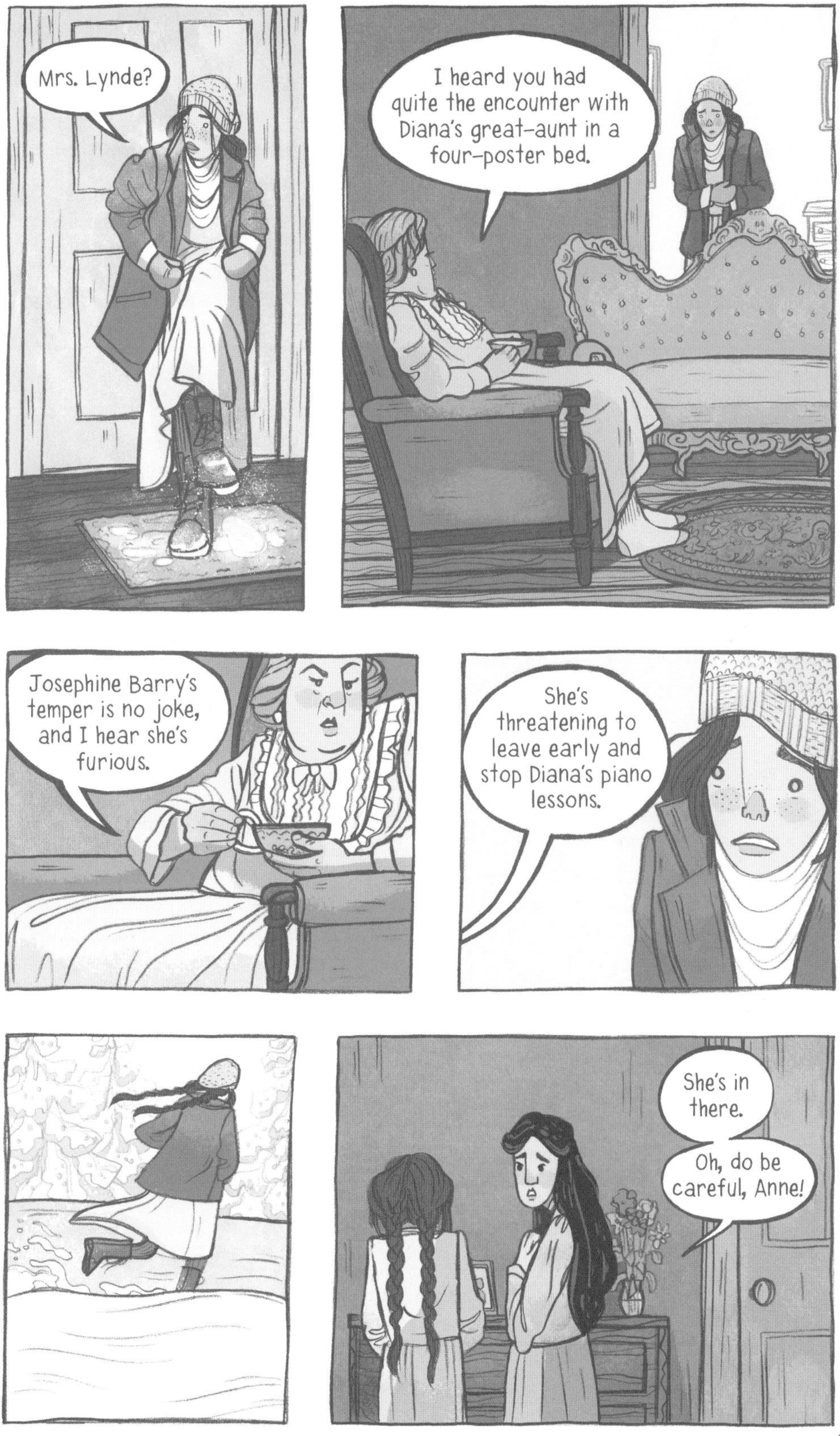
Mrs. Lynde?
I heard you had quite the encounter with Diana's great-aunt in a four-poster bed.
Josephine Barry's temper is no joke, and I hear she's furious.
She's threatening to leave early and stop Diana's piano lessons.
She's in there.
Oh, do be careful, Anne!

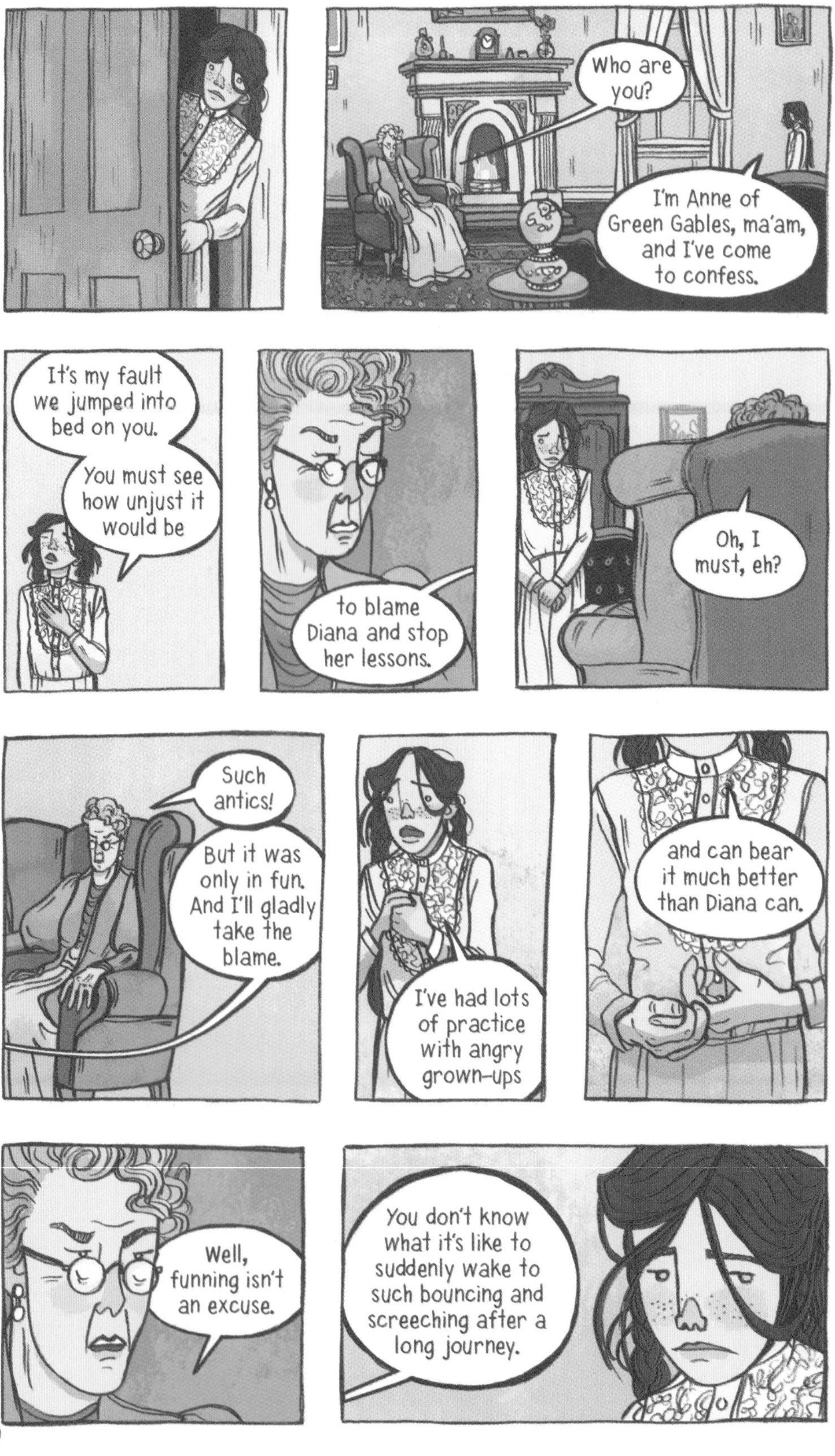
Who are you?
I'm Anne of Green Gables, ma'am, and I've come to confess.
It's my fault we jumped into bed on you.
You must see how unjust it would be
to blame Diana and stop her lessons.
Oh, I must, eh?
Such antics!
But it was only in fun. And I'll gladly take the blame.
I've had lots of practice with angry grown-ups
and can bear it much better than Diana can.
Well, funning isn't an excuse.
You don't know what it's like to suddenly wake to such bouncing and screeching after a long journey.

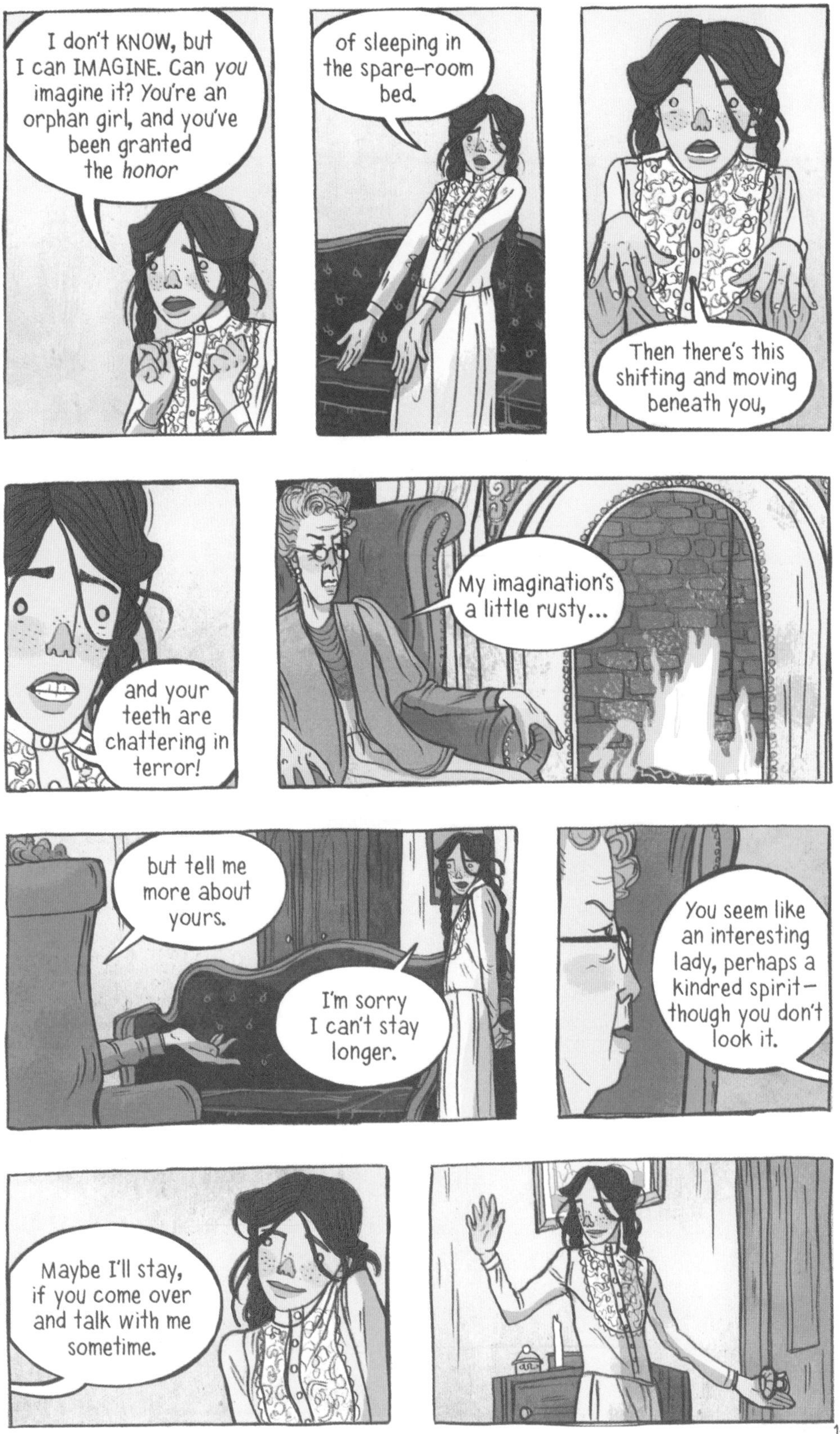
I don't KNOW, but I can IMAGINE. Can *you* imagine it? *You're* an orphan girl, and you've been granted the *honor*
of sleeping in the spare-room bed.
Then there's this shifting and moving beneath you,
and your teeth are chattering in terror!
My imagination's a little rusty...
but tell me more about yours.
I'm sorry I can't stay longer.
You seem like an interesting lady, perhaps a kindred spirit—though you don't look it.
Maybe I'll stay, if you come over and talk with me sometime.

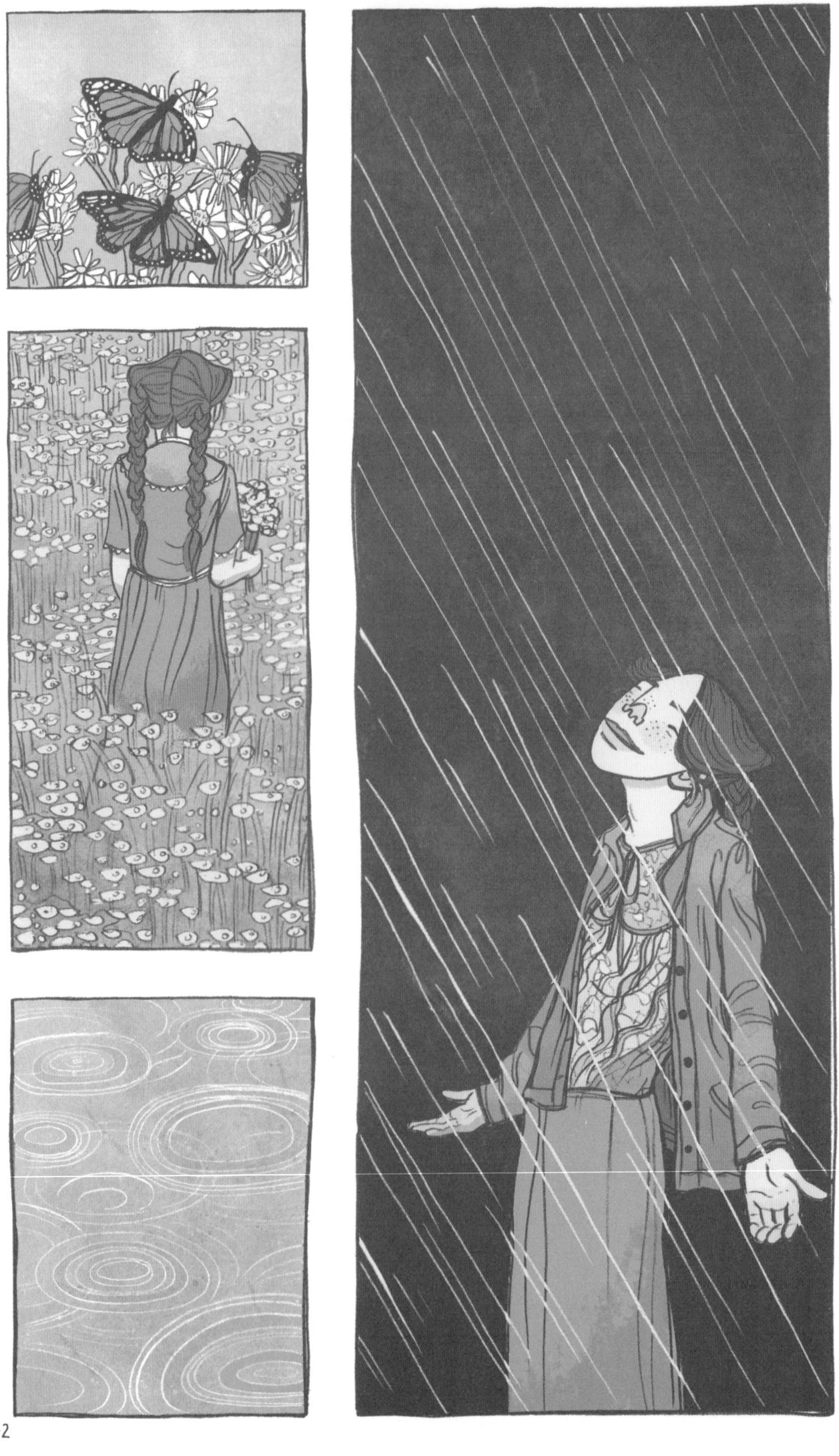

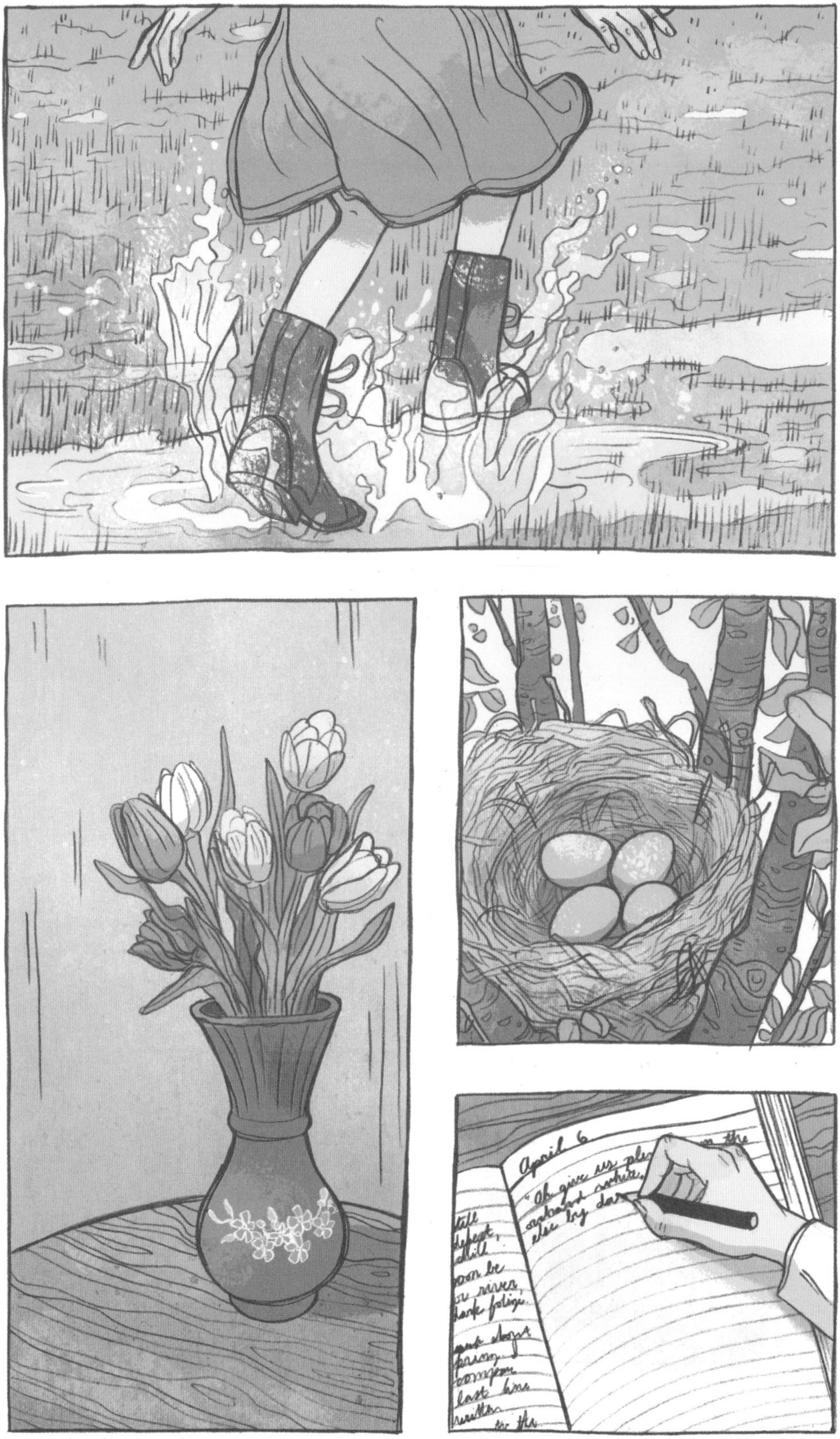
April 6

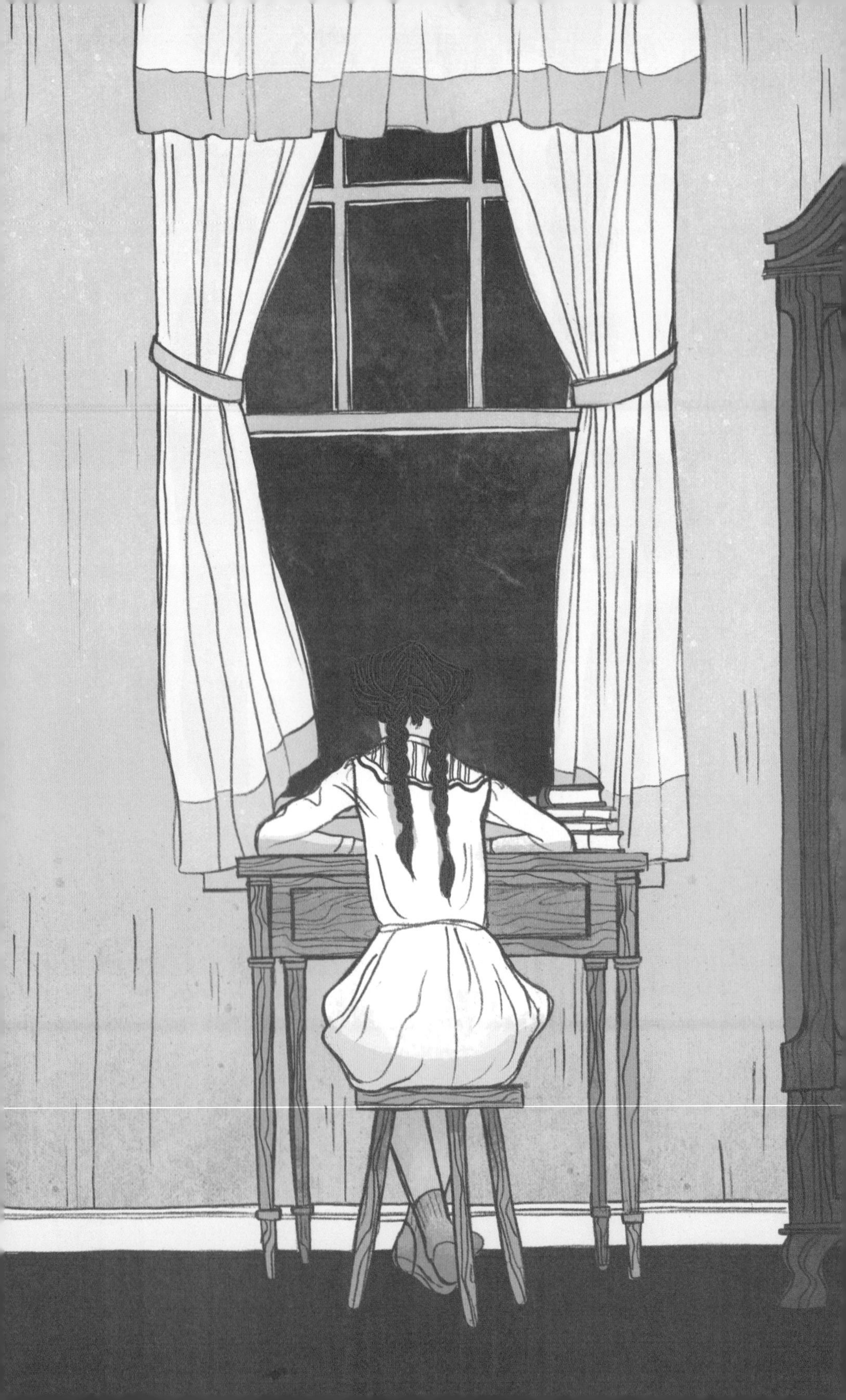

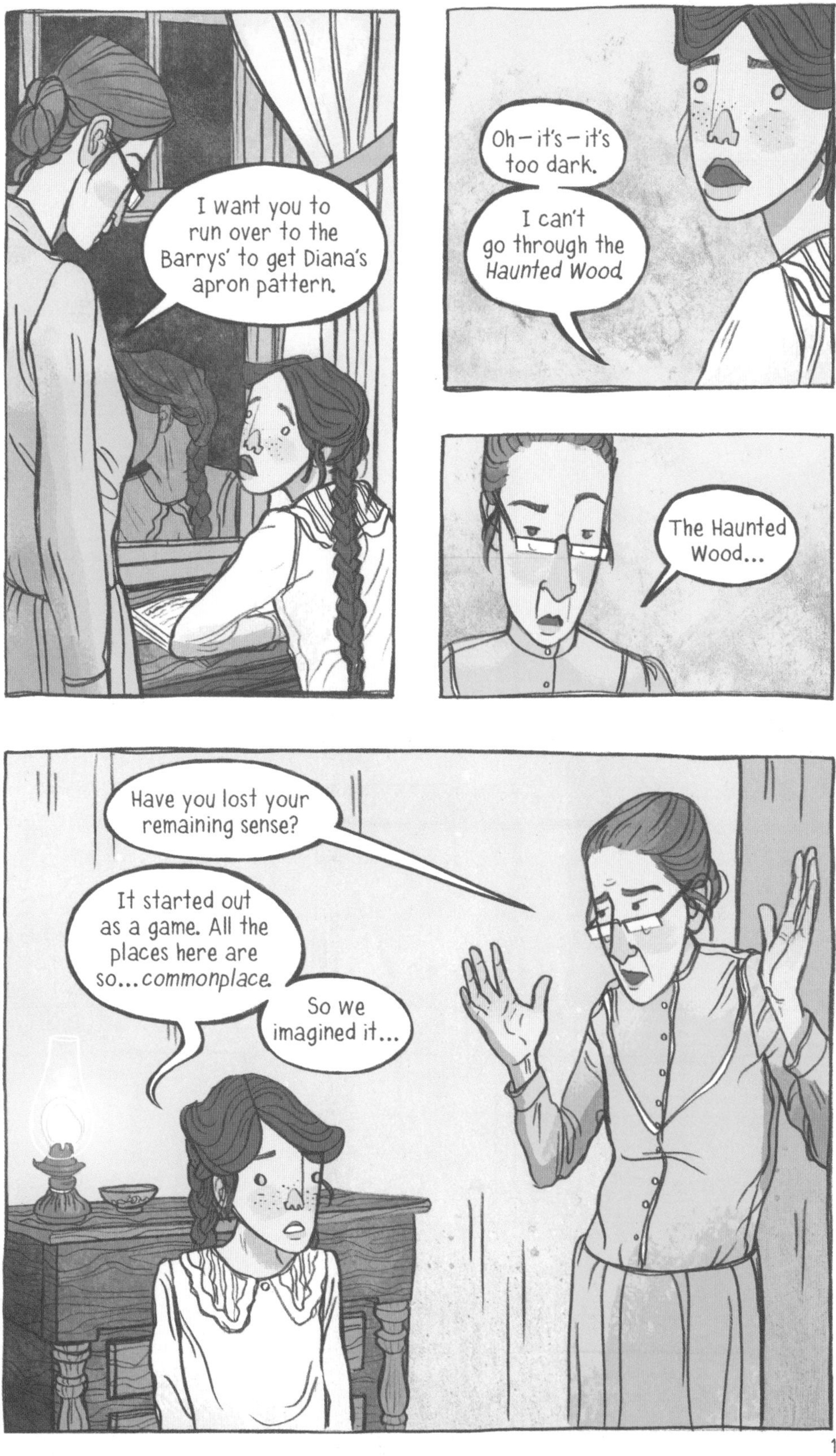
I want you to run over to the Barrys' to get Diana's apron pattern.
Oh – it's – it's too dark.
I can't go through the *Haunted Wood*
The Haunted Wood...
Have you lost your remaining sense?
It started out as a game. All the places here are so... *commonplace*.
So we imagined it...

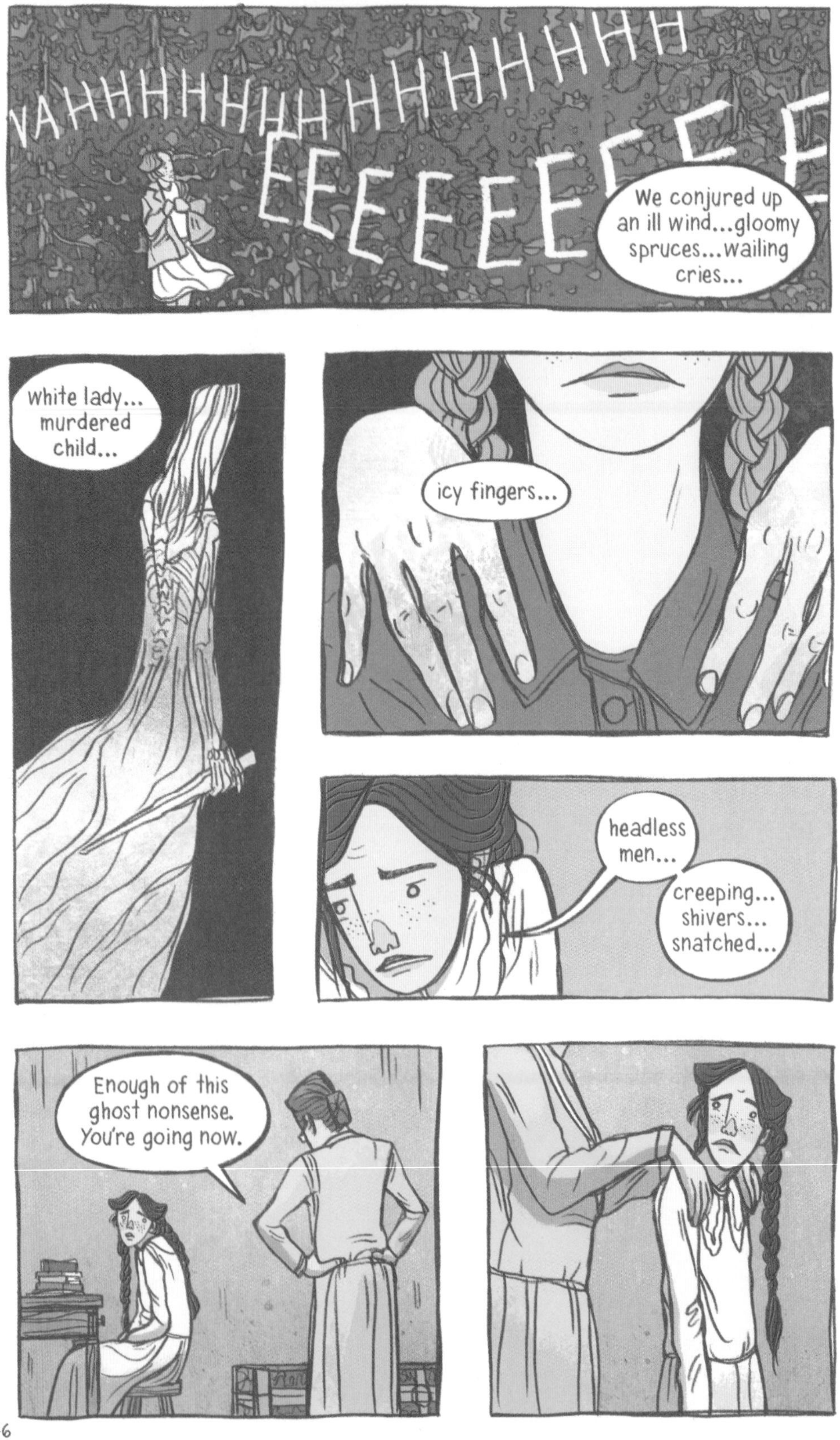
VAHHHHHHHHHHHHHHHHHHH
EEEEEEEEE
We conjured up an ill wind...gloomy spruces...wailing cries...
white lady... murdered child...
icy fingers...
headless men...
creeping... shivers... snatched...
Enough of this ghost nonsense. You're going now.

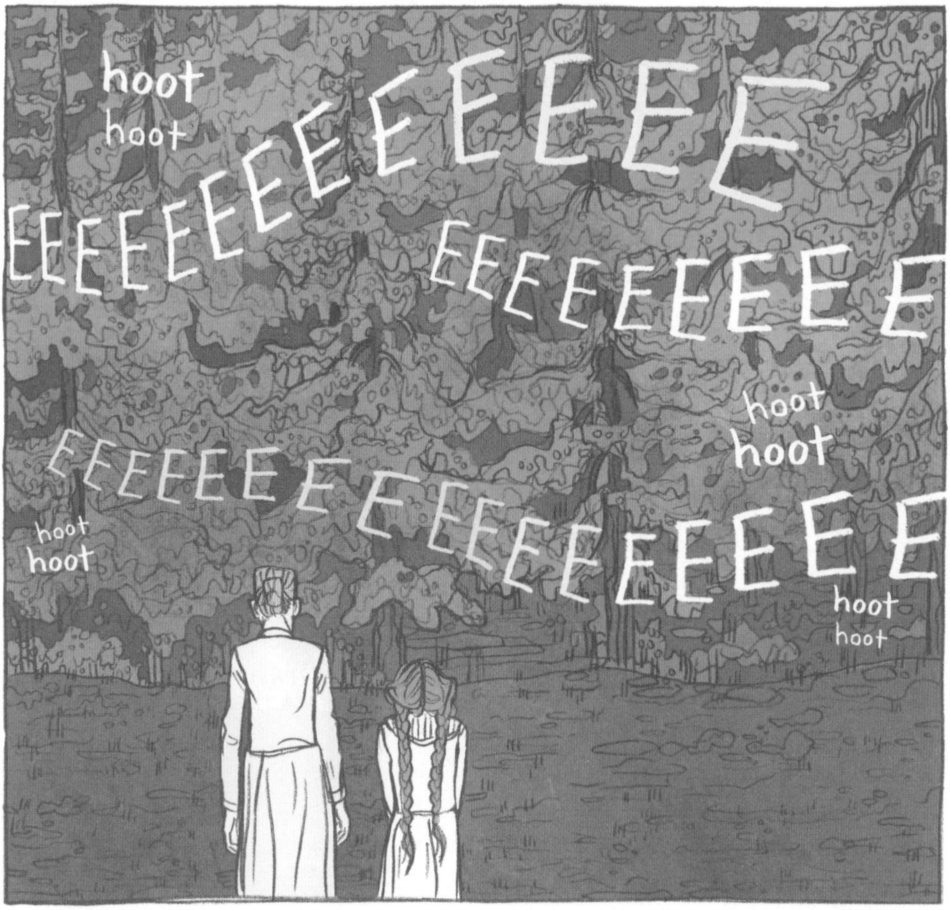
hoot
hoot
EEEEEEEEEEEEEE
EEEEEEEEE
hoot
hoot
EEEEEEEEEEEEEEE
hoot
hoot
hoot
hoot

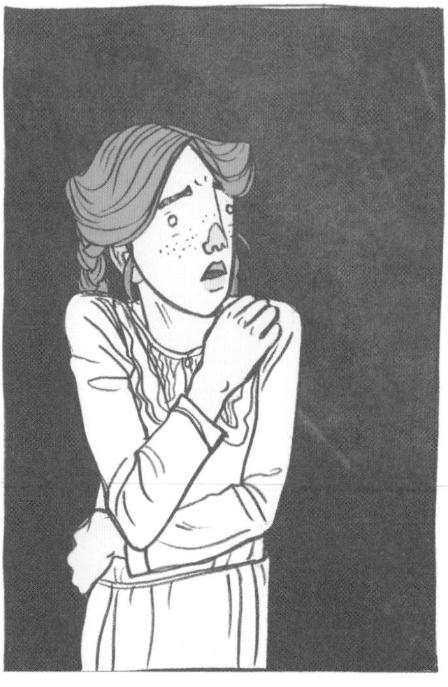

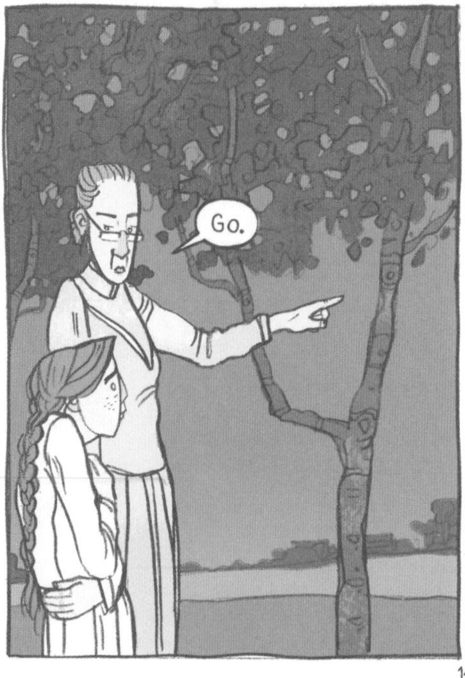
Go.

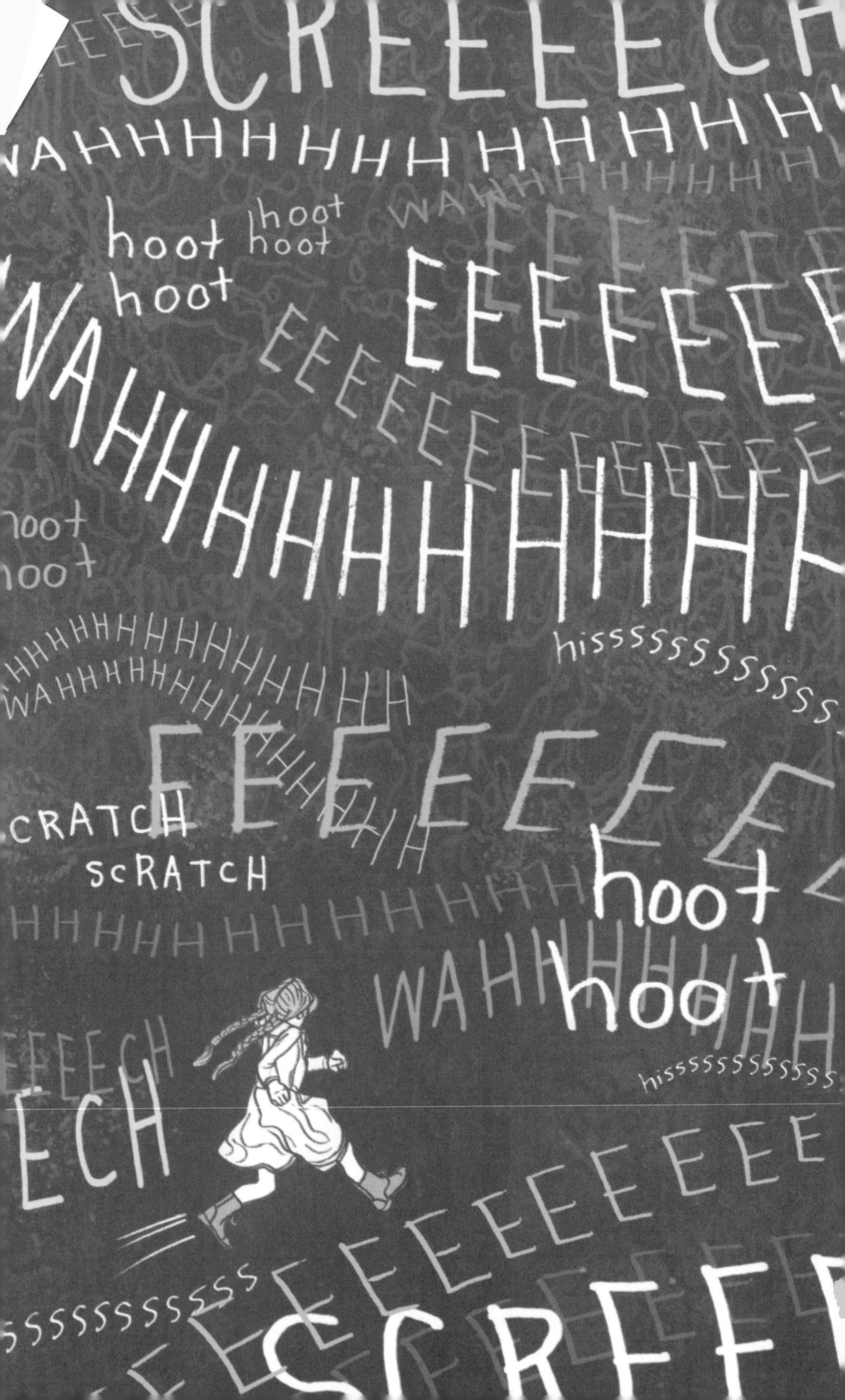
SCREEECH
WAHHHHHHHHHHHH
hoot hoot
hoot
hoot
EEEEEEEE
WAHHHHHHHHHHHHH
hoot
hoot
hisssssssssss
CRATCH
SCRATCH
hoot
WAHHHHHHH
hoot
hissssssssssss
ECH
EEEEEEEEEE
ssssssssss
SCREEE

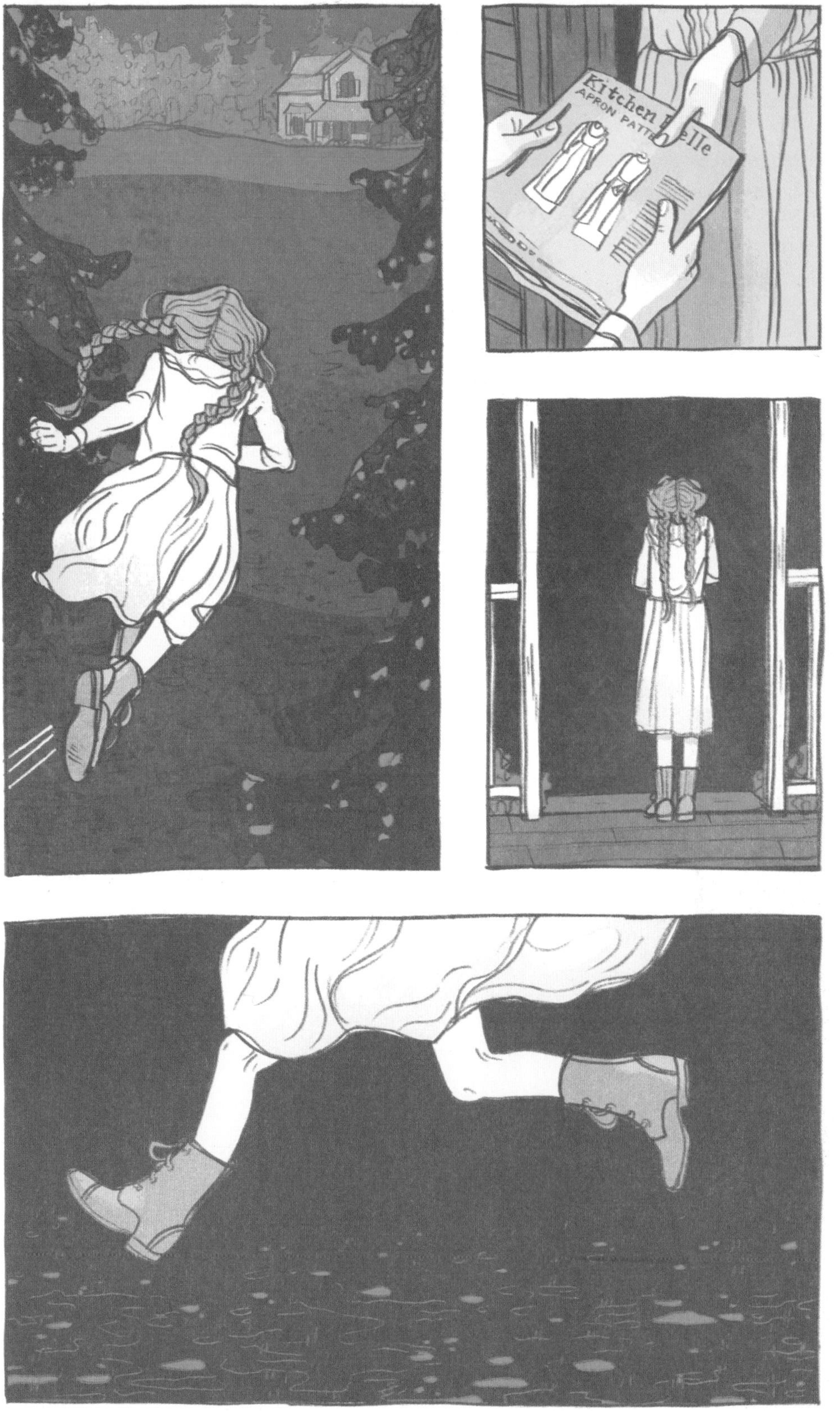
Kitchen

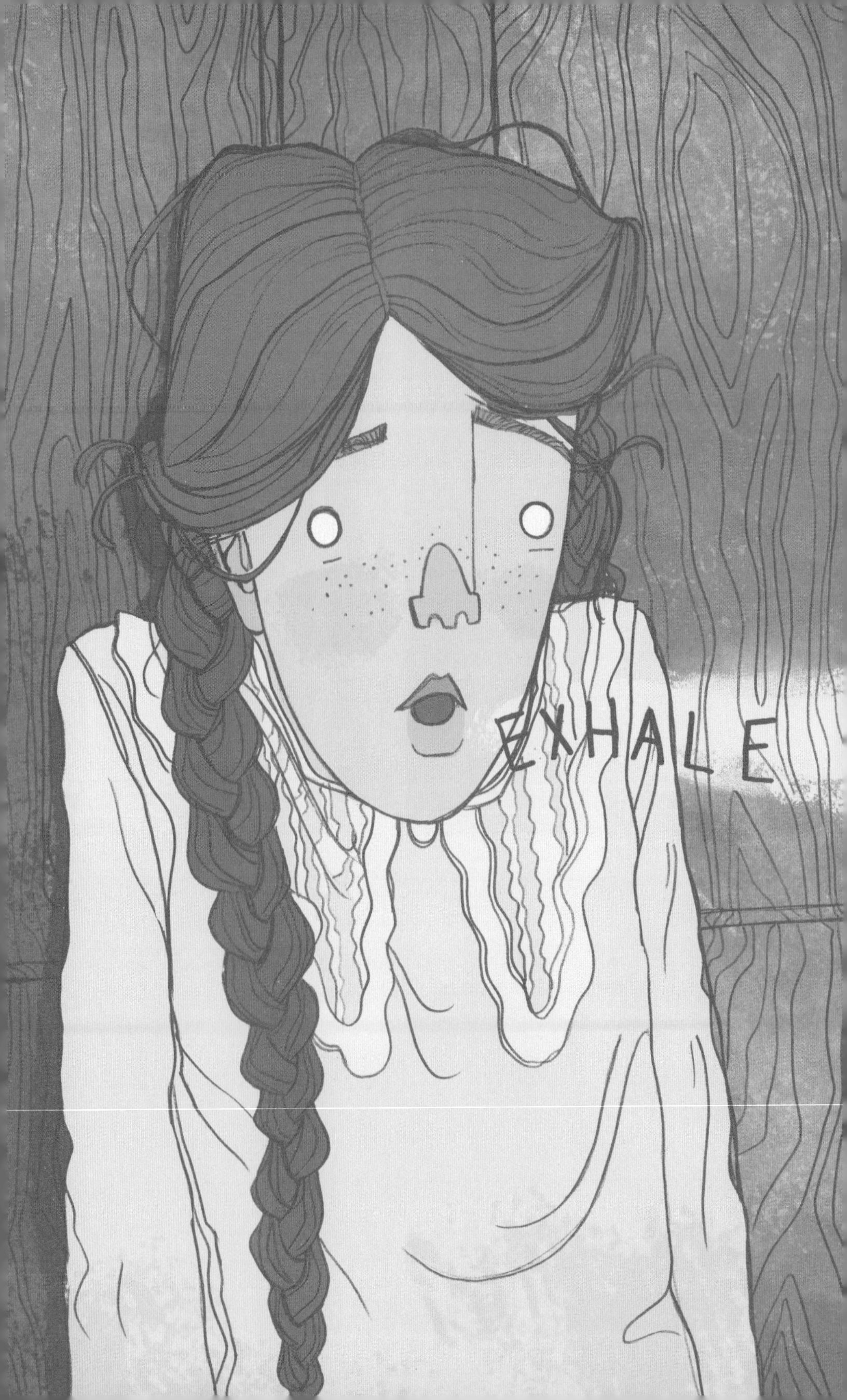
EXHALE

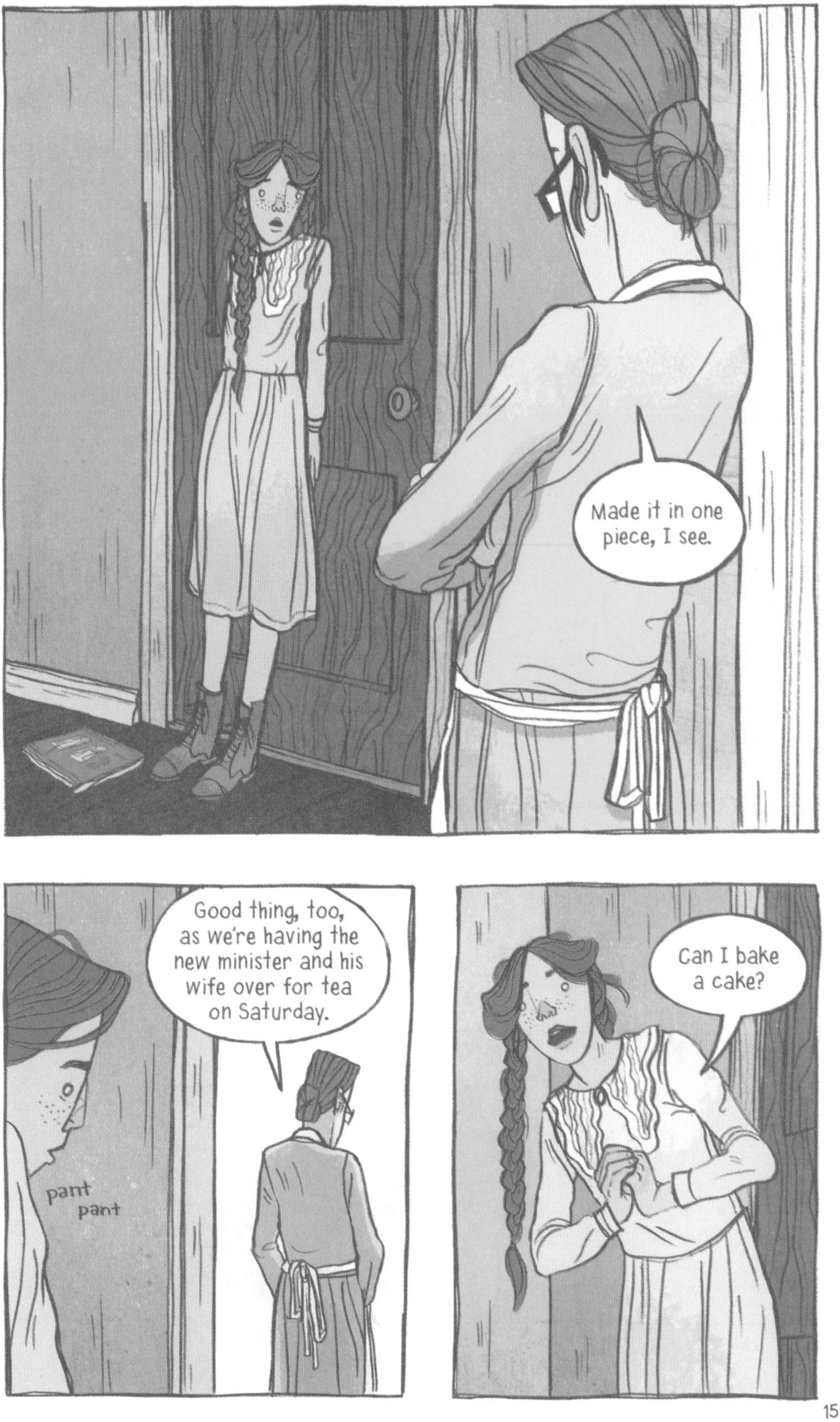
Made it in one piece, I see.
Good thing, too, as we're having the new minister and his wife over for tea on Saturday.
pant pant
Can I bake a cake?

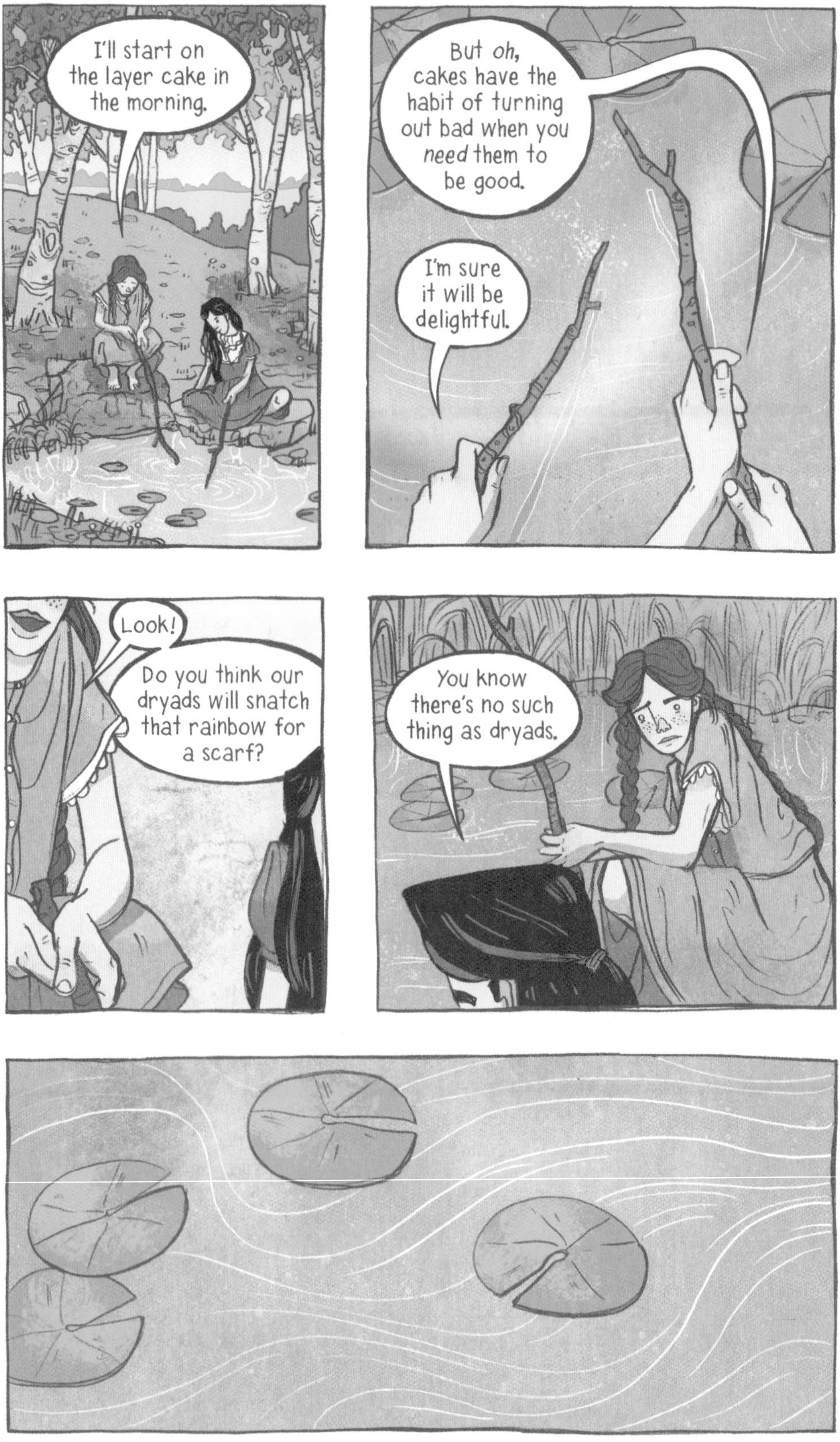
I'll start on the layer cake in the morning.
But *oh*, cakes have the habit of turning out bad when you *need* them to be good.
I'm sure it will be delightful.
Look!
Do you think our dryads will snatch that rainbow for a scarf?
You know there's no such thing as dryads.

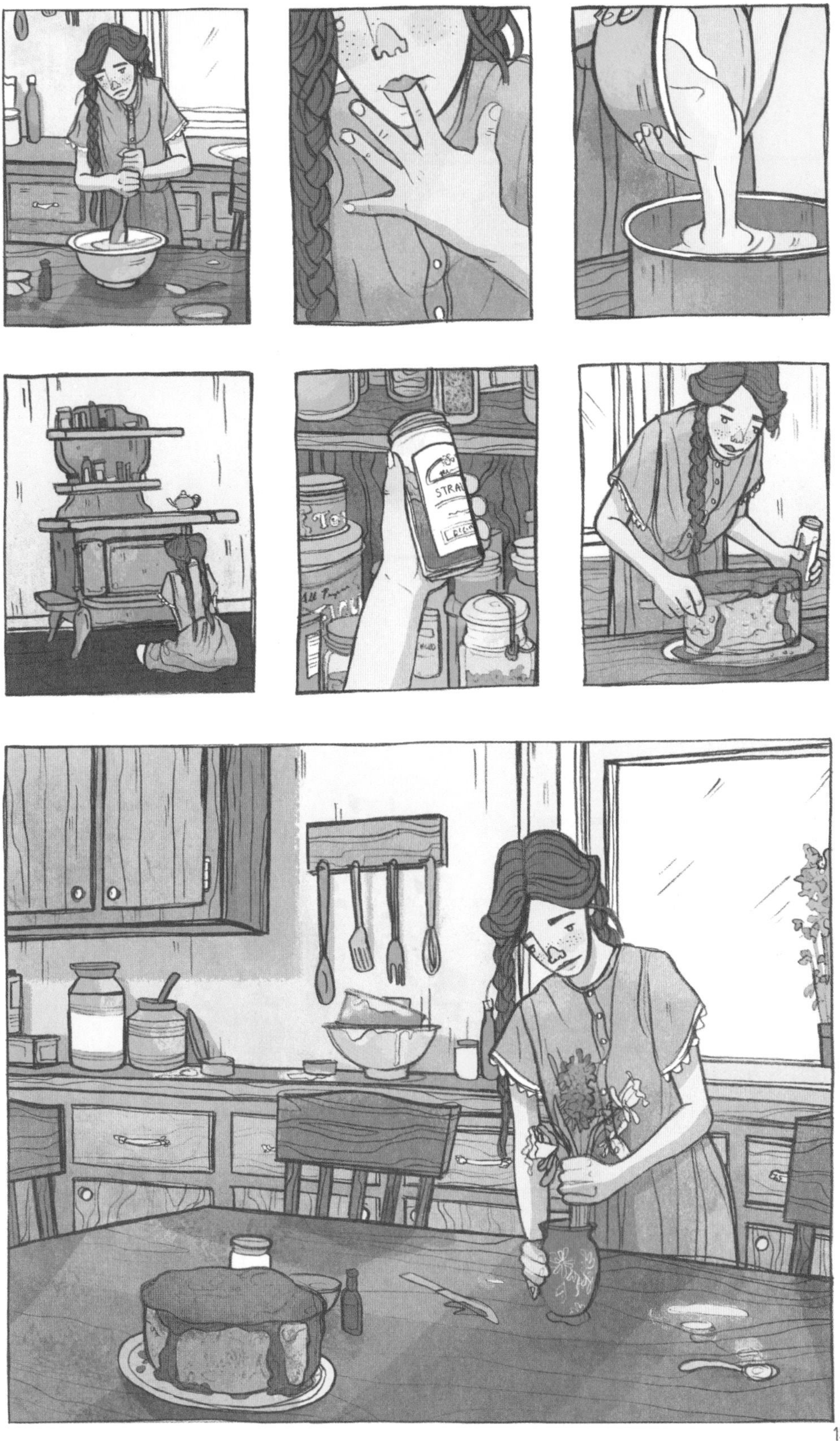

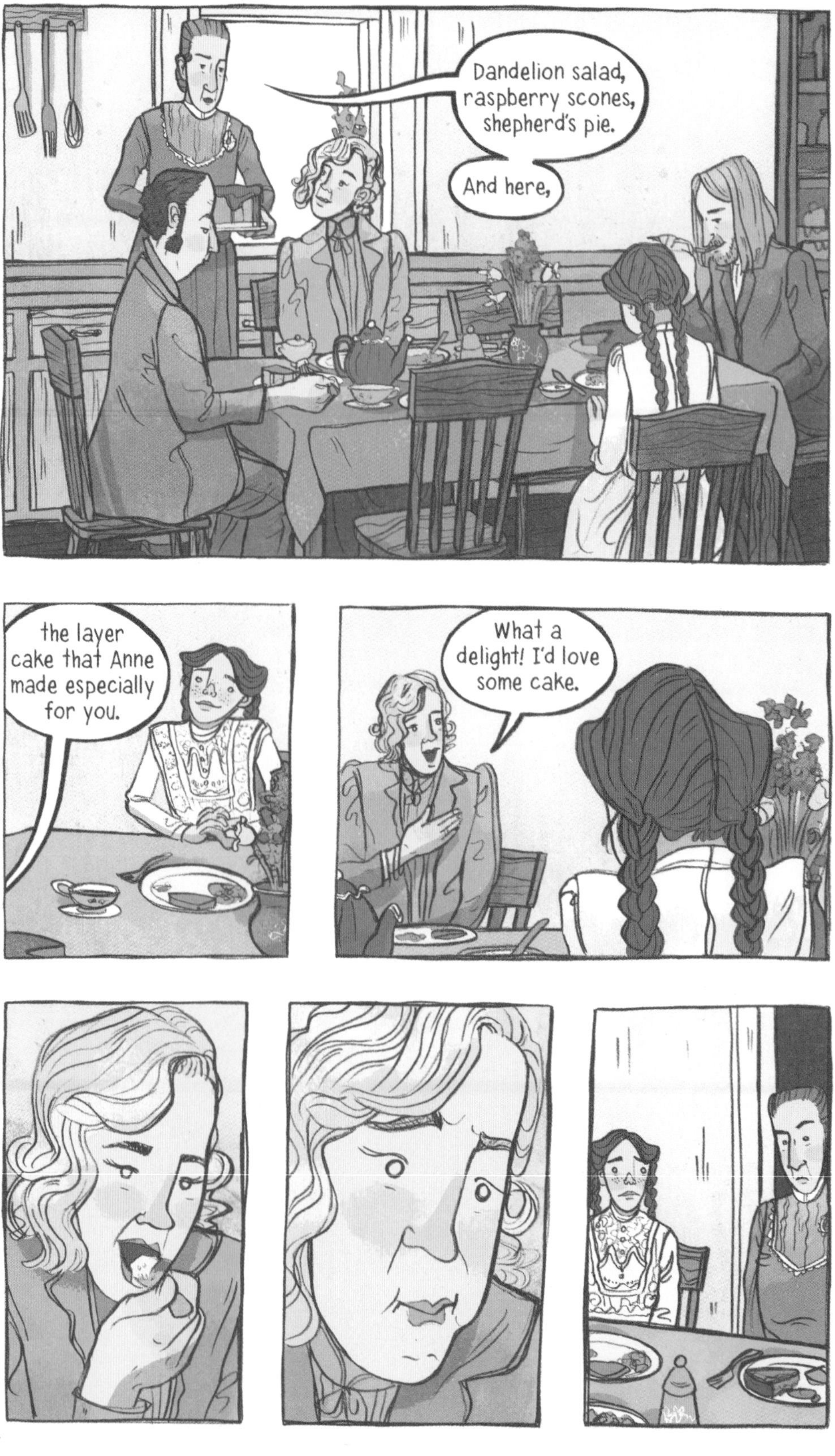
Dandelion salad, raspberry scones, shepherd's pie.
And here,
the layer cake that Anne made especially for you.
What a delight! I'd love some cake.

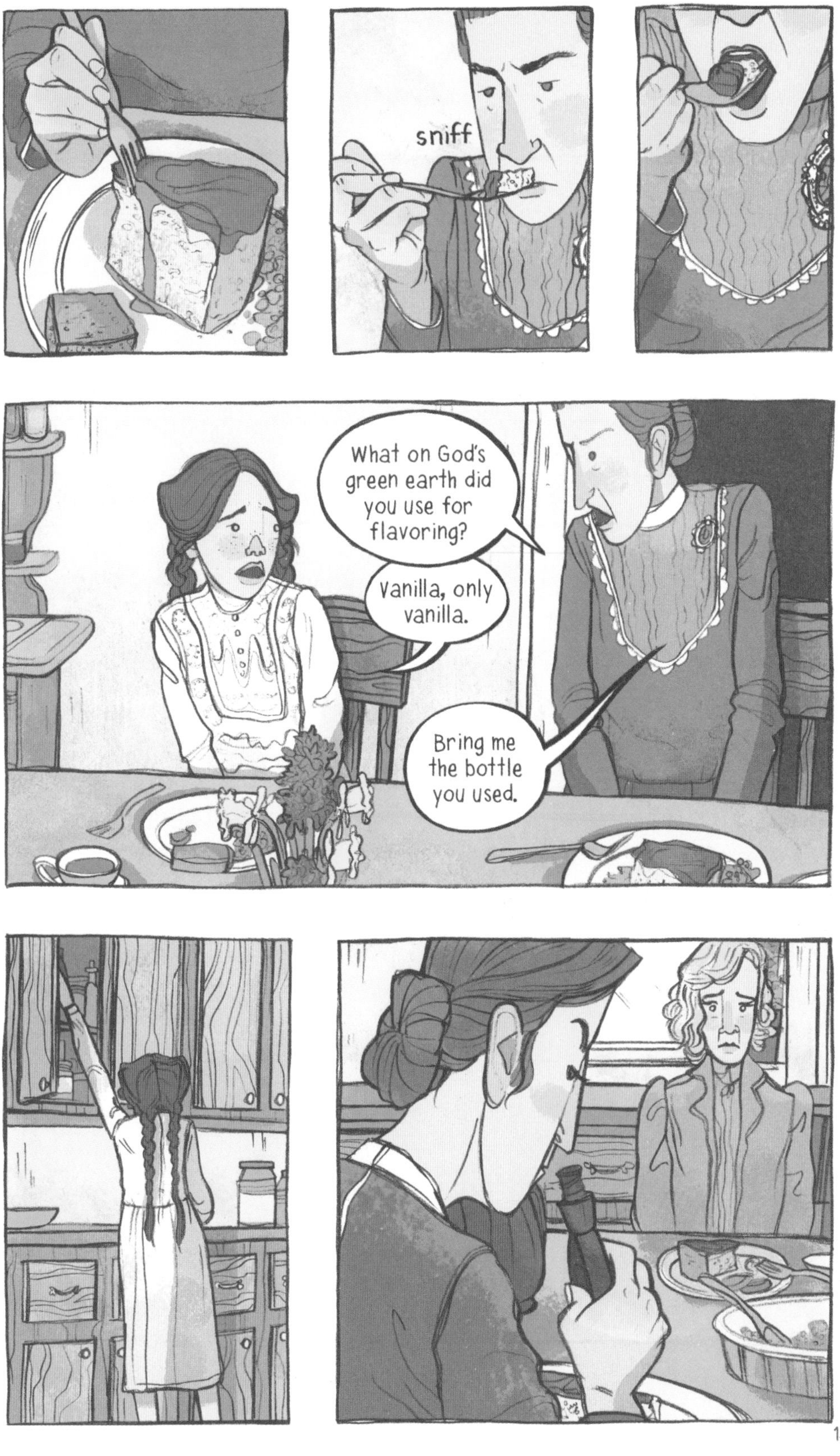
sniff
What on God's green earth did you use for flavoring?
Vanilla, only vanilla.
Bring me the bottle you used.

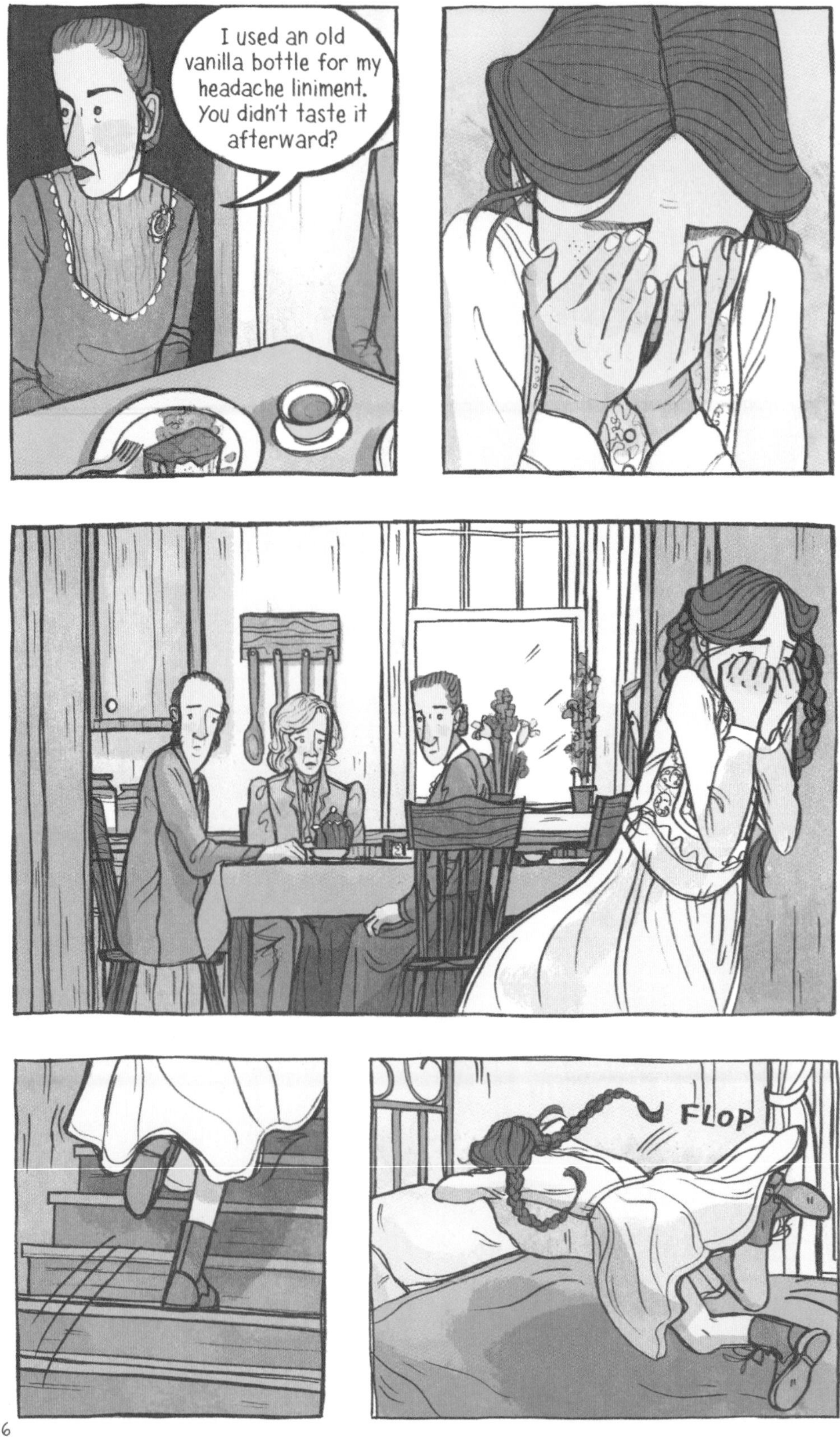
I used an old vanilla bottle for my headache liniment. You didn't taste it afterward?
FLOP

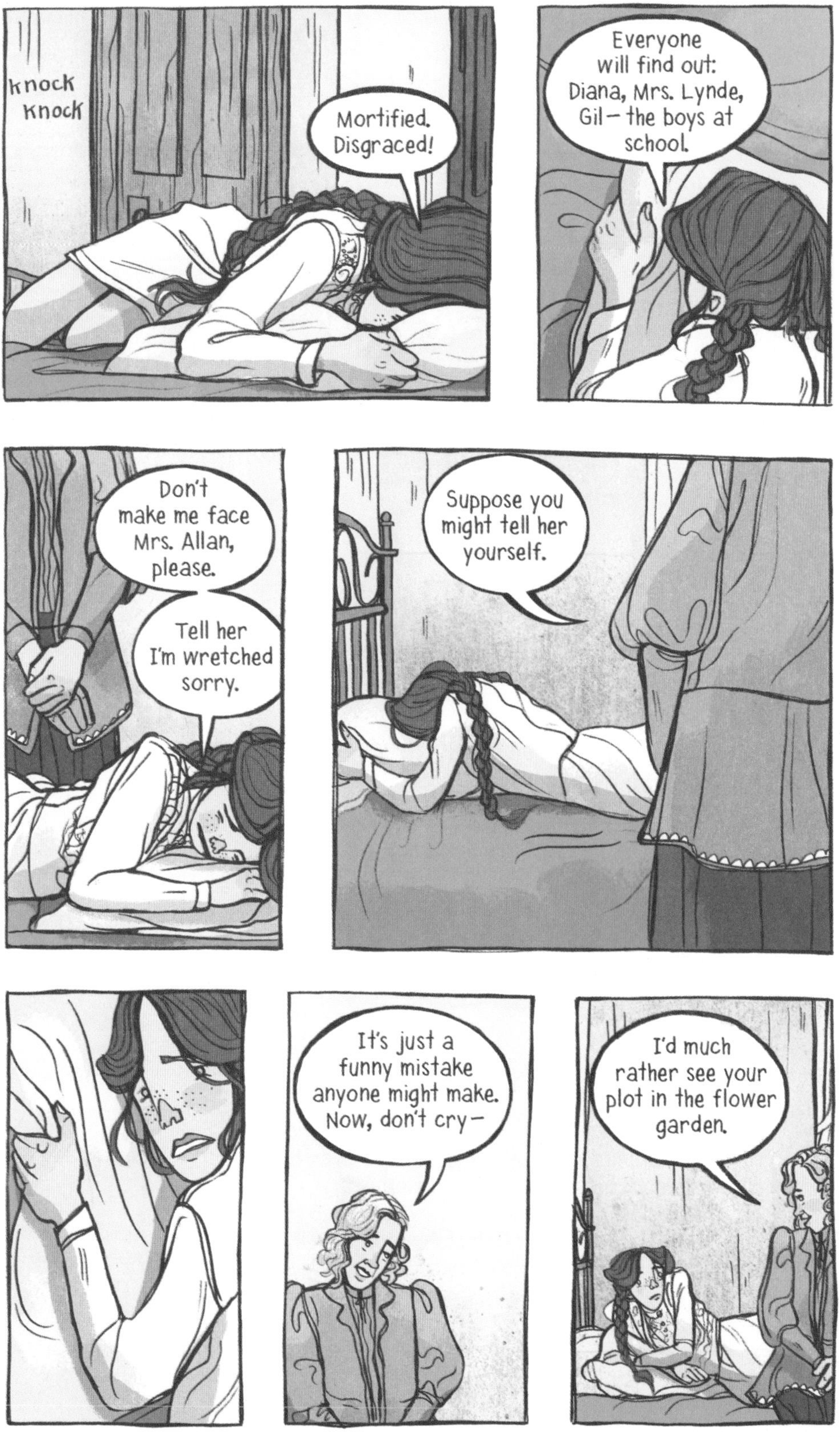
knock
knock
Mortified. Disgraced!
Everyone will find out: Diana, Mrs. Lynde, Gil—the boys at school.
Don't make me face Mrs. Allan, please.
Tell her I'm wretched sorry.
Suppose you might tell her yourself.
It's just a funny mistake anyone might make. Now, don't cry—
I'd much rather see your plot in the flower garden.

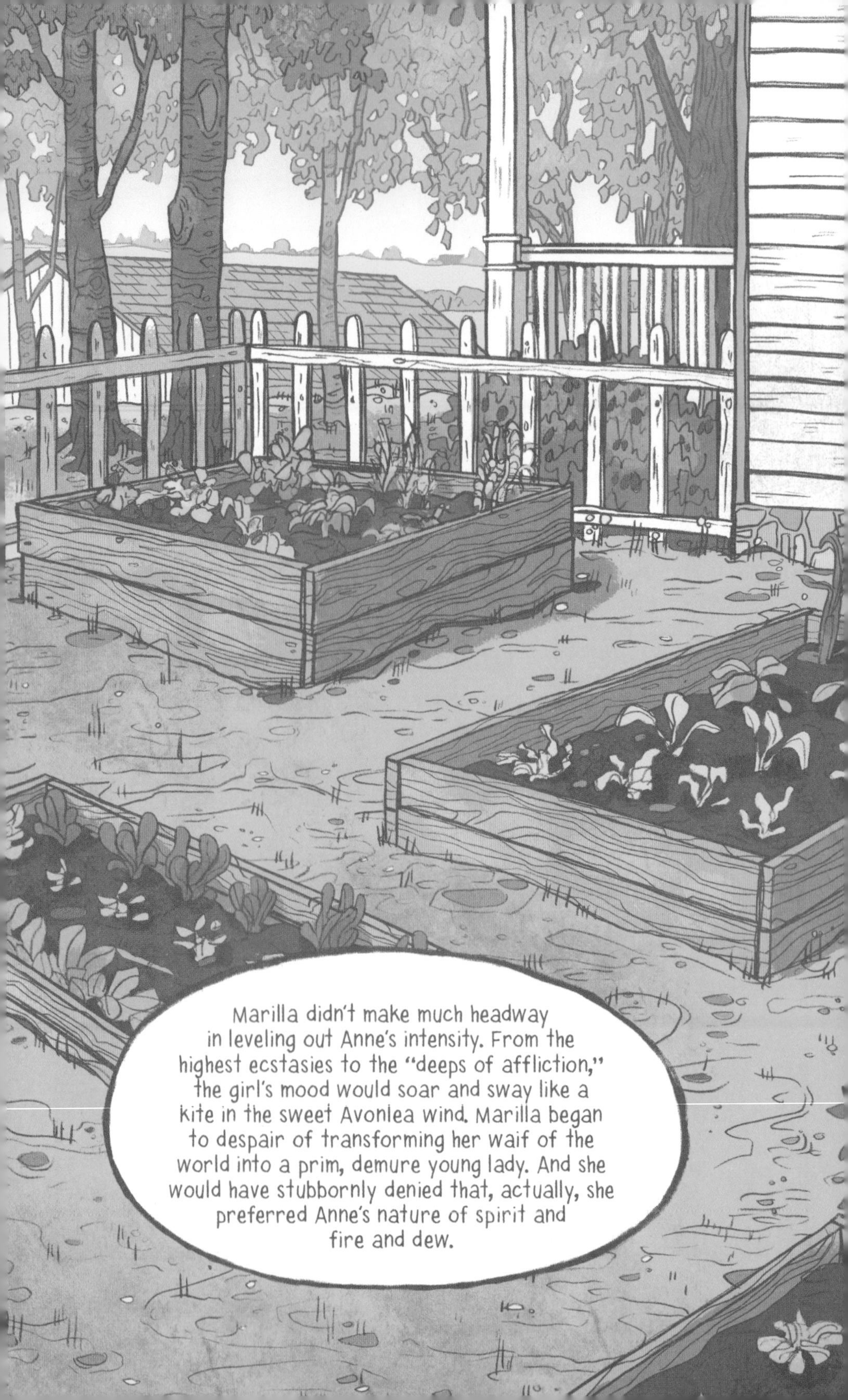
Marilla didn't make much headway in leveling out Anne's intensity. From the highest ecstasies to the "deeps of affliction," the girl's mood would soar and sway like a kite in the sweet Avonlea wind. Marilla began to despair of transforming her waif of the world into a prim, demure young lady. And she would have stubbornly denied that, actually, she preferred Anne's nature of spirit and fire and dew.

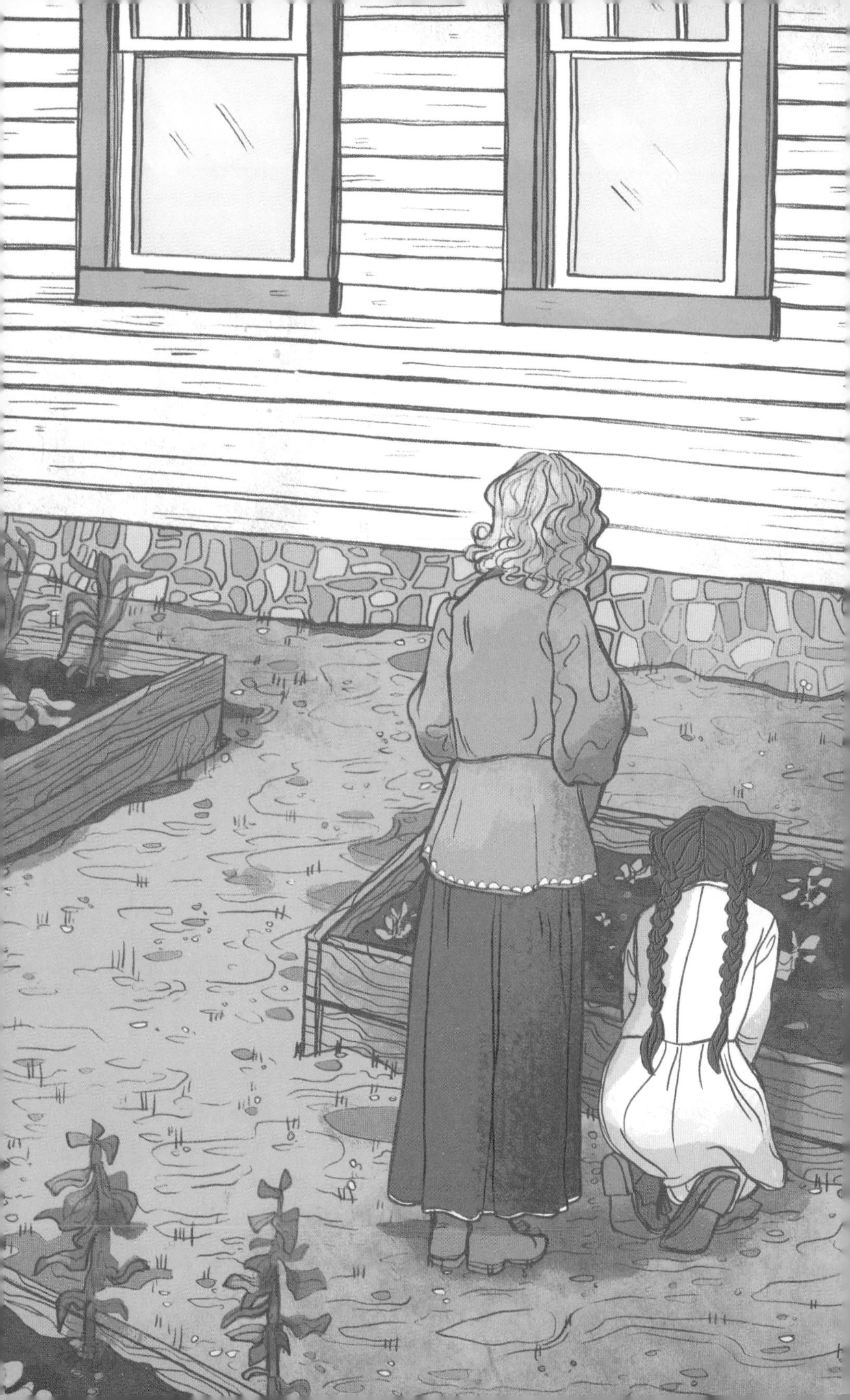

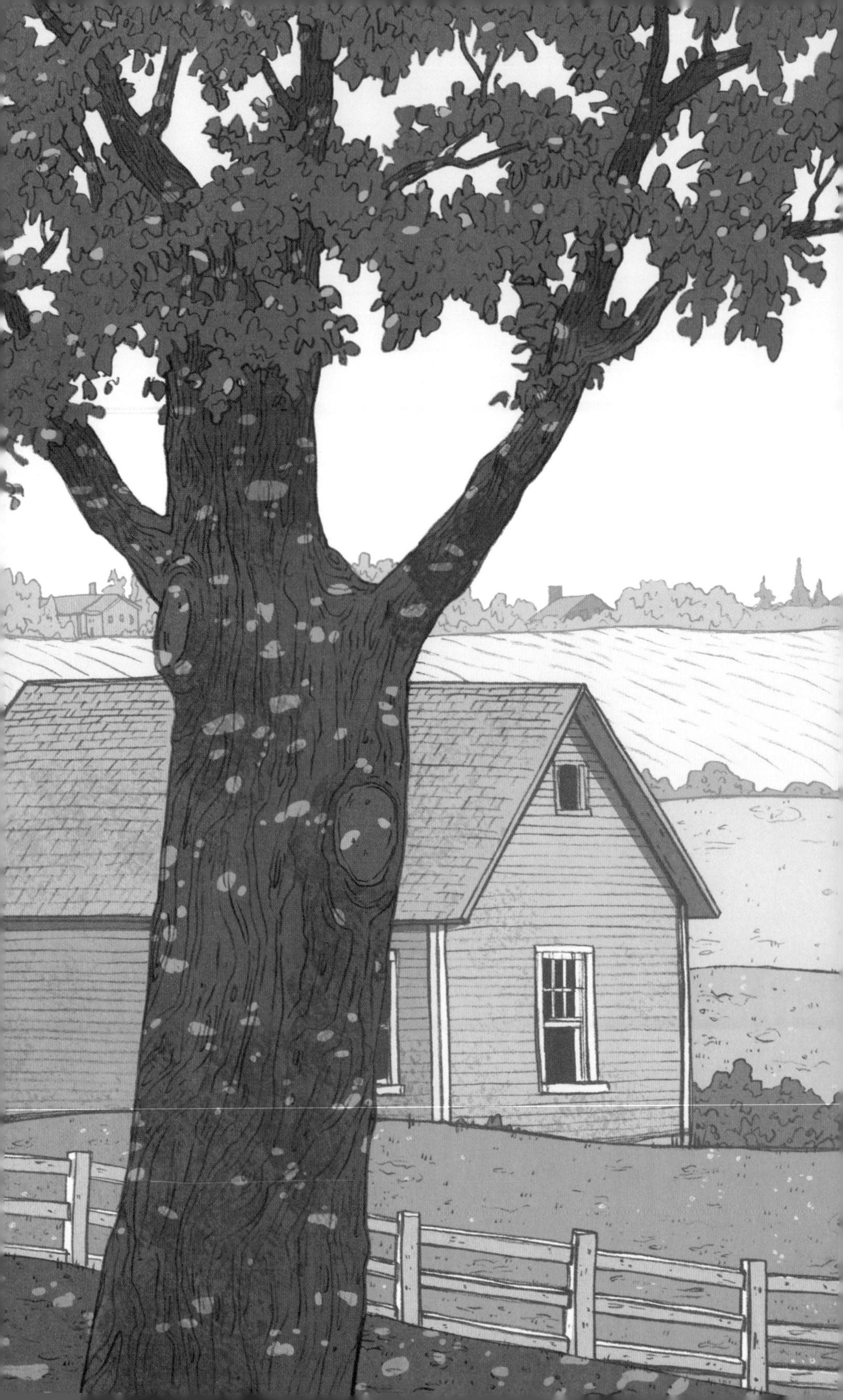

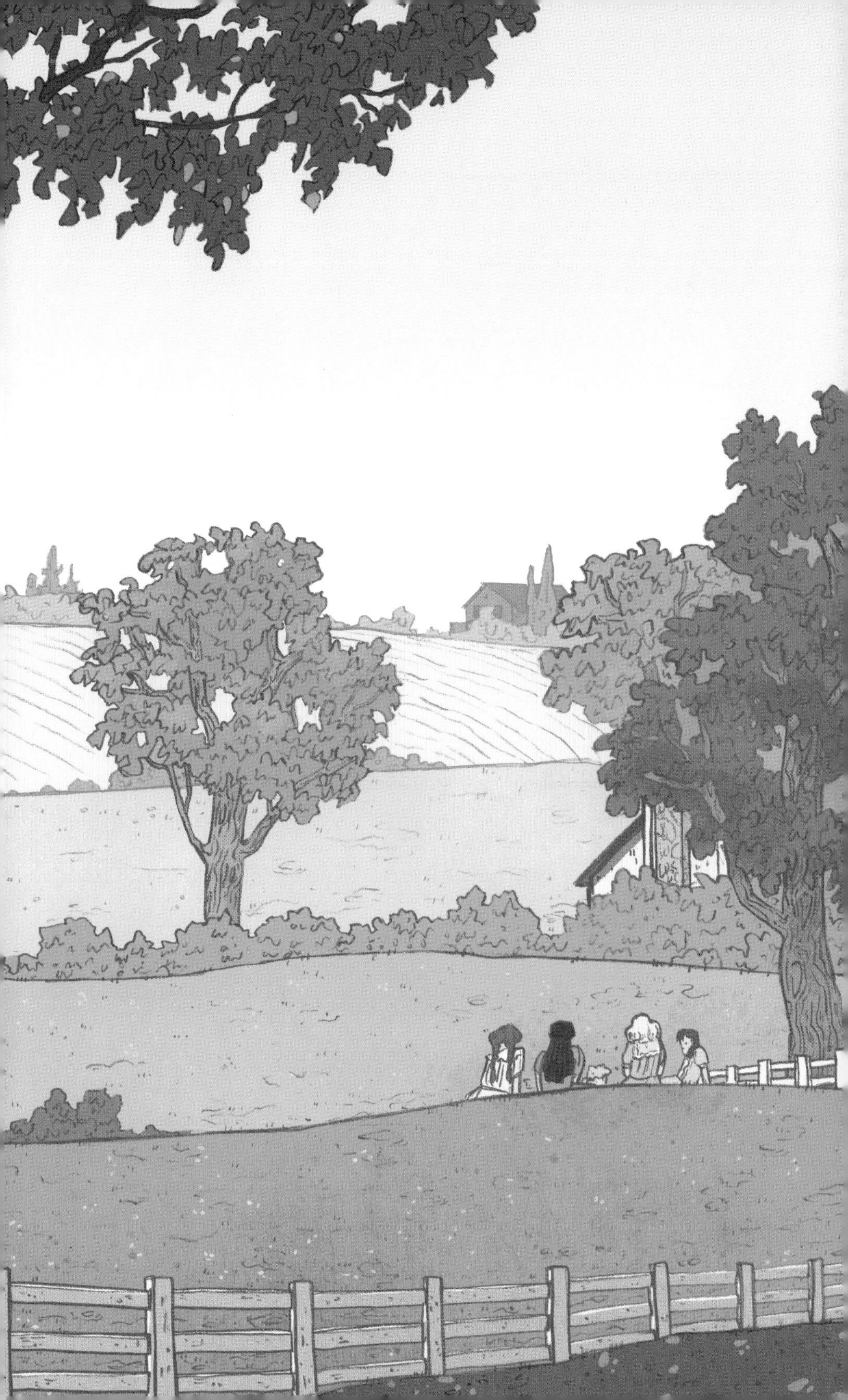

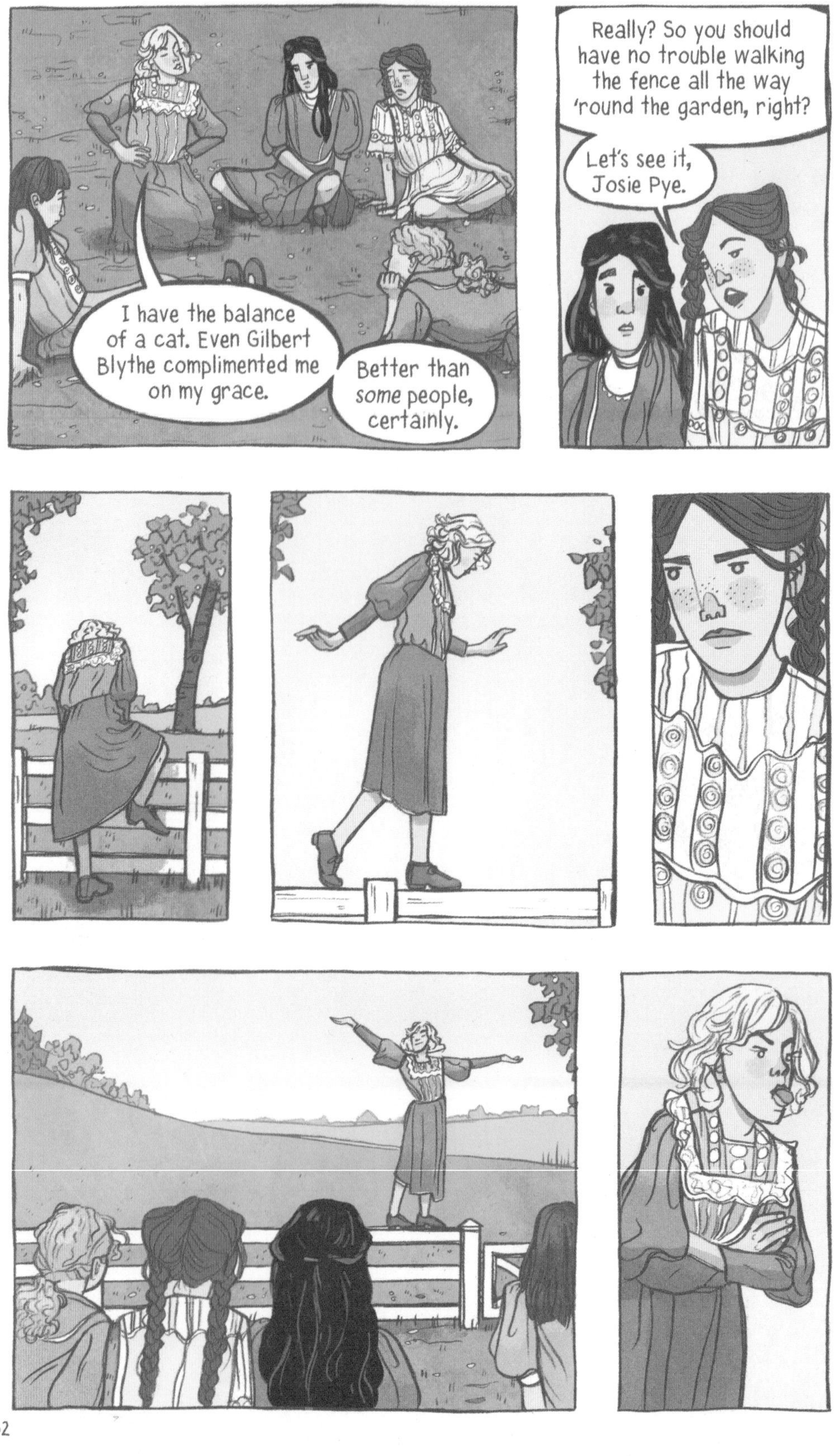
I have the balance of a cat. Even Gilbert Blythe complimented me on my grace.
Better than *some* people, certainly.
Really? So you should have no trouble walking the fence all the way 'round the garden, right?
Let's see it, Josie Pye.

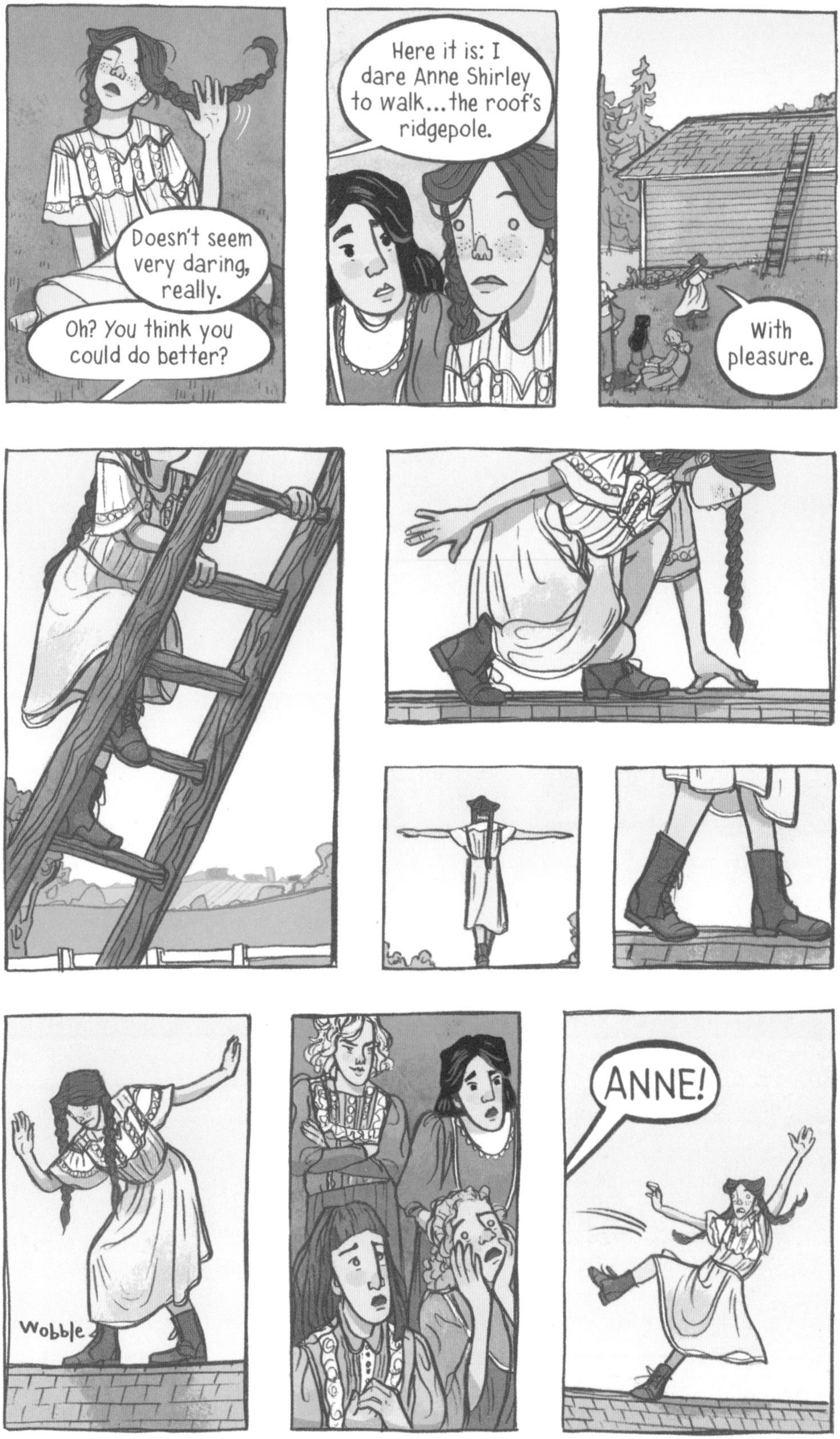
Doesn't seem very daring, really.
Oh? You think you could do better?
Here it is: I dare Anne Shirley to walk...the roof's ridgepole.
With pleasure.
Wobble
ANNE!

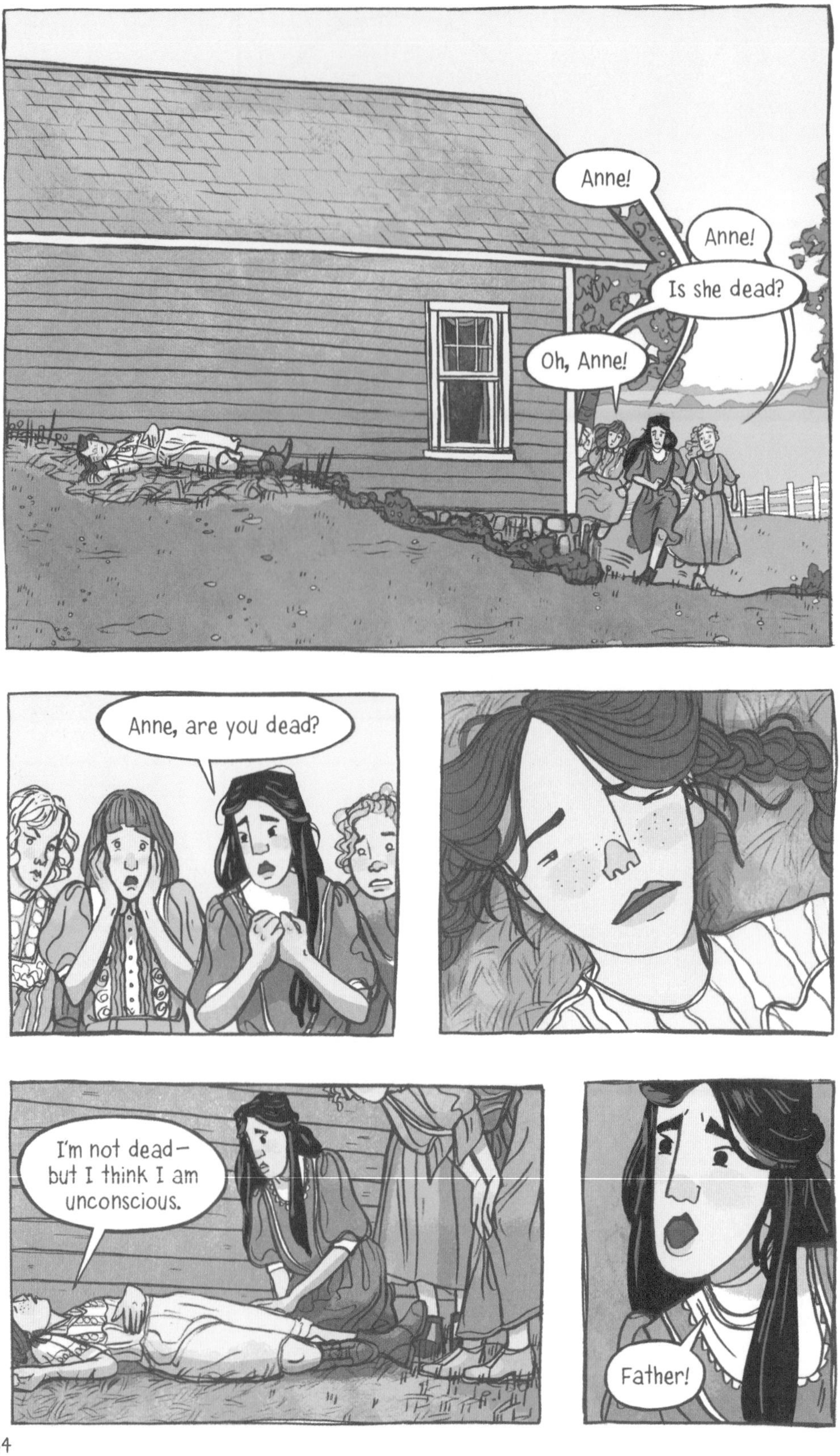
Anne!
Anne!
Is she dead?
Oh, Anne!
Anne, are you dead?
I'm not dead—but I think I am unconscious.
Father!

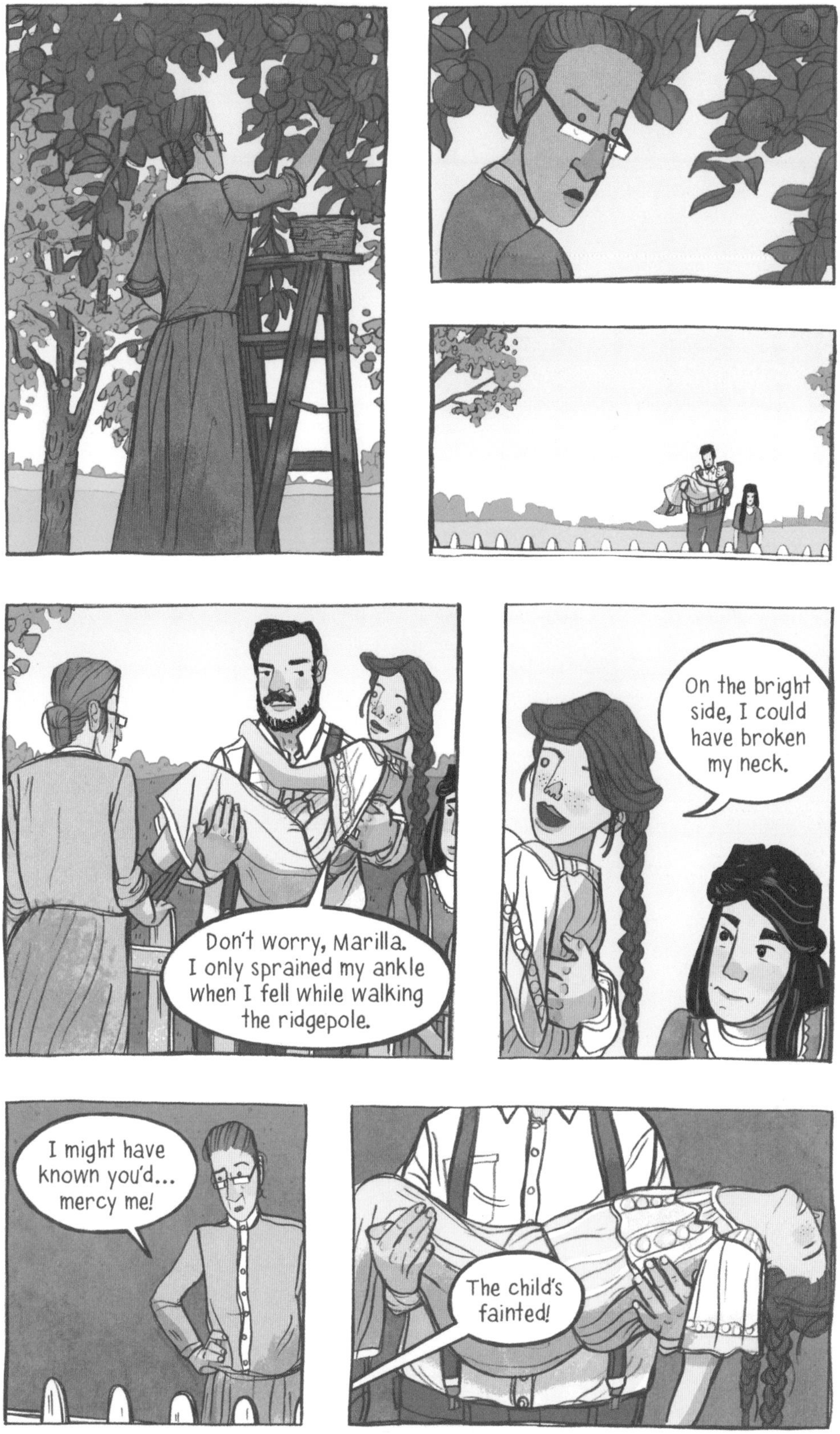
Don't worry, Marilla. I only sprained my ankle when I fell while walking the ridgepole.
On the bright side, I could have broken my neck.
I might have known you'd... mercy me!
The child's fainted!

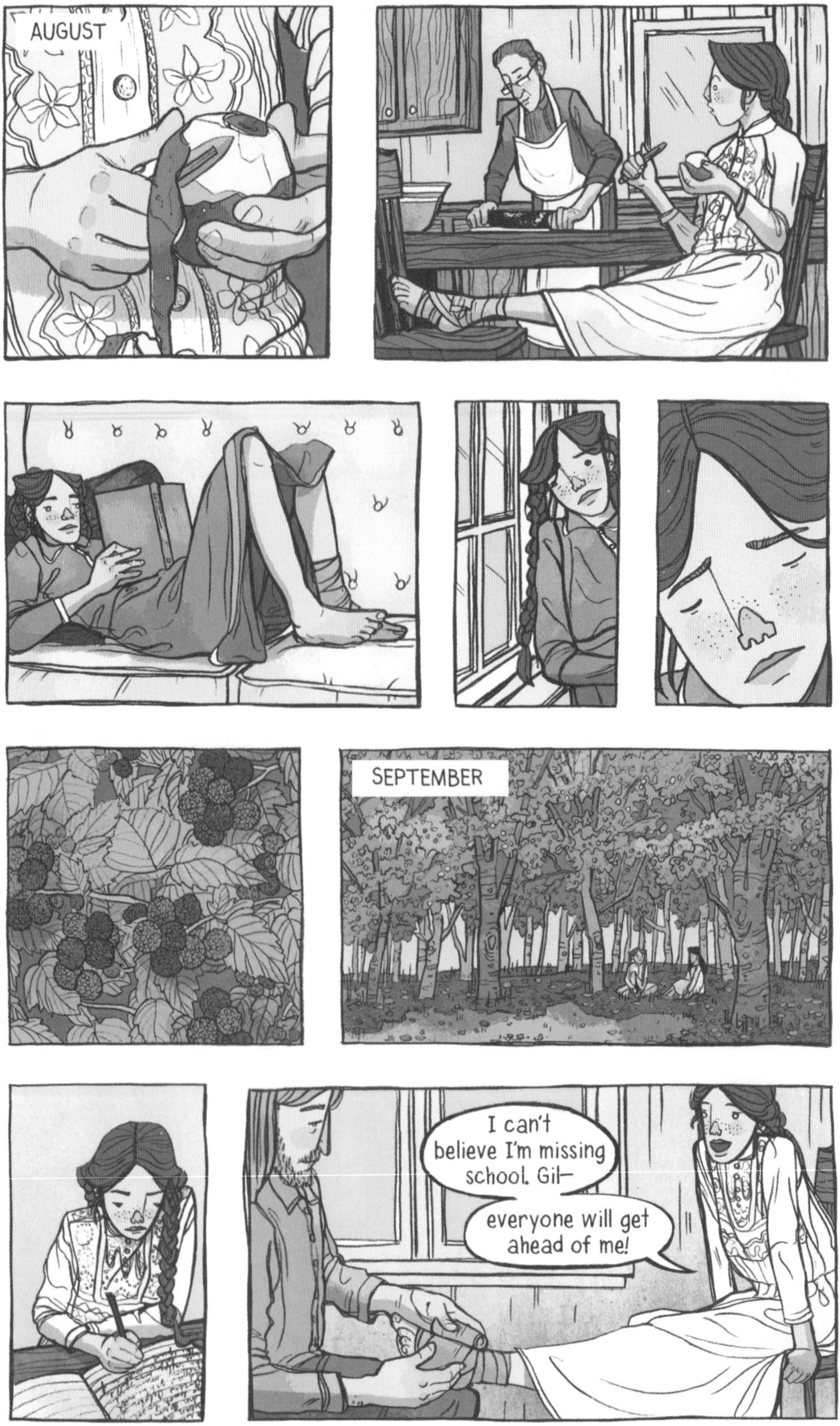
AUGUST
SEPTEMBER
I can't believe I'm missing school. Gil—
everyone will get ahead of me!

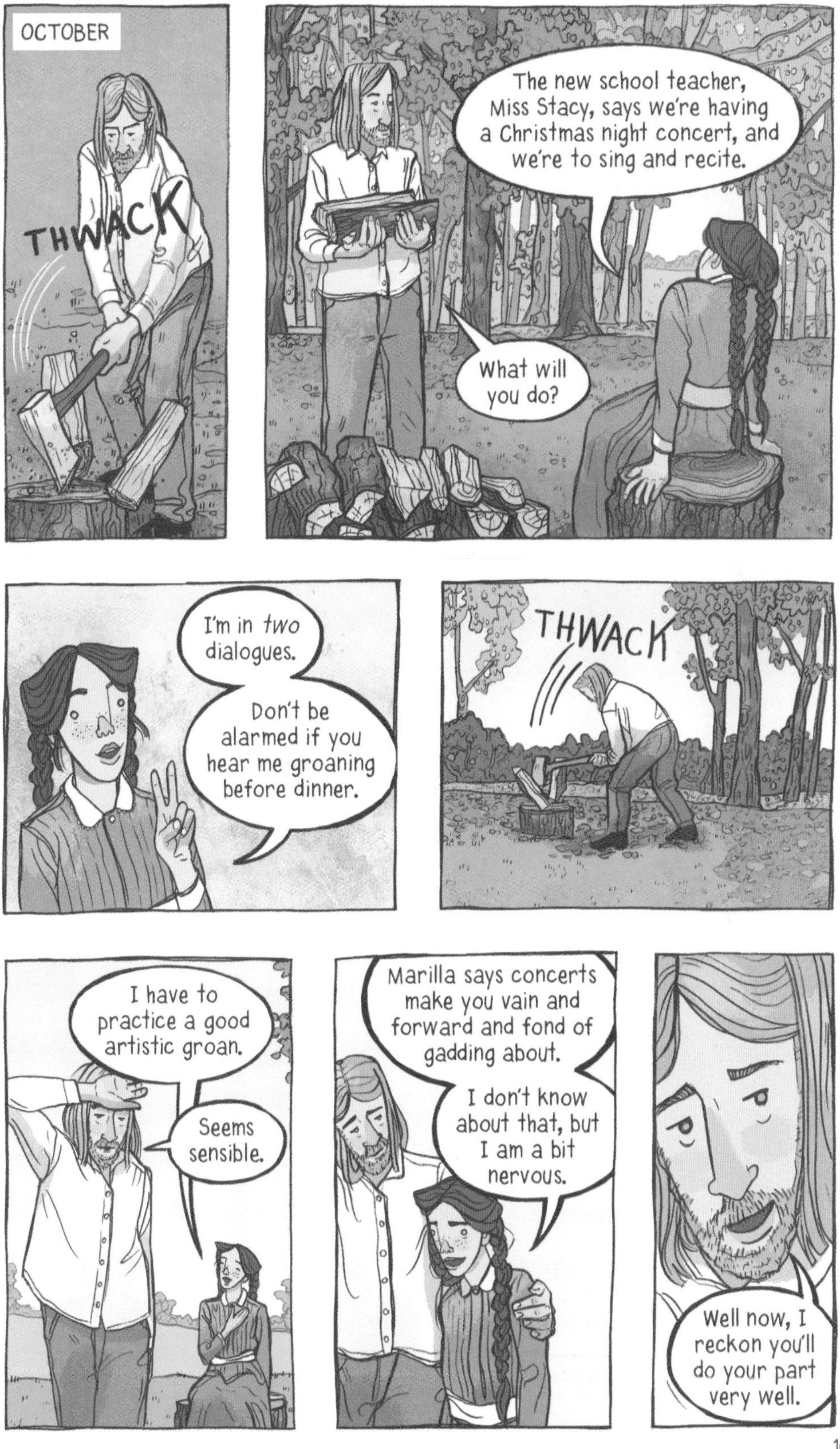
OCTOBER
THWACK
The new school teacher, Miss Stacy, says we're having a Christmas night concert, and we're to sing and recite.
What will you do?
I'm in *two* dialogues.
Don't be alarmed if you hear me groaning before dinner.
THWACK
I have to practice a good artistic groan.
Seems sensible.
Marilla says concerts make you vain and forward and fond of gadding about.
I don't know about that, but I am a bit nervous.
Well now, I reckon you'll do your part very well.

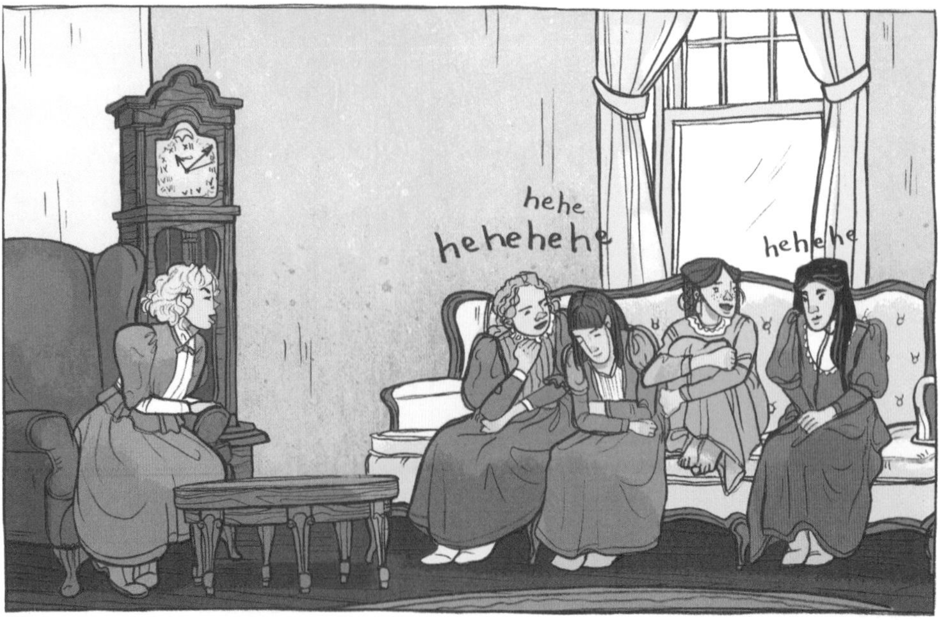
hehe
hehehehe
hehehe

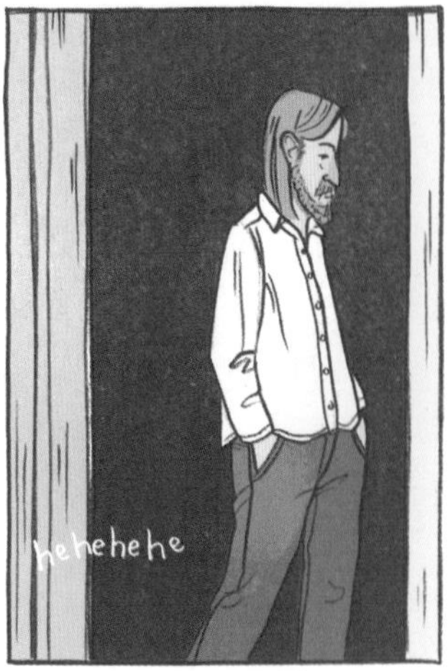
hehehehe

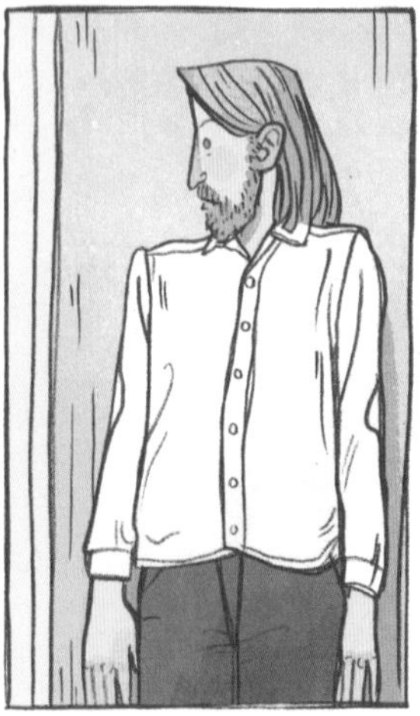

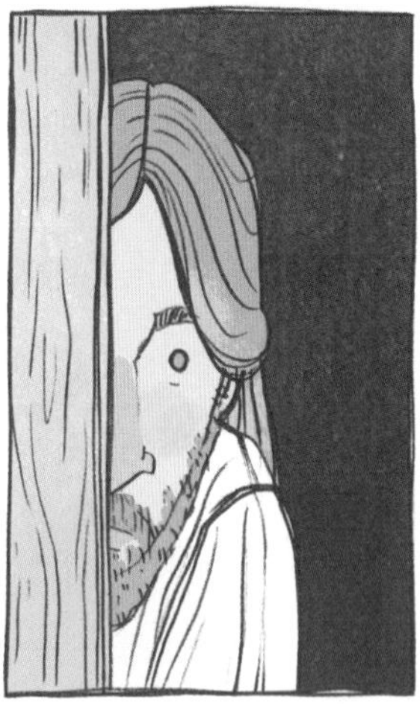

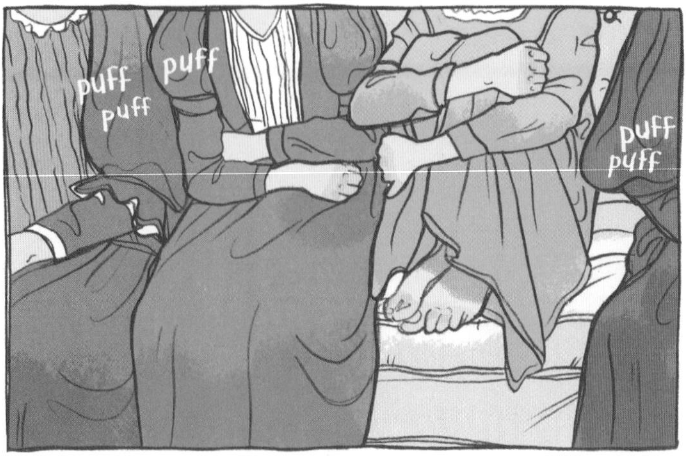
puff
puff
puff
puff
puff

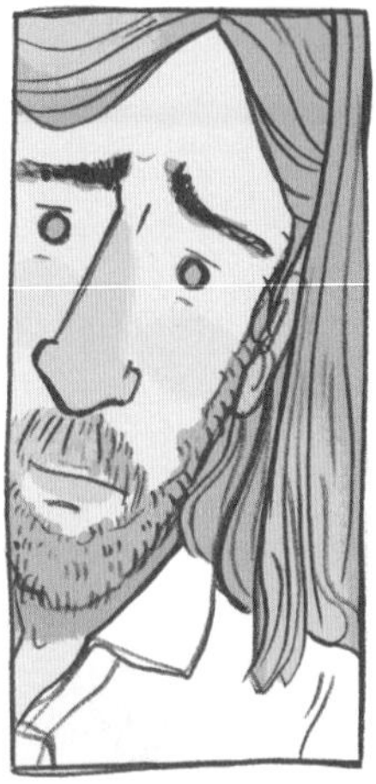

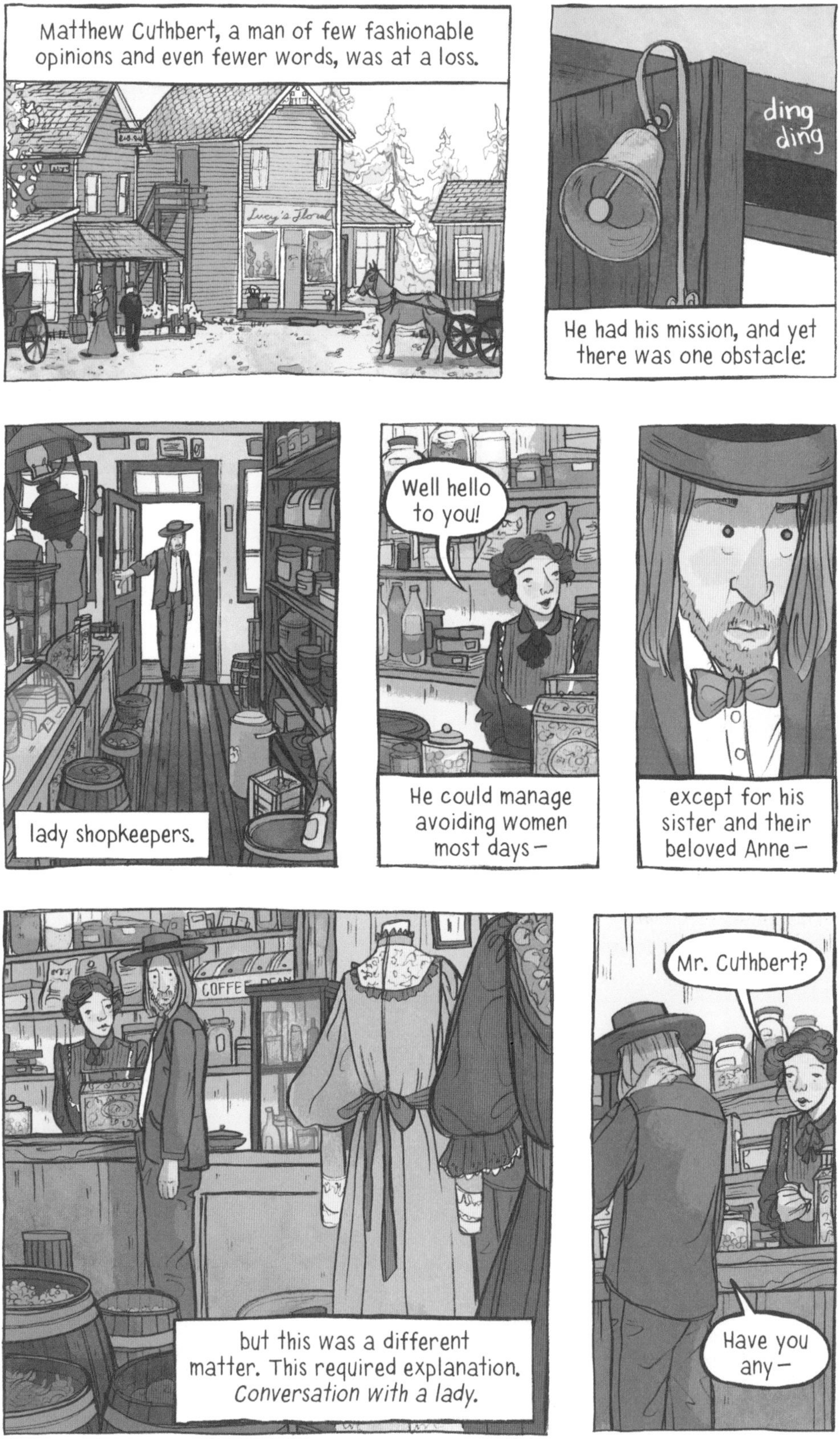
Matthew Cuthbert, a man of few fashionable opinions and even fewer words, was at a loss.
Lucy's Floral
ding ding
He had his mission, and yet there was one obstacle:
lady shopkeepers.
Well hello to you!
He could manage avoiding women most days—
except for his sister and their beloved Anne—
COFFEE
but this was a different matter. This required explanation. *Conversation with a lady.*
Mr. Cuthbert?
Have you any—

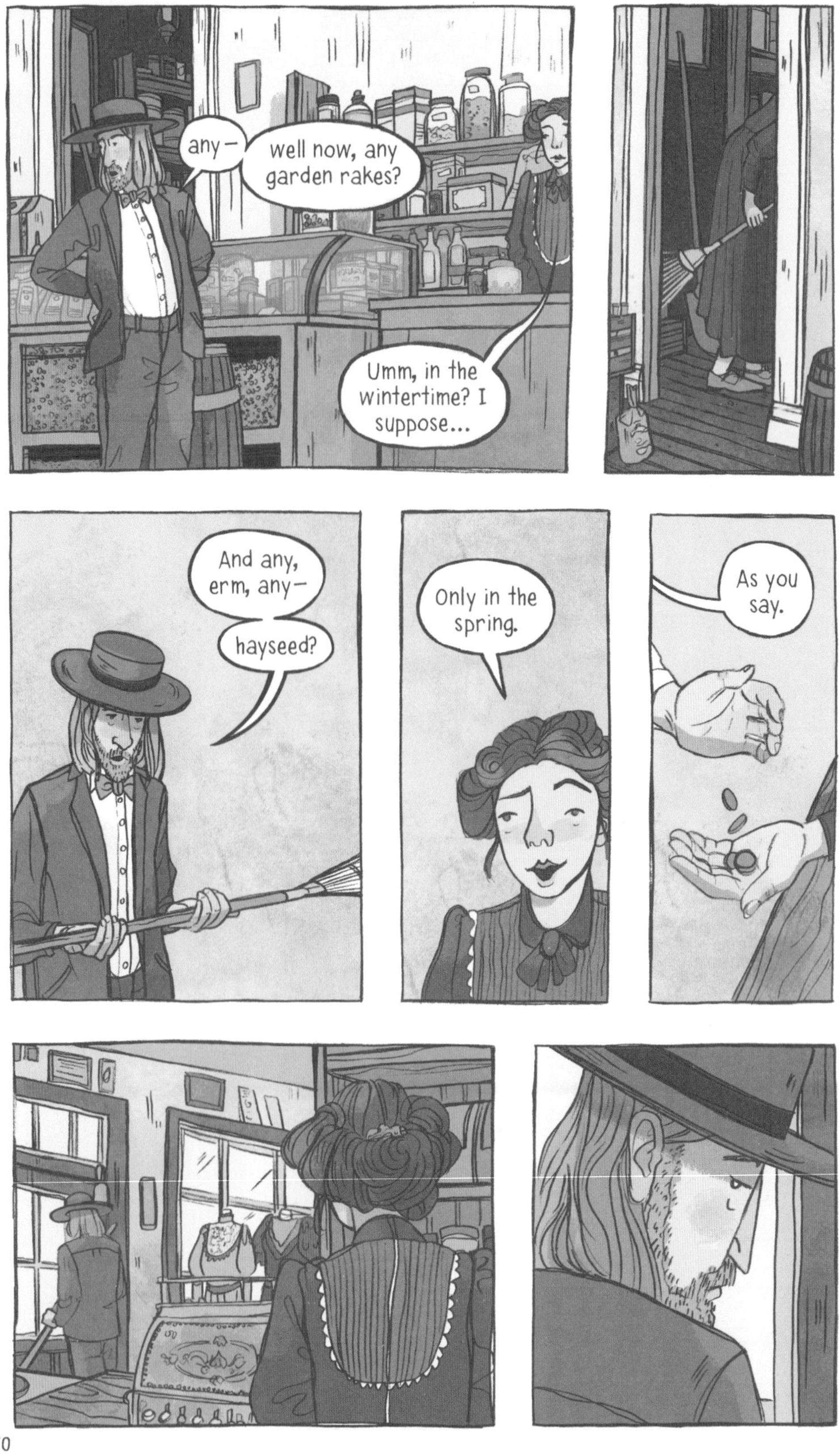
any—
well now, any garden rakes?
Umm, in the wintertime? I suppose...
And any, erm, any—
hayseed?
Only in the spring.
As you say.

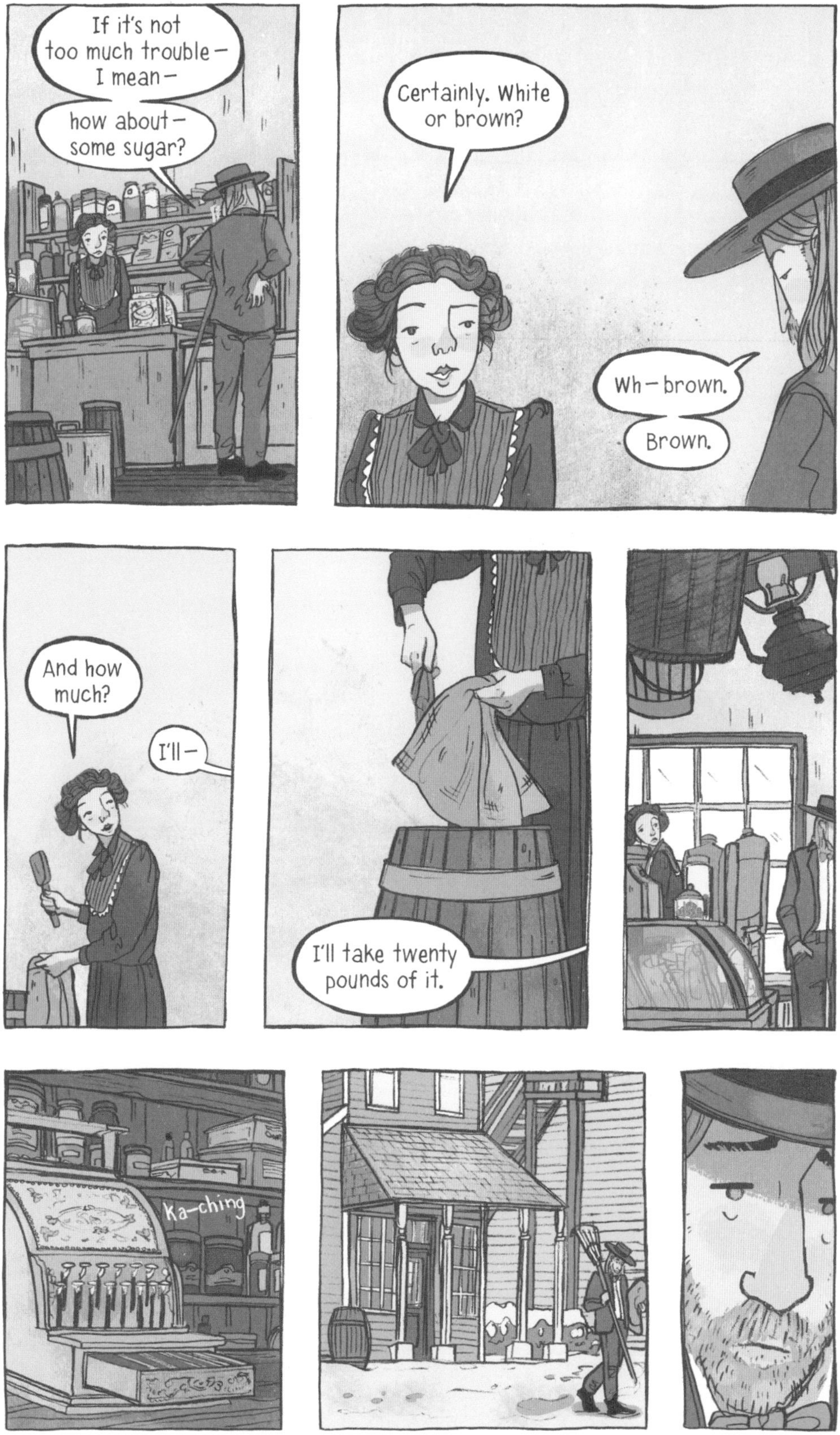

If it's not too much trouble— I mean—
how about— some sugar?
Certainly. White or brown?
Wh—brown.
Brown.
And how much?
I'll—
I'll take twenty pounds of it.
Ka-ching

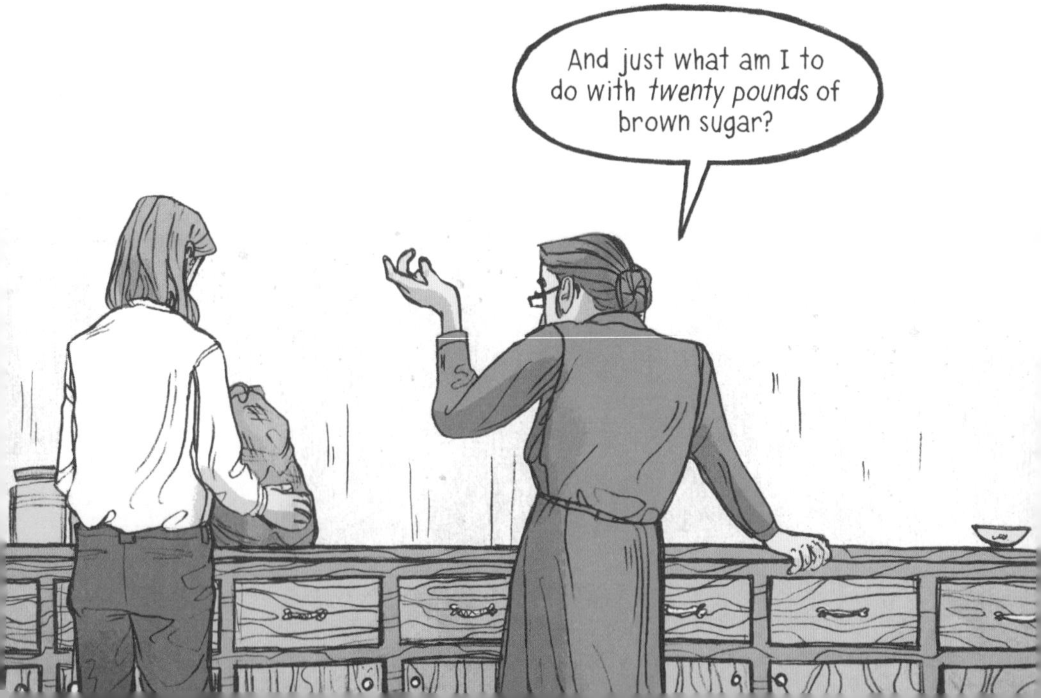
And just what am I to do with *twenty pounds* of brown sugar?

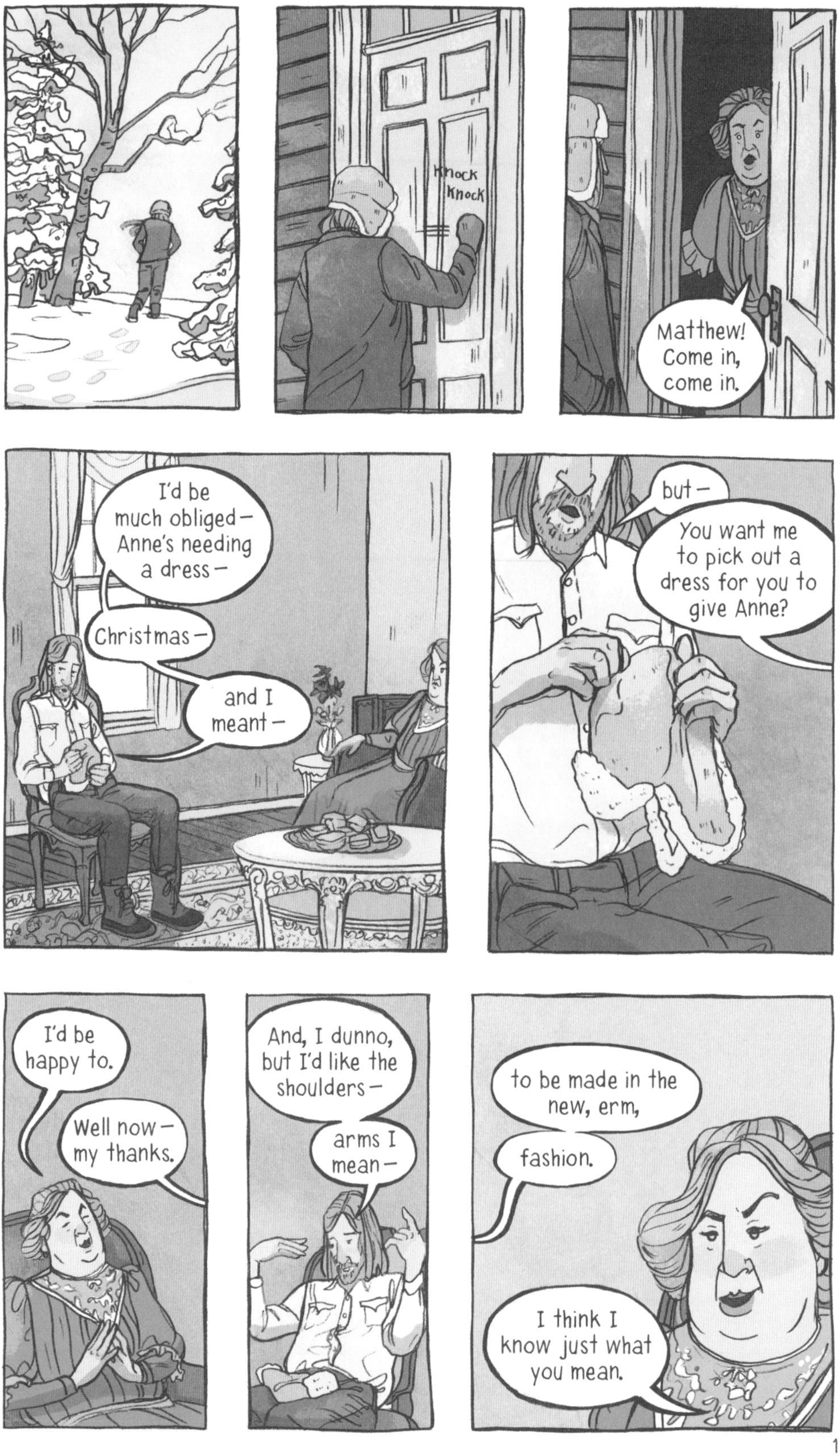
Knock
Knock
Matthew! Come in, come in.
I'd be much obliged— Anne's needing a dress—
Christmas—
and I meant—
but—
You want me to pick out a dress for you to give Anne?
I'd be happy to.
Well now— my thanks.
And, I dunno, but I'd like the shoulders—
arms I mean—
to be made in the new, erm,
fashion.
I think I know just what you mean.

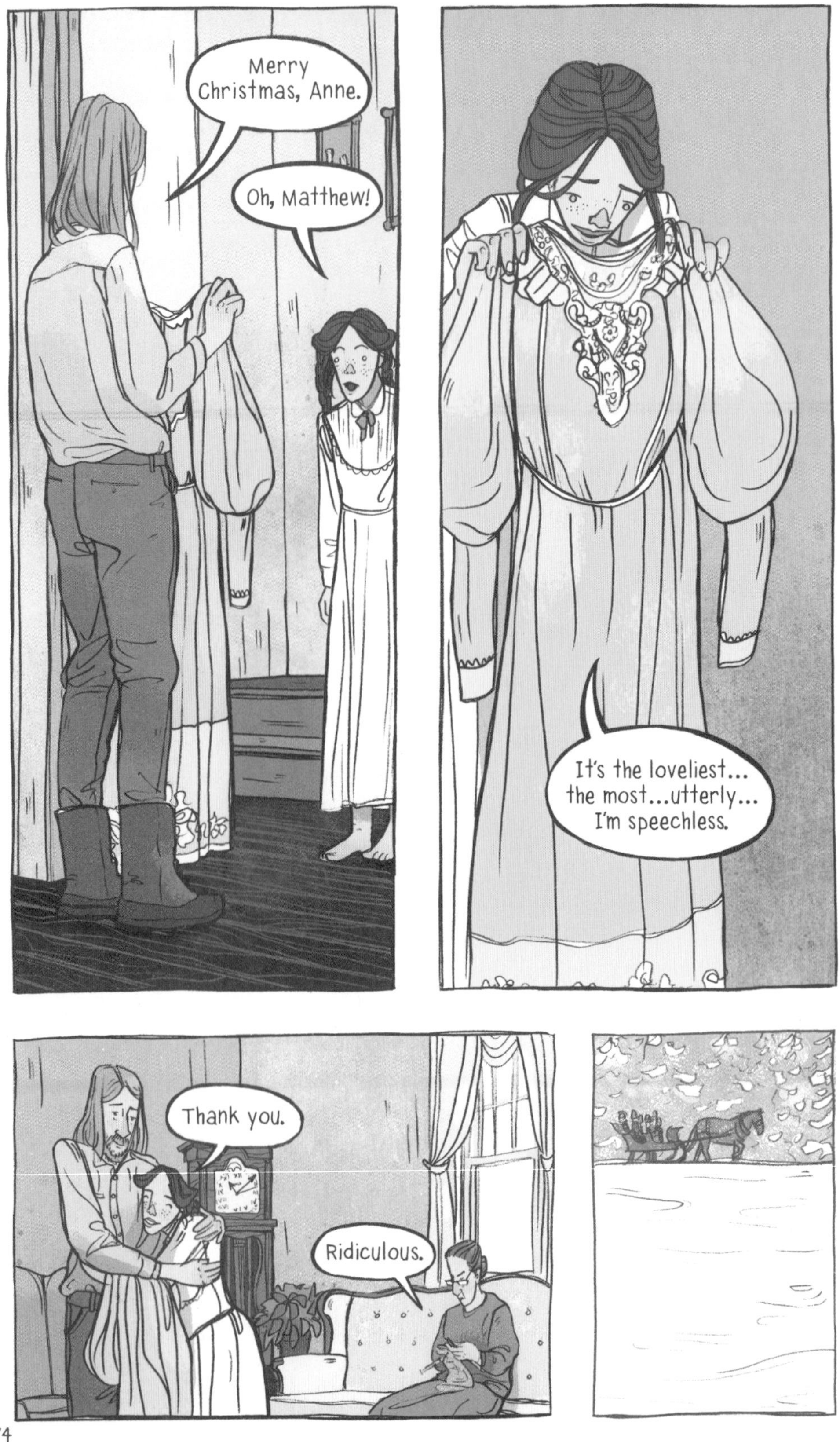
Merry Christmas, Anne.
Oh, Matthew!
It's the loveliest... the most...utterly... I'm speechless.
Thank you.
Ridiculous.

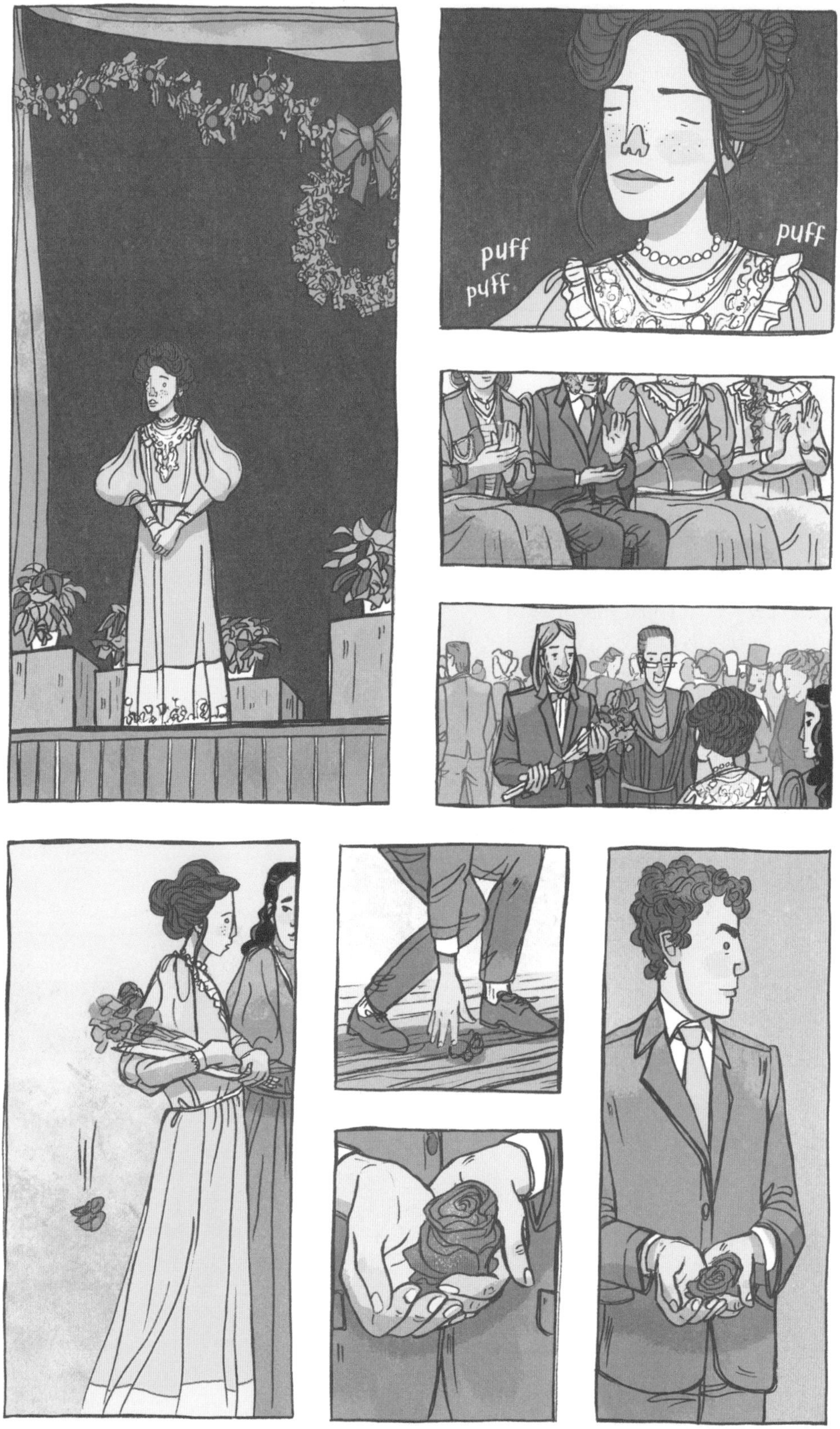
puff
puff
puff

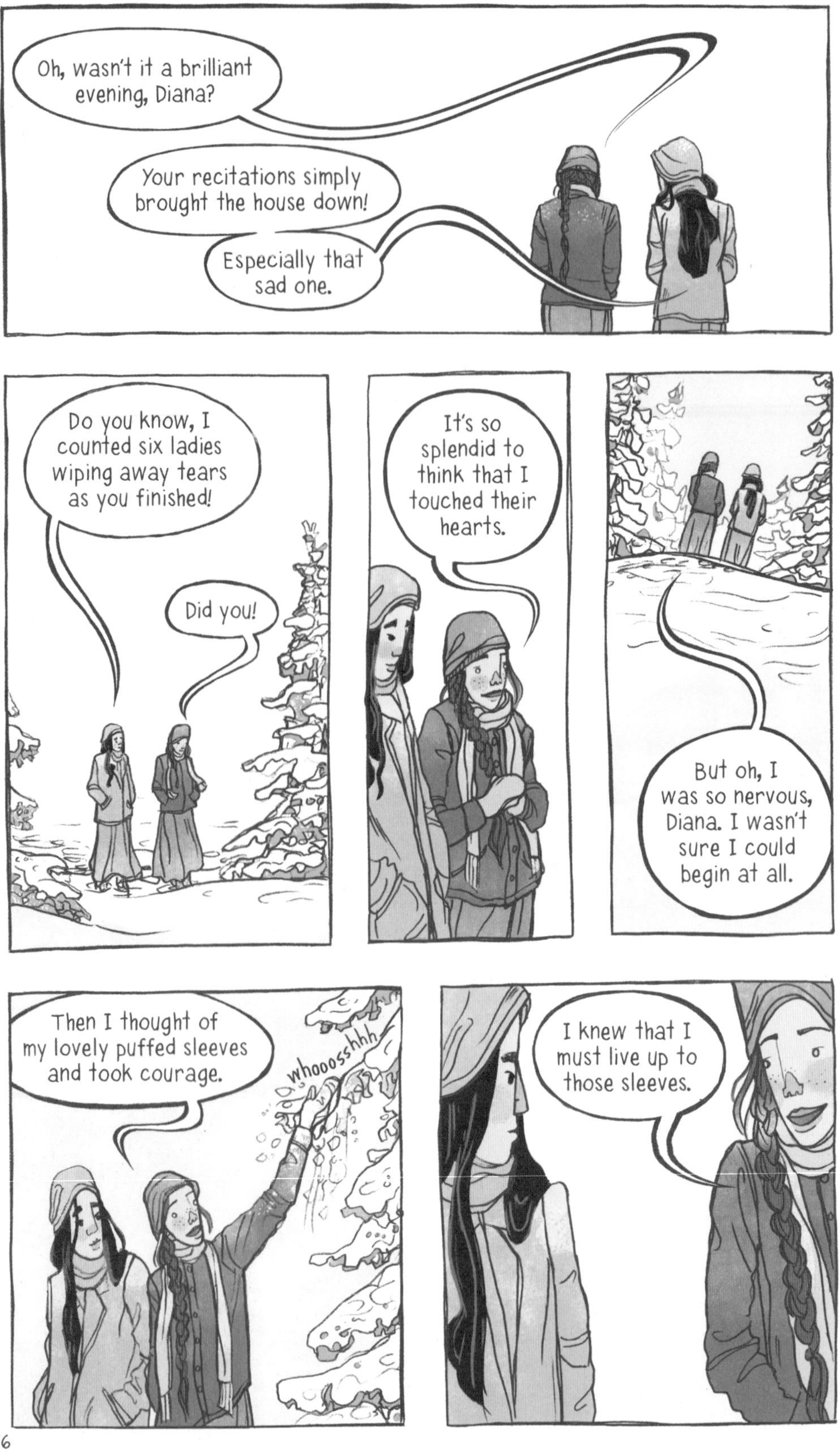
Oh, wasn't it a brilliant evening, Diana?
Your recitations simply brought the house down!
Especially that sad one.
Do you know, I counted six ladies wiping away tears as you finished!
Did you!
It's so splendid to think that I touched their hearts.
But oh, I was so nervous, Diana. I wasn't sure I could begin at all.
Then I thought of my lovely puffed sleeves and took courage.
whhoosshhh
I knew that I must live up to those sleeves.

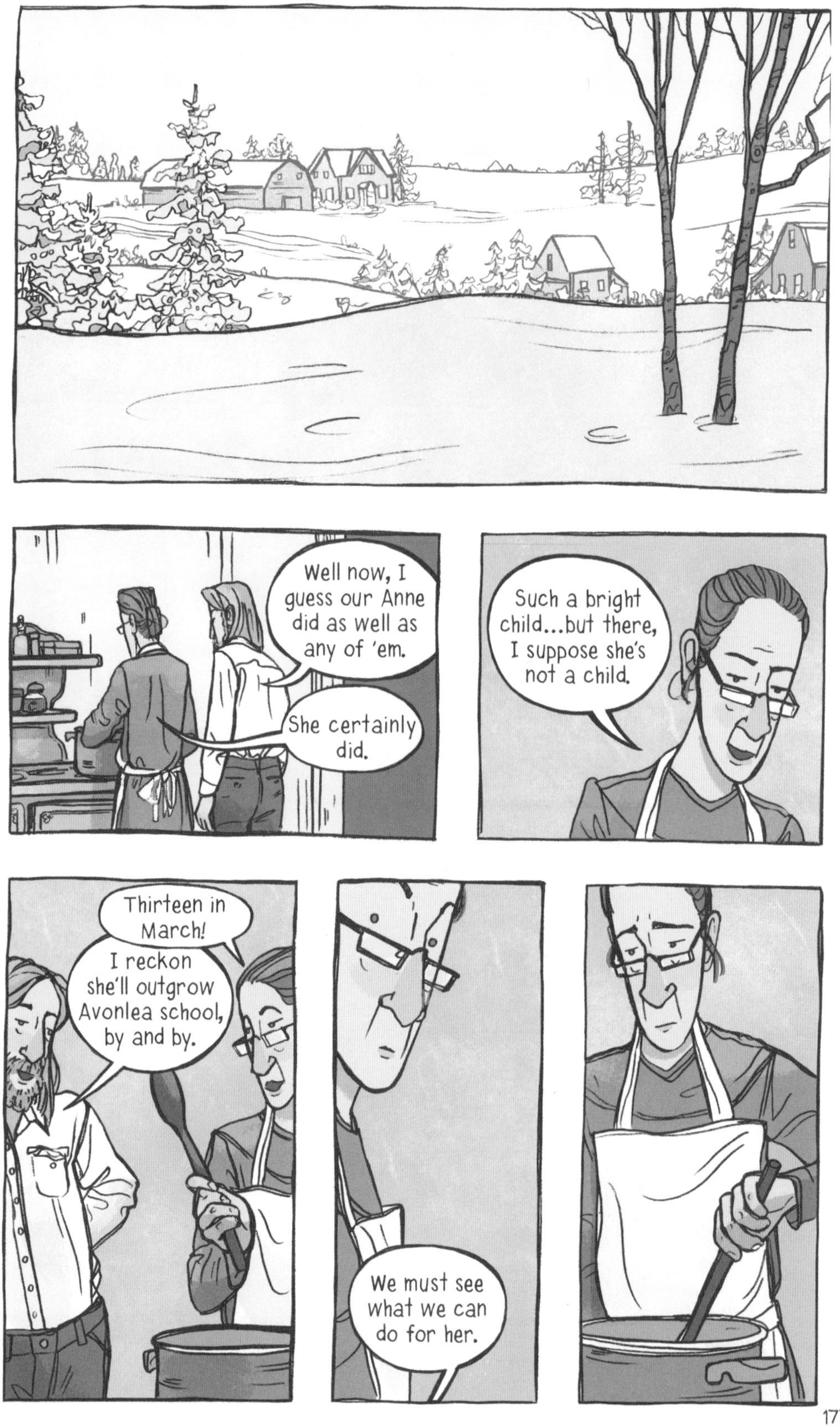
Well now, I guess our Anne did as well as any of 'em.
She certainly did.
Such a bright child...but there, I suppose she's not a child.
Thirteen in March!
I reckon she'll outgrow Avonlea school, by and by.
We must see what we can do for her.

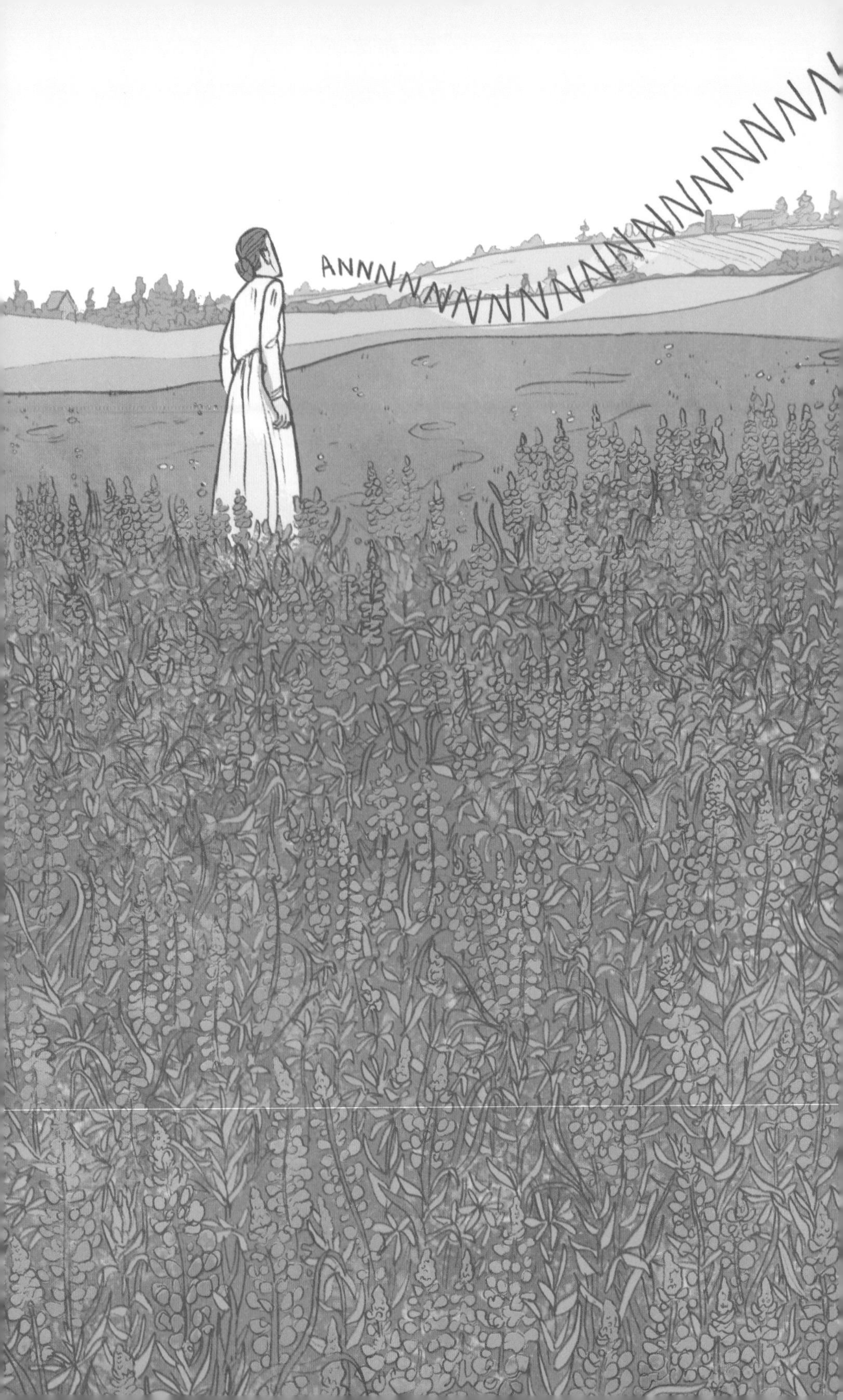
ANNNNNNNNNNNNNNNNNNNNNN

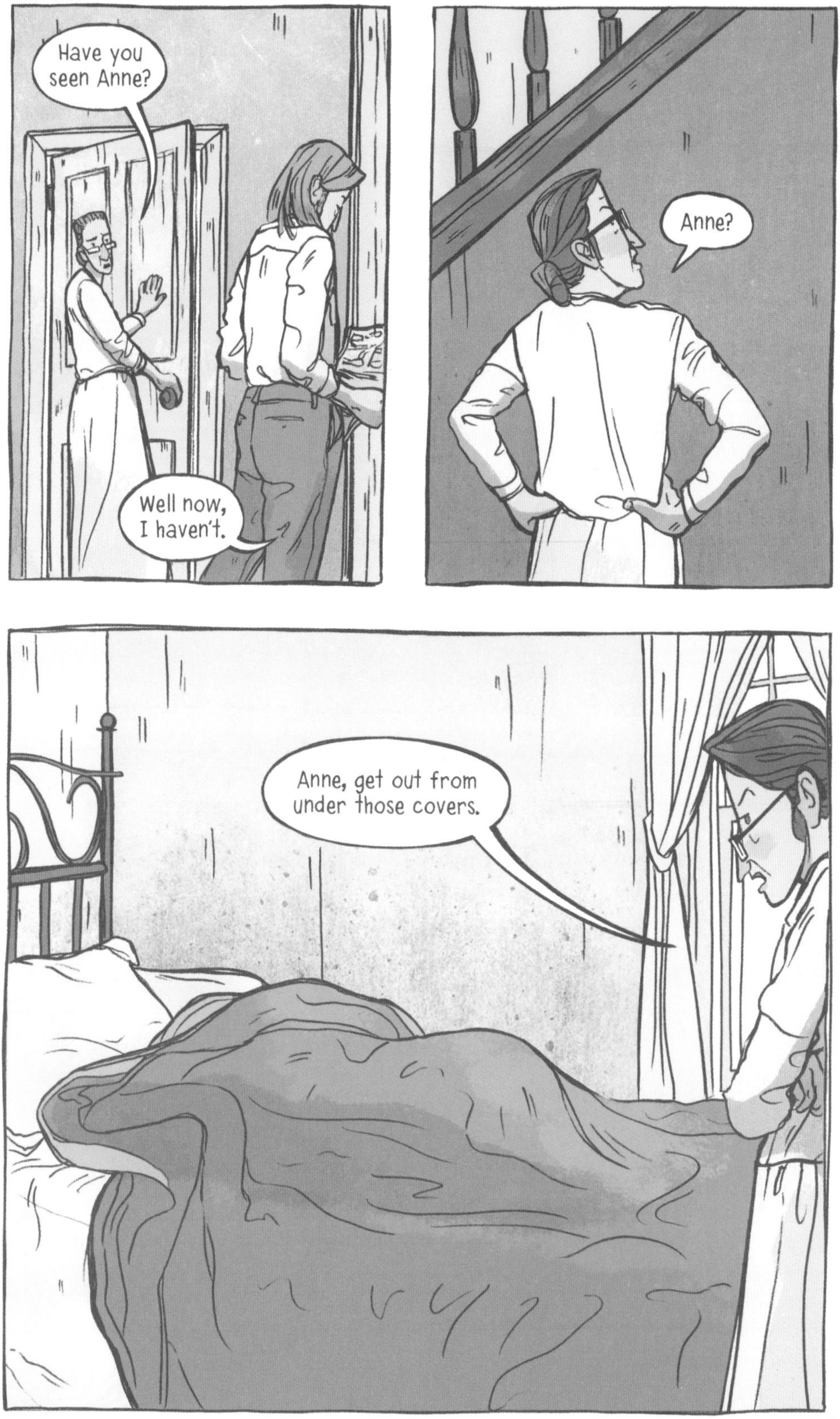
Have you seen Anne?
Well now, I haven't.
Anne?
Anne, get out from under those covers.

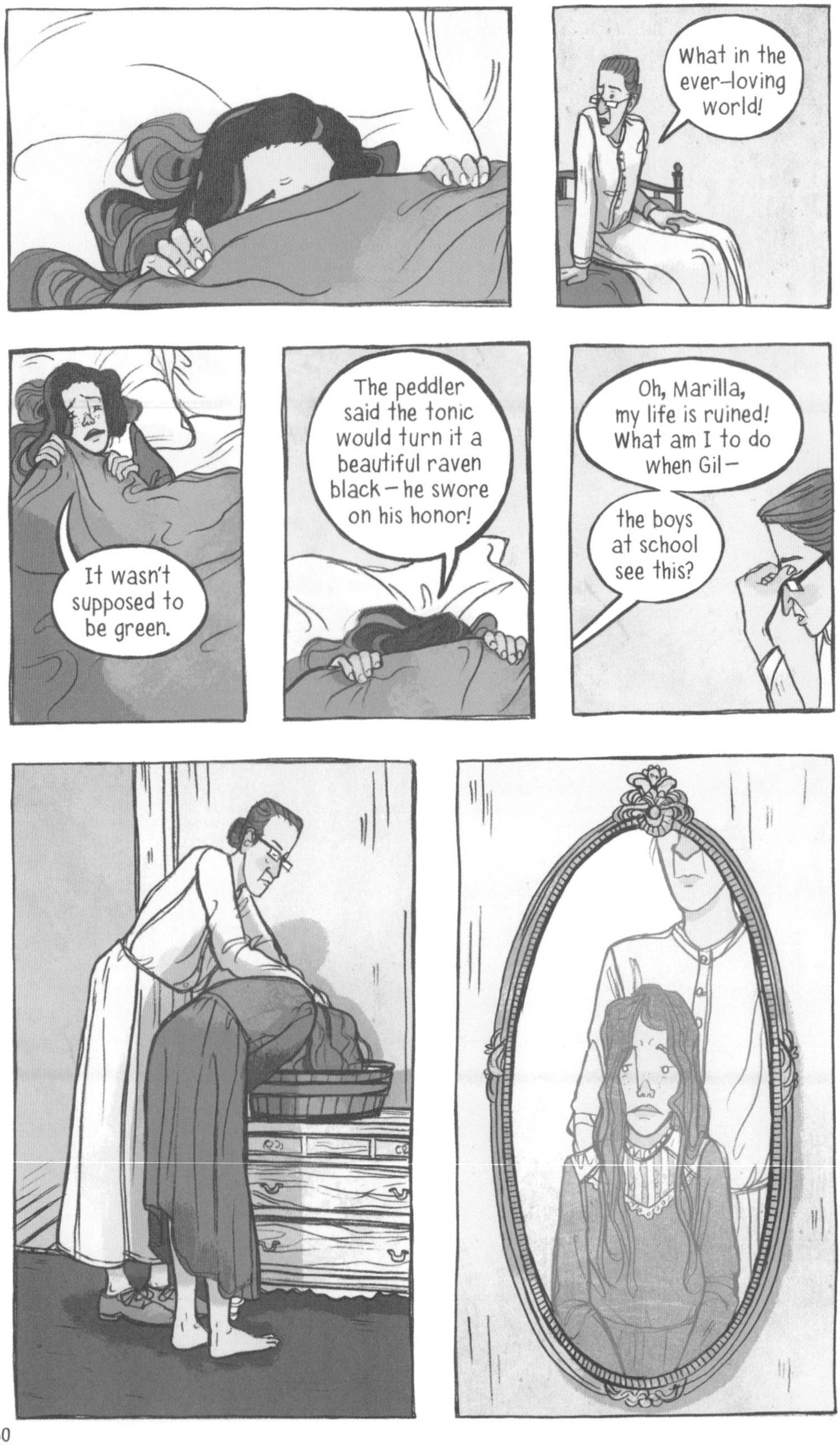
What in the ever-loving world!
It wasn't supposed to be green.
The peddler said the tonic would turn it a beautiful raven black—he swore on his honor!
Oh, Marilla, my life is ruined! What am I to do when Gil—
the boys at school see this?

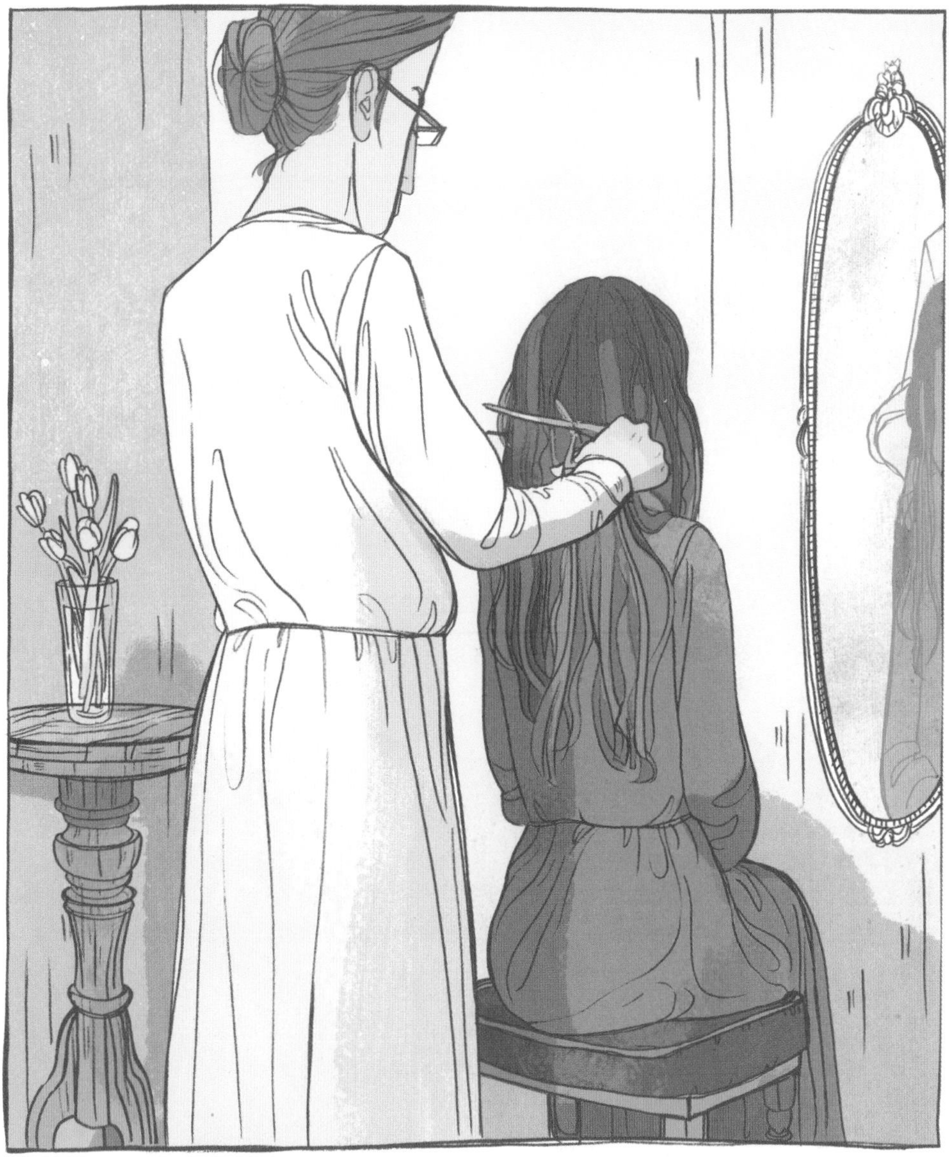

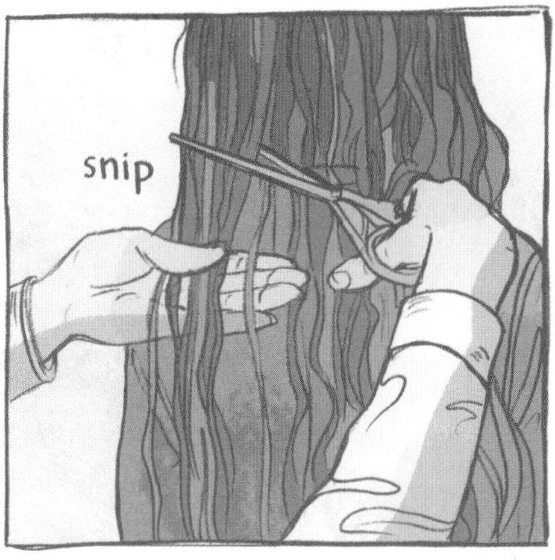
snip

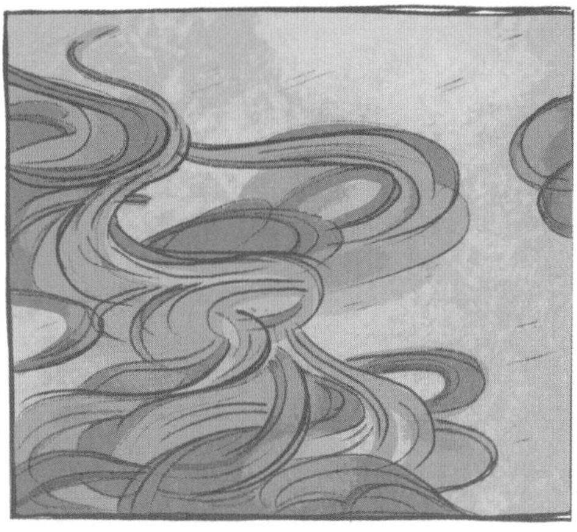

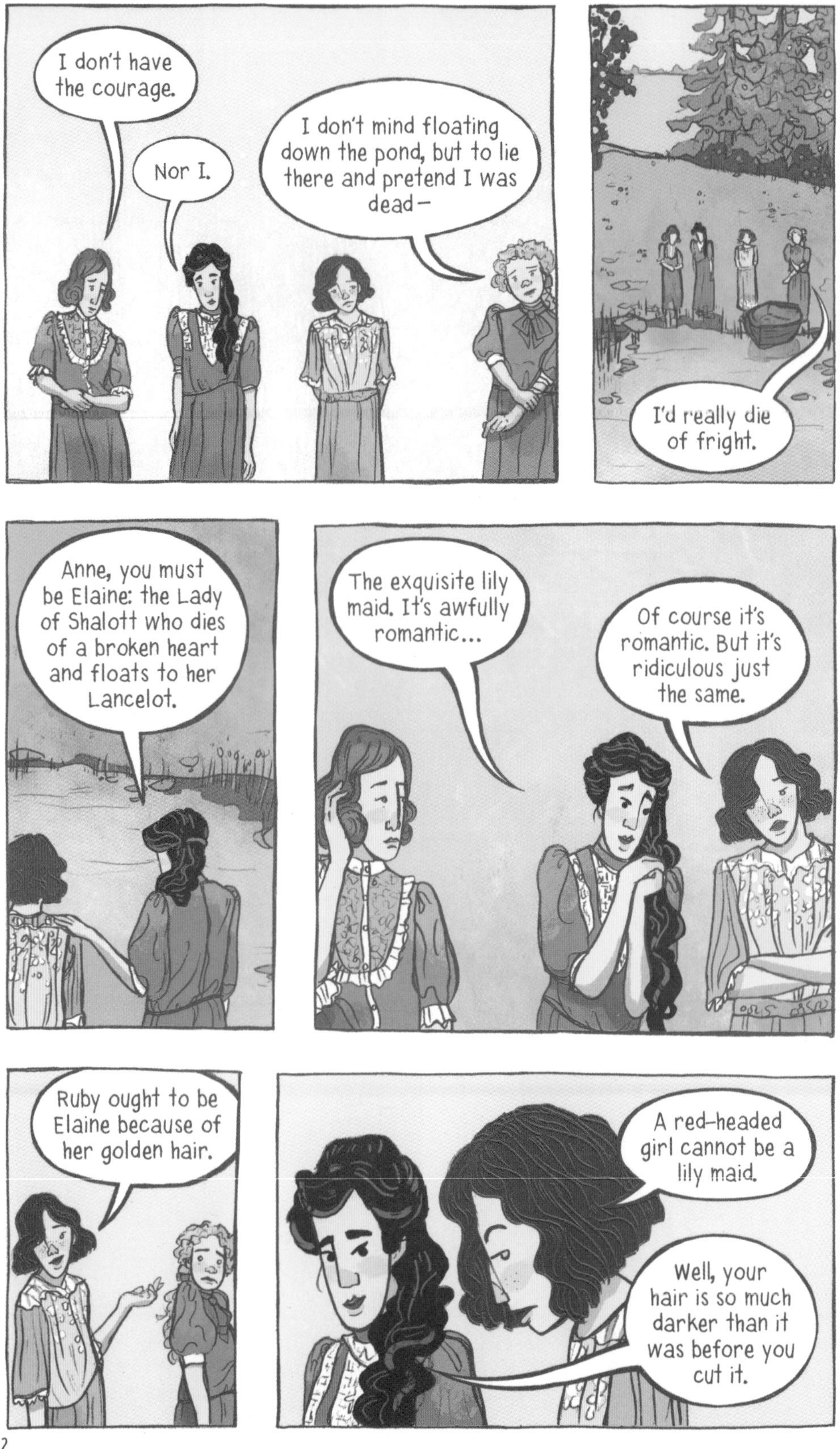
I don't have the courage.
Nor I.
I don't mind floating down the pond, but to lie there and pretend I was dead–
I'd really die of fright.
Anne, you must be Elaine: the Lady of Shalott who dies of a broken heart and floats to her Lancelot.
The exquisite lily maid. It's awfully romantic...
Of course it's romantic. But it's ridiculous just the same.
Ruby ought to be Elaine because of her golden hair.
A red-headed girl cannot be a lily maid.
Well, your hair is so much darker than it was before you cut it.

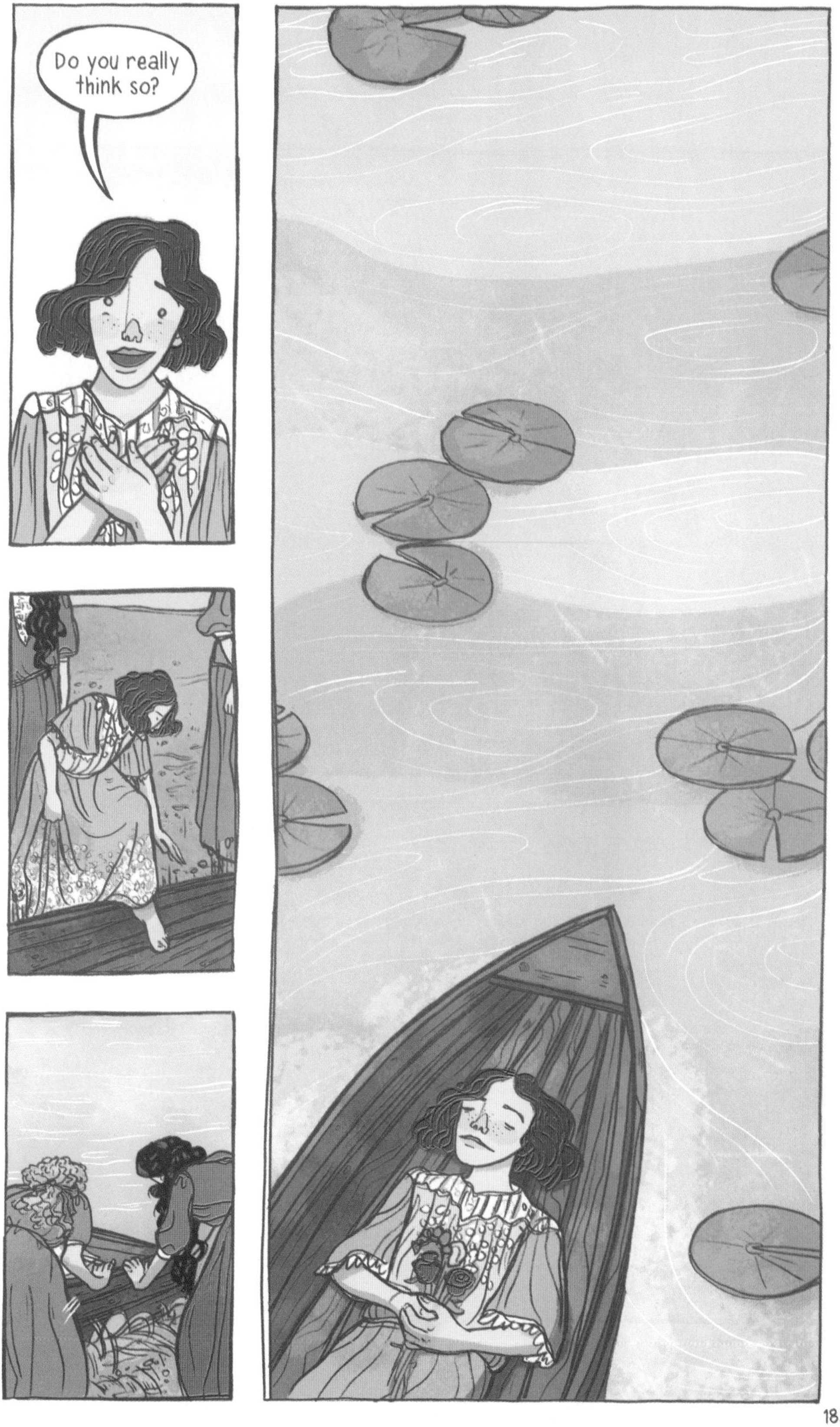
Do you really think so?

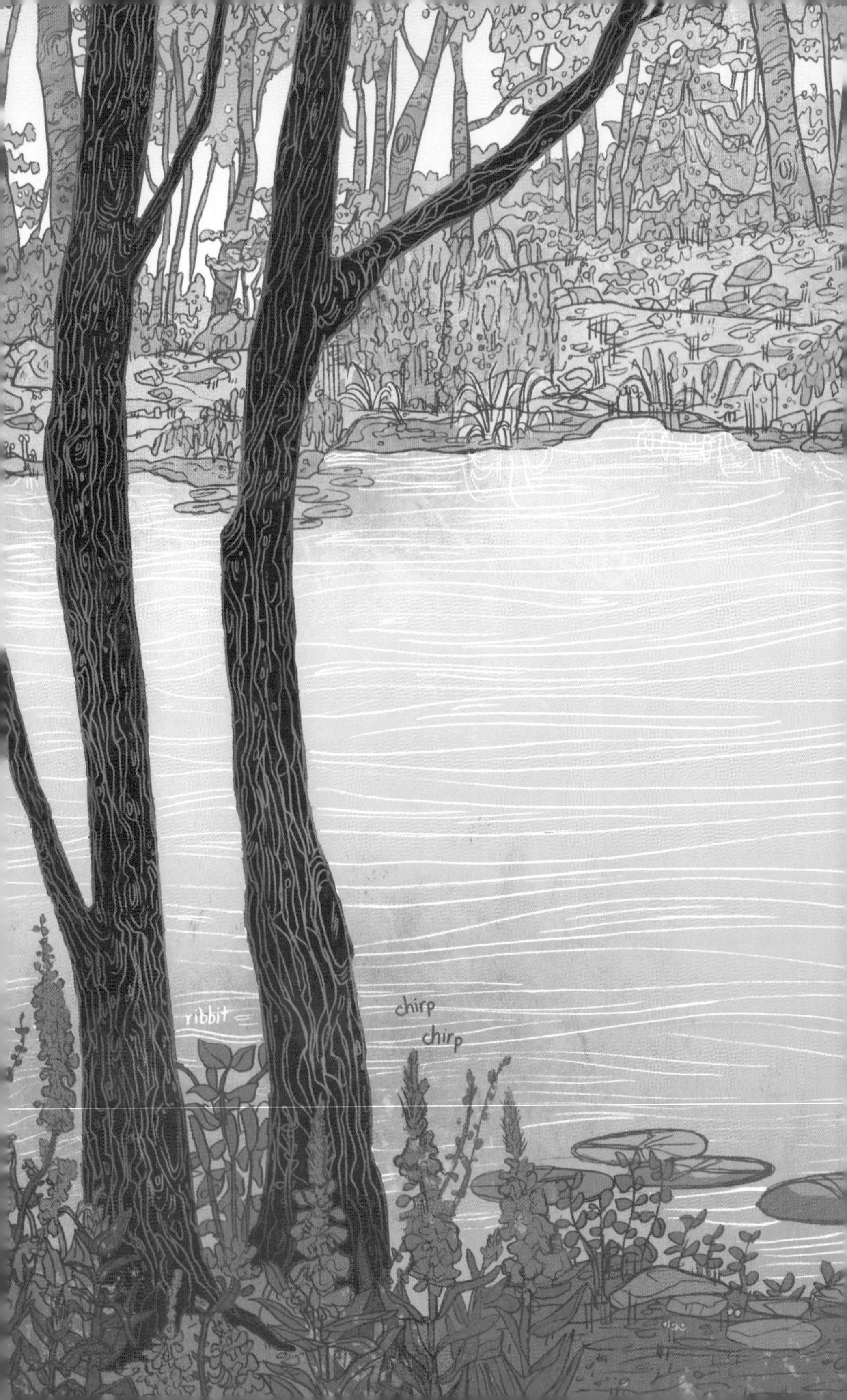
ribbit
chirp
chirp

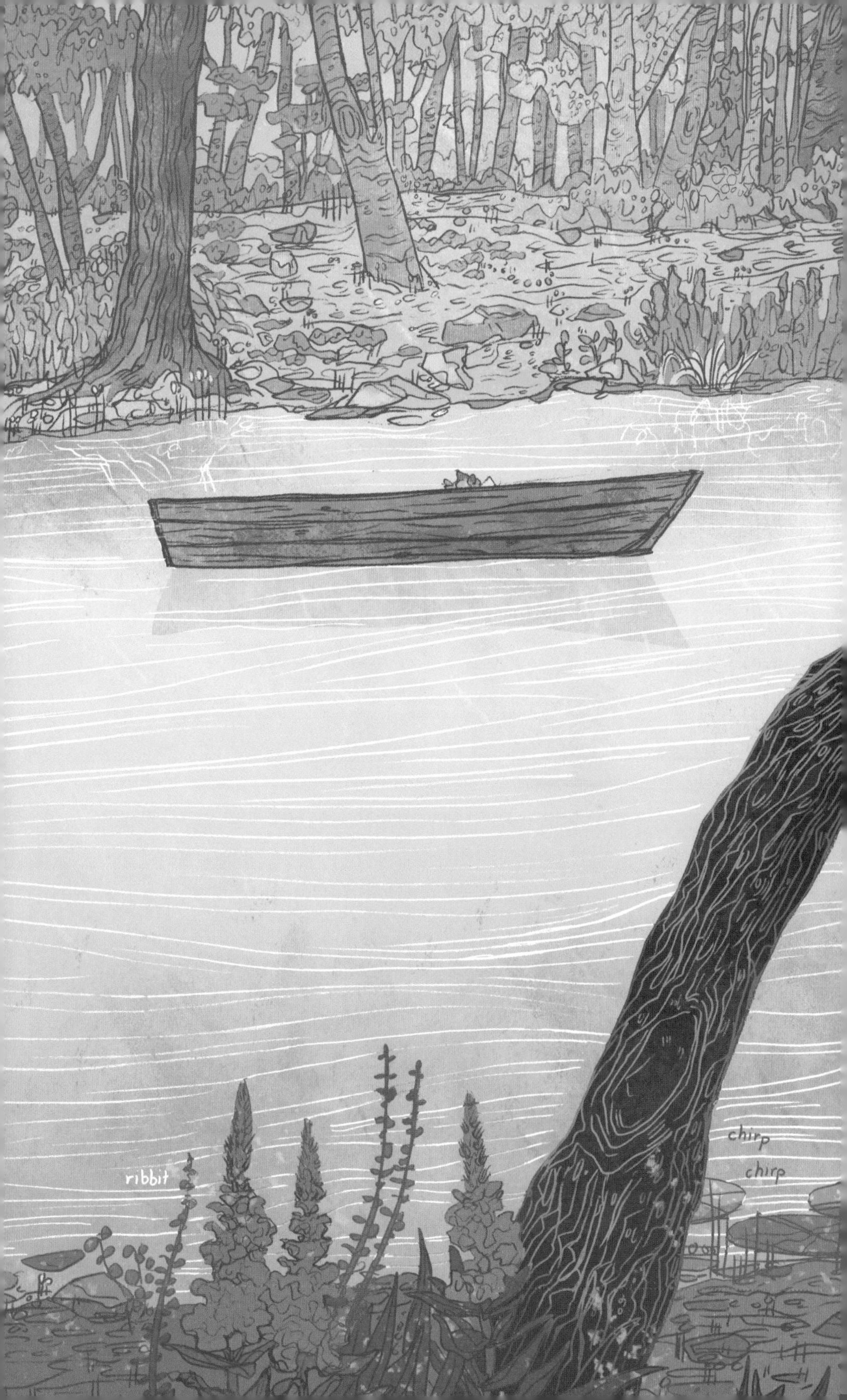
ribbit
chirp
chirp

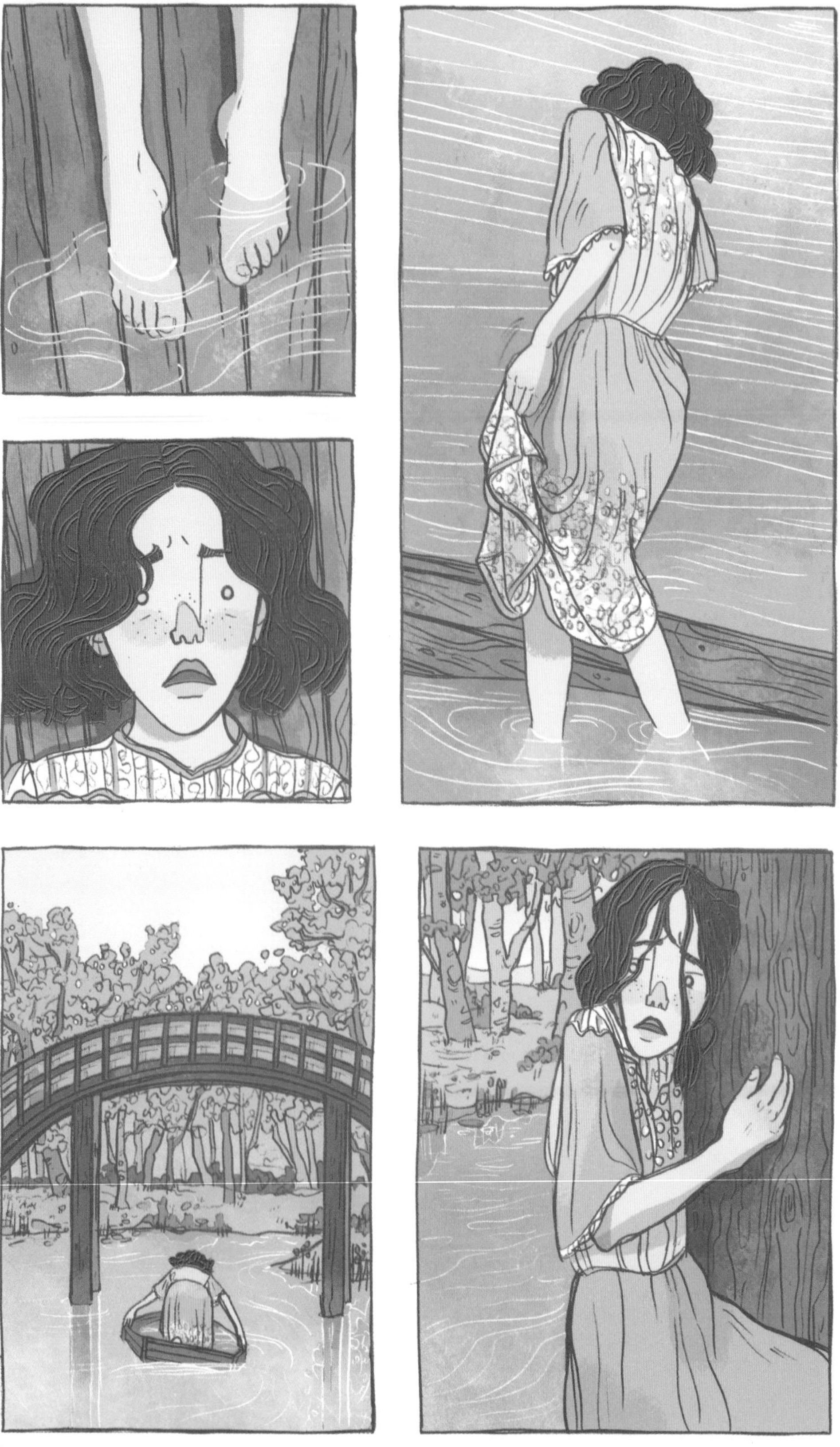

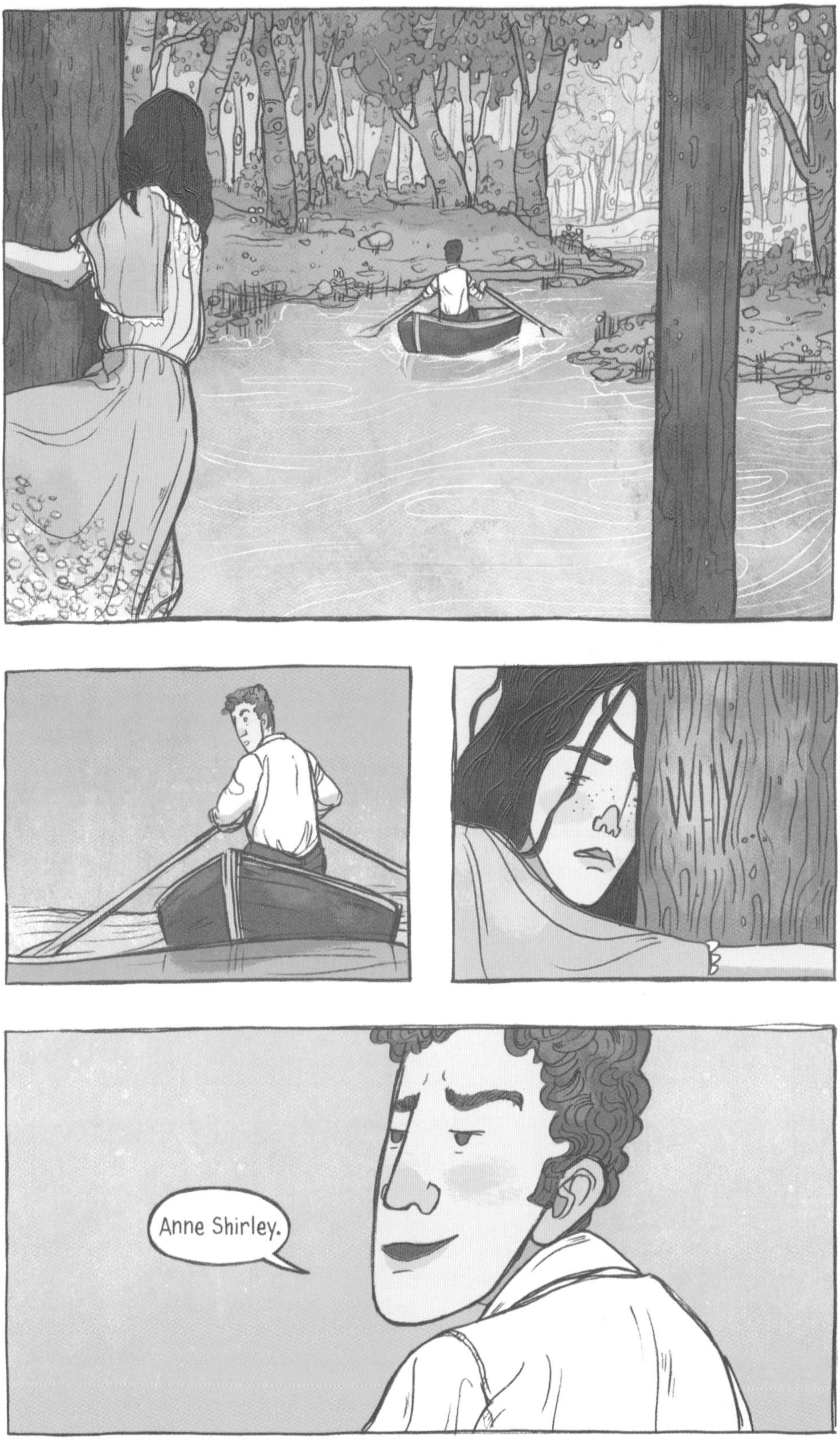
WHY
Anne Shirley.

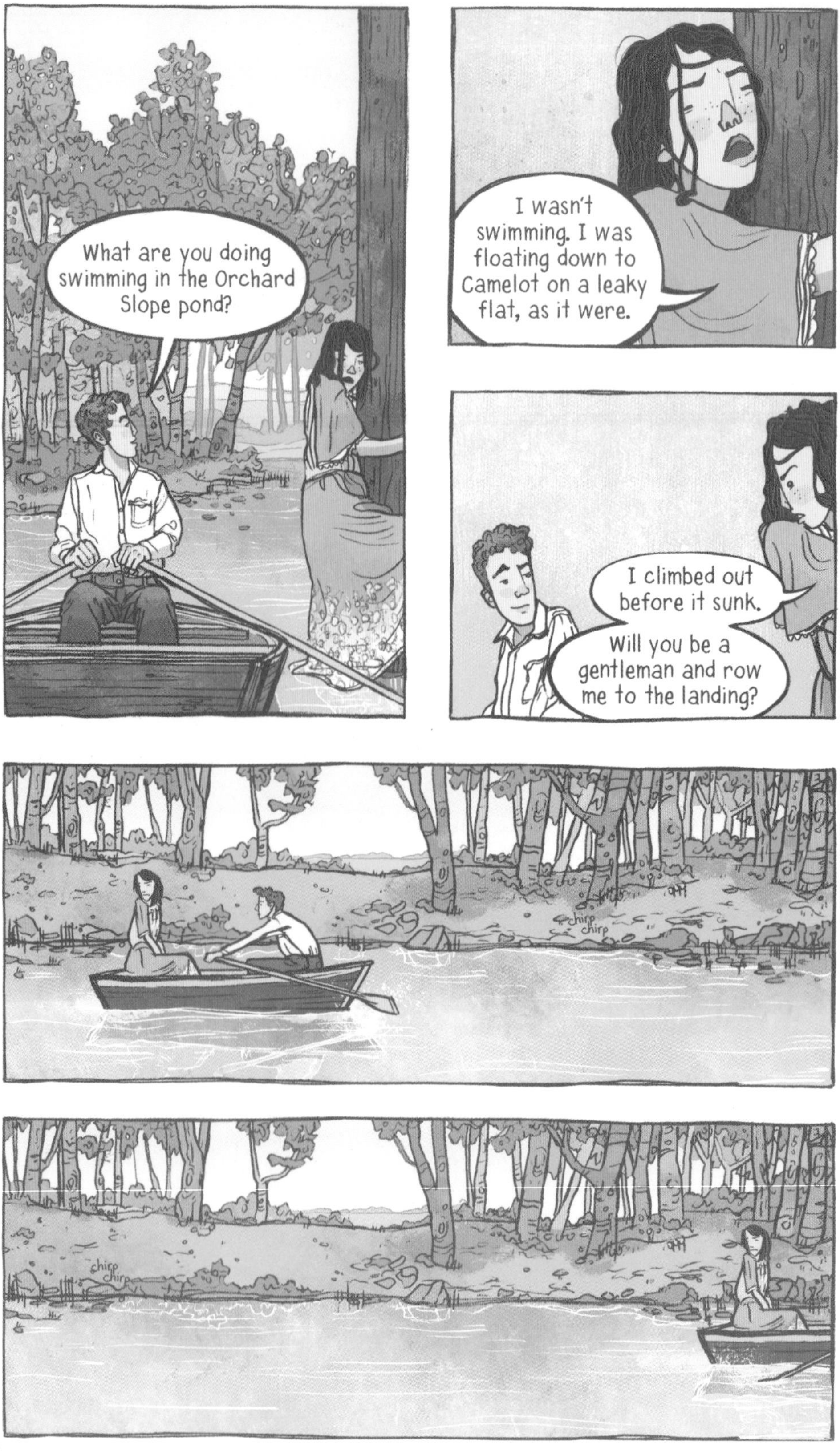
What are you doing swimming in the Orchard Slope pond?
I wasn't swimming. I was floating down to Camelot on a leaky flat, as it were.
I climbed out before it sunk.
Will you be a gentleman and row me to the landing?
chirp chirp
chirp chirp

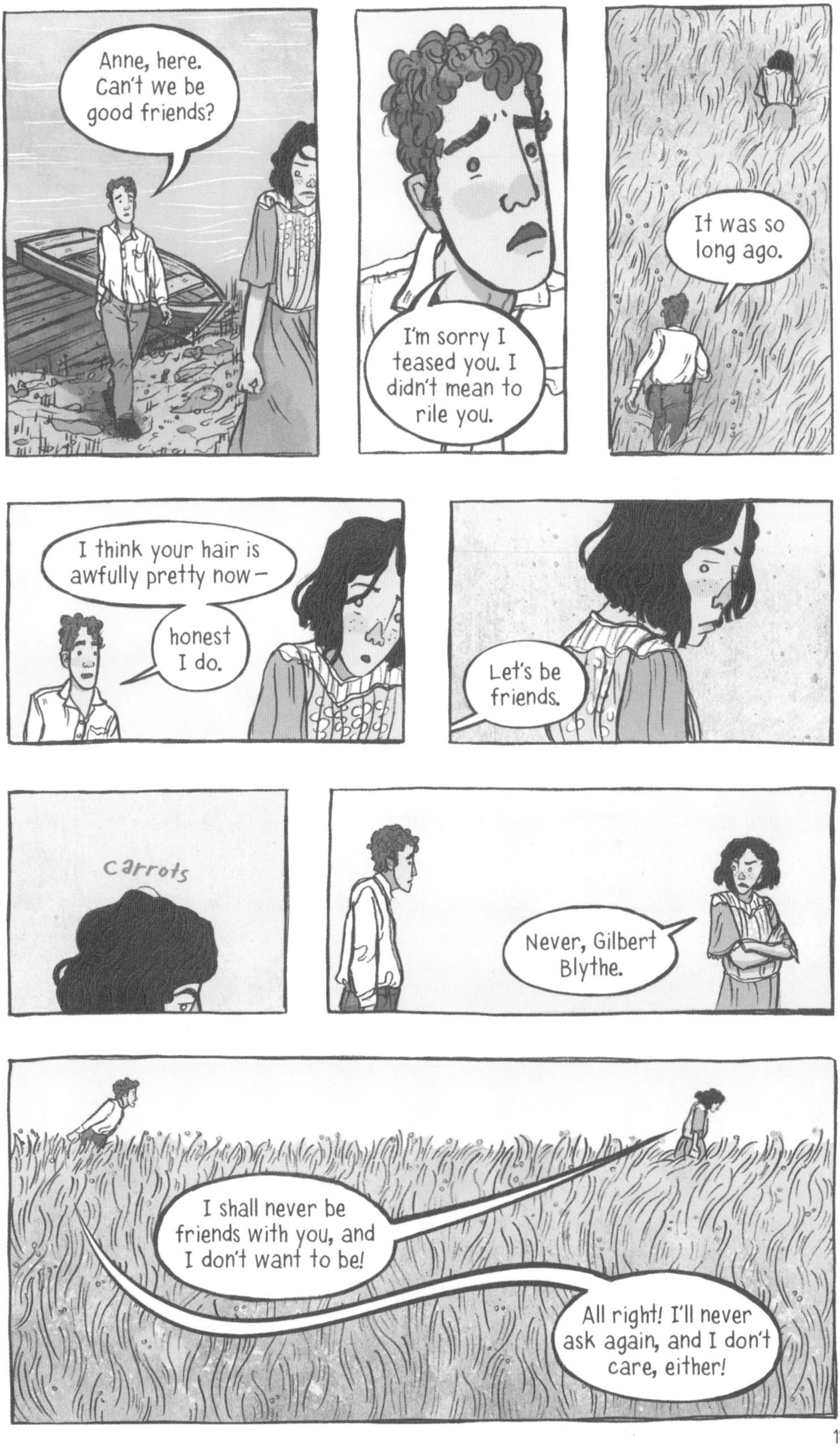
Anne, here. Can't we be good friends?
I'm sorry I teased you. I didn't mean to rile you.
It was so long ago.
I think your hair is awfully pretty now—
honest I do.
Let's be friends.
carrots
Never, Gilbert Blythe.
I shall never be friends with you, and I don't want to be!
All right! I'll never ask again, and I don't care, either!

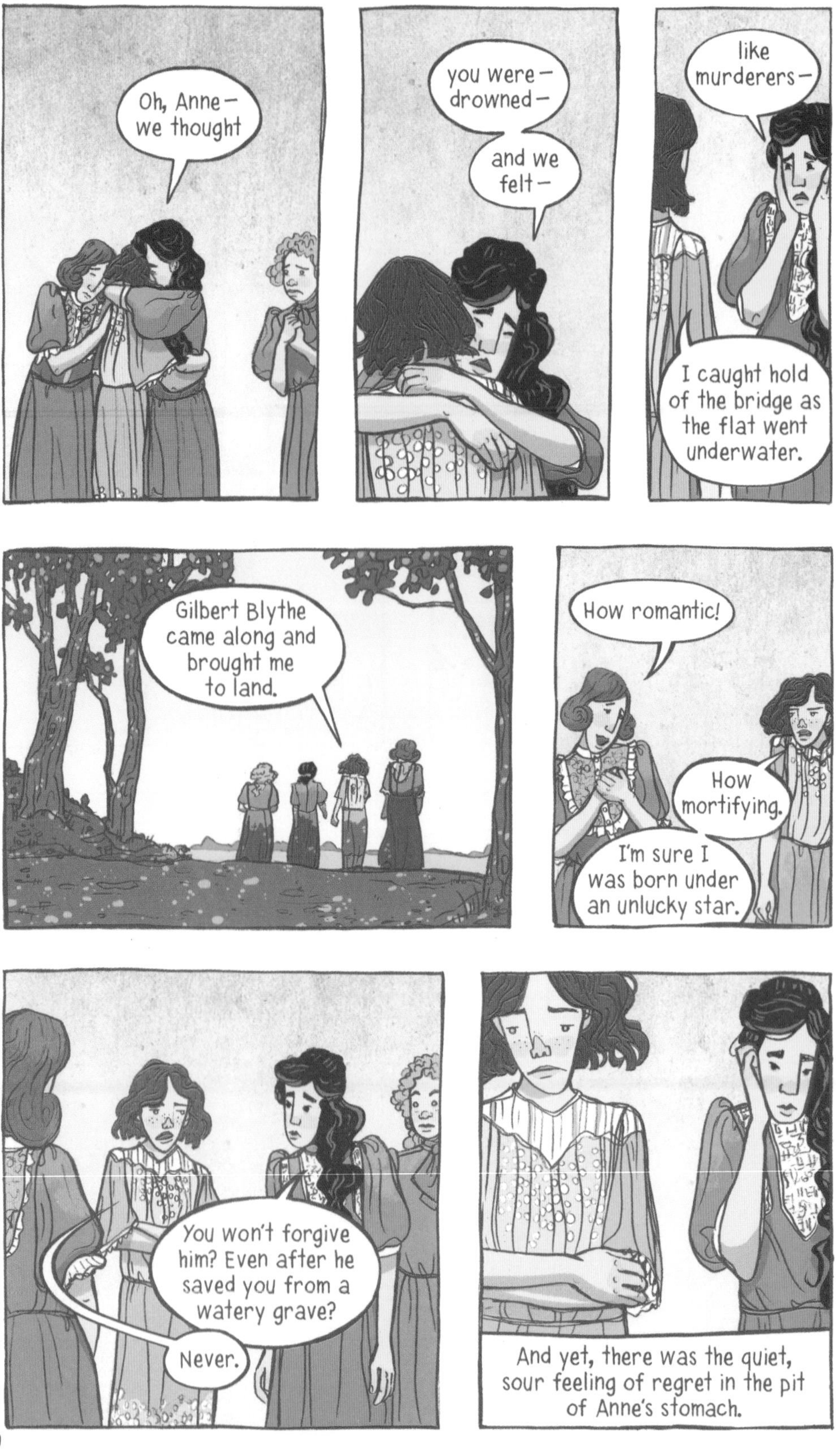
Oh, Anne—
we thought
you were—
drowned—
and we
felt—
like
murderers—
I caught hold
of the bridge as
the flat went
underwater.
Gilbert Blythe
came along and
brought me
to land.
How romantic!
How
mortifying.
I'm sure I
was born under
an unlucky star.
You won't forgive
him? Even after he
saved you from a
watery grave?
Never.
And yet, there was the quiet,
sour feeling of regret in the pit
of Anne's stomach.

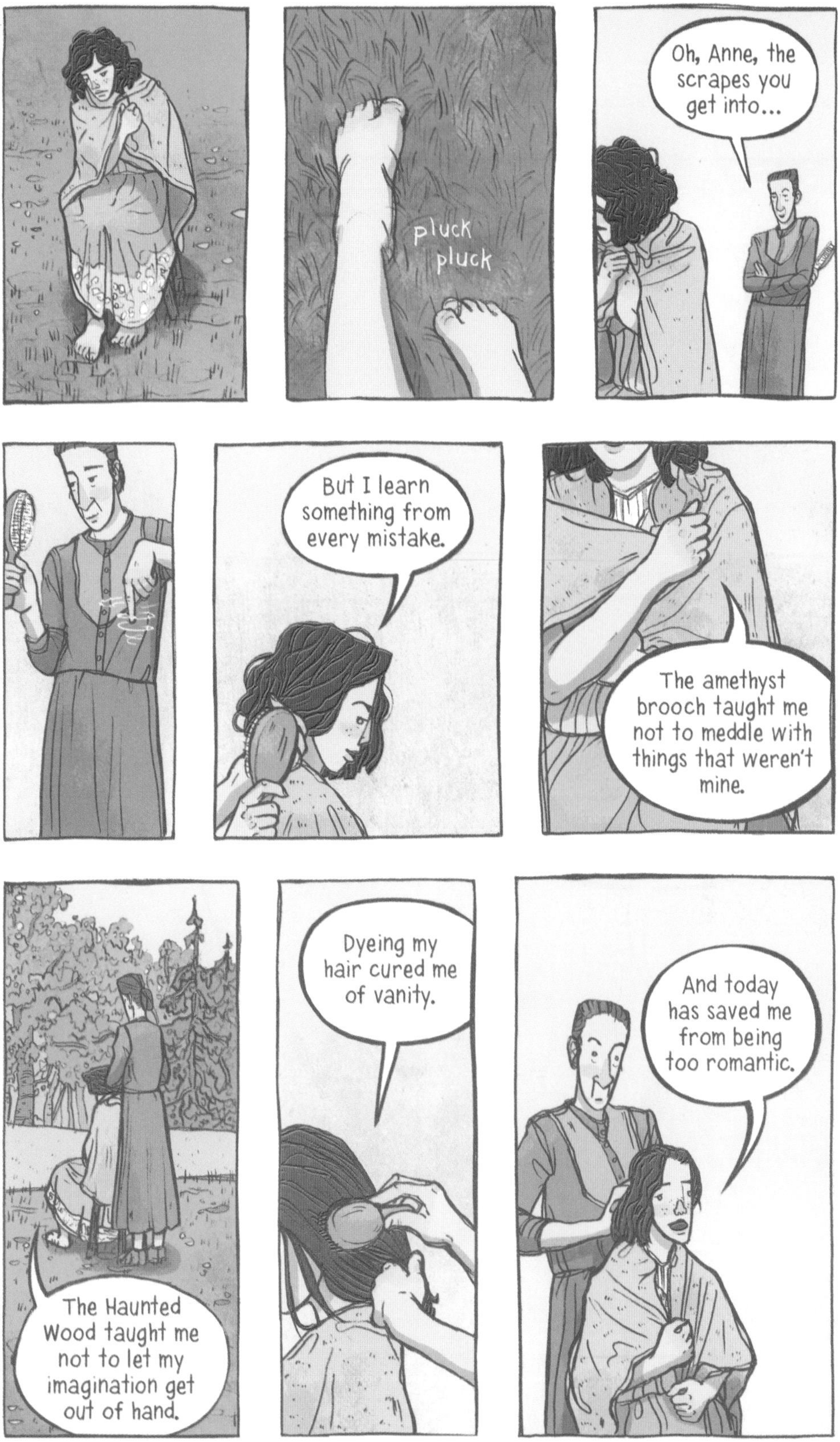
pluck
pluck
Oh, Anne, the scrapes you get into...
But I learn something from every mistake.
The amethyst brooch taught me not to meddle with things that weren't mine.
The Haunted Wood taught me not to let my imagination get out of hand.
Dyeing my hair cured me of vanity.
And today has saved me from being too romantic.

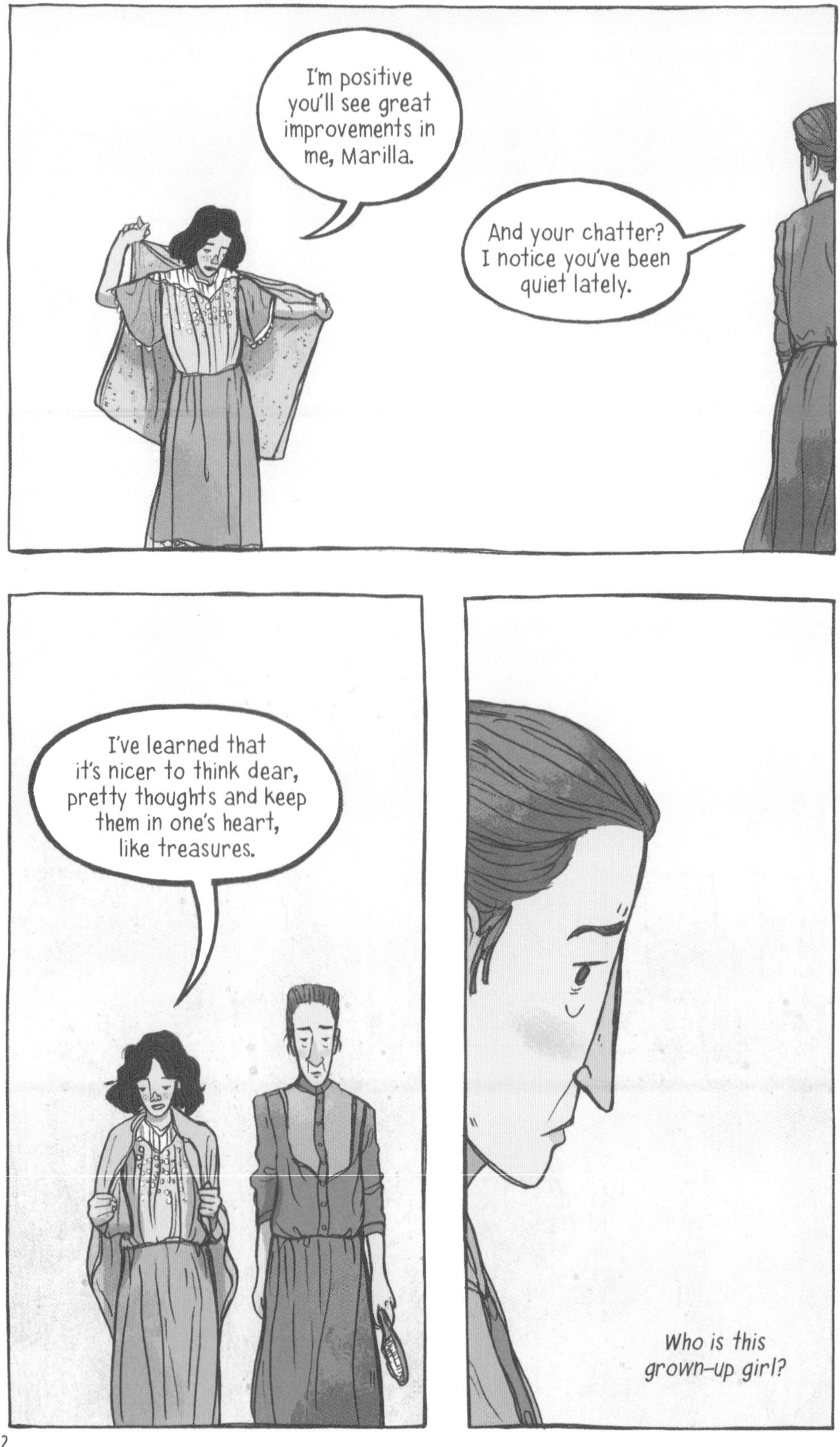
I'm positive you'll see great improvements in me, Marilla.
And your chatter? I notice you've been quiet lately.
I've learned that it's nicer to think dear, pretty thoughts and keep them in one's heart, like treasures.
Who is this grown-up girl?

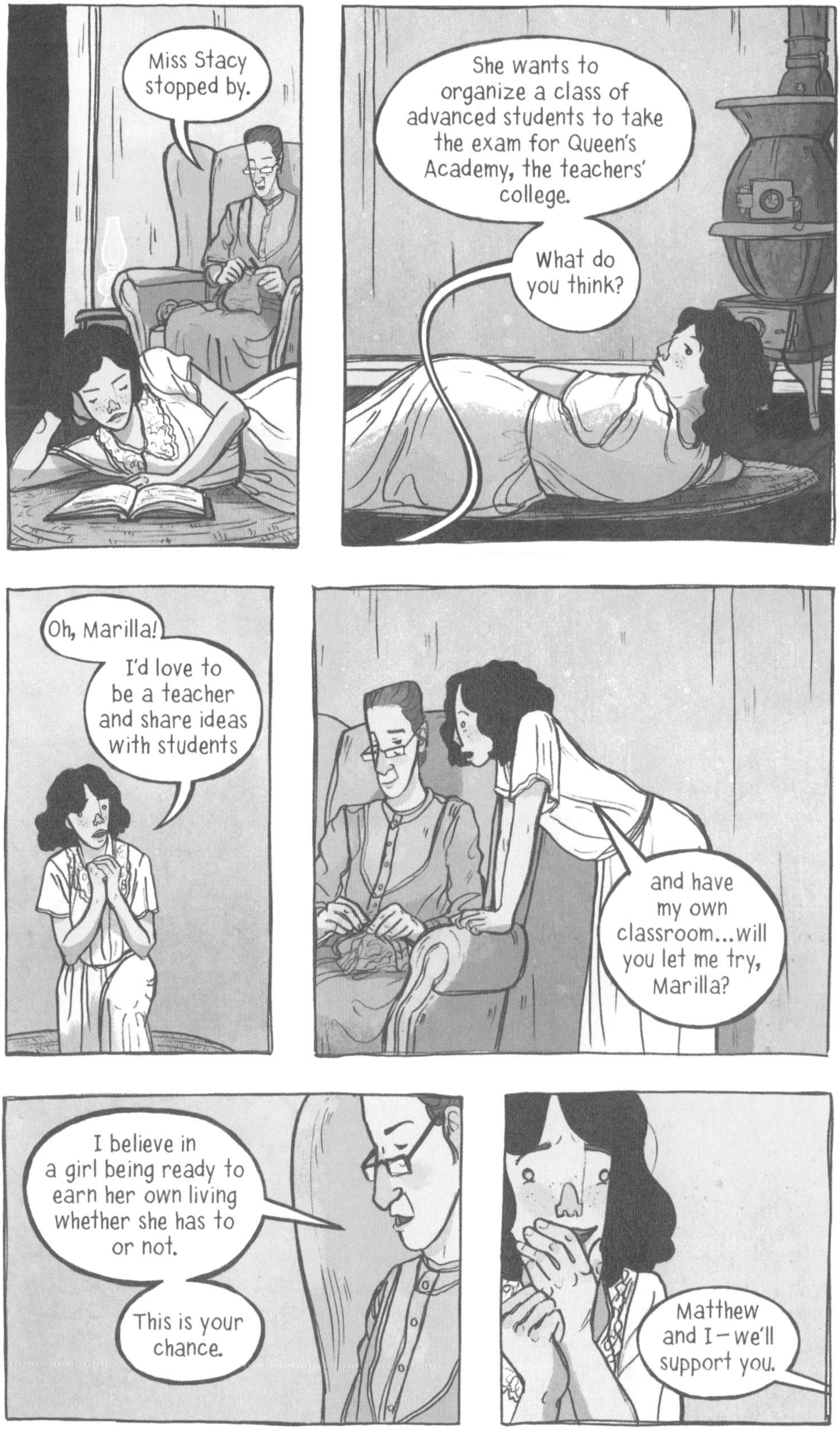

Miss Stacy stopped by.
She wants to organize a class of advanced students to take the exam for Queen's Academy, the teachers' college.
What do you think?
Oh, Marilla!
I'd love to be a teacher and share ideas with students
and have my own classroom...will you let me try, Marilla?
I believe in a girl being ready to earn her own living whether she has to or not.
This is your chance.
Matthew and I—we'll support you.

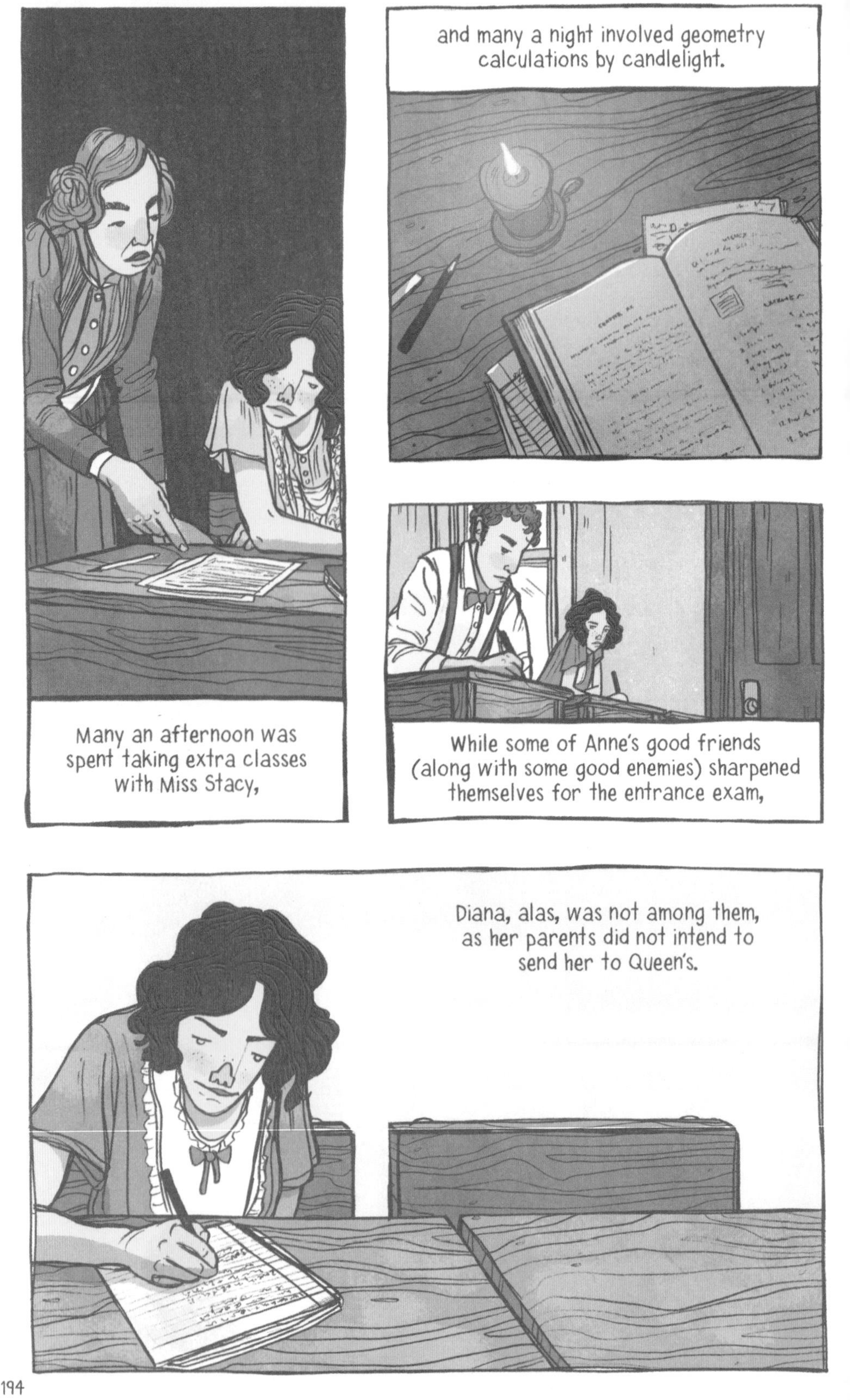
Many an afternoon was spent taking extra classes with Miss Stacy,
and many a night involved geometry calculations by candlelight.
While some of Anne's good friends (along with some good enemies) sharpened themselves for the entrance exam,
Diana, alas, was not among them, as her parents did not intend to send her to Queen's.

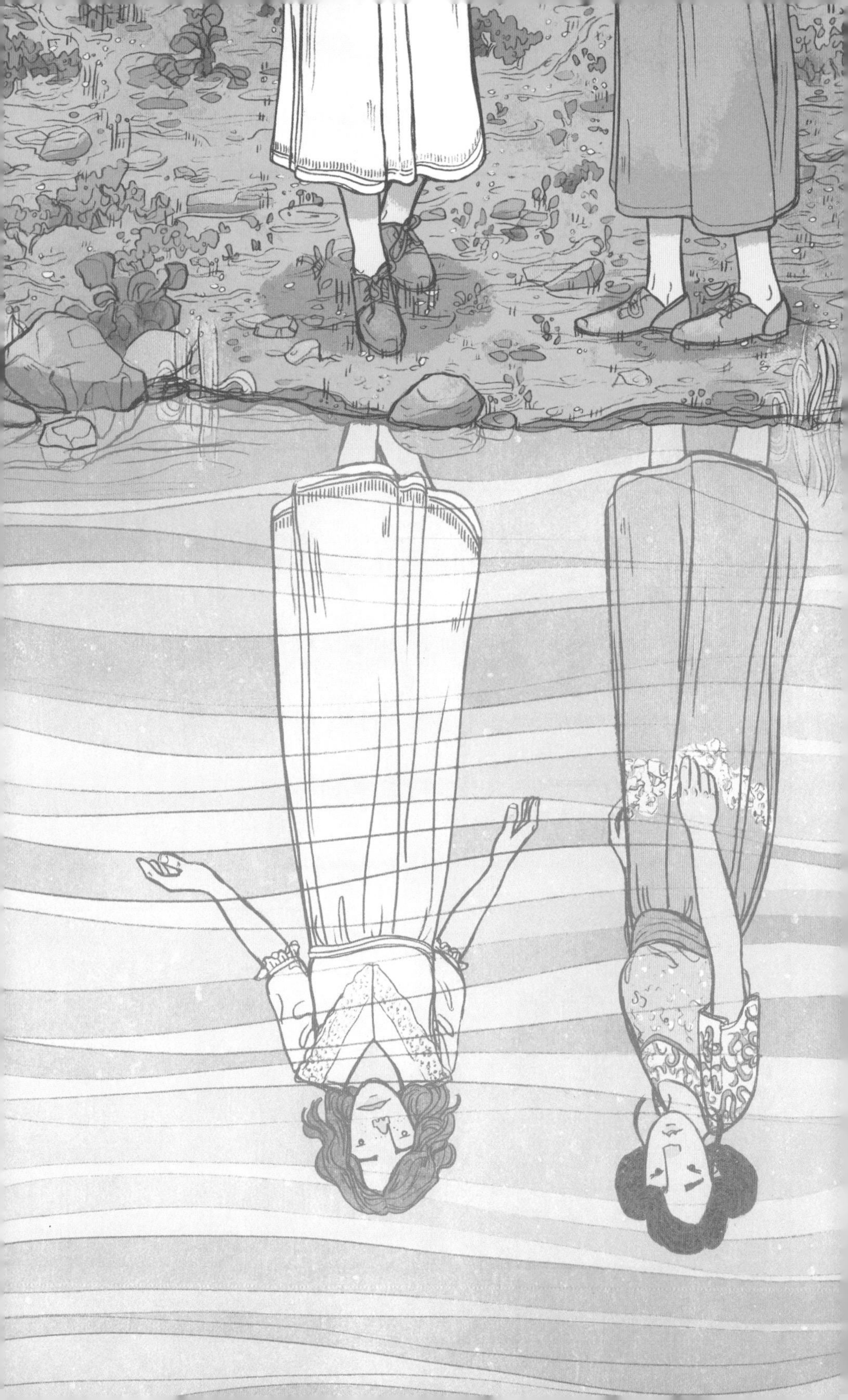

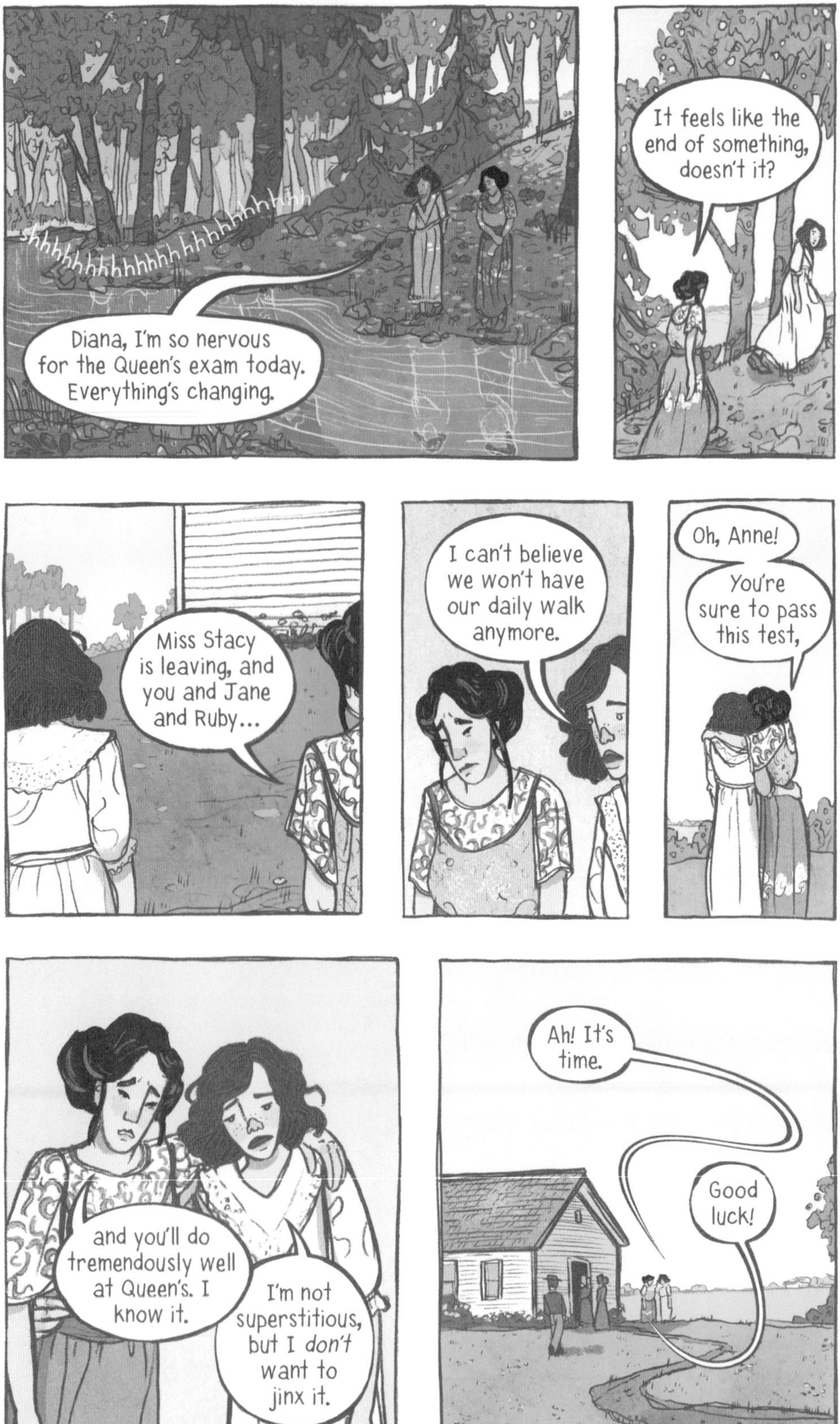
shhhhhhhhhhhhhhhhhhhhhhhh
Diana, I'm so nervous for the Queen's exam today. Everything's changing.
It feels like the end of something, doesn't it?
Miss Stacy is leaving, and you and Jane and Ruby...
I can't believe we won't have our daily walk anymore.
Oh, Anne!
You're sure to pass this test,
and you'll do tremendously well at Queen's. I know it.
I'm not superstitious, but I *don't* want to jinx it.
Ah! It's time.
Good luck!

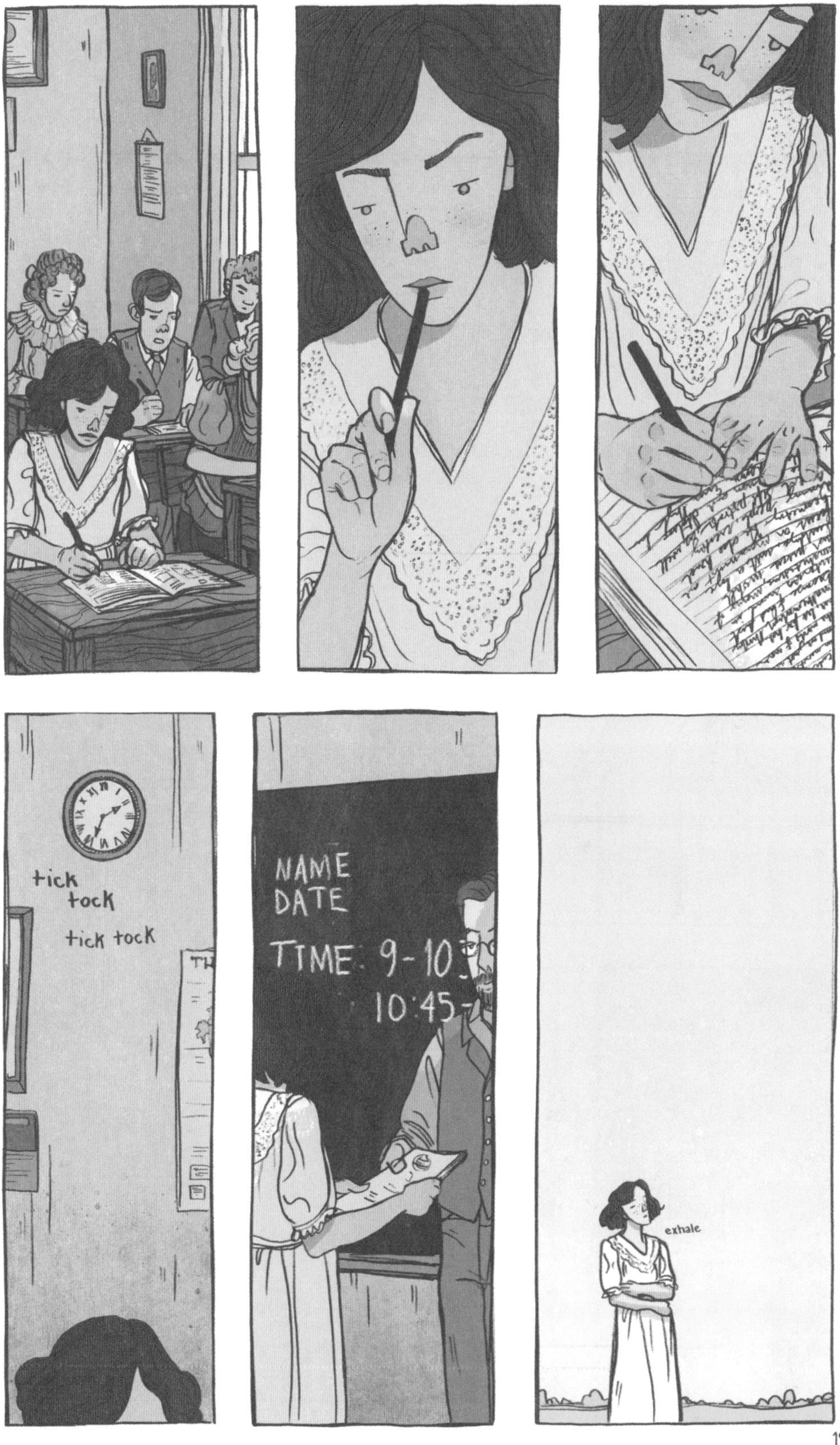
tick
tock
tick tock
NAME
DATE
TIME: 9-10
10:45-
exhale

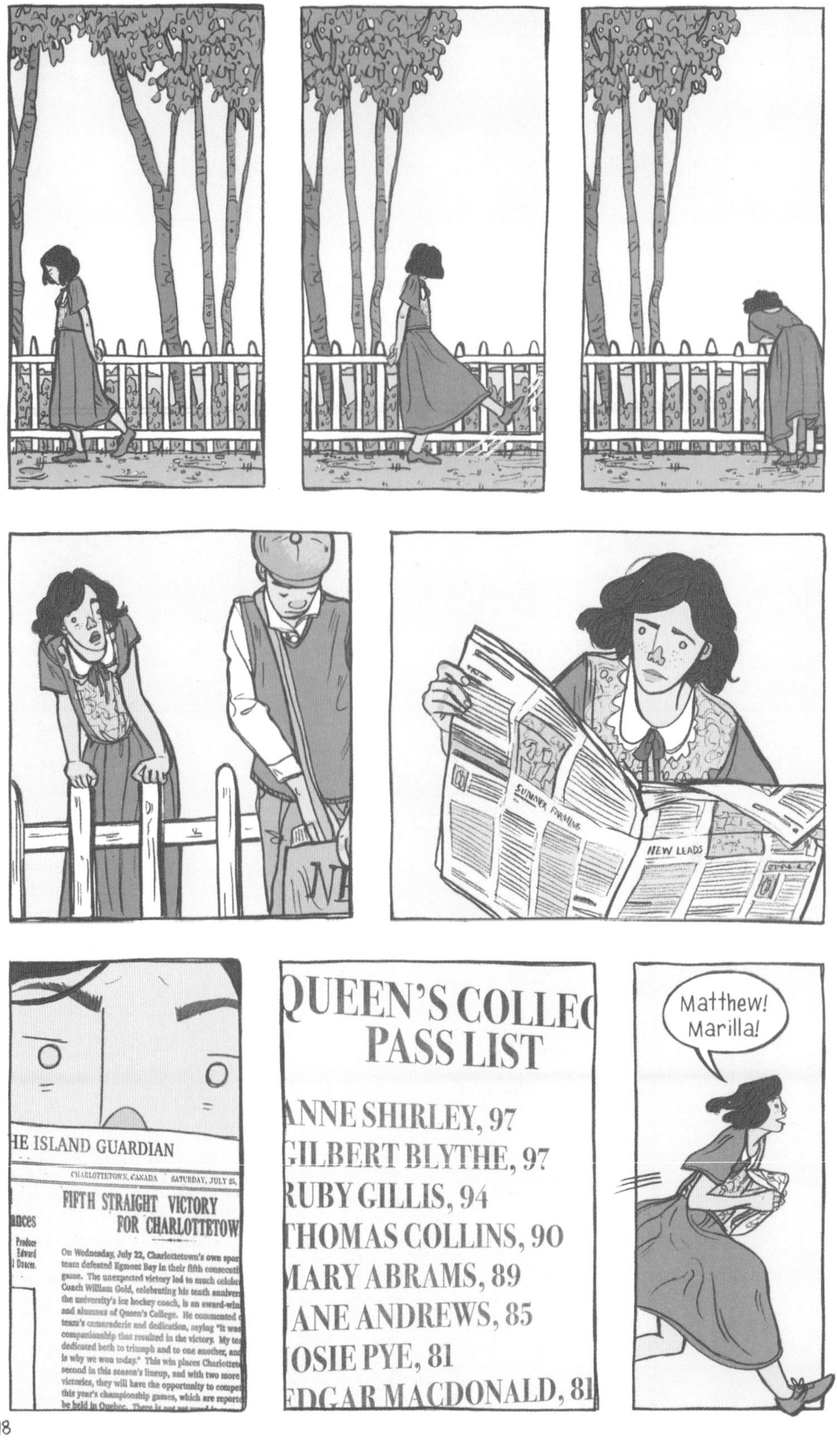
SUMMER FARMING
NEW LEADS
HE ISLAND GUARDIAN
CHARLOTTETOWN, CANADA SATURDAY, JULY 25,
FIFTH STRAIGHT VICTORY FOR CHARLOTTETOW
ances
Produce
Edward
Dances.
On Wednesday, July 22, Charlottetown's own spor
team defeated Egmont Bay in their fifth consecuti
game. The unexpected victory led to much celebr
Coach William Gold, celebrating his tenth annivers
the university's ice hockey coach, is an award-win
and alumnus of Queen's College. He commented
team's camaraderie and dedication, saying "It was
companionship that resulted in the victory. My te
dedicated both to triumph and to one another, and
is why we won today." This win places Charlottet
second in this season's lineup, and with two more
victories, they will have the opportunity to compet
this year's championship games, which are report
be held in Quebec.
QUEEN'S COLLE
PASS LIST
ANNE SHIRLEY, 97
GILBERT BLYTHE, 97
RUBY GILLIS, 94
THOMAS COLLINS, 90
MARY ABRAMS, 89
JANE ANDREWS, 85
JOSIE PYE, 81
EDGAR MACDONALD, 81
Matthew! Marilla!

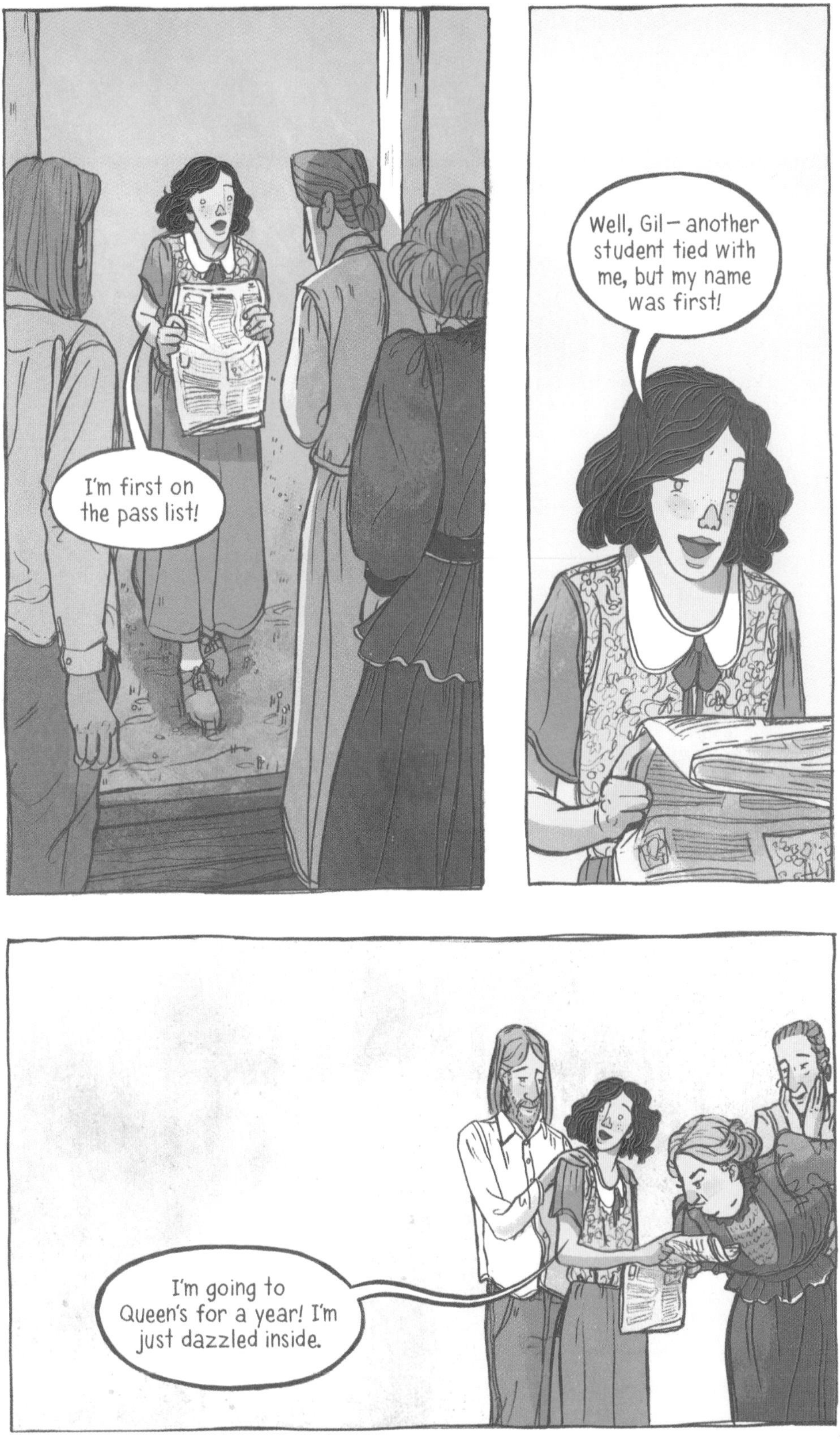
I'm first on the pass list!
Well, Gil— another student tied with me, but my name was first!
I'm going to Queen's for a year! I'm just dazzled inside.

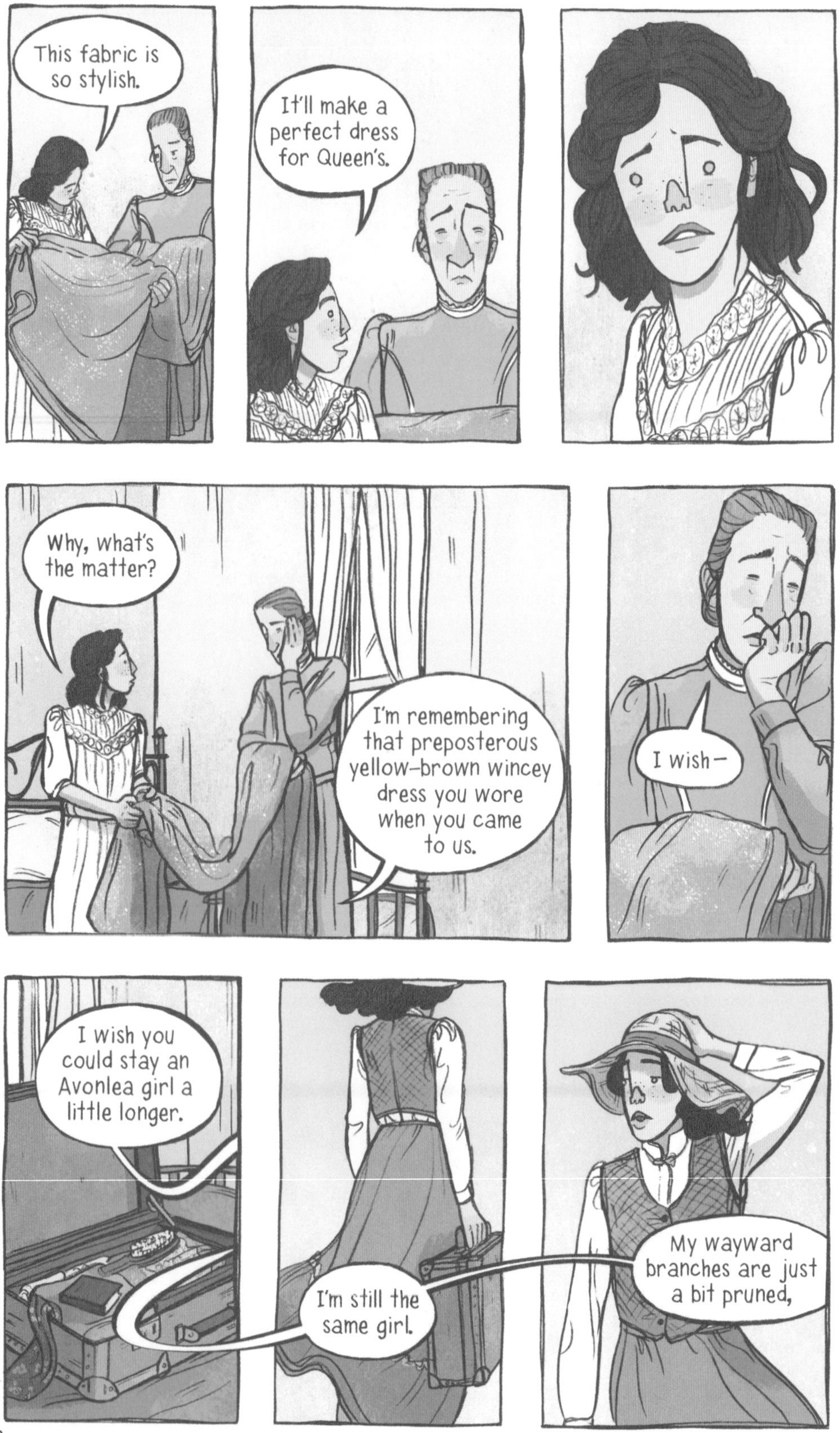
This fabric is so stylish.
It'll make a perfect dress for Queen's.
Why, what's the matter?
I'm remembering that preposterous yellow-brown wincey dress you wore when you came to us.
I wish—
I wish you could stay an Avonlea girl a little longer.
I'm still the same girl.
My wayward branches are just a bit pruned,

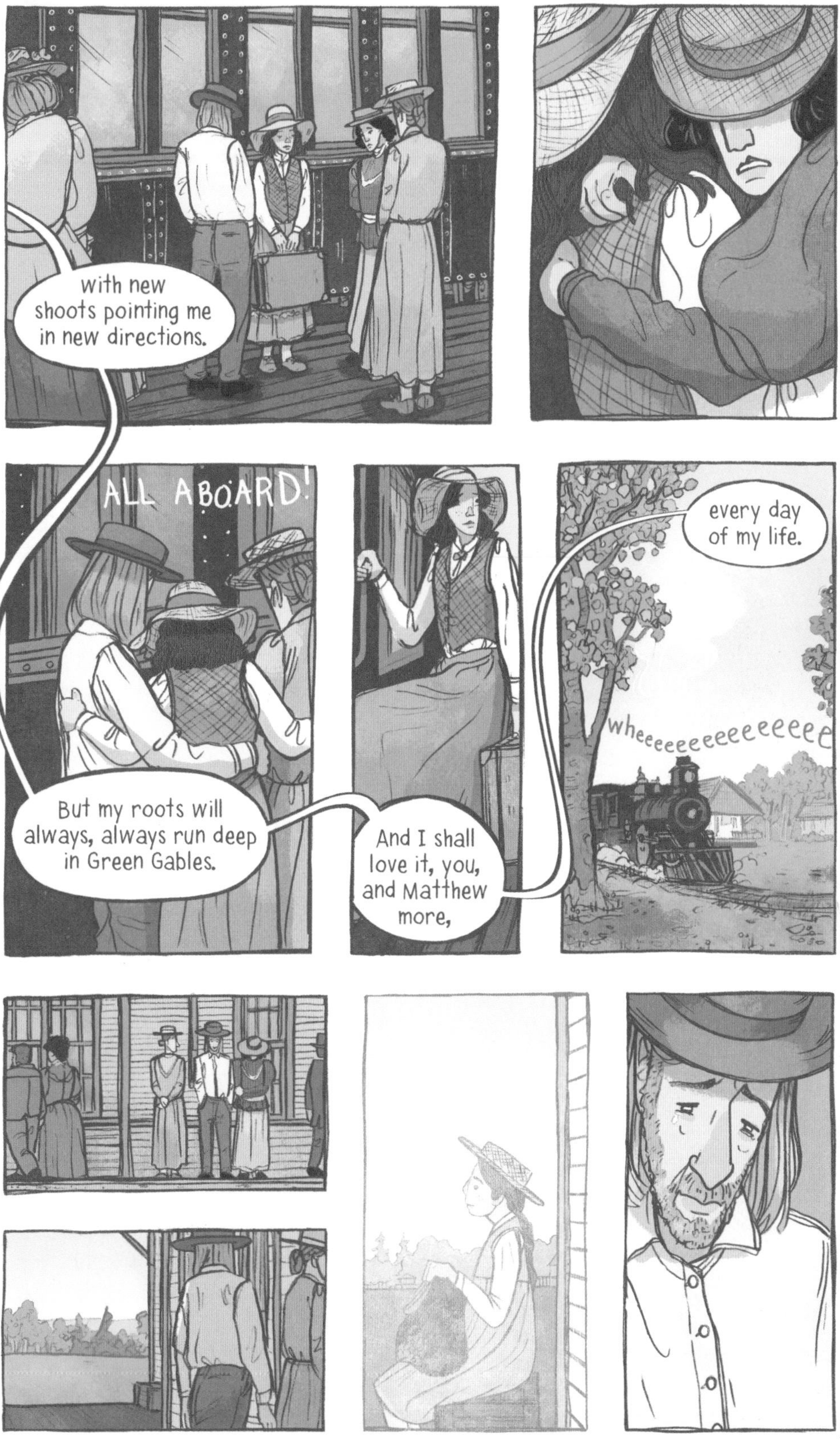
with new shoots pointing me in new directions.
ALL ABOARD!
But my roots will always, always run deep in Green Gables.
And I shall love it, you, and Matthew more,
every day of my life.
wheeeeeeeeeeeeee

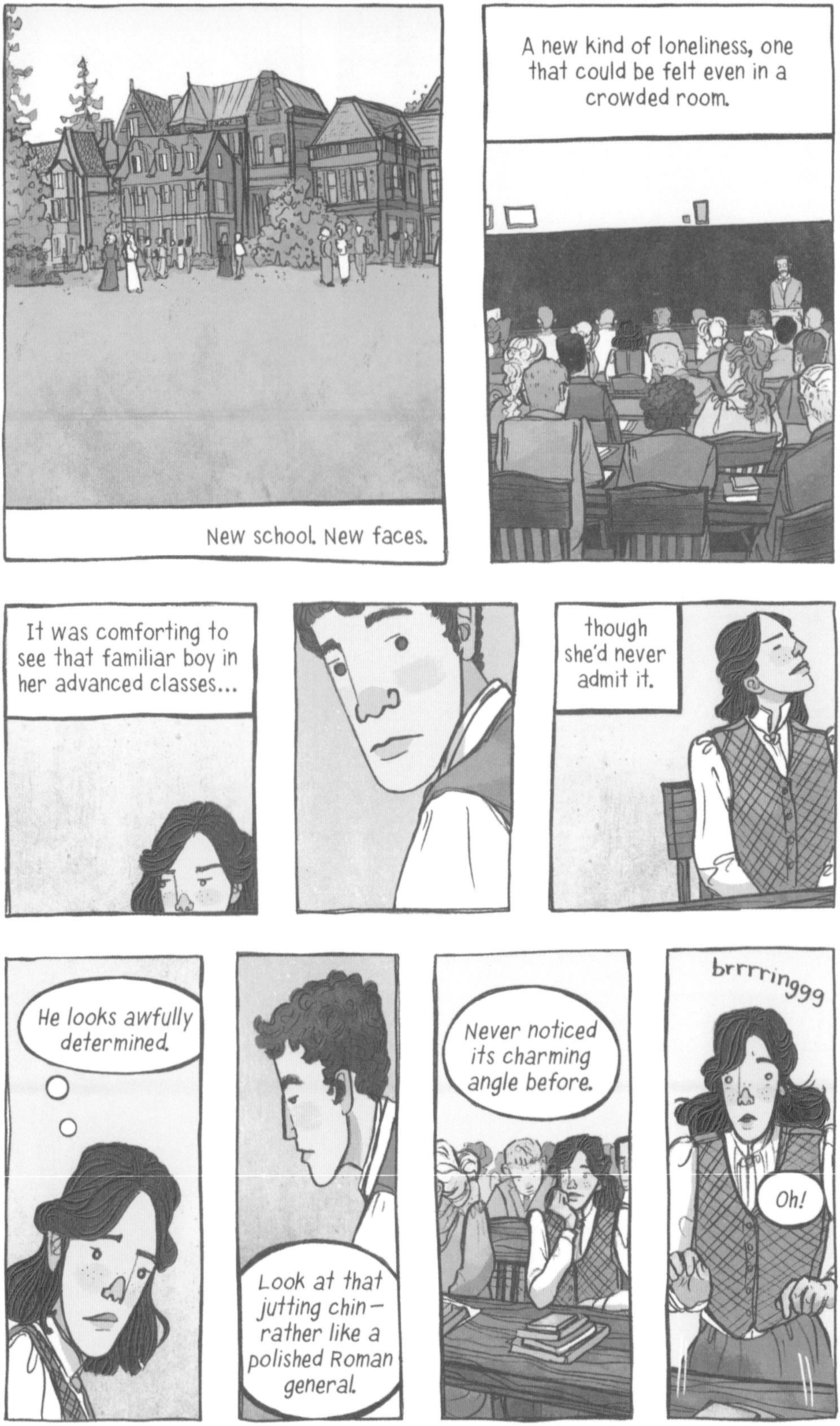
New school. New faces.
A new kind of loneliness, one that could be felt even in a crowded room.
It was comforting to see that familiar boy in her advanced classes...
though she'd never admit it.
He looks awfully determined.
Look at that jutting chin—rather like a polished Roman general.
Never noticed its charming angle before.
brrrringggg
Oh!

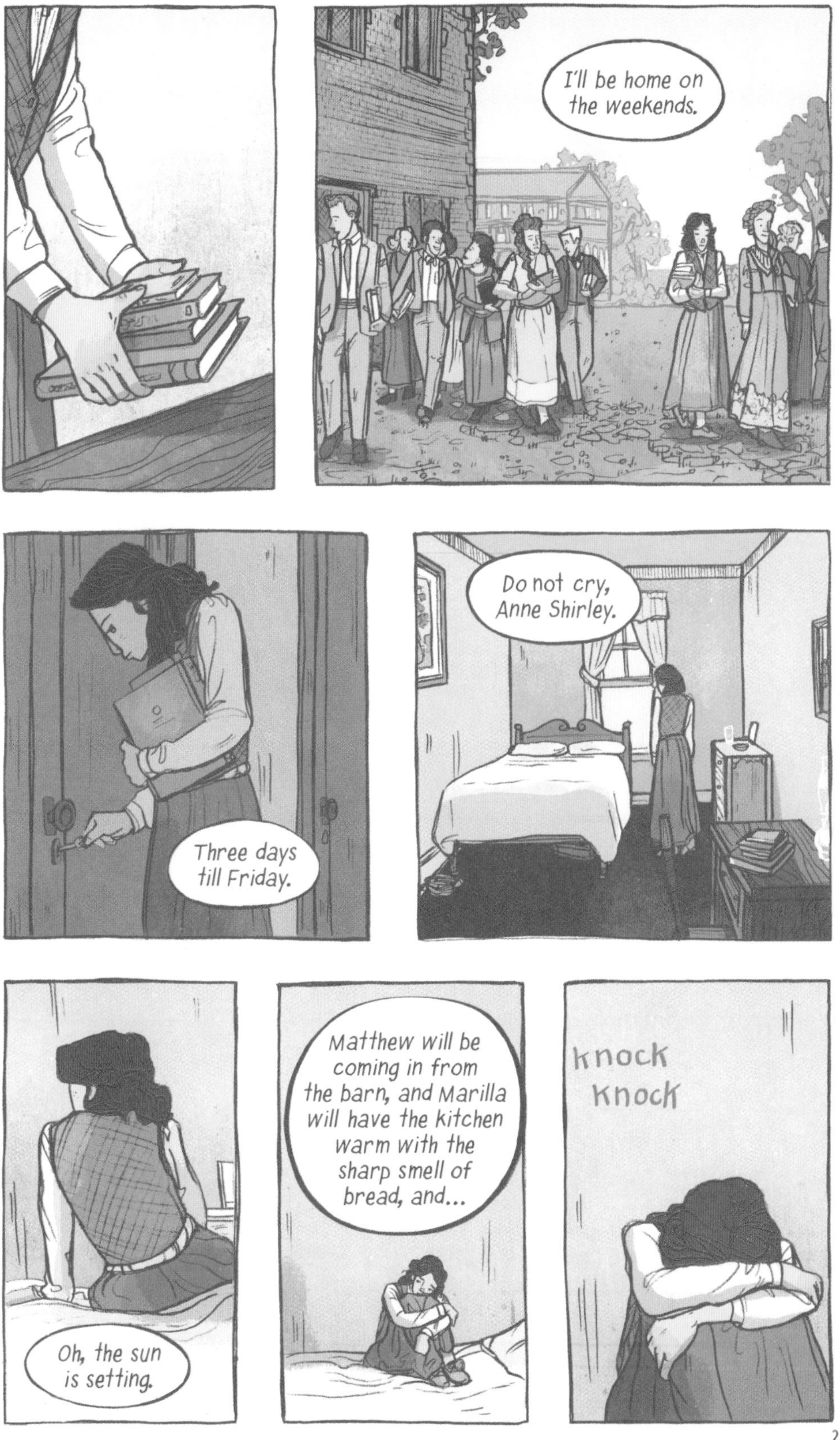
I'll be home on the weekends.
Three days till Friday.
Do not cry, Anne Shirley.
Oh, the sun is setting.
Matthew will be coming in from the barn, and Marilla will have the kitchen warm with the sharp smell of bread, and...
knock knock

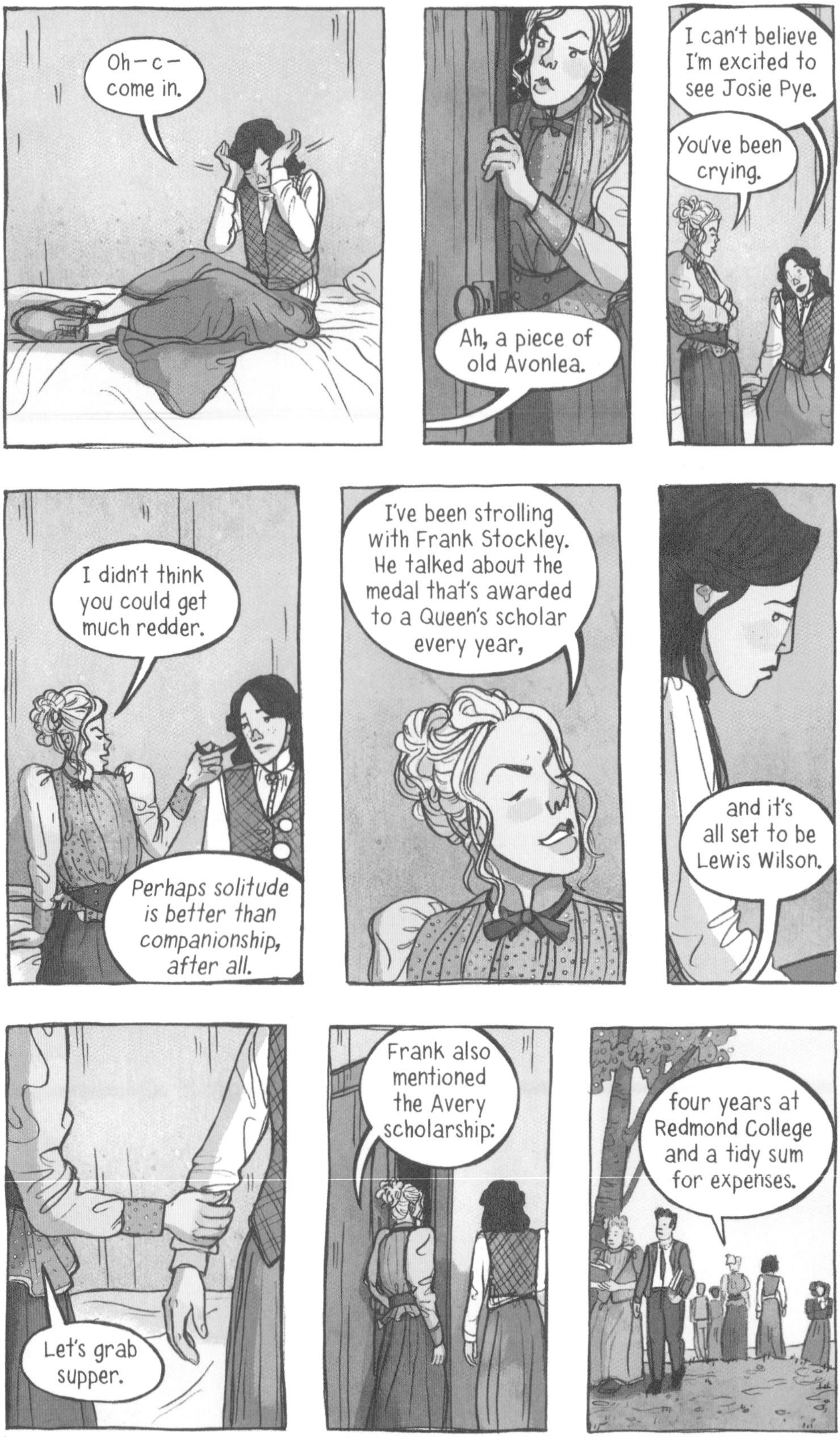
Oh—c—
come in.
Ah, a piece of
old Avonlea.
I can't believe
I'm excited to
see Josie Pye.
You've been
crying.
I didn't think
you could get
much redder.
Perhaps solitude
is better than
companionship,
after all.
I've been strolling
with Frank Stockley.
He talked about the
medal that's awarded
to a Queen's scholar
every year,
and it's
all set to be
Lewis Wilson.
Let's grab
supper.
Frank also
mentioned
the Avery
scholarship:
four years at
Redmond College
and a tidy sum
for expenses.

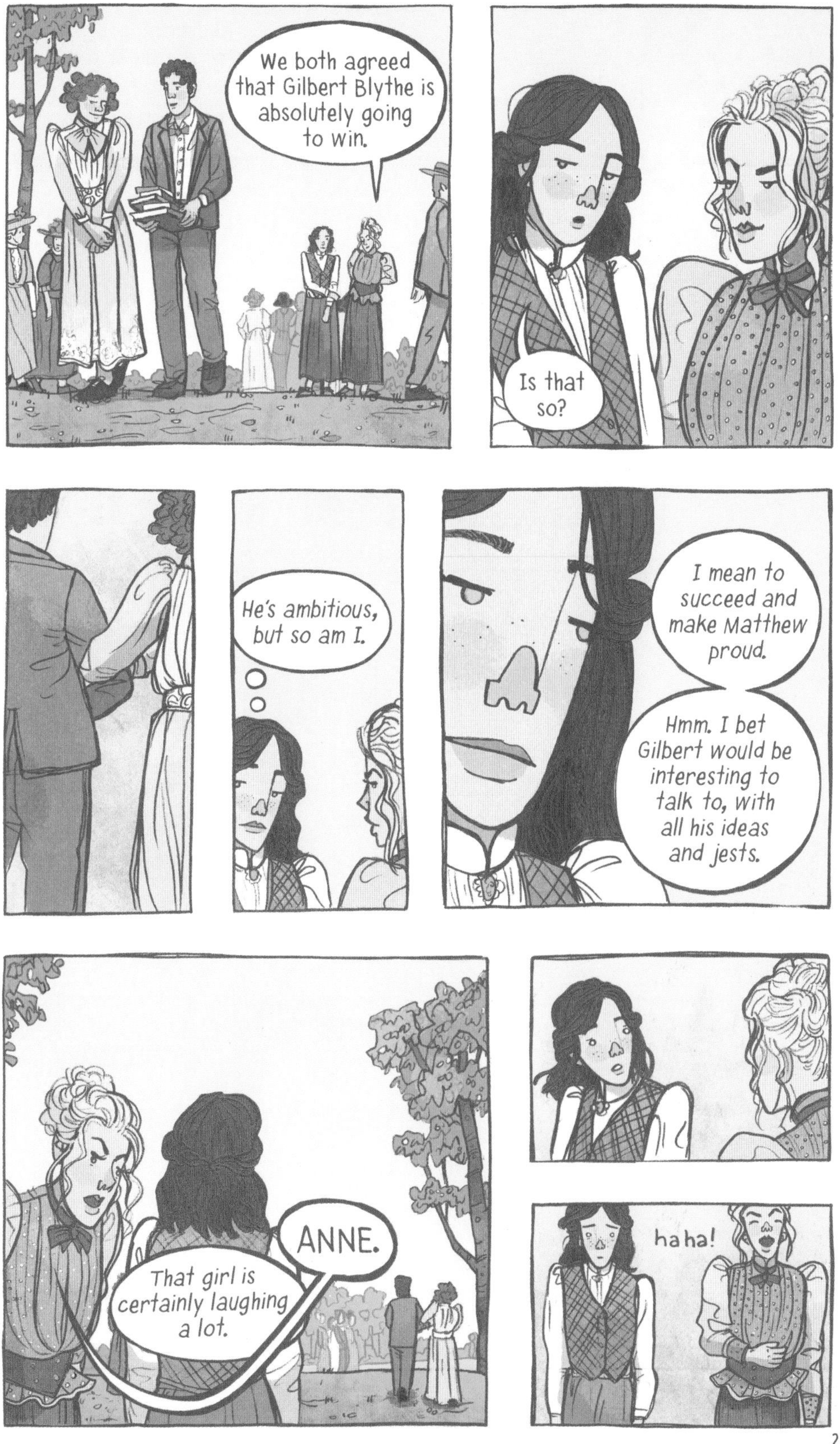

We both agreed that Gilbert Blythe is absolutely going to win.
Is that so?
He's ambitious, but so am I.
I mean to succeed and make Matthew proud.
Hmm. I bet Gilbert would be interesting to talk to, with all his ideas and jests.
That girl is certainly laughing a lot.
ANNE.
haha!

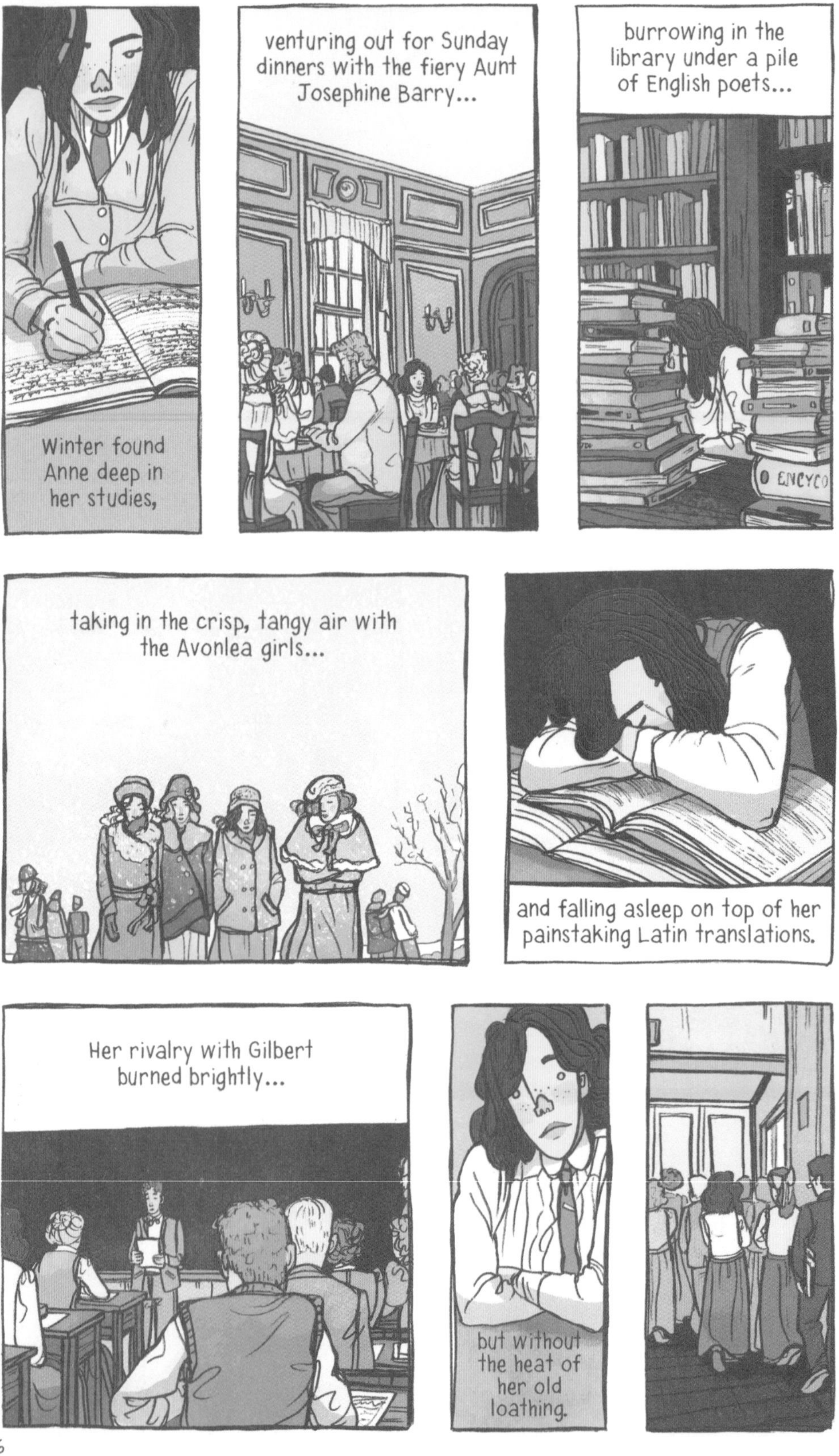
Winter found Anne deep in her studies,
venturing out for Sunday dinners with the fiery Aunt Josephine Barry...
burrowing in the library under a pile of English poets...
ENCYCO
taking in the crisp, tangy air with the Avonlea girls...
and falling asleep on top of her painstaking Latin translations.
Her rivalry with Gilbert burned brightly...
but without the heat of her old loathing.

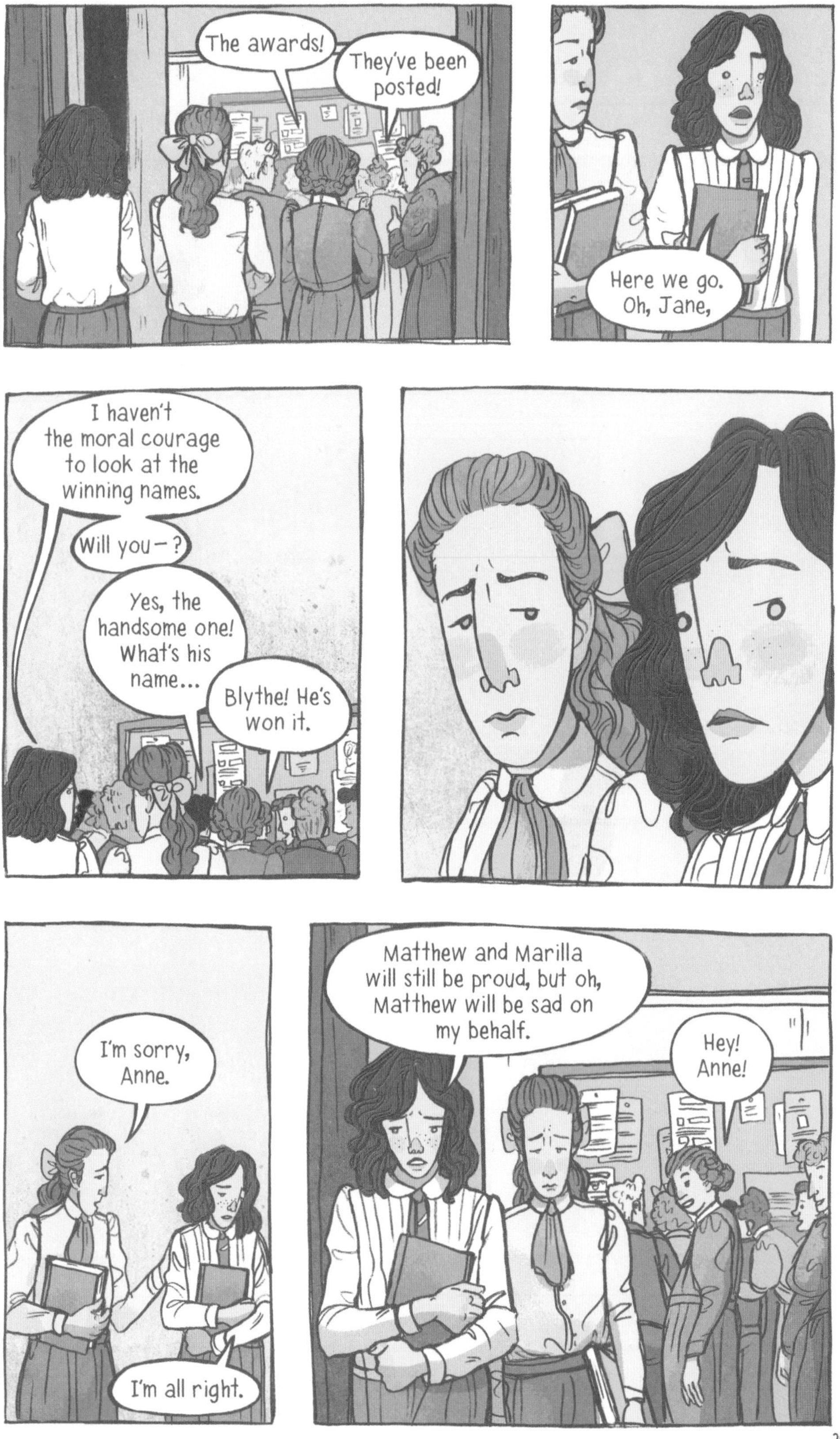
The awards!
They've been posted!
Here we go. Oh, Jane,
I haven't the moral courage to look at the winning names.
Will you—?
Yes, the handsome one! What's his name...
Blythe! He's won it.
I'm sorry, Anne.
I'm all right.
Matthew and Marilla will still be proud, but oh, Matthew will be sad on my behalf.
Hey! Anne!

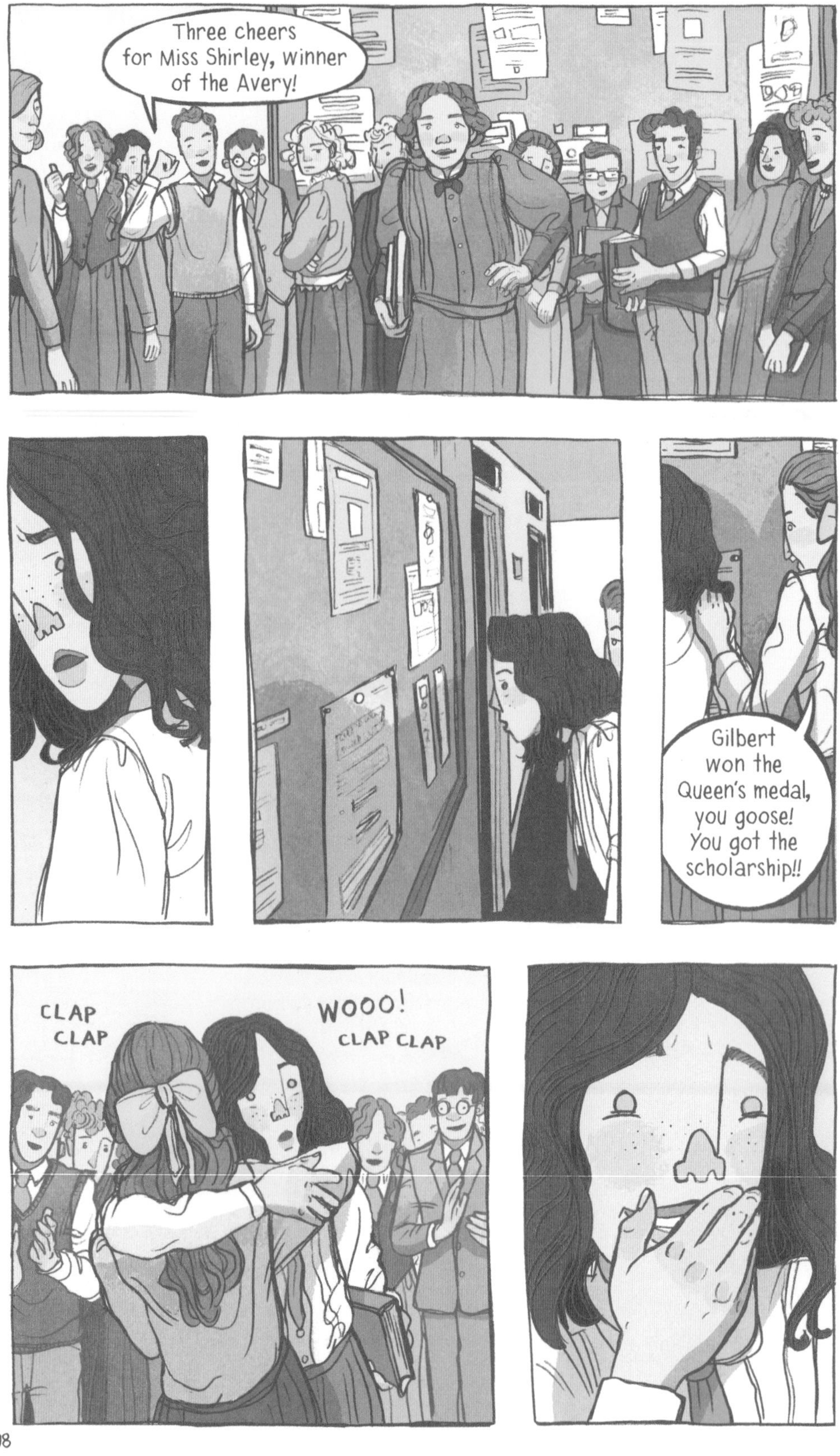
Three cheers for Miss Shirley, winner of the Avery!
Gilbert won the Queen's medal, you goose! You got the scholarship!!
CLAP CLAP
WOOO!
CLAP CLAP

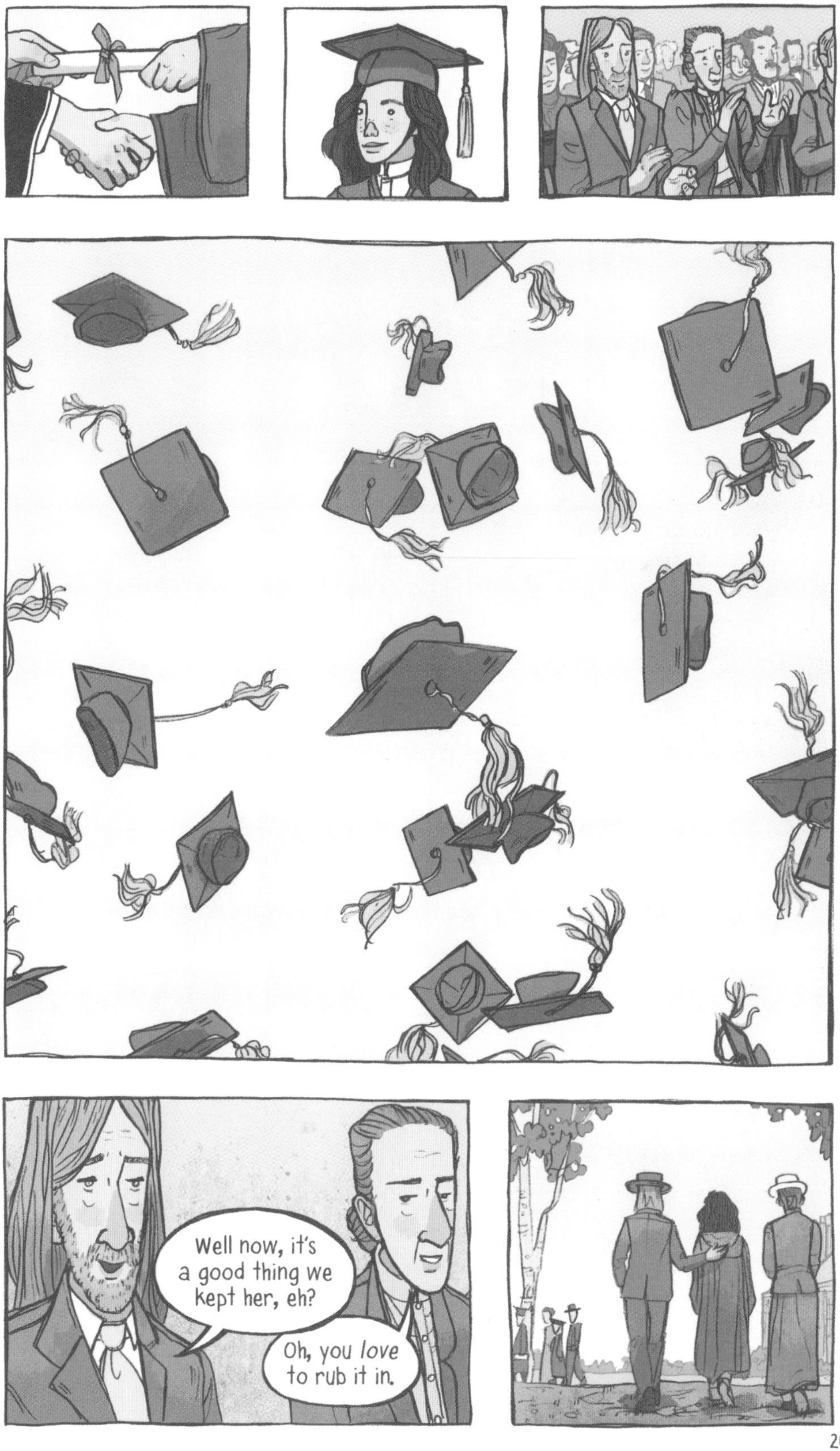
Well now, it's a good thing we kept her, eh?
Oh, you *love* to rub it in.

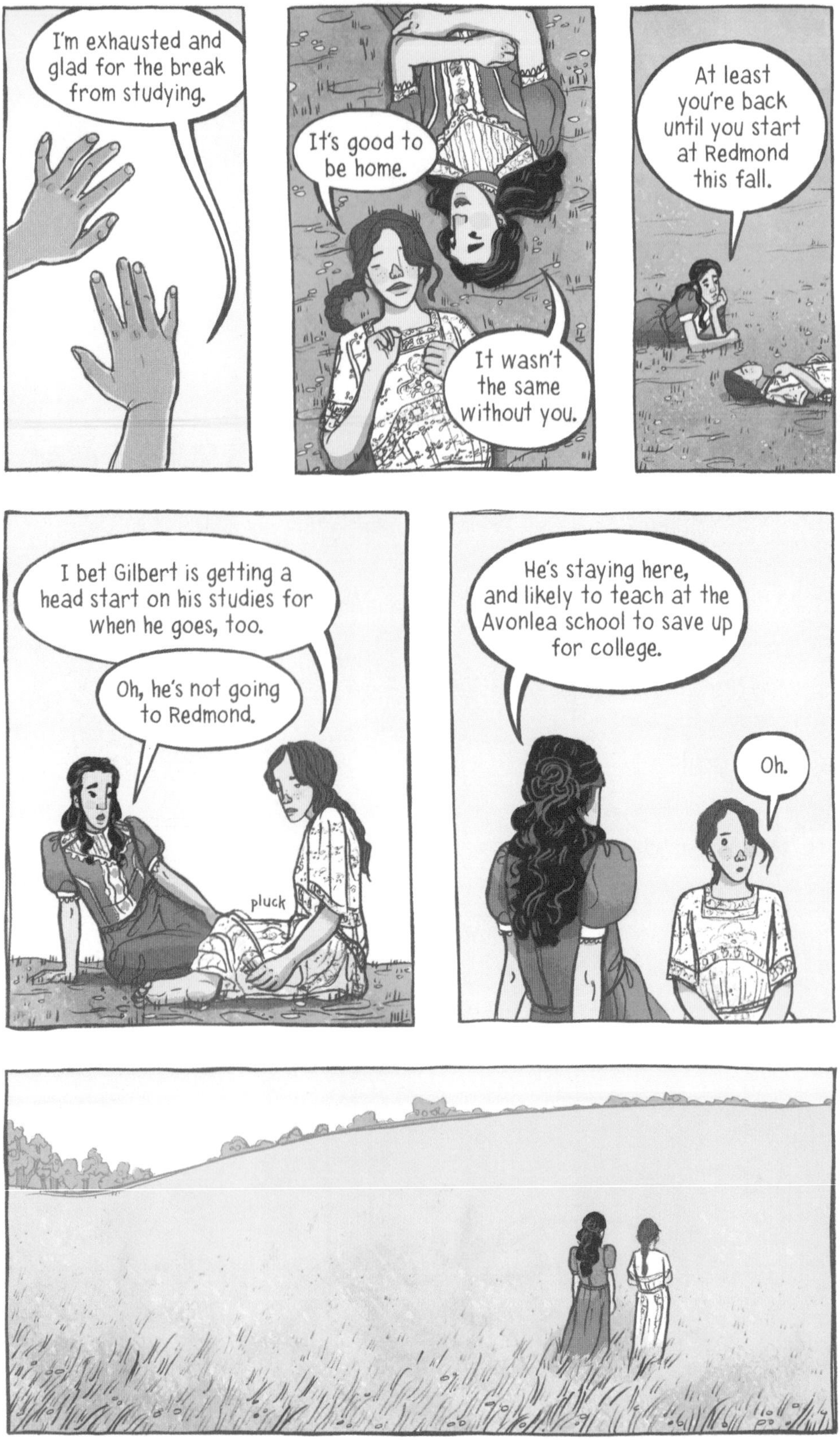
I'm exhausted and glad for the break from studying.
It's good to be home.
It wasn't the same without you.
At least you're back until you start at Redmond this fall.
I bet Gilbert is getting a head start on his studies for when he goes, too.
Oh, he's not going to Redmond.
pluck
He's staying here, and likely to teach at the Avonlea school to save up for college.
Oh.

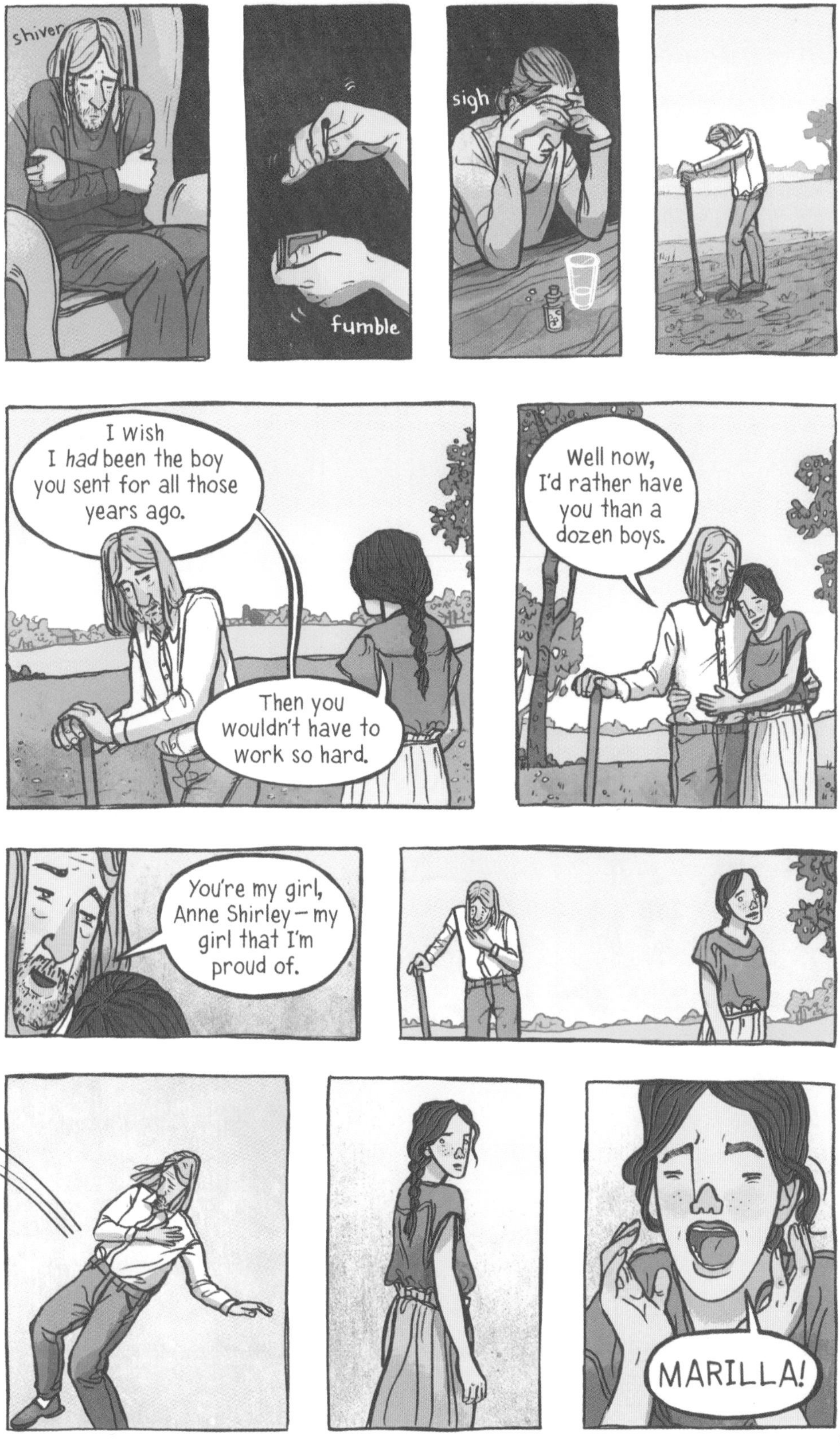

shiver
fumble
sigh
I wish I *had* been the boy you sent for all those years ago.
Then you wouldn't have to work so hard.
Well now, I'd rather have you than a dozen boys.
You're my girl, Anne Shirley—my girl that I'm proud of.
MARILLA!

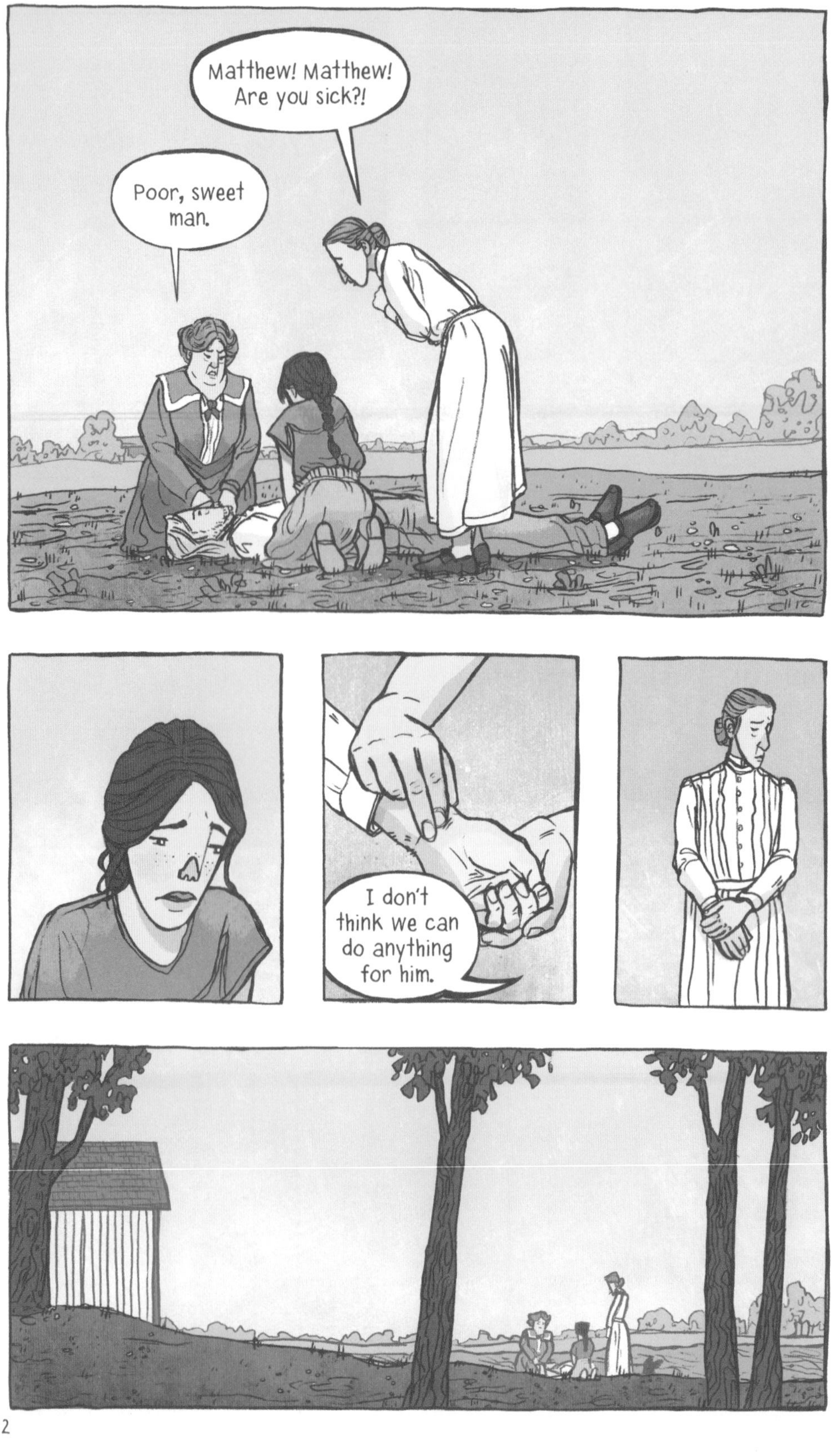
Matthew! Matthew! Are you sick?!
Poor, sweet man.
I don't think we can do anything for him.

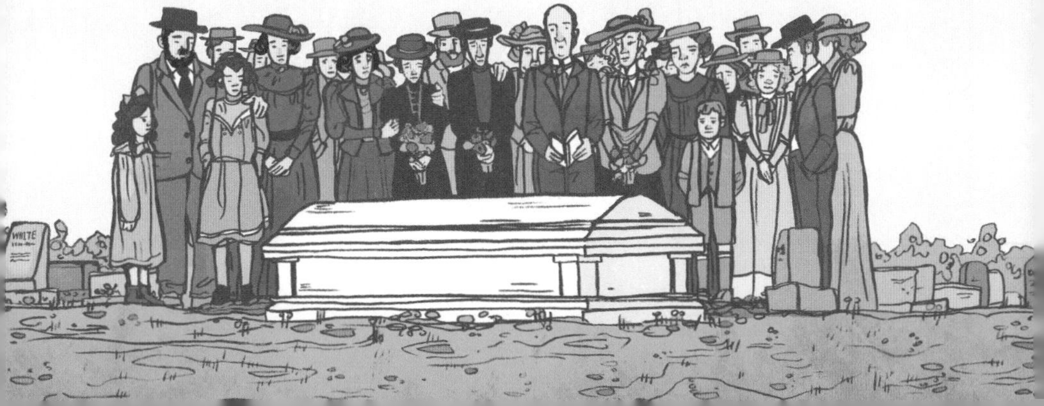
WHITE

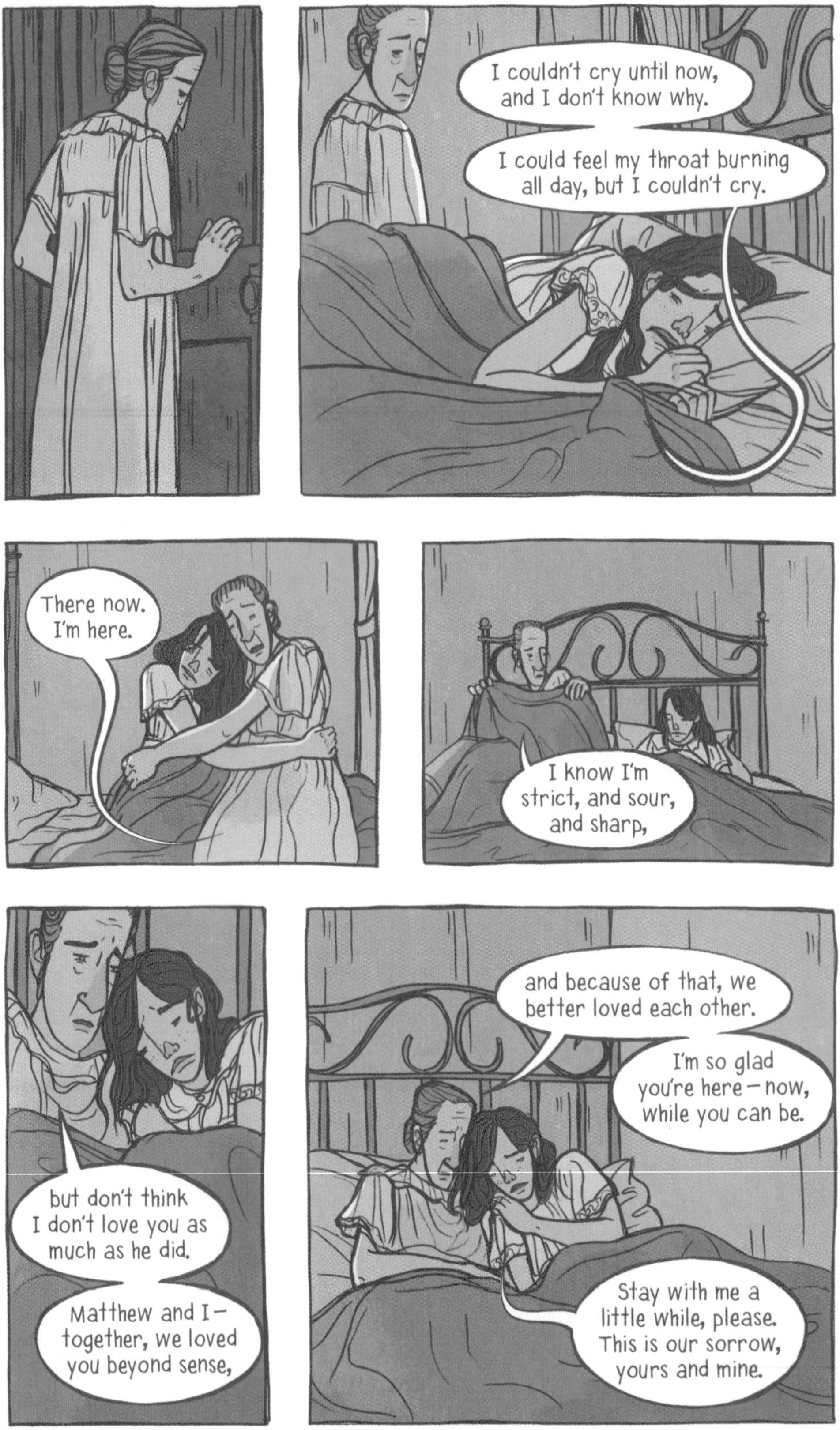
I couldn't cry until now, and I don't know why.
I could feel my throat burning all day, but I couldn't cry.
There now. I'm here.
I know I'm strict, and sour, and sharp,
but don't think I don't love you as much as he did.
Matthew and I— together, we loved you beyond sense,
and because of that, we better loved each other.
I'm so glad you're here—now, while you can be.
Stay with me a little while, please. This is our sorrow, yours and mine.

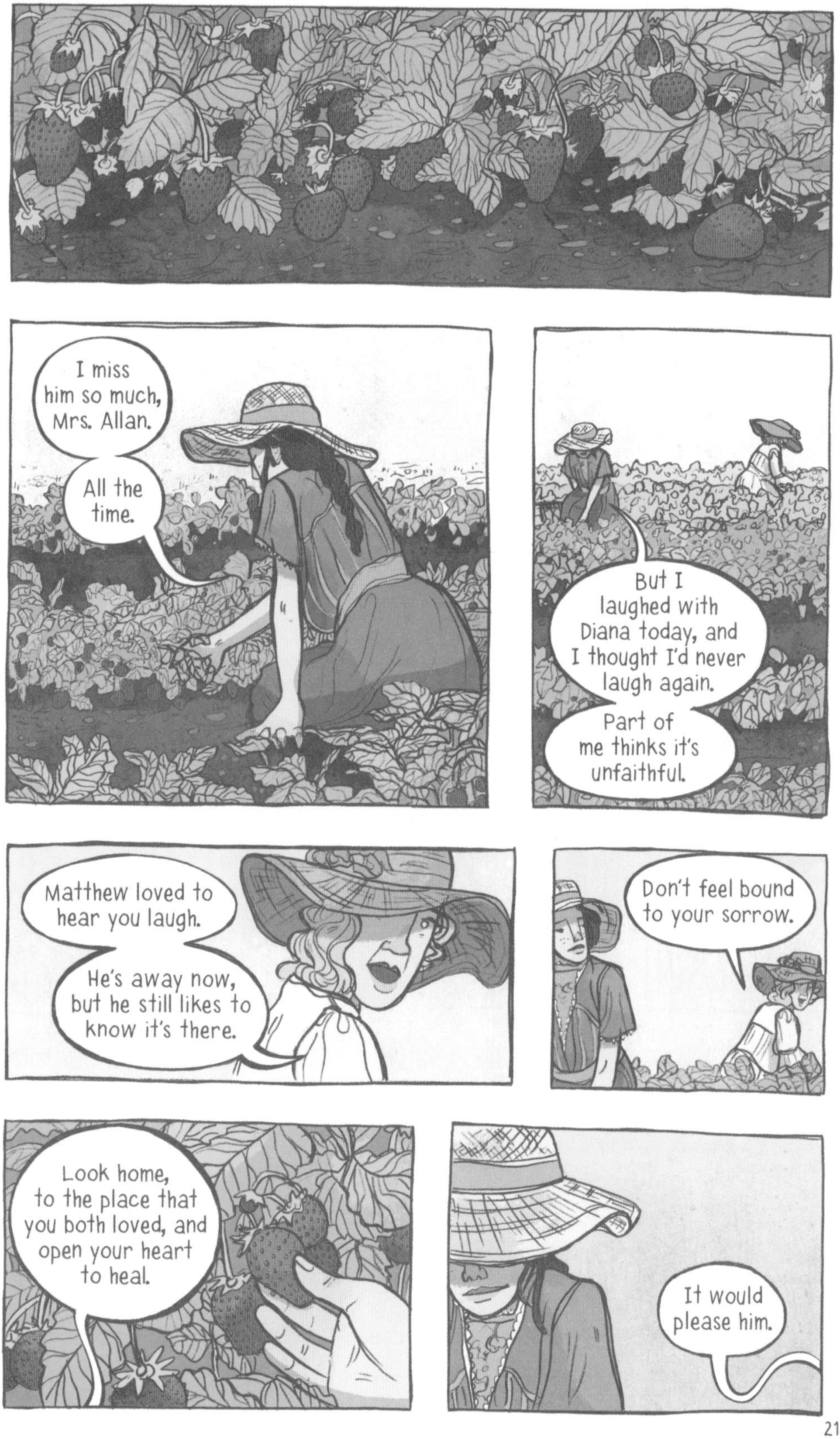
I miss him so much, Mrs. Allan.
All the time.
But I laughed with Diana today, and I thought I'd never laugh again.
Part of me thinks it's unfaithful.
Matthew loved to hear you laugh.
He's away now, but he still likes to know it's there.
Don't feel bound to your sorrow.
Look home, to the place that you both loved, and open your heart to heal.
It would please him.

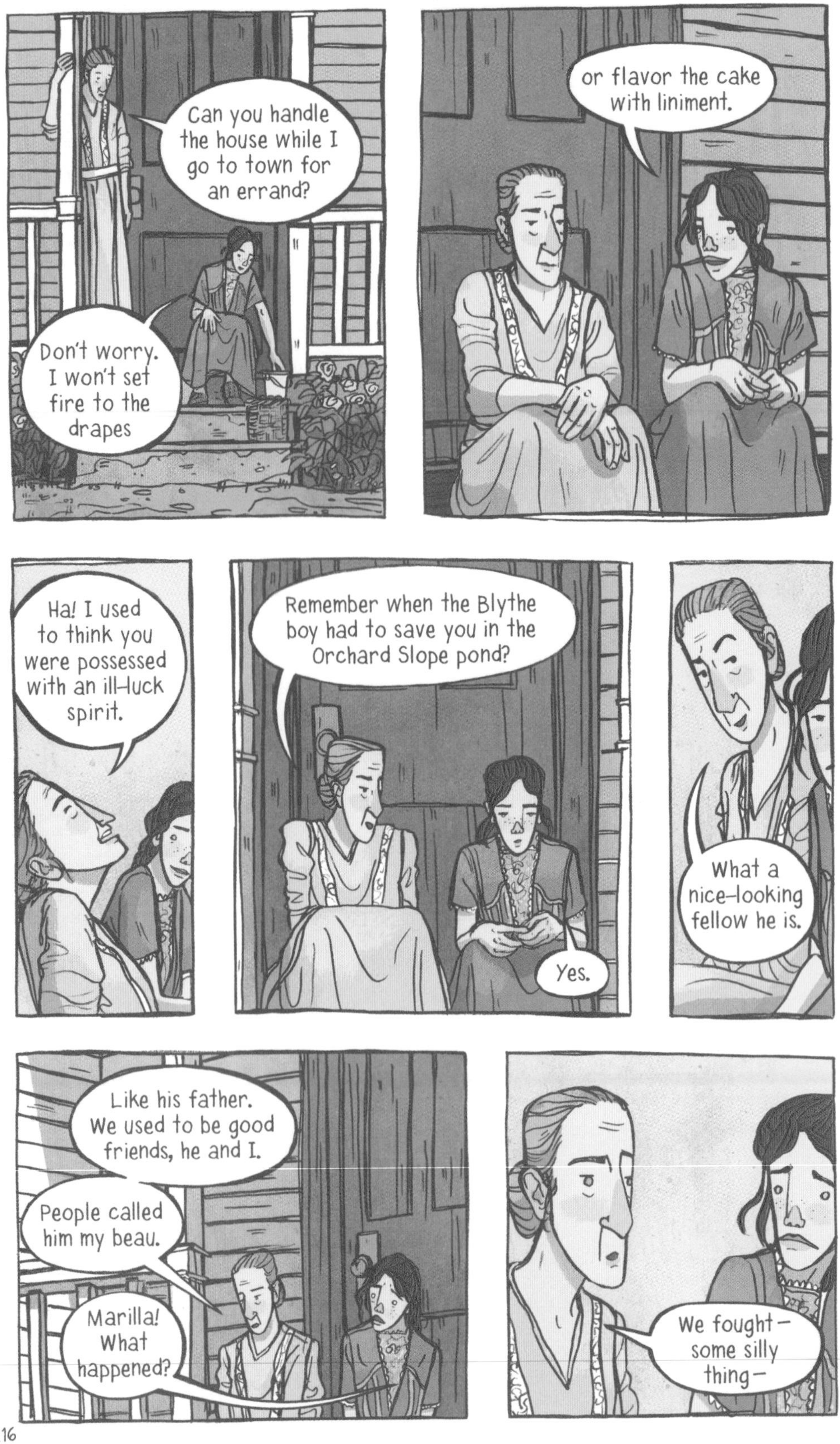
Can you handle the house while I go to town for an errand?
Don't worry. I won't set fire to the drapes
or flavor the cake with liniment.
Ha! I used to think you were possessed with an ill-luck spirit.
Remember when the Blythe boy had to save you in the Orchard Slope pond?
Yes.
What a nice-looking fellow he is.
Like his father. We used to be good friends, he and I.
People called him my beau.
Marilla! What happened?
We fought— some silly thing—

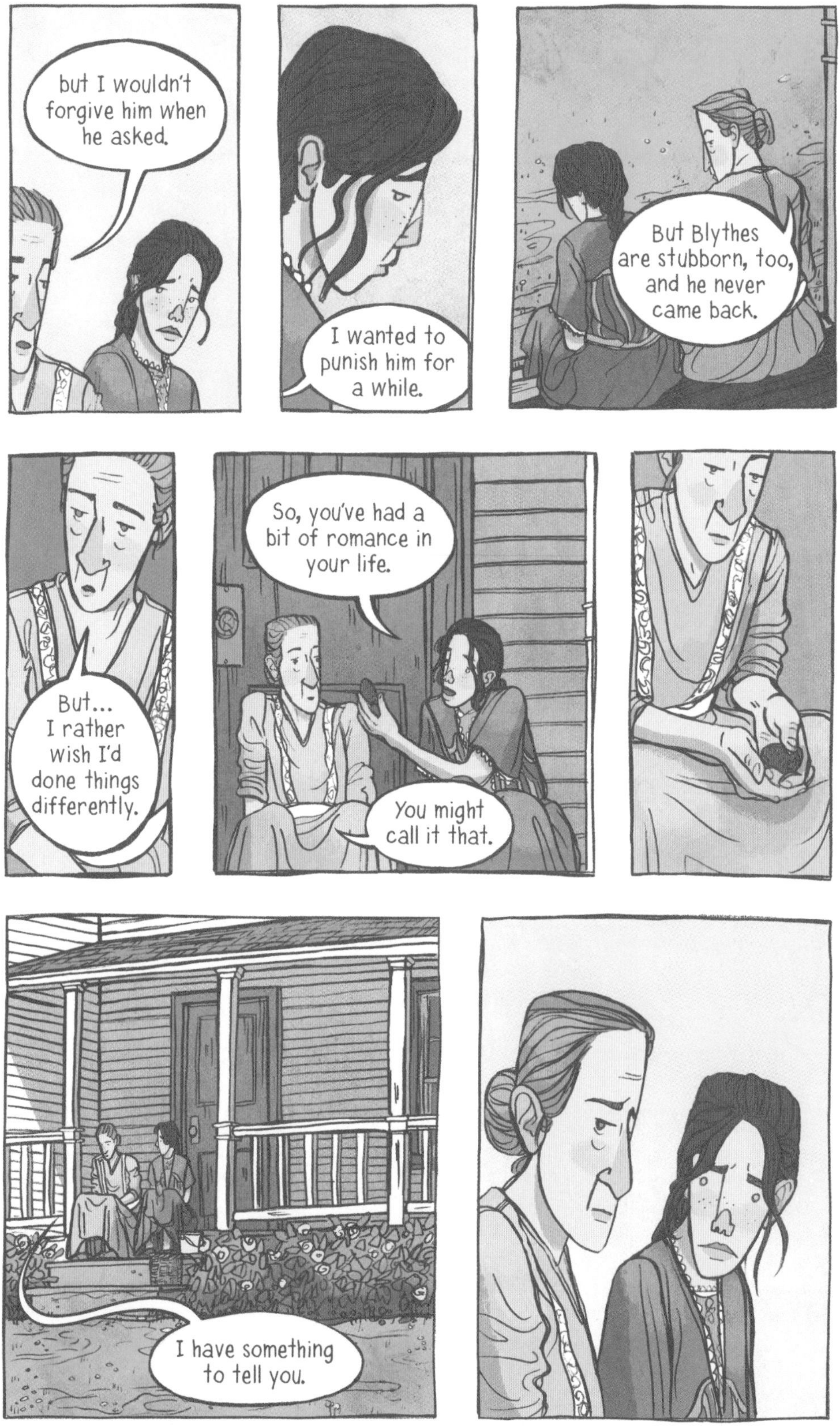
but I wouldn't forgive him when he asked.
I wanted to punish him for a while.
But Blythes are stubborn, too, and he never came back.
But... I rather wish I'd done things differently.
So, you've had a bit of romance in your life.
You might call it that.
I have something to tell you.

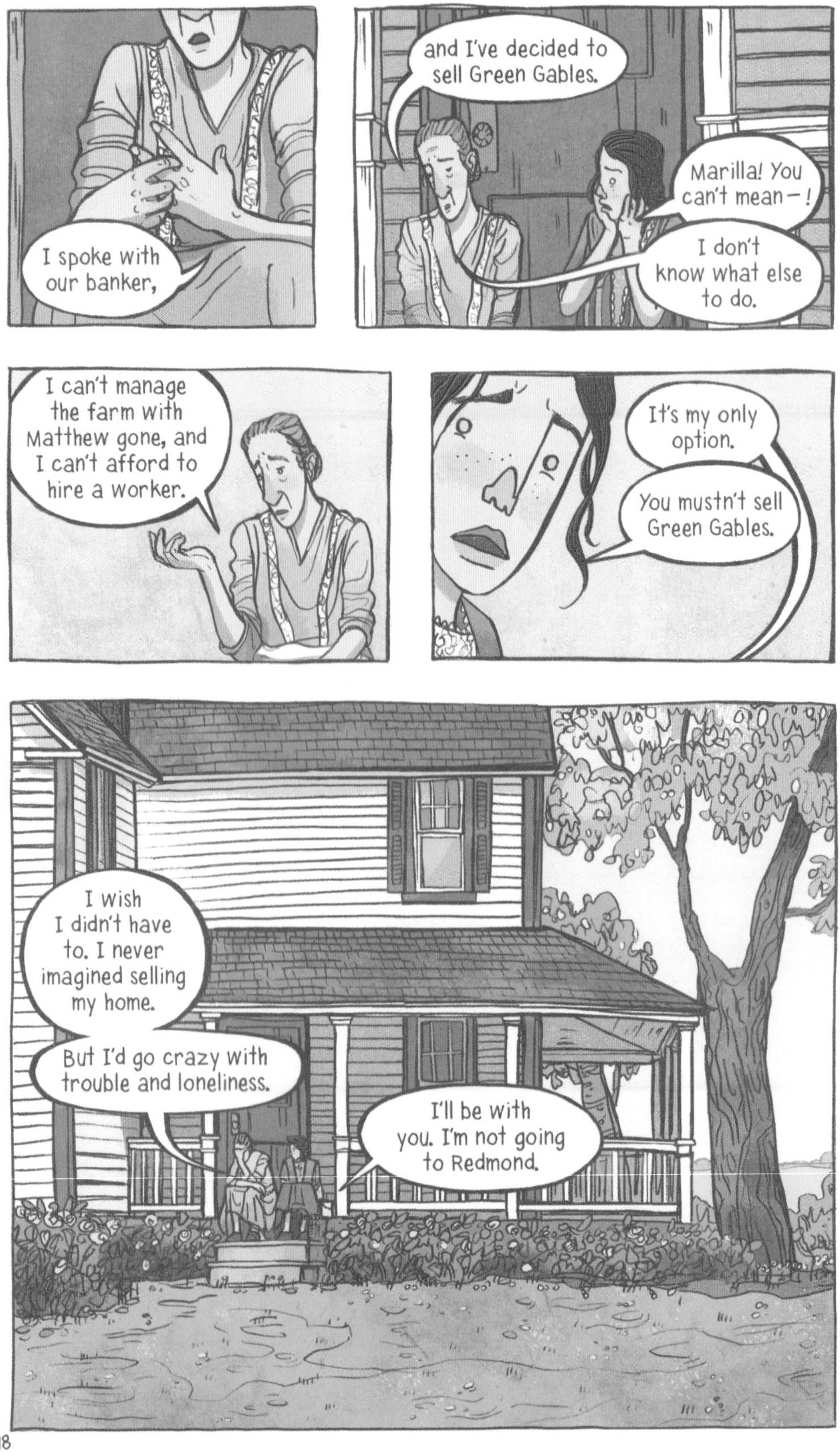
I spoke with our banker,
and I've decided to sell Green Gables.
Marilla! You can't mean—!
I don't know what else to do.
I can't manage the farm with Matthew gone, and I can't afford to hire a worker.
It's my only option.
You mustn't sell Green Gables.
I wish I didn't have to. I never imagined selling my home.
But I'd go crazy with trouble and loneliness.
I'll be with you. I'm not going to Redmond.

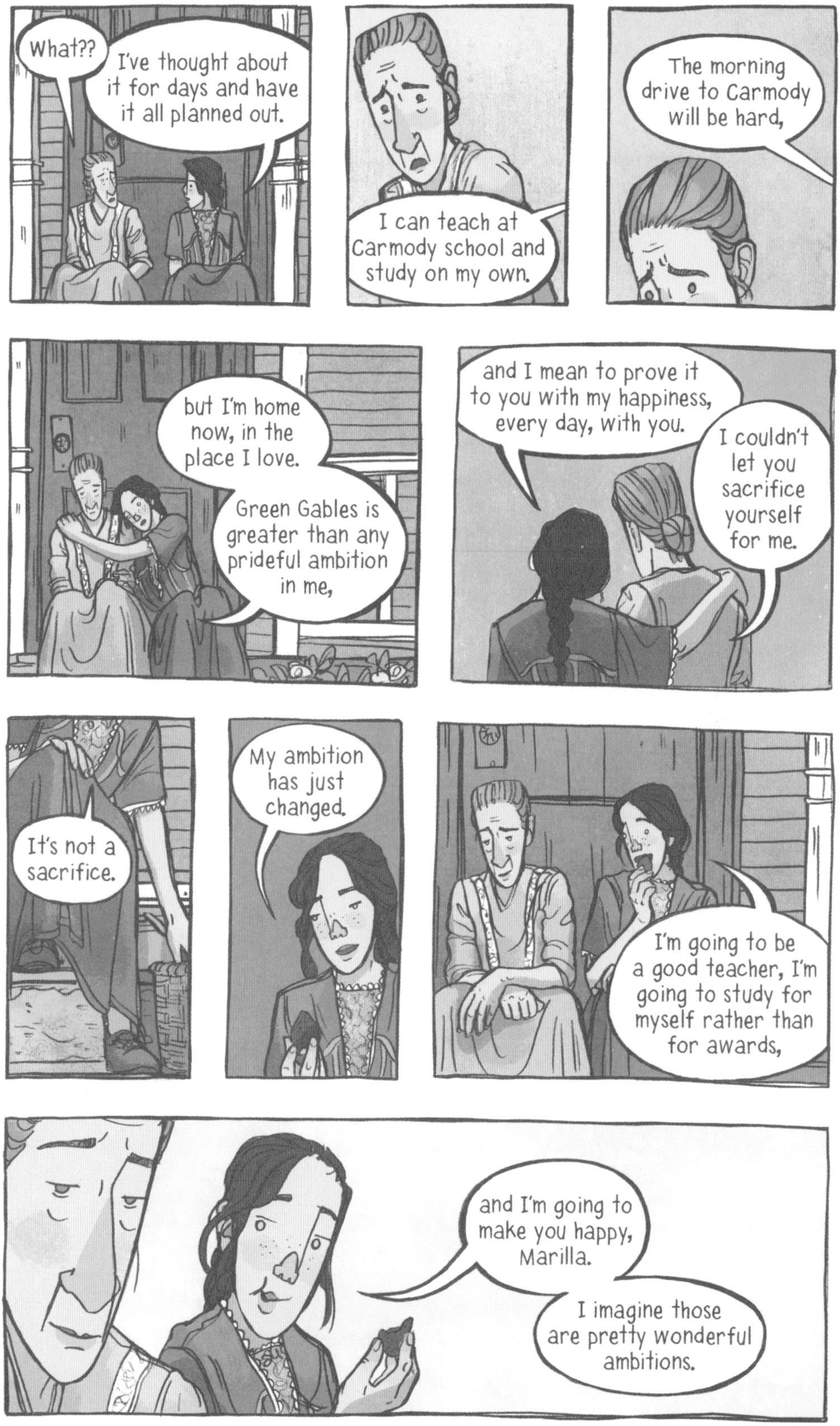

What??
I've thought about it for days and have it all planned out.
I can teach at Carmody school and study on my own.
The morning drive to Carmody will be hard,
but I'm home now, in the place I love.
Green Gables is greater than any prideful ambition in me,
and I mean to prove it to you with my happiness, every day, with you.
I couldn't let you sacrifice yourself for me.
It's not a sacrifice.
My ambition has just changed.
I'm going to be a good teacher, I'm going to study for myself rather than for awards,
and I'm going to make you happy, Marilla.
I imagine those are pretty wonderful ambitions.

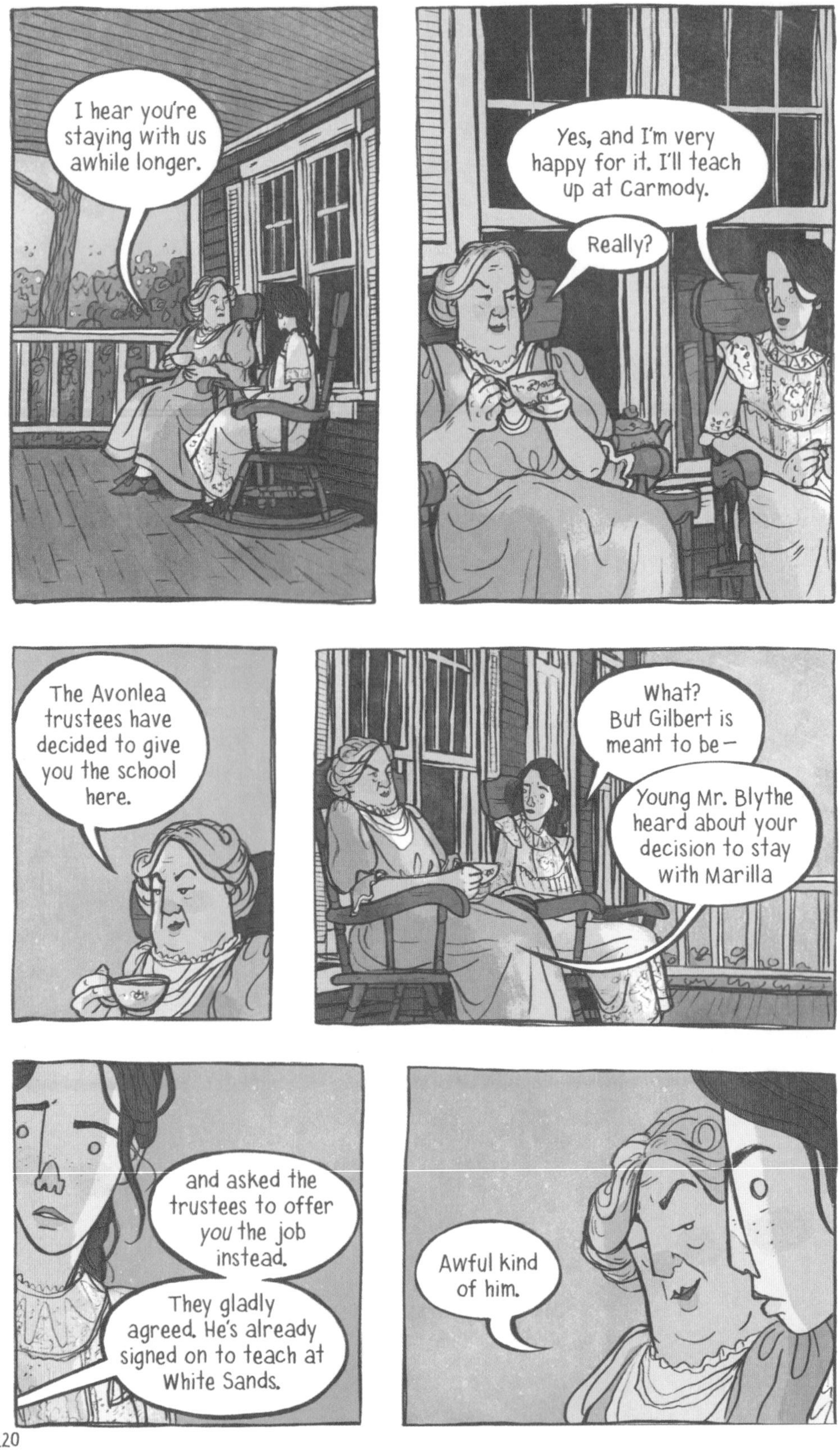

I hear you're staying with us awhile longer.
Yes, and I'm very happy for it. I'll teach up at Carmody.
Really?
The Avonlea trustees have decided to give you the school here.
What? But Gilbert is meant to be—
Young Mr. Blythe heard about your decision to stay with Marilla
and asked the trustees to offer *you* the job instead.
They gladly agreed. He's already signed on to teach at White Sands.
Awful kind of him.

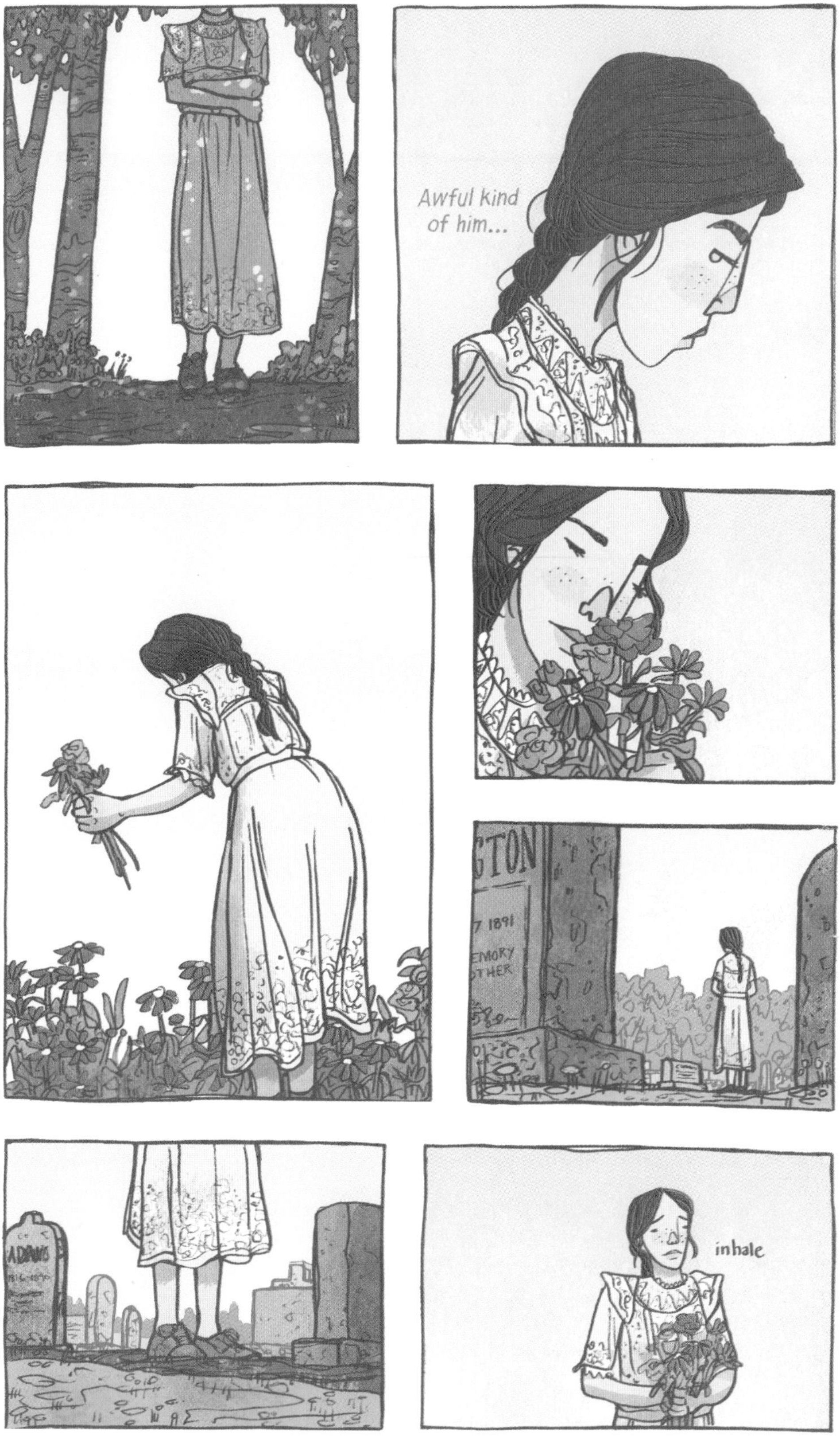
Awful kind of him...
inhale

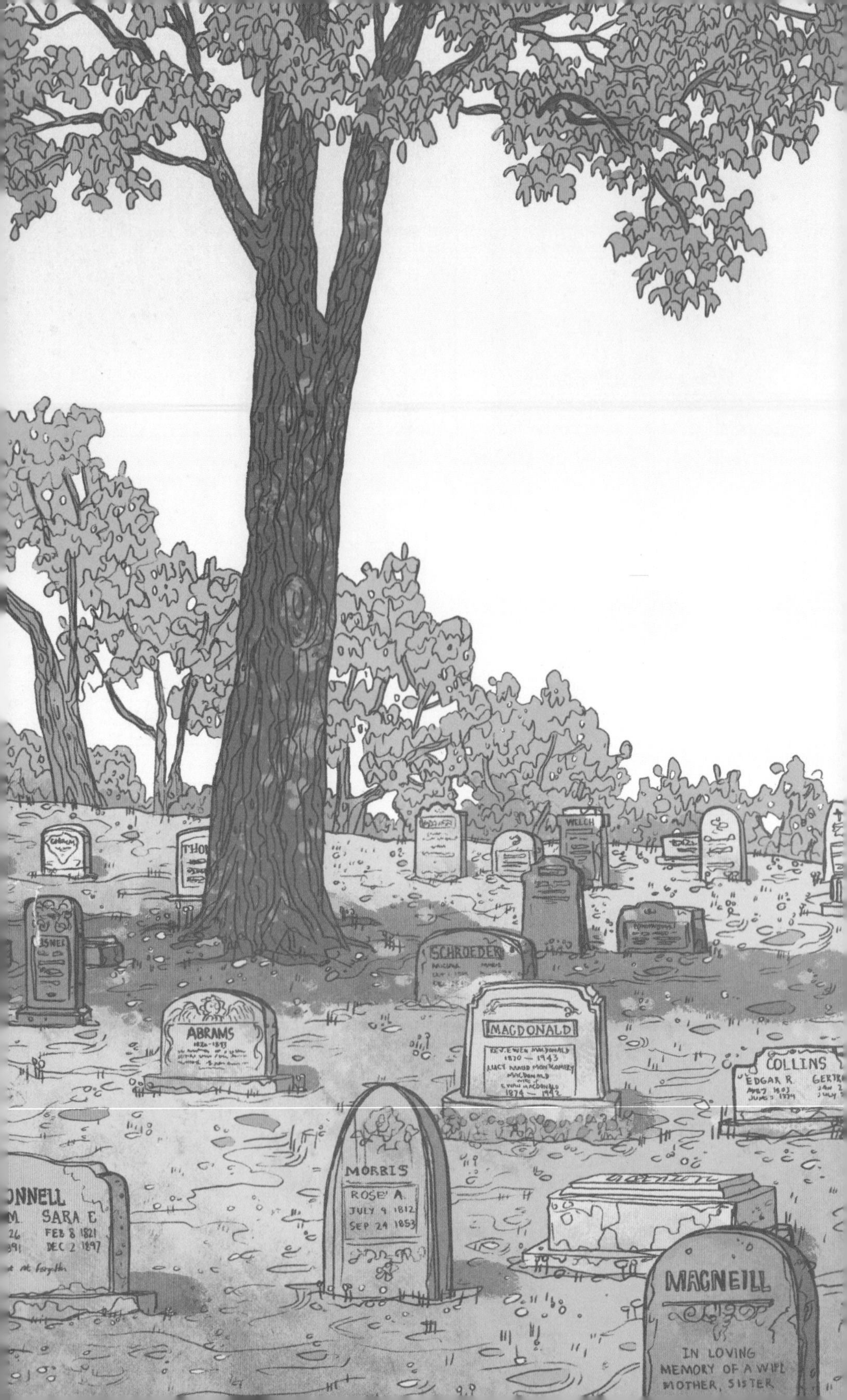

WELCH
THO
SCHROEDER
ABRAMS
MACDONALD
REV. EWEN MACDONALD
1870 — 1943
LUCY MAUD MONTGOMERY
MACDONALD
WIFE OF
EWEN MACDONALD
COLLINS
EDGAR R.
ONNELL
SARA E
FEB 8 1821
DEC 2 1897
MORRIS
ROSE' A.
JULY 9 1812
SEP 24 1853
MACNEILL
IN LOVING
MEMORY OF A WIFE
MOTHER, SISTER

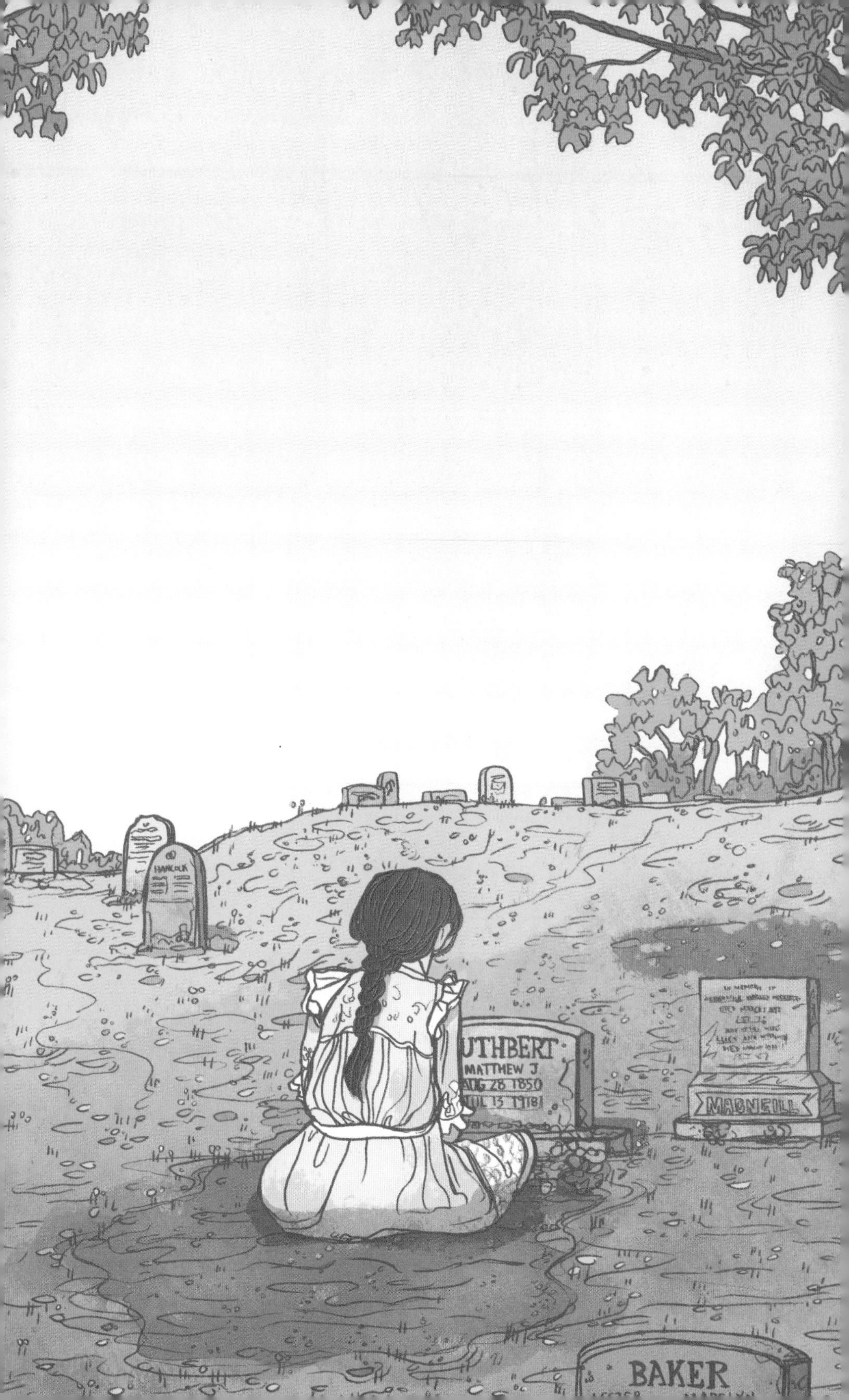
HANCOCK
UTHBERT
MATTHEW J.
AUG 28 1850
MACNEILL
BAKER

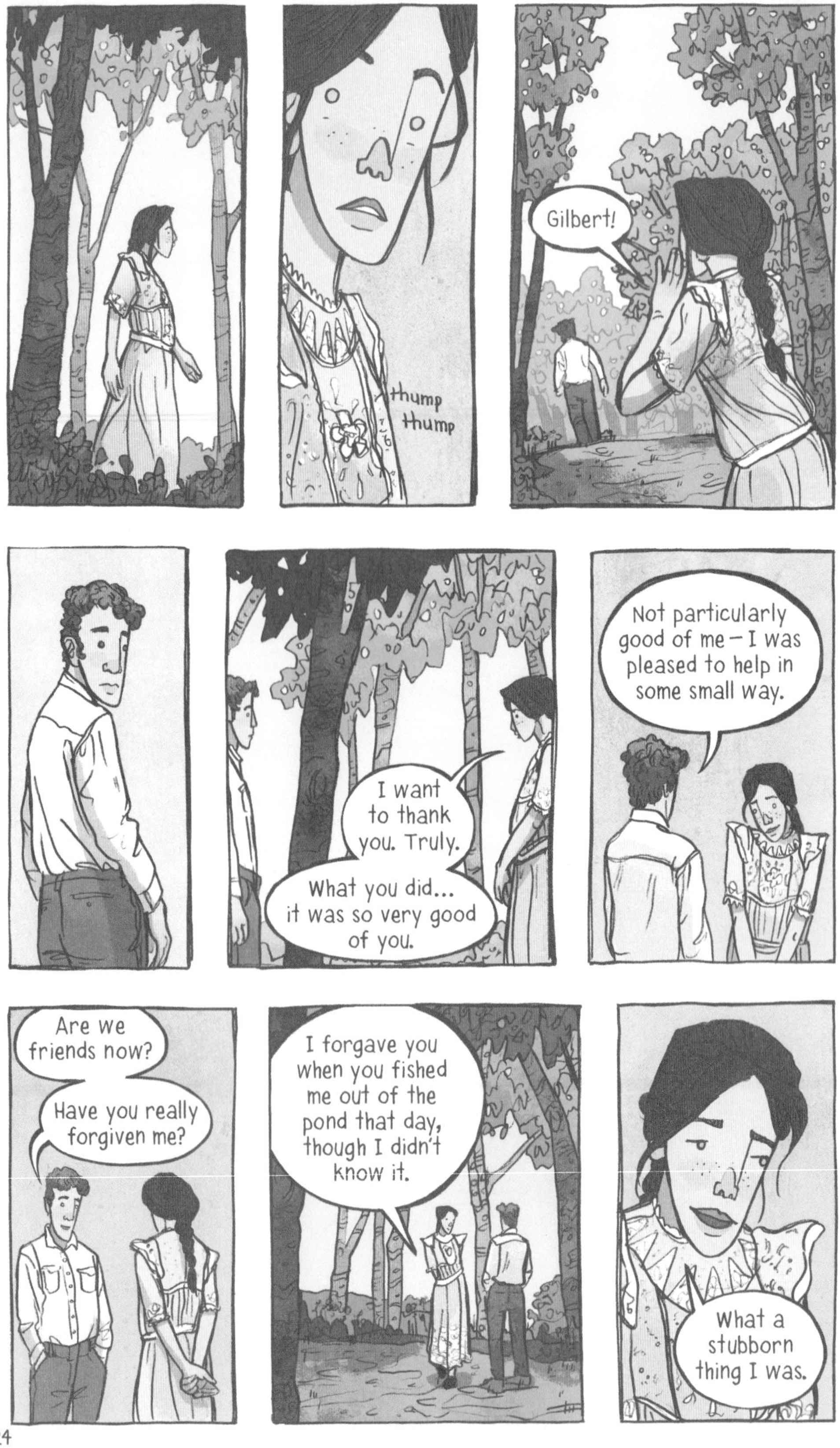
thump
thump
Gilbert!
I want to thank you. Truly.
What you did... it was so very good of you.
Not particularly good of me — I was pleased to help in some small way.
Are we friends now?
Have you really forgiven me?
I forgave you when you fished me out of the pond that day, though I didn't know it.
What a stubborn thing I was.

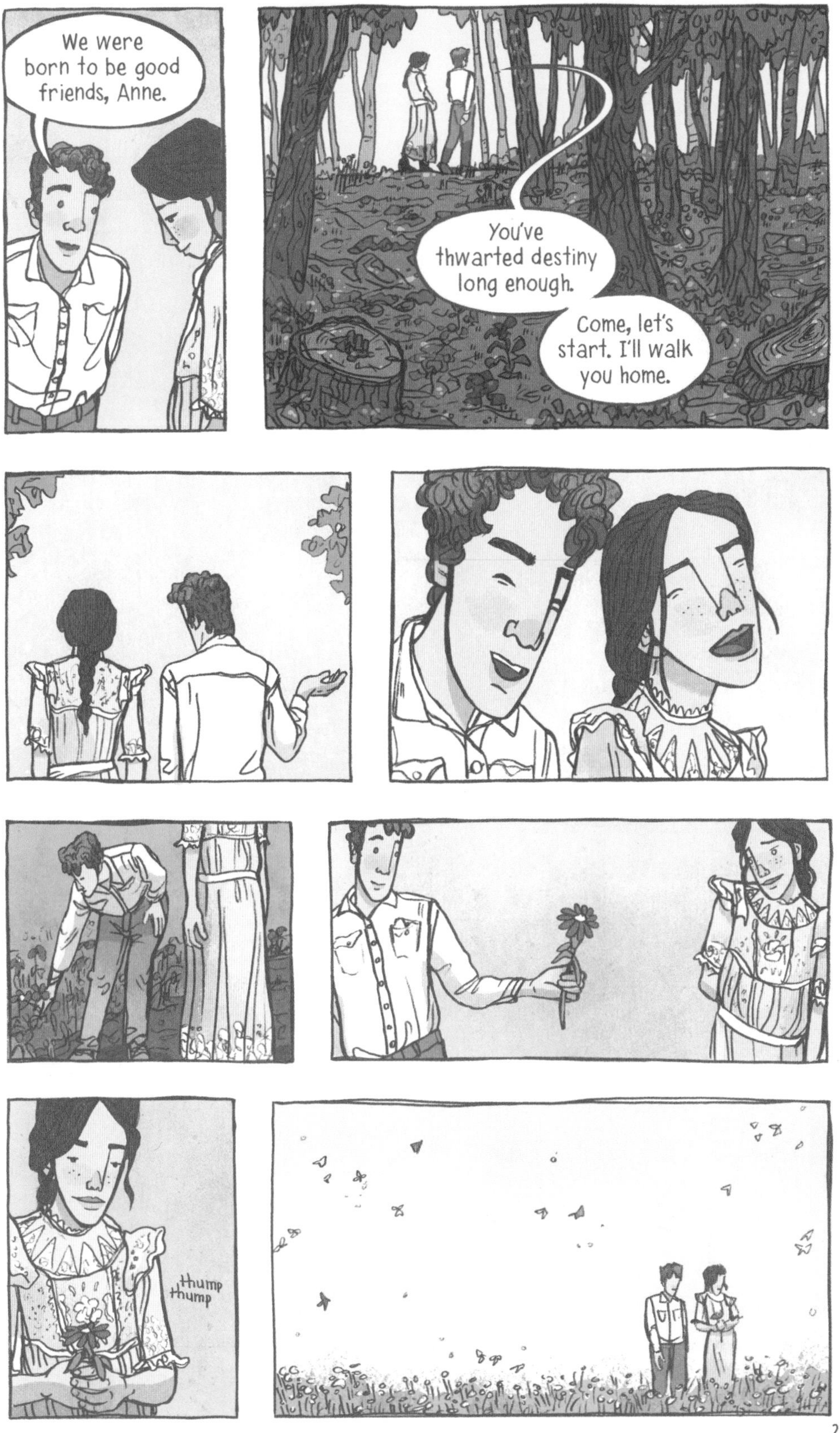
We were born to be good friends, Anne.
You've thwarted destiny long enough.
Come, let's start. I'll walk you home.
thump thump

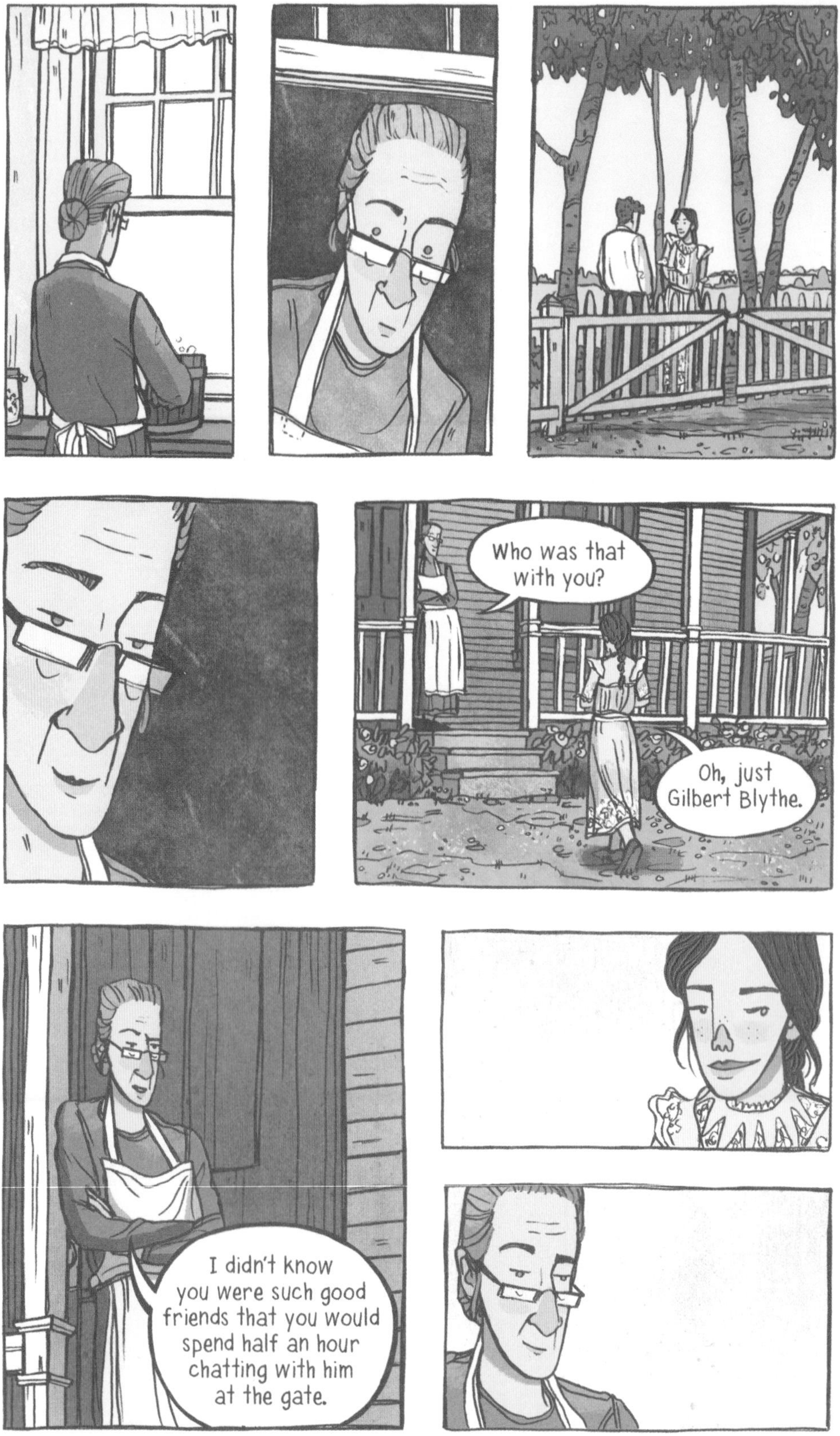
Who was that with you?
Oh, just Gilbert Blythe.
I didn't know you were such good friends that you would spend half an hour chatting with him at the gate.

*Was it really
half an hour?*

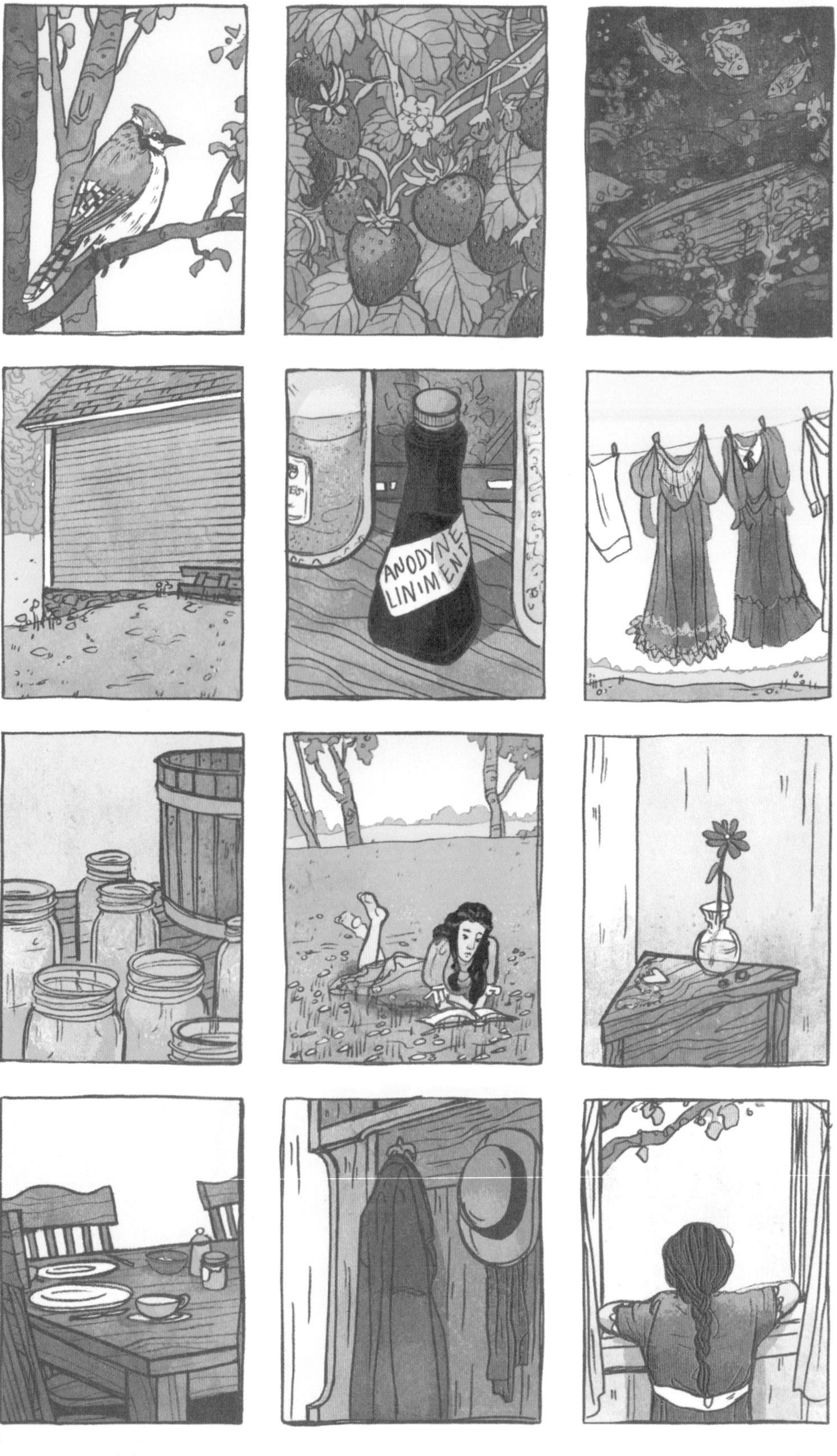
ANODYNE
LINIMENT

Anne could see her life through the window of Green Gables—a future filled with worthy work, sincere friendships, and unknowable adventures—and she realized that her world was bigger than she had ever imagined it to be.

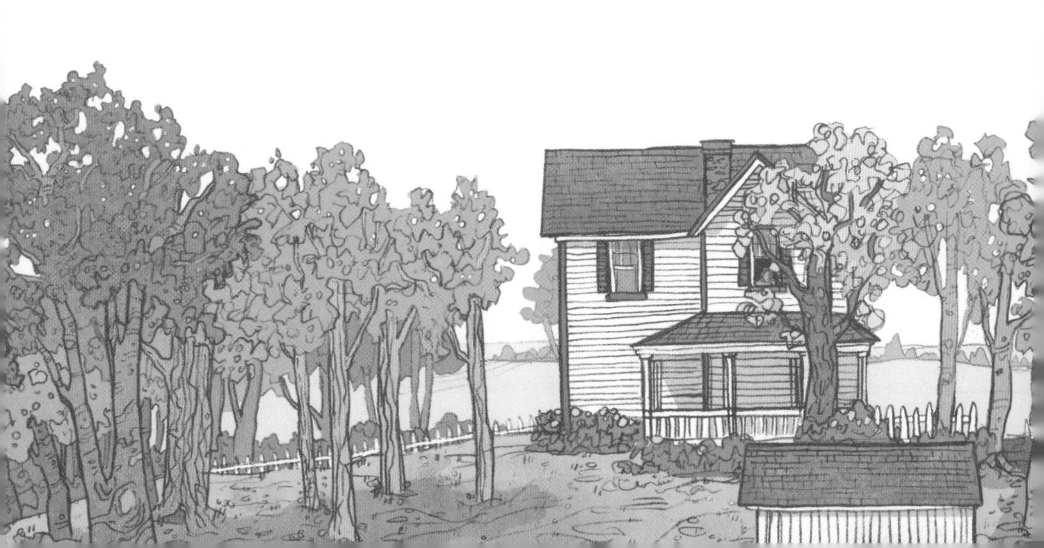

Mariah Marsden spent her childhood hunting for
faeries amidst the old hills of the Missouri Ozarks.
She began telling stories to pass the time on her
family's farm, and she hasn't stopped since. A former
children's librarian, she earned her MFA in Creative Writing
and Media Arts from the University of Missouri–Kansas City.
She writes about the dreams and difficulties of girlhood,
the folklore of her region, and the complexities of rural life.
She's still on the lookout for faeries.

Brenna Thummler grew up in northwestern Pennsylvania,
where she developed a great love for nature trails,
peanut butter, and, above all, drawing. A graduate of
Ringling College of Art and Design, she was named the
Society of Illustrators Zankel Scholar during her junior year.
Since graduation, she has done editorial and advertising work
for such clients as the *New York Times*, the *Washington Post*,
Razorfish, and Empathic Films LLC. *Anne of Green Gables* is her
first graphic novel but won't be her last: she's currently
writing and illustrating her own, entitled *Sheets*.
In those rare moments she's not creating art, you might
find her dancing, making music, baking cheesecakes,
or spending time with kindred spirits.

PRAISE FOR *ANNE OF GREEN GABLES*

"The spirit of Anne is alive and well in Mariah Marsden's crisp adaptation, and it's a thrill to watch as the beloved orphan rushes headlong through Brenna Thummler's heavenly landscapes. Together Marsden and Thummler conjure all the magic and beauty of Green Gables. Like Anne herself, you won't want to leave."

— Brian Selznick, *The Invention of Hugo Cabret* & *The Marvels*

"From the first panel, I was enchanted...Thummler's illustrations are beautiful, inviting, and lovely...I read it in one sitting, and it stayed with me long after. This was a delight!"

— Georgia Dunn, *Breaking Cat News*

"The illustrations are incredible, and Anne is such a captivating character...I finished reading this book and then immediately read it again."

— Dana Simpson, *Phoebe and Her Unicorn*

Andrews McMeel Publishing
a division of Andrews McMeel Universal
1130 Walnut Street, Kansas City, Missouri 64106

www.andrewsmcmeel.com

20 21 22 23 24 SDB 15 14 13 12 11

ISBN: 978-1-4494-7960-2

Library of Congress Control Number: 2017932307

Made by:
King Yip (Dongguan) Printing & Packaging Factory Ltd.
Address and location of manufacturer:
Daning Administrative District, Humen Town
Dongguan Guangdong, China 523930
11th Printing — 5/25/20

Based on the novel by L.M. Montgomery

Author: Mariah Marsden
Illustrator, Designer: Brenna Thummler
Editor: Kendra Phipps
Creative Director: Tim Lynch
Production Editor: Erika Kuster
Production Manager: Chuck Harper

ATTENTION: SCHOOLS AND BUSINESSES

Andrews McMeel books are available at quantity discounts with bulk purchase for
educational, business, or sales promotional use. For information, please e-mail the
Andrews McMeel Publishing Special Sales Department:
specialsales@amuniversal.com.